THE DEPTHS WITHIN

PART 2

The Depths Within: Part 2 © 2024 Matthew Cirson.

All Rights Reserved. No part of this book may be reproduced in any form or by any electronic or mechanical means including information storage and retrieval systems, without permission in writing from the author. The only exception is by a reviewer, who may quote short excerpts in a review.

This book is a work of fiction. Names, characters, places, and incidents either are products of the author's imagination or are used fictitiously. Any resemblance to actual persons, living or dead, events, or locales is entirely coincidental.

Printed in Australia
First published July 2024
This edition first published 2024

Cover design by Melinda Childs
Internal design by Jessica Chaplin

Paperback ISBN 978-1-7637529-2-4
eBook ISBN 978-1-7637529-3-1

More great titles can be found by visiting www.matthewcirsonauthor.com.au

A catalogue record for this work is available from the National Library of Australia

THE DEPTHS WITHIN

PART 2

MATTHEW CIRSON

Also by Matthew Cirson

The Depths Within: Part One

50% of author's proceeds from the sale of this book will be donated to "Soldier On," to assist with the health and mental wellbeing of current and ex-serving ADF personnel.

SHEPHERD

*'I have said these things to you,
that in me you may have peace.
In the world you will have tribulation.
But take heart,
I have overcome the world.'*

John 16:33

The world lay in darkness, at least for the moment. Only seconds remained; the sun had already begun to rise. That suited him fine. Everything that had happened on the face of this earth had been for a reason. Every nail hammered into a board did not just pierce the splintered hide of the top, but wedged itself deep into the structure below to hold its charge in place. He was such a nail. In the same token, Tamworth and its regions were plotted out in the fields and hills. He was driven through the heart of that town to ensure that he and his flock would not only remain, but flourish.

He threw the doona to the side and exposed his nakedness; he stood as his morning hardness swayed about in front of him. The remnants of the passion from last night dried into a milky crust that clotted the thin hairs that shrouded his manhood. As he stretched, he looked back at the bed and the gleaming white flesh of the girl's ass. She was young and pretty, but she fucked like a corpse. At first he had been excited, too excited to enter her. Perhaps it was the softness of her breasts, or the way she squirmed under him, but that was where it ended. The tears and sobs had started, followed by her refusal to even look at him while he drove himself deeper into her; her response hadn't fuelled his lust, but had driven an icy anger into his gut. She fucked like a corpse, alright, and if that's what she wanted to act like in his suite, then why shouldn't her wish be granted permanently?

He yawned again as he turned away from her. His manhood continuously wagged back and forth as he strolled to the free-standing mirror. The image in the failing darkness of the room was pale. He blinked and tried to free his eyes from the sleep that still shrouded them. This was the best room the Tamworth Hotel had to offer. The carpet was soft and lush under his feet; he almost felt as though he partially sunk a fraction of an inch each time he took a step on its patterned pile. The cornices were decorative and bright with the new coat of paint he had ordered applied. The smell of paint, although was mostly subsided, still lingered, which disappointed him, while the detail of the fleur-de-lis wall paper met his approval. New drapes, sourced from the windows of the wealthiest houses in town, were hung for his pleasure. Likewise, with the clamshell lounge suite that sat awkwardly to the side. However, his most prised possession was his oak desk, ornately carved from a tree that had held such splendour inside of itself. Its surface had been lacquered nearly fifty times to give the timber the impression of a floating pool of water. The leather top was the hide of an elephant, pale and wrinkled to look at. But a softer feeling leather could not be found, not even on the pale ass of the girl that stirred in his bed.

He smiled at his reflection. He studied the rows of the gleaming whites of his teeth, the small lines that formed at the corner of his eyes and the peaks of his lips. Good, but not perfect. He relaxed his face and rubbed at his cheeks with his hands. Again, he smiled, this time he looked at the eyes and the dullness in them. He needed to work on that. He had heard it said many a time before that when people smiled, they did so with their eyes. His were still asleep, that, or unwilling to hide their true nature. As the slits of light slowly illuminated the room, the old salesman sparkle glinted in his eyes at the first hint of the day. He spread his lips a final time and felt the muscle memory kick in; his back straightened and his shoulders slid back.

'Good morning, handsome,' he whispered to himself. He winked and allowed himself a small moment to admire the shape of his body. Everything had been done for a reason, every stone shaped a certain way by the winds to run its course through time. He was shaped, etched and crafted to persuade. Some called it a con. In many ways, everything about him was a con, but that was the dark of the night speaking. There were times for darkness, for cons and lies. Then there were times for daylight, smiles and persuasive comments or suggestions. The moment he stepped out of his suite door, he needed to be in day mode.

As his eyes ran over each perfectly shaped line of his body, his manhood gave a new pulse of vitality. He looked down at his greatest asset, his most loyal soldier, and he smiled softly.

'What a man does the moment he wakes is his defining character.' He looked over to the pile of blankets, and shrugged. 'Let's see if a goodnight sleep has put some vigour into those bones.' He strolled over to the bed, roughly threw the covers off, and took her from behind. She screamed anew.

At first, she was dry and gritty, the flesh grabbed as it parted way. Then her body betrayed her and the machine began to slicken. A gasp escaped his open mouth as he climaxed and panted as he felt the heat in his skin. It always took him longer in the morning, but at least it got his heart pumping. He left her without a word, and showered.

While he cleaned the sex from his loins, he whistled to himself. The sound echoed off the gleaming white tiles and resonated in the sparkling brass shower fittings. He continued while he dried himself, used the plush soft cotton towels that were once again seized from the richest households and dressed himself. Once he was dressed, he returned to the mirror. The light of the morning now fully lit the room; he practised his smile once more.

As he did, he took moments to inspect his attire. A man who wished to win the hearts and minds of his followers needed to present humble, he thought to himself. The R.M Williams' long sleeved shirt, belt and boots combination gave the impression he worked on the farms, a shoveller of shit and a herder of stock, though his hands had never seen a day of hard labour in their life. His labour was persuasion.

The door to his suite opened behind him and he watched in the reflection as a boy carried in a tray of silver, burdened with the glimmering cloches and utensils. The smell of bacon and salt hit his nose, and his stomach growled in anticipation. He adjusted the shoestring tie around his neck while the child placed the dishes noisily on the dining table.

'Good morning, Michael!' Shepherd proclaimed. His well-practised smile radiated from his face. 'I trust you slept well.'

The boy stood in silence at the foot of the table. He stared at the silverware, a blank expression on his face. 'Yes sir, good morning, sir.'

The lines around Shepherd's face deepened as he sat. 'Now Michael, I told you that you don't need to call me *sir*. Shepherd is fine.' He removed the shining dome from the plate and a cloud of steam rose. Crispy bacon, golden scrambled eggs, sirloin cooked mid-rare and two plump sausages, the flesh of which trembled as the hot grease bubbled beneath. He lifted a second smaller dome to reveal four slices of deep thick golden-brown toast. He took a long, deep breath in through his nose and then closed his eyes and bowed his head and sat in silence for a few seconds. The idea of this was to give everyone the impression that he was thanking the Lord; a godly man was easier to trust. In reality, he took this time to plan his day and the labours he must undertake.

When he opened his eyes, his hands had already moved to pluck the silver utensils from their place on the cotton napkin to his right. The boy had learned quickly. He had taken it on himself to hand pick a certain number of 'newcomers' to serve in his household. Mostly, he had picked the girls. He let them settle themselves in their false dreams of maid work and cookery, then night by night he called upon each of them to serve him as he had fully intended. So far, he had not been pleased. The longest he had held a girl in his service so far was a week. She had been well spirited, the fight within her was deep and hard wired, however she too, like the others, had become withdrawn and silent before long and that just wouldn't do.

To take the boy on had been a new idea of his. His house servants were not allowed in public sight and his guards had worked tirelessly at first to keep that so. However, the more he spent amongst the people (his people), the more he realised he needed to be seen as a type of father figure, to help persuade them that he indeed thought of them as his flock.

When he had first revealed himself to the country community, he had done so as one of them. A man in the row of chairs that filled the sports field, that spoke up against the then mayor. That fat, bumbling idiot didn't even know what was happening to him as the weeks unfolded. He kept on pledging that the town's police and the army would do nothing but protect the people of Tamworth. How easy it had been to raise the point that by protecting the town, all the town needed to do was give up their sons and young men. Say goodbye to them and send them away. From the row of chairs, he had created dissent.

Then in the church halls he had spoken his mind in the mass while he had volunteered to read the morning psalms. At first the father had been concerned, but the old smooth talking and persuasive tones, with a few bible references thrown in here and there to be sure, had won the congregation. The idea of the flock and that they should hold their strength together had been one of his greatest. He continued to spread his word, person to person, to groups when he could. Once it took hold, he had created his own domino effect. Families convinced other families, friends and neighbours. When the town officials came knocking, looking for the young men to join the ranks, they refused. Mothers stood in front of sons, fathers slammed the doors in the faces of well-dressed officials.

Then it had happened. He knew it was inevitable as he had told his small group of trusted followers back then, Lewis especially. Everything had been placed on this earth for a reason. Each man only walked the path that God had set out for him and by the righteousness of that God above, they walked their path now. The officials had arrived to take the Murray boy from his family; he had turned eighteen and his time for glory had come. The father had another idea and had threatened the officials with an old rusted shotgun. The officials had drawn their own side arms and the Lord himself held his breath. The town's fate was sealed the moment the young constable had shot the father. Word soon spread and the plans were made.

The more he spoke about that night and the sad story of the Murray household, the better his rendition became. Masses cried out in anger, mothers wept and fire burned in the bellies of men and boys alike.

Lewis helped with the plans; he and his northerner friends had been invaluable to his ascension. As the Lord had once risen from his tomb, he had risen to power. Mobs had lined the streets, they broke down the doors of the lawmen, the mayor and the other town elite.

They dragged their naked bodies out into the street.

The final fall of the old town had happened where its decline had first begun, in the southern sports field. The mayor cried and shrieked as the nails were driven through his hands and feet and the cross was raised in the grounds. All of this was to Shepherd's surprise, he hadn't even thought of crucifixion. However, once the rails of chaos had been laid down, the mob was helpless but to follow.

He stood In front of them that night, while the mayor died in agony, the stoned bodies of his family at his feet. In the burning disorder and the death of the old way, he spoke to them about peace, and how a good community should stick together and how he would take each and every one of them under his wing to protect their folk alike. They had held their hands to him and called his name, all the while he had smiled.

That had been over a month ago now, and so much had happened. He had called his flock in; towns like Kootingal, Uralla and Walcha were the first to fall. When he had sold the idea to his flock, it had been about strengthening against the Chinese oppression and they had bought it. The men from Tamworth and the farms that surrounded it, were already absorbed into the militia, the women were put to work on the fields and handled the stock mostly.

The new souls that they needed were for work forces. They needed men to build ramparts. He already had men to stand on them and so, they had taken the families from these towns. Those that came willing when he had first sent out his call were treated well enough, there weren't enough houses, so some were given land to live on while hundreds dwelled in communal shelters formed out of long-standing structures, the town hall was one such example. Those that complained were dealt with before the dissent could start again.

Idle hands were the devil's work he knew, so every man in the town had a job. Doctors, teachers and engineers were rounded up.

Schools continued, the sick continued to get treated and work began. Those that didn't wish to come were forcefully taken. Their possessions were absorbed and they had a choice: work or die. Most decided to work as he thought they would.

However, there were those that came into the town to spread rumours about him and his cruelty. He knew it was the case, and he continued to make public announcements in person, his smile as warm as it had always been. They continued to look to him as he spoke of holding hands and how sticks are stronger in a bundle than on their own, all the while quoting 'Revelations' or 'Psalms.' The crowds once again looked at him and decided that the rumours couldn't be true.

The one thing that had sealed his grip on the town was the defeat of the Chinese. In truth, he couldn't take the credit for that little gem; they had destroyed themselves mostly in mutiny and desertion when the fuel had dried up, that he could take credit for. By the time the soldiers had marched down the road into town, arranged in a sloppy formation behind their last running tank, Shepherd had smiled. Only a thousand men of the Western contingent had arrived to conquer them. He saw the complete collapse of morale when the tank shuddered and came to a huffing halt only three hundred feet from the first house. He saw the desperation as they walked, and hoped for supplies. The militia had allowed the small column to enter the town entirely before they fell upon them. Rifles rattled from the windows of houses. Farmers ran onto the street with machetes and farm implements in a brilliant display of bravado and stupidity and like another Domino in his game of glory, the Chinese had fallen.

He witnessed a mutiny in their ranks, where soldiers turned on one of their own officers and dragged him to the ground. He screamed as they pummelled him with the butts of their rifles.

He saw lines of men break and turn to flee, only to find waves of Australians behind them. Finally, while men died up and down Peel Street, hands were thrown into the air and they surrendered.

In total, he had been left with no more than four hundred of the Chinese to deal with. Lewis had found a translator and offered those that were left the same choice as he'd offered his new lambs from the other towns: work or die. Some he had amalgamated into his militia, others he sent to work on the farms, spread out amongst the other workers under the watchful eyes of those he could trust. The farmers loved him; they had all the hands for work they had ever needed and didn't have to pay them a dime. Some grumbled at the need to feed their workers and suggested that the township should arrange the food. Shepherd had simply reminded them of the attitude they had once rebelled against and had told them to thank the Lord for the help they now received in these troubled times. Most smiled at him, confusion rampant in their minds, then they nodded and left.

As he finished his breakfast, he looked at the boy who had continued to stare blankly at him while he ate. Here was where he found his new labour, that, or the solution to a problem.

'Tell me, Michael, how is the arena coming along?' He dabbed at the remains of the egg on his face with the napkin.

'Jonathan said to tell you they were on track,' the boy replied flatly.

Although to the rest of the town, Shepherd had pretended to have taken this child as his adopted son, in reality, he had taken him for his page. At first, he had shown laziness and a small will to defy, but a firm hand had broken him and constant beatings at mistakes had proven him to be a fast learner.

'I beg your pardon?' His smile faltered.

'He said to tell you they were on track, Shepherd.'

'Very good.' His smile returned to its usual brilliance. 'How is Riley?'

Michael hadn't blinked at any of these questions. However, their eyes met as he spoke the words, 'He's dead, sir.'

Shepherd held his gaze as he tried to see if there was some sort of joy beyond that blank expression. As if Riley's death was a victory for him. 'Now that is a crying shame.'

Riley had been there when they had brought this boy, the girl and the collapsed giant in. He had taken it upon himself to claim the giant's rifle. Instantly, he had become withdrawn and silent, a man that had usually been loud, jovial and outspoken, they had all put it down to off days. Two nights ago, he had burst into the Tamworth Hotel, brandished his new rifle and had shot down five men in the common room.

Shepherd himself heard his rantings before he fired; he was not himself. In the last moment, through the tears and undistinguishable language, he had tried to turn the rifle on himself, but had succeeded in only severing his lower jaw. When Shepherd had come downstairs to see what had happened, Riley had just lay there, holding the rifle close to his chest and rocked back and forth. Everyone else had cleared out. Shepherd took the rifle from his hands, and the horrible feeling that had come with it unnerved him.

He looked at the mirror in the corner of the room, at the wall beyond, and shuddered.

'You know, son,' Shepherd said as he returned his attention to his reflection, 'I think it's time we paid your brother a visit and see how his treatment is coming along.'

Michael remained silent. In the five days since their arrival, Michael had not been permitted to see his brother. Shepherd had gotten most of everything out of him the first time they had sat down and 'had a talk.' The boy was Michael Baker, the big sick man was his brother Jack Baker who had been attacked by dogs. He knew where they had lived and that they had moved South to escape their father, who was a drunken bully. But when the questions turned to that rifle, the answers had stopped. No matter how hard he slapped the boy, or pinched his nipple, he wouldn't answer. Shepherd had finally decided that he couldn't answer and had left it.

'Doesn't that make you happy, Michael?' he asked. 'To see your brother? I hear he is healing up fine.' He met the child's gaze and forced his smile to return.

Michael no longer held his eye contact, instead he had returned his focus to the silverware and had begun to tidy up. 'Is he awake?'

Shepherd stood up to have a piss. He placed a hand on the boy's shoulder and turned his head up to look at him. 'Not yet, but maybe today.' He continued to whistle as he urinated, partially to drown out the sobs of the girl that seemed to have regained her consciousness in the bed. He wondered if there had been any more stragglers picked up on the road and whether his trip to Ryan and the prison would present any other specimens for him to view apart from the sleeping giant.

The remains of Billy's face had been a good indicator to suggest that this unique individual would indeed make for the spectacle he was looking for. Poor Billy had been brought back unconscious, along with the rest of them. Jonathan had had a hell of a time trying to lift the big son of a bitch into the back of his LandCruiser with Riley.

Not only had everyone heard that story more than once, but on eight separate occasions, he had brought up his thoughts that he deserved a special reward for bringing the big bastard down. Everyone in the Tamworth Hotel was sick of the story that changed in every retelling of how he heroically beat the crazed bastard within an inch of his life.

Although his effort was admirable, Shepherd was not impressed. The fact that his best doctor, a thin man with glasses by the name of Dyson, had worked tirelessly since his arrival just to keep Jack Baker alive and stave off the infection, had taken a lot of the danger from Jonathan's story. No doubt, Dyson would already be in the cell tending to his patient. Shepherd fastened the zip on his jeans and left his room.

The drive from the Hotel to the prison was a short one. They kept Jack Baker in the largest cell of the police station. Having no need for a fully operational station, they had converted most of the rooms into cells. Shepherd ignored the pleas of the inmates that recognised him as he walked by. Ryan was at his heels and the small boy brought up the rear. The sound of their footfalls echoed through the concrete halls, only contested by the groans of some and the requests for forgiveness of others.

'He stirred this morning. We all near shit thought he was coming to,' Ryan panted as he struggled to keep up.

'I think it's still too early for that,' Shepherd remarked, uninterested. 'He was too far gone when they brought him in. Patience is a virtue and is one that I am well equipped with.'

Ryan hated the God bothering statements, he knew that. Every day he planned to visit the old station, he had made sure he thought of at least three possible proverbs that he could work into conversation. Why Lewis had decided on picking that man to run the prison was beyond him, but he trusted Lewis and had no need to question his decisions.

Jack Baker's cell was at the end of the hallway. The tunnel-like corridor stretched forty feet into the darkness. Small light globes protruded from the concrete roof every five feet; the conduit of wire ran crooked along their path. The result was that of a poorly lit underground tunnel that he likened to those of the French catacombs. Cells only lined the left side of the hallway. To the right was a solid concrete wall where folding chairs were placed sporadically for guards to rest their fat asses as they patrolled. He could hear Dyson's nasal voice as they neared the end. He mumbled something to one of his assistants while the fat guard at the end stood outside the cell door, and leaned on the steel bars as he looked in.

Three men stood over the body of Jack Baker, pulling the stinking white bandages from his skin. They cringed as they threw the puss-ridden gauze to the side and dabbed alcohol onto the wounds. The giant lay on his back, his eyes closed, the deep heavy breaths rasped through the cell doors as if they belonged to that of a beast. The wound on his face had been the worst. Although he had never been a totally handsome man, they had been forced to cut away the flesh, which distorted the features on his right side. However, from what Shepherd could see under Dyson's moving hands as he lifted the gauze and dabbed more alcohol onto the flesh, he had healed faster than any of them could have thought.

'I'm going to need a hand moving him,' Dyson requested, as he struggled to lift the man's enormous head.

With the doctors' assistants busy tending to other parts of the giant's body, Shepherd looked to the fat guard by his side. 'Are you deaf, son?' The guard shot his head in his direction, a puzzled look on his face.

'No, sir?'

'Well, the good doctor asked for your help.' His smile was as bright and wide as he had ever practised. The guard looked back at the sleeping giant and then nodded his head. He fumbled with the keys and ran the shaft into the lock. There was a loud metallic clunk as the lock released and he slid the door open. As he entered the cell,

Shepherd slid the door closed behind him and snapped the lock once more. The guard turned back to him. 'Safety first, young man.'

While Dyson, his two assistants and the guard worried over Jack, Shepherd turned to Michael. The boy had his hands around the cell bars and his face pressed close. The look of concern on his face was endearing; it was the first time he had seen the boy show any form of emotion apart from defiance. He placed a hand on his shoulder and felt the slight flinch. He knew that Michael wanted to pull away but he knew better than to. 'I'll leave you with your brother for a while. I need to talk to Ryan here about some business.'

He gestured toward Ryan, and they walked about twenty feet down the tunnel. 'Ryan, my good man, you haven't happened upon any newcomers?'

Ryan panted as he continued down the tunnel. He almost ran right into Shepherd as he stopped to turn and look at him. Ryan looked bewildered, 'Ahh no sir, we haven't found anything that I think you would find to your liking.'

Shepherd closed a fist around the collar of Ryan's shirt and pulled him close. 'Well by Christ, young man, you better keep looking.' He glanced over Ryan's shoulder and saw Michael crouch next to the bars, he heard him say his brother's name in a soft voice. Shepherd turned back to Ryan. 'You can send someone to pick up the sorry soul that you left me last time. And don't take—'

From the cell at end of the hallway he heard Dyson cry out. Someone else said, 'Jesus Christ.'

Then a deep roar that made Shepherd's heart skip a beat, ripped through the tunnel. Michael had stepped back to the concrete wall. He saw the arm of the guard reach through, as he tried to unlock the door, then the arm was ripped back into the cell. Shepherd ran back down the tunnel, Ryan close on his heels. He could see the keys still jutted out of the lock. Michael was frozen with his back to the wall, a look of horror on his face.

The sounds that came from within the cell were horrific. People screamed and howled over the sounds of squelches and snaps. Shepherd didn't even look into the cell as it came into view, his vision was fixed on the keys. Without seeing anything else, he rammed the key over to lock side, to make sure it was secured and pulled the keys out. In that exact moment, he saw the blur of a faded navy uniform as the guard's body was slammed into the bars directly in front of him. He stumbled back and felt his back press against the concrete wall. He finally looked up and saw the figure that stood in front of him.

Beside him, Ryan yammered, 'Jesus. Fuck!' as he pulled his pistol from his belt. Shepherd held out a hand as Ryan raised the pistol and he pushed down on the barrel. His heart hammered in his chest. On the floor of the cell lay the twisted, broken remains of what could only be Dyson and his two assistants.

Their limbs were twisted into positions that were not natural. Even as he watched, their coats became a deep red as the blood flowed from their wounds. One of the men's heads had been crushed against the concrete wall, the blood splatter traced the roof and the three solid walls. Beneath his crushed skull, a pool of red stretched outwards.

Jack Baker stood with his nose to the bars, as tall as the door itself and seemed to take up the whole width. His bandages had unravelled in the carnage and hung loose around him, exposing the black flesh and oozing wounds. As before, his face was the worst. Black lines ran from the hole in his cheek and down his thick neck. The flesh seemed to writhe with each breath he took and each time he clenched his jaw. What gave Shepherd pause were his eyes. They were black, as if his pupil had taken up the entire surface. There was no correlation between his iris and the white globes; the whole things were as black as the dead flesh on his face.

Although he couldn't tell, he was sure that the black eyes were trained on him. It made him uncomfortable even to look at them, but he couldn't turn away. Michael stepped forward to his left, and looked up at his brother.

'Jack?' he sobbed. The dark eyes turned to him. One hand came up and grasped the bars, his palm was so large he was able to wrap his fingers around one bar and his thumb around another.

'No,' the big man said in a deep raspy croak, 'not Jack.'

'Where is he, you sick fuck?!' Michael spat at him. 'All of this was you, wasn't it? All of it!' His voice was shrill and tears had begun to form in his eyes. Inside the cell, the man began to laugh; the cackle was sickening.

Shepherd grabbed Ryan. 'I think it's time you took our young friend to get some rest. He is obviously upset.' Ryan turned to him, his face still pale. As he nodded his jowls shook and he turned. 'Ah, Ryan?' He turned back, his hand on Michael's shoulder. 'Leave me the gun, please.'

Ryan handed it over and escorted the loudly sobbing and swearing Michael out of the tunnel. The metal of the pistol's frame was cool in his hand and it sent shivers up his spine. Everything was too cold down here and the dark didn't help. The man inside the cell still boomed with laughter. He laughed louder the further Ryan led Michael down the hall. Shepherd waited until he heard the steel door slam shut at the end of the tunnel before he turned back.

No sooner had the steel door shut had the laughter stopped. When Shepherd had turned back to the cell, the black eyes were on him once more. Jack's lip was curled into a snarl and he snorted out of his nose like a bull.

'Open this door,' he said calmly.

'Now, son, you and I both know that isn't going to happen.'

The tyrant shot his hands up and slammed them against the bars. They shook in their frame and dust listed down from the roof.

'You call me son one more time and I'll bust through these fucking bars and push your head out through your ass.' He wrapped his hands around the bars again and the metal groaned as the giant began to clench his fist. Metal flaked above his hand and sifted down to the ground.

'Okay. Okay.' Shepherd pushed the pistol down the back of his pants and held his hands up in a pacifying gesture, as he forced his smile once more. 'What do I call you then? Because apparently, I can't call you Jack.'

It was the right question; the bars fell silent as the fists relaxed. The brute pushed his face closer to the bars, a horrible sneer spread across his face. 'Are you a religious man?' He looked Shepherd up and down.

'I am a man of God—' he began.

'Horse shit!' he bellowed. 'You say that you are and they fall for your shit, the fucking sheep.'

Shepherd pulled over the folding chair and sat down. 'No. You aren't a sheep. You're right about that, and no, I'm not a pious man you're right about that too. I read people. That's my talent, and I see that you aren't a man for bullshit.' The big man snorted. 'So, if you're not a sheep, you're not Jack. Who do I have the pleasure of talking to?'

He snarled back instantly, 'Even though I'm behind these bars, don't talk to me as if you have any power over me.' He spat as he paused. His black eyes never seemed to move from Shepherd's face. 'You're the one that has me locked up here, you tell your name and I'll decide what I tell you.'

'Shepherd.'

He laughed that horrible cackle again. Then he became serious in a snap once more and clenched the bar. With a roar, the bars groaned and screamed as they noticeably moved under his strength.

'Liar.' As he pushed his face close to the bars, the soft light washed over him. Shepherd saw the darkness in the eyes clearer, saw how they rolled in their sockets. 'You ask who I am, you should ask *what*. But your kind doesn't understand, you can't understand. I'll ask you a question and you better tell me the truth.' He pushed his face into the bars. 'Where is it?'

Shepherd paused. He looked to the ground, he needed to choose his words wisely. He thought about Riley; he thought about the new wallpaper. 'It's safe.'

'Safe isn't a place!' he sneered.

'But it wasn't a lie,' Shepherd retorted.

The body of Jack Baker spun away from the cell and paced back and forth. In another fit of rage, he raced back to the bars, and spat as he screamed. 'Where is it?!'

'I had to hide it.' Shepherd came back. 'Something—'

'Something,' he leered. 'Riley.'

Shepherd's smile wavered. 'How do you know his name?'

The sneer was back. 'He was weak.' He laughed as he said this. 'You touched it as well. I couldn't get you though, you didn't hold it long enough. Wasn't it nice though? Didn't you just want to hold it, look at it? Use it?'

Shepherd went quiet. He thought about the horrible feeling that worked through him when he took the rifle from Riley. That odd sensation that crawled through his spine each time he looked to the spot that only he knew existed behind the wallpaper, behind the mirror. He searched deep inside of himself. He was the persuader here not this… *thing*.

'I have it and if you want it back, you'll need to help me with something.' He stretched his smile out there for good measure.

'Help you?' it laughed. 'I don't need to help you. You're so insignificant you can't even think past yourself.'

'That may be so, but you'll never get it back if you don't.' His smile, for the first time in a long time, actually seemed genuine. He had this bastard. 'On the other hand, I could bring it here, in pieces, ground down to nothing more than what it was when It was a piece of bar stock.'

The face darkened. 'I'll fucking—'

'You'll do what you're asked otherwise the boy might have an accident as well.'

The giant turned away. 'I don't care about the boy.'

'Ahh, but does Jack?' The feeling that he had lost control was gone. Shepherd had him now, and they both knew it.

'Jack doesn't matter anymore.' He grumbled, his back to the cell door, his head down. 'He's too weak.'

'And what about his body?' Shepherd probed.

'I make his body strong. He didn't even know what he had.' It turned back to the door. 'In Riley, I felt slow and weak. I felt like how I always do in your kind, like nothing. But in this. Even now, sick and broken, I feel strong. For the first time, I don't even know how strong.' Then he placed his hands around the bars again. 'Do you want to find out?'

Shepherd leaned forward, tempting fate. 'Why don't we find out together?' The fist remained relaxed. Deep breaths were the only sound the hallway. 'You need that body. I'll fix it for you. In return I have a—' He paused. He needed to say it right. 'A favour to ask.'

'Favours?' it snarled.

'It doesn't even have to be for me. All I need is something that people will remember. I need a champion. In return, you'll get well. You'll have the chance to,' he gestured to the bodies behind him, 'to do what you are good at.'

For some time, it remained silent behind the bars. It didn't move or talk, it just stared at him. Then with a deep rushing exhale it said 'Let me ask you something.' As it bent down and grasped the limp guard who still lay at his feet, by the head. He lifted him with one hand and stood him on his feet.

To Shepherd's surprise, he was still alive, their eyes locked as he sobbed. He murmured the words, 'Please God' over and over again, but no one paid him any mind.

'Do I frighten you?' The tyrant asked as he pushed the guard's face gently into the bars.

Shepherd took a moment; the guard's sobs weren't helping his situation. He felt like he was about to lose control of the situation once more, and he didn't like it.

'Any man would be stupid not to be cautious of someone your size,' he said, hopeful that it would placate the man.

'That's not what I asked,' The tyrant snarled as he pressed the guard's face into the small space between the bars. Screams came again, as horrendous as they were short lived. The guard's skull crunched and splintered as his screams died.

Shepherd watched as the guard's head, deformed and broken as it was, squeezed through the bars toward him. His nose protruded out further than it should; his eyes bulged from their sockets, then burst from the strain. Blood and fluid ran down the dead man's face and into his mouth, where it pooled and dribbled from the corner of his lips. When the hand relaxed, the crushed head slid down the bars until the frame of its collapsing body stopped it.

'I scare the shit out of you, is the answer. I know it's true.' They stood there for some time. Neither of them spoke. 'You fix this body, keep the boy safe and it. You do that and you have your champion.'

With the smile gone from his face, Shepherd turned to leave. He walked four paces when it called out to him. He stopped. He didn't want to look back, and he didn't have to.

'Remember what you saw today. If I get my hands on you, no God will save you.'

RANKIN

*'All lies and yet,
Still the man hears what he wants to hear,
And disregards the rest.'*

Simon and Garfunkel – *The Boxer* (1970)

Gooseflesh erupted on his shoulders and his forearms; his body trembled. The rain hammered the shell of the Holden and the thunder shook the body on its chassis. The ground quaked beneath the tyres, either afraid of the roar from the heavens or the blatt of the V8's exhaust. He sat in silence as Chris navigated the hull down the empty highway and his eyes were drawn to the centre of the crack in the windscreen.

Rankin watched as the water ran over the crack. It torrented over the ridges and jagged edges of the glass. Then slowly, a bead formed in the centre and dripped onto the dashboard. The small windscreen wipers worked tirelessly, yet they seemed to have as much hope of clearing the water as Chris did of finding his wife.

He turned and looked at his driver, the middle-aged man. Solemn, with eyes sunk into their sockets, the bags of a thousand years of insomnia under his eyes. His skin was pallid from malnutrition and his beard was an ashen grey. Chris would drive for, say, twenty minutes, then burst out in laughter about a joke that Rankin obviously had not been privy to. Either that or he would cry. Or both. Rankin decided that things like this could only happen to him.

Only he could go through what he had, just to find himself further in the shit each time he opened his eyes.

In the short time he had known Chris Lowe, he had seen more sides of him than of all of his old friends from Vietnam put together. Hope came with the first light of dawn. Despair and the relapse into depression came with the fires of dusk every night. The anger that swelled out of him when he questioned the soldier back in Brisbane. Which could only fuel the fierce power of his old body that had not yet given up the ghost. Bursts of humour and witty one liner's that came from nowhere and without warning, no matter the mood he was in. Then at night, when Rankin tried to sleep, if they decided to pull over at all, Chris would sit there behind the wheel of his Holden, his bayonet across his lap while his revolver hung loose from his hand. His mouth moved as he whispered to himself. At times in the light of the moon, he thought he saw the glint of tears on his cheek as they melted into the scruff of his beard. His mouth ran off words of no correlation to anything Rankin knew. The fog or the mist, the smoke over the road, as if he recited a prayer to himself each night, or to her.

Below it all, he saw the desperation of a man who had lost absolutely everything in his life. The desperation that left him to cling to a piece of metal that he called Pestilence. Rankin smiled softly as he brushed the cool brass at his hip. He was no better. As he looked into the poor man's face, the exhaustion evident in his expression. He wondered if he was actually there in the forefront, whether the pilot light in his head still flickered.

Seven days and six nights they had travelled. The going was slow beyond the waste of life that was Brisbane. Each town needed to be watched for signs of life, or patrols. Any hint of the elements of the Chinese rear was dealt with.

Rankin had always enjoyed being in cars, especially those with some power. He couldn't remember many times in his life where he had been scared for his existence, but this car and the way it was driven, was one thing that chilled him. It wasn't like he was scared to look at the thing or sit in it but when it was driven at fifty miles per hour straight into the side of a stationary jeep while he sat in the passenger seat, he felt he had reason to be concerned. In fact, he was more than concerned, he was scared shitless.

Since the LandCruiser incident back in Brisbane and the jeep, they had rammed two more jeeps at high speed and one small personnel carrier. Rankin had counted himself lucky to be alive more than once, but the sight of the lightly armoured hull as it rapidly grew in size through the already cracked windscreen, turned his stomach while the driver next to him spat curses and howled in anger. He thought of the stories he had heard about the Japanese kamikaze pilots in the Second World War. The pilots that had so much honour that once they had run out of munitions to slay their enemies, they had flown their vessels directly into them. They gave up their lives for the furtherment of their nation's cause, but this was beyond a joke.

The personnel carrier incident had happened on the first day, just after they had left the side of the highway. Shortly after, they had found Rankin some clothes. He had pulled the denim over his legs while the unbuttoned wings of the plaid shirt jostled. Although Rankin was happy to wear some warmer clothes, the stark red and blue was not something that he envisioned as a suitable camouflage. In the same token, he supposed a pale Holden with a worked V8 and straight through exhaust couldn't be classified as the stealthiest of the vehicles ever made. He was happier when he found the stash of cigarettes. The town had been ransacked, each building turned upside down in the search for food, water and fuel. He thought about the looter that had gone through his pockets and thanked Christ that the son of a bitch hadn't been present in this store. Two cartons of Benson and Hedges sat on the counter proud as punch, as if they waited just for him. He had run out of smokes the previous day and Chris had shown little empathy, seeing as though one full cigarette had been lost to him, when Chris tossed it out of the window.

Rankin smoked happily as he threaded the buttons across his chest, the cigarette clamped between his lips. The town had been mostly silent, only disturbed by the clinking glass beneath their feet as they entered shops and houses. The clatter of rubbish that skittered across the ground as one of their careless feet disturbed its rest. But slowly a sound that Rankin despised had crawled up on them, the sound of tracks on bitumen.

'Fuck. Armour,' Rankin muttered to Chris, before they slunk back to the Holden, his cigarettes in his arms. The V8 fired up and Chris trumped the throttle briskly as he pushed the shifter into gear.

'Ease up man, we don't want the whole army to hear us,' Rankin scolded. He spoke almost in a whisper, realising as he did how stupid it was.

Chris simply laughed at him and continued to reverse the utility down the road. The steering system groaned as he turned the wheel and the front end swung around. He backed the utility off the road and down a narrow alley between two old shops. The exhaust baffled back onto them. He killed the engine and pushed his head out of the window to listen.

'They wouldn't hear this over the tracks of that thing.' Chris nodded in the direction of the street.

Rankin popped his door open and slid out. As he made his way around the cabin, he kept his body low. They had still not found any ammunition for the SLR and Chris hadn't allowed him to touch the revolver since their escape. So, he slipped his old faithful brass dusters out and clenched his fist around them; instantly, he felt better. He pulled himself over the stone face of a brick wall, and his boots thudded heavily onto the gravel below. Three buildings now stood between him and the battered utility. He moved to the small concrete walkway and squatted with his back to the wall. With his body concealed from the road, he let his ass slide onto the ground and slowly he leaned himself out so that he could see the street.

The clatter of the vehicle's tracks had become louder, but if it was a tank, it still seemed a way off. Then he heard the voice of a soldier who seemed too close and he snapped his head back. Another voice laughed in response to the first, further away, but the clattering was closer still. He leaned out once more and slid further down the weatherboard to allow only the tip of his head to reveal itself from cover. He saw the silhouette of a soldier disappear behind the shop wall. The man was headed back up the street. On the far side, he saw two men armed with AKs as they walked close together. The flat nose of a light armoured transport edged into view. No wonder he'd thought the tank sounded far away; it only made half the noise. He let the vehicle come full into sight and waited as long as he could to see if there were more men.

Rankin ran as fast yet as quietly as he could. He vaulted the brick wall and landed in a sprint. He rounded the rear end of the Holden and heaved himself in as he shut the door.

'Three infantry, maybe four, two this side, two on the far side. Light troop carrier working up the middle.'

Chris nodded, and he flicked the ignition to on.

'Hey, what are you doing? Just let them pass man, they don't know we're here.' Rankin grabbed Chris by his arm, but he was focused on the windscreen. His eyes looked dull and unfocused. Chris raised the revolver so he could easily fire from his open window and a smile worked over his lips.

'Someone said to me once that a man plays the cards he's dealt,' Chris said to him as he pumped the throttle, priming it for the ambush. He had sat in silence, for some time until the very tip of the armoured vehicle had become visible. Then he spoke as he turned the key, 'But I reckon a wiser man rigs the deck.'

Rankin did not even have a second to register the words before it all happened. The engine didn't even turn once and it caught. Chris pressed the accelerator as soon as the first piston fired and it went immediately into a high throated roar that rattled Rankin's window in its channels as the exhaust echoed back. The tyres hooked and the utility shot down the alley. There was no point in saying anything; Rankin was as much a prisoner in that ute as he was a collaborator. He sunk himself back into the soft fabric of the seat beneath him as the opening of the alley whisked toward them, as did the armoured side of the carrier.

He hadn't seen the first soldier step out. Not at first, but as the Holden exploded out of the alley, there was crunch of meat and metal and a slap as a limb caved in. The speed only increased, as if the impact had meant nothing on the track to its target. As the curb stepped down, the Holden soared into the street. Rankin was frozen. He had no idea of the speed they travelled at; he was in too much shock to look over at the speedo. He braced himself against the dashboard and pushed himself deeper into the seat. The engine revved high as the wheels spun in the air and then they crashed into the side of the carrier.

There was a tremendous crunch and the sound as steel ground and scraped against the tracks that continued to try to push the lightly armoured carrier forward. The steel on the side of the carrier was heavy enough to withstand penetration from rifles, but it stood no chance against the force that was put behind the hardened steel track.

As if in slow motion, Rankin saw the side give in as they continued to push forward, the tail of the utility still high behind them as it drove inwards and then he was thrown forward with such force. He heard a horrible crack and he thought for sure that his legs had been broken, then his side crashed into the dash and he felt all the air go out of him as the board crunched beneath him. Then they were still.

As he gasped for air, he opened the passenger door and spilled out onto the road. The taste of blood was in his mouth and a horrible ache thrummed in his ribs. As he lifted himself up, he spat and a motley glob of blood and snot spread out over the bitumen. He steadied himself and then fell to his knee; he gasped in a breath of air that stung him horribly as his chest expanded. He heard a pistol shot and he lifted his head.

One of the soldiers on the far side of the road had moved around onto him, his AK raised as he walked. He looked up, helpless and unarmed, in too much pain to move as he saw the black hole of its muzzle. Then another pistol shot and the soldier's face became taut with pain and he dropped his rifle. His two hands went to the hole that had appeared in his chest as blood began to pour through his fingers. Below the grinding metal of the pinned troop carrier and the ticking of the Holdens stalled V8, Rankin could hear the gurgle of the soldier's last struggled breaths.

Rankin crawled over to the rifle that lay at the dying man's feet. Each movement felt like a dagger in his side and for a moment he thought he had been stabbed once more, the scar of his old wound torn open. He felt the fabric of the rifle's sling, and he dragged it over to him. The over oiled timber was warm in the palm of his hand and he tried to move his finger onto the trigger, but the brass knuckles prevented him.

He groaned and gasped as he swore into the air in a spray of blood and spit. He swapped his grip and held the rifle as if he were left-handed, as the top of the troop carrier opened. A man's head appeared, blood ran down his face as he screamed. Rankin pulled the trigger and the AK rattled to life in his hand. The clunky fire in his left hand felt horrible and odd to him. Bullets sprayed over the heavy frontal armour and ricocheted into the air.

Finally, he caught the screaming driver of the carrier under the chin and silenced him. There was a thud as his body fell lifeless back into the hull.

Automatic fire sounded from the other side of the road and the back window of the Holden exploded inwards. Rankin rolled onto his side and hissed at the pain of movement as he saw the soldier they had hit, his legs destroyed beneath him. He held his rifle in one hand as he tried to support himself with the other. The recoil forced the rifle to move violently with each shot and bullets sprayed off the bitumen, the steel sides of the Holden, and into the weakened side of the carrier. Until Chris used his final shot in the revolver and put an end to the skirmish.

When it was over, Rankin would have liked nothing more than to have driven his fist into Chris' mouth, but the way he felt, he doubted that he would have been able to swing. Chris' face was dark. He was angry about something. He climbed onto the carrier and peered into the roof hatch.

'Fuck!' he yelled into the street, 'Fuck!'

'Wh-What?' Rankin gasped, as he finally stood under his own power but hunched slightly from the pain that seemed to soak into his whole body.

'We didn't leave any alive.'

Rankin saw red once more. They had almost died, both of them and his biggest concern was that none were left alive, no doubt so that Chris could show them the photo of his wife and ask where she was. Somehow, his side felt better and the urge to punch Chris swelled up once more.

'We're fucking lucky to be alive, you idiot!'

Chris looked at him, the anger still hot on his face. 'Ahh bullshit.'

'Bullshit nothing, you have to stop this shit. You're going to kill yourself and more importantly, me.' Rankin hobbled over to him, and pressed the butt of the rifle into his hip as he held it out sideways, which for some reason alleviated the pain. 'I said I'd help you find her. I didn't say I'd help you run fucking suicide missions on every Chinese patrol we come across from here to Sydney.'

The darkness in Chris' face lifted a little and he dropped his gaze to the ground. 'That was close.' His mouth started to work and Rankin sighed. Was he about to cry? But no, a large toothy grin spread across Chris' face instead.

'What is there to smile about?' Rankin asked, even further aggravated by this mood swing.

Chris laughed as he jumped off the carrier's roof. The soles of his boots slapped the bitumen as he landed. 'Watch this,' he said as he leaned in the window of the Holden. The transmission clunked into neutral and then the starter motor whirred. The engine turned over once, twice and then fired and amazingly, ran perfect. The engine blasted its monotonous note into the empty street as if nothing had happened. Chris opened the door and slid behind the wheel. The transmission clunked once more and the wheel started to turn, pulling the Holden from the side of the steel wreck in front of it. At first, it was hung up, trapped by the treads that had finally stopped turning. Then with a screech of steel, it came free and backed away.

The bar had not moved an inch. Marks of green paint and blood still marked its bonnet, but the structure of the Holden wasn't even twisted. Rankin shook his head as Chris brought the ute to a stop and leapt out of the driver's seat to do an inspection. He clapped his hands together as he saw the strength of his work and held his hands out to it.

'That is what I'm smiling about. And to think, a roo almost wrote this baby off.' He laughed and pointed back to the caved in side of the carrier. 'You should see what happened to the poor bastard sitting next to that wall.'

Rankin decided he preferred not to and climbed into the ute. He took the AK with him, and lit a cigarette. When Chris went to say something, Rankin lifted the barrel of the rifle and looked at him. 'You fuckin' try it mate, one isn't going to hurt it.' Then Rankin looked to the dash and whistled, his body had destroyed the entire passenger side of the dash. That was the crack he had heard. 'Shame your dash isn't as strong as your chassis.' He said before a deep raucous laugh took him, even though it pained him severely to laugh in that matter, it was worth it. He laughed while he looked at Chris, the driver's face was pouty at the sight of the crumpled metal and cracked veneer.

That was four days ago. The ache in his ribs had mostly subsided and he moved freely once more. To carry a Chinese AK was another experience for him; the Chinese built assault rifle was poorly made and clunky compared to the Australian SLR. However, the SLR lay in the bed of the Holden, with no ammunition to run it. While the AK sat awkwardly in the cab, a pile of magazines floated amongst his feet. Rankin snorted softly in a laugh, 'the cards we're dealt.'

The rainwater continued to bead in the centre of the spider's web in the windscreen and drip occasionally to the buckled dash. The vision out of the windscreen was poor, he estimated he could only see about forty feet in front of the bar. Although Rankin had the crack to contend with, he doubted whether his driver could see much further. The rain swept across the road in sheets of intensity. One moment it lapsed and he felt as though it was finally about to lift, then the grey line of water moved toward them and the road in front dissolved into water and hazed lights once more.

How Chris was able to keep the ute on the road in this weather was beyond Rankin. He himself had never been much of a driver. If his life hadn't gone to shit the second time, and if he had stayed on as a mechanic, he eventually would have owned a car or a truck of some sort. He'd enjoyed working on cars more than he'd realised. He frowned. Perhaps one day he still would.

The lights reflected off a green road sign, which was large with white lettering. Rankin struggled to read it through the over washed glass and the water that spattered in through the smashed rear window. Rankin thought that it would have been a disaster when it started to rain. He smelt the moisture in the air and felt it on the back of his neck, but Chris didn't seem deterred.

At first, the wind rolled over the roof and swirled back into the cab through the gaping hole. However, as Chris adjusted his speed, they found they could minimise the water ingest by holding the speed at thirty. They cruised pretty happily at that speed, as they coursed through northern New South Wales. Even though at times Rankin would have preferred for Chris to slow down in the wet weather, he appreciated being mostly dry.

The road sign whisked past. Rankin barely caught half of the word. 'TAM…' Rankin spoke out. He had to yell due to the increased road noise. Chris raised his eyebrows and looked over at him, a confused look on his face.

'What did that sign say?' Rankin asked, his eyes on Chris.

'What sign?'

'The one we just…' Rankin started to look back out the windscreen as he spoke and saw the unmistakable shape of a Chinese tank's hull emerge from the darkness and rain. 'Shit!' Rankin yelled as he pointed forward.

Chris turned his head back slowly. His reactions had become woefully sluggish. His mouth opened in surprise as the tank's body came closer by the second. Rankin felt the wheels lock underneath them. In a panic, Chris slammed his foot on the brake. The Holden slid and Chris began to turn the wheel wildly. The car went into a horrible slide, but thankfully, the vehicle's momentum took it to the right of the tank. Rankin sighed, but they weren't out of the woods.

Chris pumped the throttle and the back end snapped to attention and came around fast in the opposite direction. The headlights washed over the faces of people that stood behind the tank. Rankin saw a plaid jacket and others in blue overalls. He turned his head to look at them, but they had vanished in the rain. Chris pumped the throttle again and this time the back end listed the other way, but too far. Rankin heard the tyres grind over the wet bitumen as the car went into another long slide and then it all came to an abrupt halt with the all too familiar sound of crunching metal.

Rankin was thrown onto Chris, whose head smashed through the driver's window. Chris groaned underneath him as the rain now poured in through the two windows. Rankin lifted himself back and he pulled Chris with him, his head lolled on his neck and as he folded over, the faint sight of blood in his hair.

This was the last thing they needed, a Chinese tank in the road and now the driver knocked out. Rankin swore. He reached for the AK. His hand closed around the chunky grip as he heard a click, and the passenger door swung open.

More rain and water rushed in, and Rankin raised the barrel. He saw a hand come forward and force the barrel back down.

'Now son,' a smooth, firm voice came from over the rain, 'you don't want to create a problem now, do you?'

Rankin looked up. Before him was a man who would not have been a day over fifty, hunched so that he could peer in at the occupants of the car. He had green eyes and blonde hair and a smile that seemed too big for his face, either that or his teeth were too large. The smiler's eyes went past Rankin and looked to Chris, who still lay unconscious. 'Looks like your friend's in a bit of trouble.' His smile seemed to widen. 'Well, you're lucky you came by us. Put down the rifle, son.'

Rankin didn't like how this man, who had never laid eyes on him before in his life, called him *son*. He didn't like the patronising smile nor the look of him altogether, but in the end, they needed help.

'He hit his head in the crash. I think he's out to it.' He lowered the rifle and let it clack to the floor of the cabin.

The smiler's eyes squinted as it touched the carpet, then he held out a hand to Rankin. 'Here, let me help you.' Rankin took his hand, and climbed out of the Holden. It felt good to get out of the car, but the rain was horrid. 'Come on, get out of the rain and I'll send some people back for your friend.' With that, the smiler turned and began to jog down the road. Rankin watched as the plaid jacket blurred in his eyes to make a smear of red across his vision. The street was wide, with small houses to the left and a sweeping field of grass to his right that fell away from the road. He turned back to Chris, he lay in the ute unmoving.

'I'll be back mate, you'll be fine.' He patted Chris on the shoulder and closed the door. He took off after the faint image of the red plaid jacket. It looked as though the smiling man was headed to a pub: an old building with a worn porch. Rankin rushed after him, leaving the stalled Holden behind him.

The smiler waited for him under the cover of the porch. Rankin stopped once he had made it out from under the rain and wiped the water from his eyes. 'Hey man, I just want to say thanks.' He held out his hand, which the smiler shook. 'I'm Rankin Bartlett.'

His smile widened even further and his eyes squinted to create lines of crow's feet at their edges. 'Pleased to meet you, Mr Bartlett. You can call me Shepherd.' Rankin regretted shaking hands with him as soon as they touched. It was an odd handshake with not enough pressure, yet the man wouldn't let go. 'We're real happy you joined us. Come inside and get warm and I'll send some boys to get your friend.'

A sigh of relief rippled through Rankin's body when Shepherd let go of his hand. They held eye contact for a second, then Shepherd turned to the closed double doors. He held the smile until his face was mostly turned and the speed in which in vanished took all the relief away from Rankin's gut. He pushed the doors open and walked inside. An explosion of noise met Rankin's ears as he entered, music played from an unknown source while people chatted and laughed. The room was well lit and warm. It seemed as though this town hadn't been touched by the conflict, but if that was the case, then what was the story with the tank?

'Okay, I need three men,' Shepherd called out in his jovial yet forceful voice. When he spoke, it was as if he presented a speech. He stood up straight and his voice projected across the room. At the first word, the pub fell into silence. The music stopped, and all eyes went to Shepherd. 'A couple of boys came unstuck up by the tank outside of town. Lewis, I think you and your friends there could assist. Our new friend here' – he clapped his hand on Rankin's shoulder – 'is concerned for his partner.'

A surly-looking man with a long, dark beard downed his shot and glared at Rankin. His arm tensed as he squeezed the glass in his hands. His eyes were bloodshot and his skin was pale beneath his dark hair that was slicked back under his Akubra. He gestured for the barman in a gruff bark, all the while he held his eye contact with Rankin.

'Now, please. Lewis,' Shepherd spoke coolly.

Lewis took another shot and then turned to Shepherd. His eyes retained their soulless stare. 'Yes, Shepherd,' he barked, and moved to the door.

As he went, the two men that stood to his right went with him. A slick man with a green shirt and long hair, as well as a broader balding man with two black eyes and horribly disfigured nose.

'Thank you, boys. You get him down the road to Ryan's and make sure he's looked after.' They continued out the door. 'Oh. Lewis!' Shepherd called out. The surly bloke turned back and opened the doors slightly without a word. 'Take that car of theirs undercover too. I'm sure they'll appreciate it.' Shepherd's smile spread into a horrible sneer as he said it. Lewis closed the doors without another word and left them in silence.

Shepherd turned back to Rankin. 'Where are my manners? You must be exhausted. Please, sit down.' He led him over to a small circular table and pulled the chair out for Rankin as he sat. 'Davey, bring our new friend something to warm him up and put on a nice steak for him I think.'

Rankin didn't know what was going on in this place. Who was this Shepherd guy that everyone asked how high when he told them to jump? The guy in question sat down opposite Rankin and placed his elbows on the top.

Shepherd sighed. 'What a world we live in today huh? All of us brothers and sisters need to come together and help one another if we are going to come out of this.' He chuckled softly.

Rankin nodded. He didn't want to sound rude to the man that had taken him off the streets and offered him food and drink. 'You run this town?'

Shepherd looked at him with an embarrassed look that lasted only half a second. 'Oh, Tamworth runs itself. I merely help everyone' – he looked over Rankin's shoulders and gestured to all of the people in the bar – 'stay together.'

The barman arrived at their table with two shot glasses and a bottle of whiskey. He placed a shot glass in front of each of them and then filled them to the brim. Shepherd picked up his glass, spread his lips to reveal his gleaming white teeth once more. 'To the future of our people.' He threw the glass back and then placed it gently on the table.

Rankin didn't join him in the toast. Shepherd looked at him, his head cocked. His eyes went from Rankin to the glass and back again. 'It's rude not to drink when someone proposes a toast.'

He pushed the glass back toward him. 'Sorry, I don't mean to be rude but I'm kind of on the wagon.' Rankin said apologetically. 'It doesn't agree with me.' It had been close to a year since he had had a drink. He wasn't about to start.

'It brings the devil out in you, does it?' Shepherd said in a curious tone.

'You could say that.'

The man smiled with closed lips and Rankin thought it the first sign of genuine amusement in their short acquaintance. 'I have another friend that is, that way inclined. The devil is inside of him and sometimes it's a question of who's in control.'

'I know how he feels.'

The smile vanished. 'Somehow son, I don't think you do.' Shepherd held the eye contact for some time without speaking. His mouth worked as he looked at Rankin as if considering what to do. His eyes looked over Rankin's shoulder once more, locked on a position for a short while and then came back.

'You see, son, we have a problem here. Myself and my friends,' he gestured around the room once more. Rankin shifted uneasily in his seat and he only now noticed the room had remained silent. 'We are trying to keep everyone in this town. We had a small problem with the Chinese, but really they were the ones to help us see the light and we sure do not blame them for what they have done.'

Rankin's eyebrows furrowed. 'You don't blame them? For killing thousands?'

Shepherd waved his hands in a dismissive motion. 'Oh, sure, they may have been a bit brash, but weren't the English when they descended on the lambs that dwelled here two hundred years ago?' He cocked his head once more as if he waited for a reply. There wasn't any.

Behind him, Rankin heard chair legs screech across the timber boards.

'Anyway, that is beside the point now, isn't it? I said I have a problem and I think that you and your friend might be able to help me with that problem.'

Rankin still didn't speak; his eyes were focused on Shepherd. Behind him there were footsteps as one, maybe two, people moved around.

'When times are unsure, people become restless and that is a very, very dangerous thing.' He placed both of his hands together as if in prayer. 'And what better way to quell a restless spirit than to provide' – he paused, and looked upward as if to think but Rankin knew he had prepared this speech – 'entertainment, to get those thoughts of misgivings and rebellion out of one's mind.'

'I don't see how I can help with that.' Rankin spoke softly as he attempted to maintain his level of politeness.

'Oh, you will, son.' Shepherd's eyes darted to the right.

Rankin heard quick steps behind him and he began to turn when the sound of shattering glass erupted around his head and he felt himself fall. He hit the hardwood floors and the world reeled in waves of darkness and light. His ears rang from the impact and he felt someone's knee deep in his back.

Someone whispered in his ear. He felt their breathe against his cheek and smelt the whiskey. Before he faded, Shepherd said to him, 'You will.'

MICHAEL

'Seasons change with the scenery
Weaving time in a tapestry
Won't you stop and remember me
At any convenient time?'

Simon and Garfunkel – *A Hazy Shade of Winter* (1968)

Michael lay curled up in his cot. As he had never slept in anything as basic as what he now lay on, he assumed that was what it was called. The straw stuffed inside the hessian bag worked through the rough weavings with each movement of his small body and pushed their needle-like points through the fabric to stab into him like daggers in the night. He itched continuously; his back was red from the constant scratches from his finger nails and a rash had run up his right side.

His thoughts took him back to the rough woven blanket that used to live crumpled up at the foot of his bed. What he would've done to have had that scratchy old thing now. What had happened to everything back home? The Fairlane, his books, all of his home-school work shut inside of his father's office cabinet. Would they ever have new owners? Would they ever have the hands of another child run over their exterior? Or just like everything else, every person or thing left behind, would they just cease to exist at all? A forgotten dream that gave only a sense of déjà vu.

When the sun had begun to rise on his fourteenth day at

Tamworth, he rose with no real ambition left. When he had awoken at Chinchilla, he had so many things to look forward to and only a few to dread. Even when Jack had taken him into the mountains, he at least had something to wake up for. Even if it was to walk a few more miles, to follow his brother up and down the rolling hills. He still had no idea the exact reason to why Jack had taken them up there.

In the best way he could, he understood and accepted that his mother and Tony were dead and that they had been dead for days, if not weeks, before they had left. He had decided that Jack's motives could be a possibility of two things and perhaps a combination of both. Shortly after their arrival in Tamworth he had questioned one of the nicer men that held him in captivity, about why Tamworth was the way it was now. Billy, the heavy-set man with his favourite denim jacket, had told him about the invasion and the Chinese. Perhaps Jack had taken them south to escape the front lines. But as far as Michael knew, the fighting never even came close to Chinchilla.

The second possibility came in the face of the older man that visited Michael in the kitchen that time. He had only the vaguest of memories of that time and now that he tried to think back on that nice man's face, he found that he couldn't remember what it looked like. Only the twisted image that had appeared on the hedge wall inside of his dream. He had this thought before and had already come to the conclusion that Jack in no way could ever have been frightened of another man.

If it had come down to anything, Jack would rather have died than to have walked away from an insult, but perhaps Jack didn't just think about himself. All of the times that he had looked back on his life with his brother, he had always thought of Jack hurting him. Over the times that had been so, but brothers played, sometimes.

At first, they had played a lot. Then one time Jack had hurt him pretty bad, and Michael could never remember them playing at all ever since. Whether Michael had been bored and egged his brother on, Jack had only ever walked away in a silent brood. Maybe it was never his fault.

The simplest thing to do would be to walk down and talk to him, but that could never happen. Shepherd, being the sick and twisted man he was, had even offered multiple times to take Michael down there to see him. He offered his fake smile and almost pulled off a look of concern for the boy, but Michael had always turned him down. He could never quite work out whether Shepherd had just wanted to show off his new toy, or if he wanted Michael to suffer at what had become of his brother.

Instead, Michael thought of Jack now like his father, his mother, Paul Darcy, and Susan. Someone that was in his past, someone who the lines of the face would become blurry with time in his mind. He wondered if he could ever go back to the sanctuary that was destroyed just to look at the carvings on the hedge. Just to see if Jack's face had joined all the rest.

He went about his morning ritual, although it had changed dramatically now. He washed himself with the freezing water that lay in the bucket to the side of his cot. His flesh erupted in goose pimples as he ran the old, wet rag over himself. The clothes that he had been given to wear were always left on the shelf above where he slept.

The basement of the Tamworth Hotel seemed cold even in the heat of the day. It always smelt damp and no matter how much he swept the floors just to pass the time, the floor always felt dirty beneath his feet. He'd positioned his cot so that the first light would seep through the small slitted window close to the ceiling and shine on his face. Then, once he had washed himself, he would dress and head upstairs to collect Shepherd's breakfast and deliver it.

Like a rabid animal, his stomach always roared and rumbled as he entered the kitchen. The smell of the bacon and eggs, the sight of the plump sausages, all of it got him going, but he never ate right away. As if he was one of the dogs in the pack that had attacked him and Jack, he had to wait until the Alpha had eaten his full, before he was allowed to nibble at the scraps. He hated it, he hated standing there as he pretended to be polite. Forced to watch as the man that held him captive chewed loudly, as grease ran down his chin. Although Shepherd was not a fat man, he ate like one that had been starved.

As Michael stood there in silence, Shepherd often gave him his chores for the day, labours he called them. Mostly they seemed to be things that Shepherd himself should do. Things like sourcing information on the projects that he had ordered to be undertaken. Relaying orders to Ryan about what prisoners to keep in chains and what ones to send to Jonathan for the building of his grand design. He often spoke of his grand plan. Now that he had managed to safe guard Tamworth from the Chinese, he saw his position only to be threatened by the people who lived under him and so he needed to keep them happy. Michael still had no idea on how he intended to do this, but something told him that Jack played a part.

'I only have two labours for you to accomplish today, son,' Shepherd said to him through a mouthful of toast. He forced the dry toast down and took a large swig of orange juice. As he dabbed at his face with a napkin, Michael saw his sinister smile appear across his lips once more. 'I want you to head over to Ryan's—'

'I don't want to see *him*.' Michael interrupted.

The smile vanished from Shepherd's face and he slammed his open palm down on the table. The silverware jumped slightly at the slap. 'Don't interrupt me,' he growled through his teeth. 'I made a bargain with your brother that I would keep you safe. But that doesn't mean that I won't discipline you when I see fit.' His eyes burned with an anger that seemed as false as everything else about this man. Michael wondered if anything was real with him, or if it was all an act.

'I don't want to see him, sir,' Michael repeated. He added the title to try to make it seem more polite.

'Let me finish,' Shepherd growled again, picking his screwed-up napkin back up from the table where he'd thrown it. 'I want you to help him find some strong men that look like they were fighters once, or still.'

Michael remained silent; he had learned in his short time with Shepherd that silence could be taken as many things. However, when you spoke it only meant defiance unless the only words ever spoken were 'yes sir.'

The smile returned to Shepherd's face, and he continued. 'Tell him to make a list of names, and have it to me by this afternoon. We are almost ready.' Shepherd stood and walked over to the mirror that he favoured so much. Michael thought that the only thing Shepherd liked to do more than talk was to look at himself in the mirror. Shepherd smiled into the glass. 'Once you've done all you can there, then get Billy to take you to Jonathan to see how it is coming along. I expect a full description of everything.' Although his back was to Michael, their eyes locked in the surface of the mirror.

The room had begun to stink, and Michael only wanted to clear the plates and leave. 'Yes, sir,' he said in a droll tone and set about cleaning up. As he did so, he came close to the bed. The blankets and doona were piled high onto one side. When he came closer, they shifted slightly and Michael saw the face of a woman with black hair.

Tears streamed down her face, and bruises blackened the skin around both eyes. As she moved her mouth, he could see that she had lost some teeth. The sheets shifted further as she extended a hand out to him.

'My baby,' she mouthed as the sheets rolled away from her to expose her naked body and breasts. 'Help my baby.'

Michael had seen enough in the short time since his life had begun its slow spiral down into the drain. This new sight of another poor soul that had lost everything in life barely even touched him. He felt sorry for her, God knew that, but there was nothing he could do for her. Not now.

'Kill me,' were the last words she whispered before he left that room, and Michael wished that he could.

The morning air was brisk, but the jacket they had given him was more than warm enough. As Michael walked down the street, he began to overheat slightly as his old boots thudded along the path. The police station was only a short walk, yet Shepherd drove everywhere. Michael imagined that once people learned how to drive, they instantaneously forgot how to walk. All except for him and those that had no other choice. He skipped up the concrete steps to the police station and pushed his way in past the heavy timber door.

Ryan sat at the front desk, smoking a cigarette while he sipped at a coffee. He looked like shit; the bags under his eyes swallowed half of his cheeks. Stubble grew unruly around his usually clean-shaven jaw and he slumped over the mug, which steamed on his desk as he supported his head with two hands. He had always been nice enough to Michael, so he had no reason to be angry with him. Ryan only ever did what Shepherd told him to do and he supposed he couldn't blame him for that.

'Hi Ryan.' He spoke in a somewhat cheerful tone that was the complete opposite of how he felt. He wanted to laugh at himself all of a sudden, either that or cry. The time he had spent with Shepherd had begun to turn him into liar.

Ryan looked up at him with two bloodshot eyes and gave a slow blink. 'Oh, it's you Michael, thank fuck for that.'

Surprised to hear someone actually happy to see him in this place, Michael paused. 'Are you okay?'

'Yeah, I'm alright, just had no sleep. In-between that fucking monster roaring his tits off all night and the new mongrels they dragged in, I'm about ready to pack it in.' He laughed. 'Yeah, imagine your bosses face when I hand him my letter of resignation.' He cackled as his tired eyes watered. Then when he looked back at Michael, his laughter died in his throat.

Michael looked down at his feet, saddened at once by what Ryan had said. 'Is it still the bad one? Or has he woken up?'

The adult placed a soft hand on his shoulder. 'I'm sorry Michael, I'm tired and I forgot. I shouldn't have said any…'

Michael shot him a glare through teary eyes. 'Who is it?'

He averted his gaze and removed his hand. 'It's still black eyes.'

Michael nodded and sniffed, changing the subject completely. 'Shepherd doesn't want anything with him today. He wants you and me to look at people and make a list of those that could be fighters. He said he's almost ready.'

Ryan caught that Michael didn't want to linger on the subject of his brother and followed suit. 'Won't take long for that, half of those they bring in are young women for him. They kill mostly all the rest. Probably those trying to protect these girls they take. Fuckin' animals.'

He stood up and kneaded his knuckles into his eyes. Through a yawn he said, 'The two they got the other night are pretty toey, they'd be alright. Maybe a few more in one of the other blocks. I'd have to look. I can't tell shit from shoe polish at the minute.'

Michael nodded. 'Where are the new two? He would want me to look.'

Ryan looked at him, the weariness evident. 'Same tunnel as…'

'Okay, I'll look at them. He said he wants a full list this afternoon. I'll tell him about these two and say they're special. I don't know.' He shrugged.

'I'll come with you,' he said as he drained the last of his coffee.

'It's okay. I'll be fine. Have a sleep maybe and then do his stupid list later.' Michael shrugged again; he didn't really care anymore. He knew where these two were, he knew where to go and where not to go. He liked Ryan, but he didn't need a baby sitter. As Ryan agreed, he yawned once more, sagging down into his swivel chair again and closing his eyes.

Michael made his way through the station. He saw a couple of other guards, Ryan's helpers, more than anything. There weren't many. One of them let him into the tunnel, and then shut the door behind him. Michael heard it lock. They were all scared of the thing down the end, the one with the black eyes. Deep down inside, Michael felt a glimmer of pride.

They had tried to keep the cells further down empty, as none of the guards wanted to walk anywhere near that monster. Michael walked past the first cell, which held three young women all of them quite pretty. He didn't have to look much further to find the two men that the jailer had spoken of. He came to the second cell, which held two men.

Both of them were silent, yet neither were asleep. The younger one lay on his back in his cot that lined the right wall. He was calm, his strong hands were buried in his blonde hair and beside him was a small mountain of crushed cigarette buts. The plaid shirt he wore was unbuttoned, and part of it hung down over the side of the bed to reveal a scar about two inches long on his side. The older man sat upright on his bed, his wallet unfolded in his hands. Lines appeared around his aging face and his mouth worked behind his scraggly greying beard.

'Hi,' Michael said softly. The older man continued to stare at something in his wallet that Michael couldn't see, while the younger of the two lifted his head to peer over his chest at the noise. When he saw Michael, he let his head fall back down on his paper-thin pillow.

'Unless you're letting us out of here, kid, fuck off.'

Michael laughed. Already he liked this guy. 'I'm in the same boat as you.'

The younger man sat up, his stomach and chest muscles rippled as he did. 'You're out there. You walked in here by yourself. I'm in here with my mate that's losing his fucking mind.' He gestured to the older gentlemen that he shared the cell with. 'Three women next door won't stop crying, and some noisy prick down the end decides he's going to wait till midnight before going right off the deep end. Yeah mate, we walk in the same shoes alright.' Either a ghost of a smile had crept across his face, or he normally sneered while he spoke, but Michael stood patiently as he complained.

One of the women next door heard his complaints and piped up. 'Heartless bastard.'

The younger man turned his face in the direction of the noise and shouted back, 'you can fuck off too, lady!'

Michael smiled as he walked to the bars. 'I know I'm not in a cell, but I walk around here a prisoner like you.'

'Pig's ass.'

Michael lightly gripped the bars. 'The one down the end is my brother. I think their leader keeps me as like a safe guard.' The man in the cell quietened down at that. 'I don't really have a reason to talk to you, I just thought I would. He sent me down here to look for fighters, I don't know why. He normally sends me down here to look for women.' He gestured to the cell to his left.

The older one had begun to rock slightly back and forth on his bed, he whispered over and over.

His cell mate looked over to him, and shook his head. 'Shh, it'll be alright.' Michael watched as the younger man stood up and walked over to his cellmate. 'Chris, it's alright man, we'll get out of here. We'll find her soon.' He guided the older man as he lay down and he dragged a ragged blanket over him. The young man then placed a hand on the back of his friend's head and held it there for a while before he stood once more and walked to the cell door to talk to Michael.

'You said leader. What's his name?' he asked.

Michael frowned. 'Shepherd. He treats me like an assistant.'

The young man nodded. 'Yeah, that's the bastard that got me. Prick.' He turned to look back at his friend. The young man stood up. 'Why did he send you here? He's looking for fighters?'

Michael nodded. 'That's what he said. I don't know what he's doing but, after here I have to go look at the progress.' The prisoner furrowed his eyebrows and scratched at his chin.

Just then, the lock snapped on the steel door that led out of the tunnel and it swung open. Michael turned in time to see Billy come into the poor light. The boy turned back and squinted at the prisoner as if to warn him. 'I need to know if you have fought before,' he demanded.

The prisoner sneered as he looked at him and said in a cool tone. 'Yeah, you can tell your man that I've fought. I've fought in Vietnam, I fought when I came home. All I've ever done was fight.'

'Then you'll be a great asset to us, I'm sure,' Billy said as he came to a stop next to Michael and slapped the boy on the back. 'Come on son, Shepherd told me to take you over to Johnny and I'm leaving now.'

Michael took a last look at the prisoner, who looked at Billy, a scowl across his face.

Michael turned away and was walking down the corridor when

the prisoner called out,

'What's your name, kid?'

Michael stopped, and turned back, the prisoner was at the bars once more and peered out at him. 'Michael Baker.'

The prisoner nodded and retreated to his bed. 'Rankin. Stay safe, Michael.'

Billy led him outside. They walked in silence as he led him to a white utility that had a large piece of railway iron fixed to the front. The car was in bad shape and someone had smeared something red over it and done a poor job of cleaning it off; the paint looked stained and pitted by it. Billy opened the passenger door for him and Michael slid in. Billy swaggered around to the other side and slid his wide ass into the cabin.

'One of those boys you were just talking to owned this old girl.' He said with a smile. 'Mad as a cut snake.' He turned the key and the engine roared into life. Billy laughed and they cruised down the road.

Michael sat there as he looked out of the window, which looked brand-new. Now that he thought of it, most of the glass looked new. It was just too clean in comparison to the rest of the body. He watched people as they swept the gutters in the street, or fixed shop fixtures that were in various forms of disrepair. He gathered the damage was created by the skirmish with the Chinese. Some of the men that stood there to watch the workers waved to Billy as they rumbled past. He never waved back.

'I think we got off on the wrong foot, you and I.' Billy rubbed at his swollen face and shifted in his seat. 'I have a bit of a temper sometimes, and when you kicked me in the crown jewels, I saw red. Are we all good?'

Michael continued to ignore him. If he ever had the chance, he would kick him again. For the moment, however, Billy acted amiable and if it created less problems for him, he would play along.

'Sure.'

Billy nodded. He obviously felt more relaxed, as he continued to talk. 'Where were you from, son?' he asked in an attempt to be jovial. Michael sat silent. He didn't feel like talking much at the moment. 'Come on, I'm not Shepherd, Johnny or Lewis. It's okay.'

'Chinchilla. My father ran the sawmill.'

Billy shot him a look, like an alarm bell had sounded in his head. 'Chinchilla saw mill?'

Michael looked over to him, narrowing his eyes with confusion. 'Yeah, why?'

'Anyone die nearby lately?' His mouth was twitching.

Michael shook his head, still confused. 'Haven't you seen what's going on? A lot of people have died lately.'

Billy brought the car to a halt and he turned and grabbed his arms. 'Yeah, but for you this started before the invasion, didn't it?'

Michael didn't say a word. How the hell did this guy know anything about him or what he had been through?

'See son, Johnny, Lewis and I, were policemen before all this. We worked at Dalby and the last thing that we were sent to do was go and help an old lawman out at Chinchilla. This guy reckoned he was having trouble with a big bastard who had supposedly killed seven people, maybe more, and he suspected the use of heavy weaponry. Now I'm not any 'A' class detective and sure as shit Johnny isn't, but that brother of yours is one big son of a bitch, I don't think there would be too many big bastards running around with a gun like what we dragged out of his hands.'

Michael couldn't believe the words that he heard. His eyes widened with every word Billy said to him.

'We made it out there when the shit hit the fan with the Chinese, but we saw some of what had happened in Chinchilla, and it wasn't pretty. I know Lewis took it all pretty seriously. Then we found out about what was happening further north, so we headed down south and met Shepherd.'

Michael shook his head. 'We didn't do anything.'

Billy stopped him. 'It's not like I'm going to arrest you. Those days are behind me now and I suppose they are for you too.' He shrugged and let his hands fall to slap on his thighs. 'I just can't believe through all this we found you.' He lightly rubbed at his blackened nose and groaned slightly. 'I know you two are tied up with Shepherd somehow now, but heed my words son, don't let Lewis cotton on. I reckon he still thinks he is the law.'

Michael nodded, still shocked at all he had heard. He had only seen Lewis a few times. He was there when Shepherd had decided to take him. The look of anger and disapproval on his face was obvious, yet he'd said nothing. Maybe he already knew. Lewis had been out for a few days since they had managed to get the tank to work again. Michael hadn't seen him since, for the moment while he was Shepherd's pet, he supposed that it didn't matter. Yet not having Jack to stand behind left Michael feeling as small as a kitten in the jaws of the Tracker's Doberman.

Michael didn't say a word for the rest of the trip. Billy had taken him over the Peel River and then turned south. He almost thought that they were going to leave town altogether when he saw the construction. To the right of the highway that led out of Tamworth, a large circular structure had been built. The outside of it looked like pallet racking that stretched up into the air, steel sheets and timber lined the inside. Billy whistled to himself as they drove closer and he directed the rumbling ute to a section that had two shipping container doors fixed into the structure. Two men opened them as they neared, and Billy drove the ute into the structure.

Michael had never seen anything quite like it. Where a football field once stood, stone, concrete, steel and bricks had been used to create a ten foot wall around its edge. From there, rows of flat timber benches were staggered back and rose up the further they went. Only half of the seats had been fitted, and Michael saw what looked to be church pews stacked in the centre of the makeshift stadium. They had used whatever they could. Chinese soldiers, stripped of their weapons and rank, worked tirelessly with hammers and hand drills. They fitted flat planks to steel braces while Australians watched over them with the Chinese rifles in their hands. In the centre of the field, giant slabs of concrete stuck up into the air like the ruined pillars of an ancient Greek structure that never stood before.

Billy drove the ute up to this false formed structure and killed the engine. Both Michael and Billy opened their doors and stepped out. Michael was struck by the sheer size of the structure and how quickly it had risen. No doubt, it wouldn't win any awards; even he could see places where timber benches that started at the same point in one section missed their mark by feet on the other side. The same could be said with the ten foot wall, where in some places it stood fifteen and others only eight.

'Isn't she a sight, Billy, my boy,' A voice called out from above them. Michael looked up, and saw the slick, long hair of Jonathan. He stood a top of one of the concrete pillars that he had erected in the middle of the field. He had his thumbs hooked through the belt loops on his skinny leg jeans and he smiled broadly as he looked down at them.

'You could say that,' Billy croaked in reply as he spoke through his busted nose. Jonathan laughed as he leapt from his perch and landed more than gracefully in front of them. Dirt kicked up from the place he landed. As he stood up straight and looked around, he lifted his hands in the air as if in amazement.

'You know what the first show is going to be, old boy?' He looked expectantly at Michael and Billy. When neither of them answered him, he threw his arms up as if he was in a fighter's pose, 'the story of how I took that big bull bastard brother of yours down single-handed.' He spun around, and Michael knew he imagined the crowd in the stands as they cheered.

'Do you think they'll tell the story the right way this time?' Michael asked in a flat tone, as he forced a curious expression. Billy guffawed.

Jonathan laughed, 'Yeah well maybe they'll drag him out of his cell for the occasion and they can all see for themselves.' He walked close to Michael and knelt down in front of him. 'You should know, you were there.'

Michael nodded and decided it was best to hold his tongue, although all he wanted to do was spit on him, kick him, punch him. He held his silence while Jonathan glared at him, his lips spread in a shit-eating grin. 'Good boy, you keep your teeth clamped down on that tongue of yours.' With that, he stood up and turned to admire his work once more.

'Shepherd wants to know how much longer.' The slick-haired wanker threw his arms up in the air once more, as if annoyed by Michael's question.

He repeated Michael's words but in a higher baby tone. 'Two more nights' work and this baby will be ready to rock,' he pronounced after he had finished mocking him and pumped his fist in the air. 'And all thanks to me,' he said this quieter, but loud enough for the two closest to him to hear.

Billy looked around at all the Chinese workers that still laboured with each of their roles. 'Probably thanks to Lewis more like it. If it wasn't for him, we wouldn't have the Chinese to work.'

'Ahh, the Chinese are shit!' Jonathan roared. 'We could've done it in half the time without them and done a better job of it while we were at it.' Billy rolled his eyes.

Michael continued to look around, puzzled at why they had

bothered to build it in the first place. 'So, what is it?' He asked plainly.

The two adults looked at him blankly, as if confused that he didn't know. 'It's an arena,' Billy said nonchalantly.

'Yeah, I get that, but what is it going to get used for?'

Jonathan laughed aloud. 'What, you don't know?' Michael shook his head. 'Your boss is worried that now this is all said and done, all these farmers and townies are going to wake up to what he did and turn on him. So, he's built this to keep their minds off it.' He could see that Michael still didn't understand. He sighed and knelt again. 'What do people want more than anything else in life?'

Michael shrugged. He could have probably guessed at a few things, but he imagined that his ideas would have been wrong.

'Blood,' Jonathan said coldly. 'They might not admit it at first, but that's what they want. They want the good guy to succeed over the bad guy. They want to see the Aussie drive his foot up the Chinaman's ass and by Christ, that is what they're going to get.'

Michael looked up at all the Chinese soldiers, that still laboured away. They worked to build the cage they were going to die in. Slowly, he shook his head in disapproval.

Jonathan slapped him on the back. 'Don't feel sorry for those fried fuckers, it will be your brother who's doing the ass kicking.'

CHRIS

'In a caste dark or a fortress strong
With Chains upon my feet
You know that ghost is me
And I will never be set free
As long as I'm a ghost, you can't see.'

Gordon Lightfoot – *If You Could Read My Mind* (1970)

Everything was a lie. Every single word that crawled their way into his ears. Every shadow that cast themselves along the dusty concrete floor. Bars that were straight in their frame held him back from his dream and were cast out in tangled lines of darkness that twisted over him and around him to suck the life out from his lungs.

For Chris, his sense of existence had become one of those twisted chains of shadows. Like the tethers tied to the feet of a drowned man that was pinned to the depths of a river, he was tied to the depths of his own torment. The faded photograph that sat behind the plastic strip in his wallet was all he had. Yet even it had begun to lie. The features of her face had started to fade and wear against the tips of his thumbs that had caressed her likeness. The long locks of her hair had faded into the backdrop and the lines of her face had become unclear. The thing that tormented him the most was that his memory of her had started to fade along with the photo. Now when he dreamt of her, when he saw her standing there right in front of him, her hands around the bars of his cell, her face was always shielded by her hair.

Nothing had made sense since the blackout. He had awoken in the courtyard of his mind, unsure whether he remained amongst the living or the dead. The smoke rolled freely through the borders and the broken pillars. It edged toward him like the foaming waves of the ocean that broke at a snail's pace. When it hit him, it burned like the fires of hell. Every fibre of his being ached. As he used his already burned arms to raise himself, they felt as though daggers had been pushed through each joint in his hands, arms and back. Steel pushed to grind between the cartilage and bone. His eyes felt as though they were being eaten from the inside, each nerve ending being ground down by enormous discs of stone. Finally, when he breathed the smoke and it entered his lungs, he felt his heart stop and his stomach wrench. He continued to breathe, but even his brain screamed for more air. His head was split into seven pieces. Each rib had become its own saw blade, that chewed away at the flesh beneath.

Bewildered and in agony, he staggered. He couldn't see his hand if he extended it out for the thickness of the fog. He had tried only once and had been sure that he had lost it to the cloud that surrounded him. Instead, he now clambered on with his digits clamped to his chest. Each step became a labour, each movement sheer effort. Yet he could see the outline of something just beyond the wall of white, so on he pushed. Somewhere, something made a soft metallic tapping sound that echoed through his mind.

The steel links of wire that secured his courtyard emerged step by step. It cut the thick fog into diamonds as it pushed through; the substance almost held its shape before it melted into the air once more and pushed forward. The steel for once was cool to the touch, and offered some respite to the pains of the fog. He pushed his fingers through the wire and supported his weight as much as he could, while he led himself down the fence, finger hold by finger hold. The steel gate with reinforced edges clattered against its frame as he neared. A soft breeze sucked it away, then gently pushed it back. He watched as the bolt of the gate's lock tapped against the frame and it echoed all around him. Each time it struck, the fog seemed to pause in the air as if paralysed by the sound. Then, as the echo dissipated, the fog carried on.

Chris pushed himself to the opening, swinging the gate wide open. Through the gap and the fog, he saw her. She stood with her back to him, her head hung low. The hem of her dress bristled in the slight breeze that carried the fog with it.

'Hey,' he whispered in her ear as he moved up to her, but she didn't turn to look at him, she only began to sob. 'Shh, it'll be alright.' He whispered again. He tried to move around her, but each step he took seemed to get him no closer. He stretched his arm out slightly and went to touch her. The moment his fingers felt the warmth from her skin, she changed. Her sobs stopped immediately and she raised her head. From the point of where he touched her body, she had begun to decay. A line of white ran up her arm; the flesh that was left behind looked lumpy and pale. Her fingers had become translucent, the further the line progressed up her arm. She began to turn toward him, yet the line had moved up and had already washed over her face. Its course had already run down to the tips of her hair by the time he saw her face.

If he had passed her in the streets, he would not have recognised her. The face was lumpy, and unclear; her hair was that of a ghost, grey and wispy. As she raised her hand to touch his cheek, he started to be able to see straight through her and by the time the fog that filled her hands brushed against his face, she was gone. Standing there, he was consumed by the remnants of her being. He tried to breath her in, but with the first breath he took he had already lost her in the fog.

Finally, he had made it beyond the gate. Although the road was ahead of him, he could not see it for the fog but there was something, a sound. He strained his ears and thought he could hear the footsteps of many on tar. Tentatively, he took a step toward the noise. Maybe she would be amongst them, maybe he could find her amongst the people. He whispered again and hoped she would hear him as he struggled with his agony.

'Shh, it'll be alright.'

A pair of soft hands fell on his shoulder and he turned. Rankin stood over him; he looked concerned and tired all over. His plaid shirt was open and the edges flew out behind him in a sudden gush. It was like something didn't want him to get to the road. 'Chris, it's alright man, we'll get out of here. We'll find her soon,' he said softly as he began to turn him and lead him back through the haze. Together they walked through the gates and Chris heard the gate shut firmly and the bolt slam home behind him.

Chris seemed to see Rankin as much as he saw Angie. It was the only face he saw clearly anymore. He supposed Rankin was his only friend. His face seemed to appear from the fog and guide him, protect him. If he couldn't follow Angie, he would follow him. If not just to pass the time, until he caught her scent once more.

Chris awoke in the cell, but something seemed different. For the first time, he could feel the blanket that covered him, he could feel the cold that radiated up from the concrete below his bunk. The darkness seemed to surround and strangle him with tenfold the force of the shadows. He gasped as he sat upright. His head reeled as he rose; pain shot from a point on the right side of his head and ran all the way down to his toes. His stomach rolled and he gagged as he pushed himself forward to the edge of the bed. Everything came out. He couldn't remember the last time he had eaten, but something had come out; he hoped it was for the better.

He felt the two hands on his shoulders once more.

Rankin said to him, 'Come on man, they're here for us.' Chris turned to see Rankin's face above him once more. He had changed and wore what looked to be military greens, but in the wrong shade. Rankin helped him sit up and as Chris turned, he saw a set of clothes piled at the head of his bed, the same shade and style as Rankin's. Chris slowly stood under his own power and wiped the residue of vomit from his bristled beard.

'Wh-What the fuck?' he said in a dreary tone, he still felt weak. He looked to his friend once more for guidance.

Rankin pointed to the cell doors, where two men stood and watched them. One was heavy-set, his hands jammed into the pockets of his denim jacket, his face looked horrendous. The other man leaned on the bars and rapped his batons edge along the rails as he watched them.

'It's time,' the one in the denim said solemnly. 'Best not muck about.' He turned and leaned up on the wall, he hung his head and rubbed at his swollen face.

'For what?' Chris asked, still confused where he was and why.

'For you to die a glorious death.' The one with the baton smiled, revealing a set of yellowed teeth and blackened gums. He rapped a steady rhythm out on the bars, like that of a marching beat and he began to laugh.

'Come on,' Rankin said to Chris as he felt hands tug at his shirt. When he looked back, he saw that Rankin had started to unhook the buttons. Together with the help of his friend, Chris dressed in the oddly coloured greens that were washed, but still worn. These clothes had once belonged to another.

The cell door rattled open as the man in denim drew a revolver. 'You boys walk in front and no acting up.' The two walked out of their cell. For Chris, this didn't seem odd as he had only just woken up in it; he had no idea how long he had spent in this cold place. Perhaps he would have to ask his friend once whatever this was, was over.

They were directed at gunpoint through what looked to be a small police station. They walked up a narrow set of concrete stairs where another guard led them, and Chris often looked back over his shoulder. When they reached the heavy timbered front doors, Chris sighed as he saw what waited at the curb for him.

Pestilence as scarred and as battered as ever, waited by the curb. New glass glimmered in night sky, so clear that he had to actually look to make sure there was even glass in its place. It seemed someone had attempted to wash the car, but the paint was stained and pitted where the handprints of blood and oil had been.

He walked to the driver's door instinctually and placed his hand on the handle.

'Oi!' He heard from behind and he felt a sharp pain in his shoulder as the butt of the revolver was driven down into him. 'In the back, smart ass.'

Chris fell to a knee with the impact and Rankin had to help him up. His young friend scowled at his attacker but he didn't say a word. Together they climbed into the back of Pestilence's tray and settled themselves. The engine fired beneath them.

Chris smiled softly as he patted the steel of the tray. 'What a good old girl,' he said lovingly. His creation, his pride and joy. It had carried him all the way to this point, it seemed only fitting if he was put to death that she carried him there as well.

As Pestilence carried them away, he looked to Rankin. The young soldier sat relaxed on the passenger side, his arm hung over the edge of the tray and lightly tapped at the side. He met Chris's eyes.

'You alright?' he asked once more in a concerned voice.

Chris considered this. He had so many questions he wanted answered, but right now he couldn't think of one to ask. Things like: where are we, what are we doing? These were all good choices, but they just didn't seem relevant. The double denim dickhead's mate had told him they were going to their death, that meant he would never get to see her again. He had failed.

'I guess. Ask me that tomorrow and we'll see what the answer is.'

Rankin laughed, but said nothing further. They sat in silence as Pestilence trundled through the unfamiliar town and seemed to head to the outskirts.

An enormous circular structure had been erected out of anything they could have gotten their hands on, was the way Chris would have described it. It looked as though they had pulled the roof and sides from an old bus to line one section of the structure, the metal being so long and flat it covered a good amount. However, that was in contrast to the rusted old doors of a shipping container that just looked rushed. Pestilence pulled up at the rusting doors and they were told to get out by a slim man with long, slick hair. He smiled from ear to ear and jogged back and forth, he looked that excited.

'Glad you could make it friends, so glad,' he said through liar's lips. He wrung his hands together briefly before he gave a loud clap and ushered them over to the doors. 'You're just in time for the speech and I'm sure you wouldn't want to miss it.' Other men with batons and some with rifles had moved up behind them. The slick-haired bastard smiled as he worked the lock on the container doors. He pulled them open and they were immediately pushed through. The men with batons poked them in the backs, urging them forward, while the others raised their rifles. All of them yelled as they herded them into this pit they had made.

Just before they shut the doors, the one with the slick hair poked his head through and smiled. 'Head to centre boys, you'll get the best view from there.' He laughed as he shut the door.

The pit was enormous. It seemed to stretch forever in the artificial light. The sound inside was tremendous. Chris looked up and saw rows and rows of faces that looked down on him. Everyone chatted noisily and pointed either at the two newcomers or at something further on. Bright lights that blinded Chris as they shone down on him. They shone from flag poles extended above the heads of the people who sat behind a ten foot wall of steel, timber and stone. Chris noticed that every twenty feet or so along the wall, a man was stationed with a rifle. All of them looked to the centre, where large slabs of concrete stuck out from the ground in odd angles. Amongst them stood forty to fifty men, all of them huddled together, in exactly the same clothes that Chris and Rankin had been given.

He looked at Rankin, who had likewise taken his time as he surveyed the thousands of faces that lined the rows. The mass at the centre caught his attention and he started to walk towards it, his head slightly down.

Chris saw his hand go to his hip, as if to double check he still had his wallet. Together, the two men walked toward the mass and the concrete slabs. As they approached, Chris recognised the uniform fully and he saw that the men in the middle were all Chinese. His hands clenched into fists, his teeth pressed together, and he began to walk faster. He moved past Rankin and continued to pick up his pace, when a loud ringing shot through the air and the whole crowd went silent.

'My friends,' a smooth voice projected itself across the grounds, 'my family.'

Chris looked around and saw that all of the people in the stands had their attention drawn to a single point. He followed their gaze and saw to the right, a section of the arena that had no rows.

A podium with somewhat of a stage had been raised so all could see the figure atop it. A man dressed in a suit stood there and spoke into a microphone. A small boy who looked as miserable as Chris himself, stood beside him.

'I am so proud of you all,' the man in the suit said. Even from this distance, Chris could see the wide smile on his face. 'Together, we have gone through so much. We have stood up to our oppressors, domestic and of course of foreign as well.' With this, he gestured down into the pit at the swarm of Chinese and the two Australians that stood in there with them. People in the crowd booed and spat down at them. Some people threw things they held in their hands, though all of it fell far short of where they stood.

'Together, we the people have overcome our fears, our differences and together we stand strong.' The boos turned to cheers at this, and some clapped madly as they brayed their approval. 'To honour how far we have come as people, as a community, as a nation, I present to you our past.' Once more he gestured down at the centre, and the boos took up again.

'I present to you, all of what we wanted to leave behind. The killing, the whoring, the warring.' He paused for effect, and the crowd filled the space with cheers again. With each reaction, the man's smile grew wider and wider. 'Every breath they take is a threat to our progress, our way of life.' He paused as if to think and then he held his face closer to the microphone and bellowed. 'Well, what should we do with them?'

As the speaker held his hand to his ear and pretended to struggle to hear the words that the crowd chanted, the sickening thud of drums began. The crowd began to chant, 'Kill them.' Thousands of voices, all at once. 'Kill them,' over and over. The beat of the drums became louder and louder, the chant began to break up as people swore and spat abuse down on the men in the pit.

'That's right. That's right,' the man in the suit began again, the drums continued as the chants broke up and the abuse stopped so that all could listen. 'We will give you a show tonight.' He held up his hands, and the crowd erupted in cheers. 'In the centre of the pit, there are crates full of the weapons that our friends brought to our town, just as they brought them.' The crowd seemed to hush at this.

Chris and Rankin looked at each other and started to head for the centre.

'They will use those to fight for their lives against our community champions.' The drums thudded deeper and faster. 'They will be pitted against our best, our true heroes, in this time of turmoil. Let this be their redemption for what they have done in their life. For the crimes they have committed against us.'

Chris and Rankin pushed through the Chinese, all of which stood there and looked blankly up at the speaker. None of them apparently understood a word of what he said. Chris and Rankin pushed through face after face of confusion, exhaustion, and hunger. Each one weaker than the next, until finally they found the crates. The Chinese hadn't even bothered to look inside. Together, Chris and Rankin busted in the sides while the crowd roared around them and some of the Chinese turned to look on as the Australian men struggled with the crates.

'Let us welcome our brother, Jonathan.' The drums erupted in a flurry of beats while the crowds roared, and Chris heard the growl as an engine revved far behind him.

Finally, they broke through the side of the crate and AK-47s fell out of the side, all of them were equipped with their magazines. Chris and Rankin grabbed a rifle each. He saw Rankin turn to the men that still stood puzzled around them.

'Pick a gun up, you fucking idiots!' He pointed at the rifles scattered on the floor then to the noise of the threatening engine.

The crowd roared, yet the Chinese didn't move. The two Australians headed toward the outskirts of the mass and peered toward the doors from which they had entered.

The doors swung slowly open, but only darkness lay beyond their border. Then, two bright domes shone from the darkness and the power plant roared as a battered LandCruiser shot out into the open. The crowd went wild as it bore down on them. Its body bounced and its suspension worked as its large tyres hammered over the uneven ground. The Chinese behind Chris and Rankin had finally begun to move, Chris heard them shout in their own tongue, he heard the racks of rifles being cycle but no one fired.

As the LandCruiser bore down on them, Chris could see the laughing face of the slick-haired son of a bitch behind the wheel. He drove with his left hand; in his right he held a sawn-off double-barrel shotgun which he hung out of the window. The wagon was heavily armoured on the front to protect the engine from impact, similar to how he had engineered Pestilence. However, the glass was just glass and it wouldn't protect the driver from what he had coming. Chris racked the slide of his rifle without visual inspection. His eyes remained fixed on the LandCruiser. He raised the rifle, training the sights on the windscreen as the truck hurtled closer. Finally, he pulled the trigger.

Clack. Nothing.

Chris's eyes widened as he looked to the rifle, then back to the LandCruiser. His shoulders slumped as it bored down on him. Then he was hit with such force from the side and he tumbled to the ground as he felt the ground tremble and the hot exhaust pass by him. Rankin swore on top of him.

'They're all empty!' he roared at Chris. 'Fucking sick bastards.'

They both turned and watched as the LandCruiser ploughed into the mass of Chinese. The front line of them stood there with only four rifles raised. They pulled the triggers over and over as they wondered why the rifles wouldn't fire until the sickening thud of flesh and metal rung out. The LandCruiser drove over them. The engine laboured and almost stalled with the force of the initial hit, but the armour did its job and pushed the bodies down and away from the running gear. The crowd erupted in cheers and laughter, as the dirt in the centre of the field turned dark brown with the blood from the fallen.

The men in the centre broke, and men ran everywhere. They watched as the LandCruiser turned; the driver held out the shotgun as he swung wide around a man that had broken off on his own. The shotgun roared and the Chinaman fell to the ground, his chest destroyed by the heavy buckshot load. The engine bellowed as the driver continued to laugh. He ran down three more before he fired his second shot at a soldier that had tried to get behind one of the concrete pillars. The pattern of shot hit him low in the back and he screamed as half of his side was torn away by the power of the shotgun. The crowd cheered as the LandCruiser ran over another one, while the driver fumbled with the shotgun as he steered to avoid a concrete pillar.

Rankin grabbed Chris and shook him. 'We need to get that fucker to stop or crash or something. We need to get back to the centre.' The young soldier dragged Chris to his feet and pushed him to the scene of the impact. They stepped over the dead and the screaming, mortally wounded alike. The two Australians and the Chinese could not communicate, but fear, pain and death was a universal language. They needed to survive.

The LandCruiser left the centre to head to the outskirts of the arena and pick at those that had fled on their own. From their safety behind one of the concrete pillars, Chris watched as a Chinaman tried to climb the ten foot wall. Only to have his head blown off by the guard closest to him when he raised it above the crest. His body fell, lifeless, back into the arena and the crowd laughed and cheered for the spectacle.

Other men were crushed against the stone wall as they gave up on their escape and crouched with their hands over their heads as the Toyota ran them down. Some saw the fate that waited for them outside of the centre and they soon headed back to the concrete. Although the LandCruiser could drive in-between the pillars and into the centre itself, it could not turn sharply enough to turn through them. This was their only chance.

Chris still held his rifle and followed the Toyota as it circumvented the arena. The driver watched them as he laughed and drove around them. The body of the Toyota bounced and hitched over the bodies and the uneven ground. Then the nose turned in and the driver lined the heavy four-wheel-drive up for charge similar to the first. Chris moved to the concrete pillar that sat to the driver's side and listened as the exhaust roared closer and closer.

Guessing as best as he could, Chris launched the butt of his rifle forward as the Toyota roared through the centre. He felt a shock go all up his arm and his hand went numb as the rifle was torn from his grasp. The LandCruiser slammed into the concrete pillar which was to the left of its path. The crowd fell silent.

'Get him!' Chris roared as Rankin and some of the soldiers that remained in the centre stormed the LandCruiser. Chris heard the report of the shotgun and saw the first Chinaman to reach the driver's door collapse, his head mostly blown off. The second one to reach the door, grabbed the shotgun and the two struggled until the third and fourth then Rankin arrived.

The driver was dragged from the LandCruiser. He screamed as rifle butts, fists, feet, elbows and knees were all driven down into him; every bone in that man's body broke, every joint was shattered and still the survivors pummelled into him.

The crowd erupted in an angry roar and the boos started over again. One of the Chinaman had gotten the shotgun and brandished it above his head, screaming like a Barbarian in victory. He ran from the centre and held it out in front of him. He ran straight for the podium with the speaker and the small boy. He fired the shotgun twice. Large plumes of smoke erupted from its end but the distance between the crazed Chinaman and the stage was far too great for the pattern to be effective. The two guards that stood on the wall between the podium and the centre raised their rifles and cut him down. The shotgun fell empty to the ground and the crazed soldier fell silent.

At this, the crowd had grown restless, as if they feared or waited to see whether the Chinaman would be able to kill this speaker. However, when his body hit the ground, the voice came over the loud speaker once more and everyone fell quiet.

'How unfortunate. How unfortunate indeed.' The speaker spoke. 'Our first gallant champion has fallen. However, he fell with honour and the respect of his people. He did a fine job.'

There were sporadic waves of claps throughout the crowd, but otherwise it remained silent. The speaker looked off to the side and nodded. The drums took up their pace and the smile returned to the speaker's face. 'Our last champion, is one not many of you know about. For your safety, I have kept this man from your sight.'

There were slight murmurs from the crowd as people begun to question each other.

'If a man's flock consists of lambs, then this is the wolf that hunts them. I, as your Shepherd, have taken it upon myself not to kill the wolf, but to use it.' The speaker turned and looked at the small boy, gesturing for him to come close. The boy came forward and stood by the speaker's side.

'You all know this child by my side. I saved him from this wolf and he alone knows the horror behind his story.' The drum beats quickened once more and the crowd stirred in anticipation. The speaker pointed to the container doors as the lights of the arena died.

'Behold, our wolf!'

RANKIN

'In the clearing stands a boxer
And a fighter by his trade
And he carries the reminder
Of every glove that laid him down or cut him
Till he cried out, in his anger and his shame
'I am leaving, I am leaving.'
But the fighter still remains.

Simon and Garfunkel – *The Boxer* (1970)

Darkness enveloped the arena, leaving the failing beam of the LandCruiser's smashed glass headlamps as the sole source of light. The spectators had fallen silent. Wounded Chinese, their bodies smashed and broken by the weight and impact of the Toyota, groaned and crawled. Under it all, the rolling thud of the drums continued to pound away.

At the announcement of the wolf, Rankin had moved forward. He had discarded the rifle and stood bare knuckled at the vanguard of the thirty or so remaining men. His breath was hot in his chest, his arms hung heavy at his side, tired from the beating he had given the driver. His knuckles burned from the split skin and raw exposed flesh that was neither stranger nor friend to the feeling of the air's bite. In front of him, the container doors slammed shut and he heard the metal locking rods grind into position and slam home.

He lowered his shoulders and clenched his fists, his teeth ground together. There was a deep thud and heavy click as the furthest of the arena lights turned on and illuminated the container doors, but nothing else. Rankin breathed in deeply and settled himself.

Thud. Click.

Another row of lights opened up to illuminate the next section. Nothing. He turned his head quickly to the left. Something had moved at the far side of the light's path, big yet eerie quick. Twenty feet of darkness stood between him and that spot. He strained his ears to try and hear the sound of boots on dirt or anything, but under the thudding of the drums, he may as well have been deaf.

Thud. Click.

The next row of lights illuminated the mid-section of ground. Rankin had to close his eyes briefly at the intensity; the light was warm on his face and he lowered his head. He began to suck in another settling breath and as he opened his eyes, the air caught in his throat.

Before him stood the largest man he had ever seen. His height was matched only by the breadth of his shoulders and the large muscular arms that hung by his side. Rankin had never feared men taller than him, that American in Saigon, the brute in the prison. He had always attracted their attention and had always brought them to their knees. Yet this titan in front of him stood easily another foot taller than either of the two he had felled, and would have easily weighed another hundred pounds.

Rankin braced himself and waited for a charge, some sign of aggression, but nothing came. The wolf slouched as he drew long rasping breaths, and looked into the crowd. Rankin followed the man's gaze, and found himself looking at Shepherd. The self-proclaimed leader of this town of lunatics stood as proud as they came on his podium with Michael, the boy from the prison cell at his side. Rankin turned back to the wolf and saw the hatred in the man's face as he glared up at the podium. Rankin wondered whether the hatred burned for the boy or the man. The large man coughed a long and raspy hack and he fell to a knee. The crowd had begun to heckle. Bottles and cans of beer sailed through the air to clatter harmlessly on the ground.

Rankin turned back to the podium and shook his head. They had sent a man close to death in here to fight them.

He took a few steps to the podium, bellowed, 'Some show, Shepherd!' The anger had burned deep within his guts, the veins on his neck pulsed with his rage. 'Why don't you come down here and fuck the theatrics?'

Some people in the crowd began to laugh and he watched as a beer can was hurled onto the podium. Liquid sloshed over Shepherd's legs, yet his smile didn't waver. A small glint of hope burned in Rankin's stomach. If only the crowd would turn.

In the corner of his eye, he saw a Chinese soldier run toward the sick giant. Rankin turned to watch. The small soldier stood as tall as the giant when he knelt. He advanced to a sprint, and held an AK like a club. The butt of the rifle swung down. At the moment it hit, the lights were cut again. The arena plunged into darkness and the crowd booed and swore.

'Turn them on, turn them on,' the chant began. Their noise filled his ears and muffled the commotion that happened in front of him. He thought that the Chinaman must have really given the big guy a pounding but his eyes were not adjusted enough to see. He heard dull snap, followed by another.

'Turn them on, turn them on.' The crowd continued to hammer, their feet pounded into the deck below them. 'Turn them on, turn them on.' Something heavy and wet thudded to the ground at Rankin's feet.

Thud, Click. Thud, Click.

The light washed over them and the spectators began to cheer, then fell silent. Rankin looked down and saw the crumpled, twisted body of the Chinaman. His head had been spun a one-eighty-degree on his shoulders and then half torn off. Both of his legs had been broken inward at the knee and his calves lay under his body at the wrong angle. He continued to gape at the broken body at his feet, when he heard heavy footsteps and he looked up.

Two sunken black eyes bore down on him. The entire right side of the wolf's face was red and mutilated, many parts of it had turned to scab. On his chest and his side, similar wounds were mostly scabbed over. The way this man moved and snorted air was like that of a healthy bull, not the rasped cough of the man that had fallen to a knee. In the past, he would have said that the word roar, could only be used in conjunction with a man's voice to exaggerate it. However, the sound that shook him to his bones and made him jump even as he watched, wouldn't be given justice by the word. The giant screamed as if he was something from another world, and it terrified him.

Rankin took two steps back, but the long strides of the attacker were too large. A meaty hand swung down at him and Rankin pulled his head back; he tried to get away, and he slipped. As he fell backwards, he saw the scowl of the giant as he bent down to him and a hand closed over his face.

Fuck, this bastard's going to rip my face off, the thought raced through his mind as his vision was cut by the mass of the giant's hand. The fear came into him. Then he heard a clap and air rush out of someone and there was light again. He looked up to see Chris grapple and struggle with the giant. He laid punches into his face and his side, all the while he tried to push the big bastard back. Rankin saw Chris land a good blow on his jaw, but it had no effect. Rankin got to his feet and charged. He leapt into the air in an attempt to get the height he needed and drove his fist down into the forehead of the big bastard. His fist felt as though he had punched concrete, his hand ached and the man he hit barely even grunted.

The giant swung his left arm wild in a backhand. Rankin ducked it, but Chris bore the full brunt. He was lifted from his feet and hurled back, landing awkwardly on his upper back and neck. After a moment, he rolled onto his stomach. Rankin started to back pedal, the speed of the mongrel was the worst thing. Big men were usually slow but he feared that this one could run him down. He needed to get to the concrete pillars; his line of attack had turned into a retreat.

He turned his back on his attacker for a moment and gained some valuable ground. Chinese circled around him and the wolf. Rankin just hoped they got involved. He turned around in time to see the Wolf lunge at him, his face twisted in a snarl, the black orbs of his eyes unblinking.

Rankin sidestepped, then took a step toward him. He slammed his fist in his side, then ducked another swing and stepped to the big man's right, to bring another fist into his ribs. He took a step back and bent himself backwards as another meaty arm swung just over him. Recovering quickly, he brought his left up to connect with the jaw way above him.

The giant bellowed and bull rushed him. Two arms wrapped around him, choked him, crushed him. He slammed into one of the concrete pillars and all the air went out of him. He watched, breathless as the big man lined up for a right hook and groaned as he tried to move his head. It came down hard and accurate, but Rankin moved barely quick enough. The fist grazed his face and his left ear exploded in pain and a ringing noise that unsteadied him.

A Chinaman leapt at the giant, then another. Rankin took his opportunity to slide himself away from the fight, a hand plastered to his face. He watched with his one open eye as a hand closed over the head of one of the small men and slammed it into the concrete pillar. Only one crushing blow was required, a blood smear and the glint of white bone was left in its place.

Another man had clambered onto the giant's right arm, the one used to crush the other. The big left came up, plucked the small man from his perch like an annoying thorn. He then pinned him to the concrete pillar, while the other fist drove into his chest and caved it in. Blood spurted from the dying man's mouth and splattered the face of the titan. He relaxed his grip and let the Chinaman fall to the ground.

Rankin clambered to his feet, the left side of his face hot with pain as the giant turned to him again. With no one left to distract the monster, Rankin lowered his head and charged. He drove his shoulder low and into the tyrant's stomach. He pushed hard with his legs but gained no ground. Those arms seized him by his mid-section and then he was flung through the air. His legs slammed into one of the concrete pillars and more pain shot through him.

The colossus rampaged through the remaining men. Some of them tried to run and died, others fought and died with them. As Rankin tried to gain his feet again, he saw one man open the door of the LandCruiser and close himself inside. The whir of the starter motor filled the air for a short time before the driver's door was ripped clean from its hinges and hurled across the arena. The Chinaman screamed like the original driver had as he was dragged out; the screams continued as the wolf slammed his body back into the car with only his head above the roof. His screams were silenced as his throat was crushed against the Toyota's roof sill and his head was torn lose.

As the Wolf turned away from the LandCruiser, two more soldiers attacked him. Both of them slammed the butts of their rifles into his body. At first, Rankin thought they had injured him and he started to head toward them to help bring the big bastard down.

Then the wolf lashed out, he slammed the head of one man into the LandCruiser's fender and caved it in. The other tried to run, but he grabbed him with two hands, one around his throat and other on his shoulder. The titan roared as he strained, and Rankin watched in horror as he pulled the Chinaman apart. Flesh tore down the centre of his sternum, the soldier's eyes rolled in their sockets as his consciousness was lost along with his life. Then the two parts of his body were torn asunder and thrown to the ground like old waste.

Rankin stood there, his back against one of the concrete pillars as he watched Chris make another assault. He flung himself from the roof of the LandCruiser and clenched his fists together around the wolf's throat while he drove his knees into his back. Big arms flailed uselessly in the air, his shoulders too big to get Chris from his back. Rankin moved forward again, determined to help his friend.

He brought his fist up and slammed it into the wolf's side and felt solid meat beneath his hand. He brought another into his stomach and then one into the scabbed section on his side. The wolf roared as fresh blood ran from his wound and he staggered. Rankin kept with him, he pounded him and pounded him.

Then Rankin saw what his plan was. 'Chris, get off him!'

But his friend was too focused on putting all of his strength into his stranglehold. Rankin watched, helpless to stop as the wolf drove all of his weight into the concrete pillar, and crushed Chris between them. Rankin heard all of the air rush out of his friend and watched as the mauler's hands closed around him.

He had no choice but to use his dusters. He'd been worried about using them at first, as no one had noticed them hidden beneath his belt, even when he was unconscious in the hotel. Now, his hands slipped beneath the leather and he felt the cool brass hug close against his skin. As he closed in, a giant fist slammed into Chris' head and his friend's eyes rolled with the impact. The wolf was bringing his arm back for another strike when Rankin slammed the dusters into the back of his head.

The sound was hard and thick, but the reaction was not what he hoped for. The wolf's left elbow flew back and connected with Rankin high on his cheekbone. He was rocked by the hit and he took a few staggered steps back. The tyrant turned and threw himself at Rankin. The air rushed out of his lungs as he felt crushed by the weight of the man. He watched as a massive fist raised to the air above him and came crashing down. This time he bore it; the impact was tremendous and the world split into a shade of white and grey while everything swirled in front of him. Somewhere in it all, he saw the fist come down again and he put everything he had into rolling.

Distantly, as if ten miles away, he heard the sound of an anvil crash to the ground and he knew he had escaped the blow that would've killed him. He put everything he had into a left-handed swing and he drove it into the scarred section of the wolf's face. He watched in amazement as the giant fell off him and went to the ground, his hand held to his face.

Rankin rolled to his side and spat a lump of blood to the ground. He clambered to a knee and the world reeled again. Finally, he got to his feet and swayed slightly. The first step was filled with pain, everything ached and nothing moved in his body like he thought it should.

The Wolf had started to sit up, so Rankin drove his brass clad fist into his face again to put him down. He dropped his knees onto the wolf's chest and brought his fist down again and again. Each time he raised it he saw the black eyes beneath; they stared up at him. He could feel the hate in him. However, each blow he landed, seemed to do little to no damage.

A huge hand caught his brass clad fist, and the giant rolled atop of him again. As Rankin's back hit the ground once more, he felt the crushing weight of the colossus on his chest. He rolled his head to look at Chris. His friend laid on his stomach, his eyes open and semi-focused on Rankin. The world still turned and swayed here and there. His left ear was hot with fire and loud with noise, his mind hurt, yet somewhere in the distance he thought he could hear someone singing. The soft voice of a child. He watched his friend's chest rise and fall and thought to himself, thank God he survived. He looked back up to the wolf and saw the big man atop of him. For some reason, the fist was poised, cocked as if ready to strike.

Man, I'm sure someone's singing, Rankin thought, as his vision rolled then steadied again. He closed his eyes and took a deep breath. He felt better. Slowly, he opened his eyes once more to welcome his fate and looked straight into two brown eyes.

'Help me.'

MICHAEL

'I want to know,
Have you ever seen the rain,
Coming down on a sunny day?'

Creedence Clearwater Revival – *Have You Ever Seen the Rain?* (1971)

The crowd had not cheered. They just sat and stared at what his brother, or 'it,' had become. At first, they had begged and cried for the lights to be turned on, yet now, as Michael looked around many people had turned their heads to look away. He was shocked to see that some idiot had actually brought his child to the event. The mother shook her head and scowled at the husband while the small child cried in her arms.

The most horrific sight for all of them had been when his brother had torn the man in two with his own hands. Michael had seen the strength before, he had seen the power crumble people. He had seen what had happened to the Trackers, he had seen what had happened to his father. And now Shepherd had set him loose, to kill for entertainment.

Shepherd seemed to be the only one who hadn't lost their taste for the violence. He wrung his hands together as more and more of the Chinese fell to Jack's body. Yet he didn't realise that around him the crowd that he had designed this spectacle for threw him glances of anger. He sat on his makeshift throne, ate chunks of browned lamb and sipped at glasses of wine as red as the blood that stained the earth below them. Michael hated him. He wished nothing more than to see Jack tear him to pieces. Instead, he watched others suffer that fate.

The problem had come when Michael had seen Rankin take his fall. The young Australian fighter had stood up to Jack well, but the sight of it was saddening. Each miss of Jack's was only a near miss and the smaller man's time was near its end. Then Rankin's friend had fallen, then Rankin himself and Jack was killing him. The nice man in the prison cell, the one who had made him laugh. Michael couldn't bear it any longer.

Now Rankin looked as though he was going to kill Jack. He held something in his hand and beat him with it. Either one was going to kill the other. All for Shepherd.

He didn't know what had come over him, he just started forward. He walked to the edge of the podium and looked at the microphone. With each step he took, a fist fell on Jack's face. He closed his eyes, and sang.

SHEPHERD

'For there is no authority
Except from God.
And those that exist,
Are instituted by God.'

Romans 13:1-2

'When I was a young man, I carried me pack and I lived the free life of the rover.'

The words rung through the air, yet had sailed through one of Shepherd's ears and had washed straight out of the other. He hadn't noticed Michael leave his side, he hadn't even noticed him walk in front of him. He was too fixated on the spectacle below. The flesh that teared, the blood that spilled and stained the earth. The more he watched, the more he drank, the more he craved it and lived for it. The only problem that faced him now was once this bastard boy's brother had killed them all. How was he ever going to get more people to step into the arena with him? He was so deep in the thrill of it all, he hadn't even heard the first line of the song that was now being sung only three feet away from him.

'From the Murray's green basin to the dusty outback, well I waltzed my Matilda all over.'

The men they had pulled from the cell, the ones that had arrived in the rain and the half-destroyed Holden, had put up quite the fight, of that he was impressed. Now he was surprised to see the young man they had captured in the Hotel, give his champion a beating, but he knew it wouldn't be long. His smile spread from ear to ear. He couldn't wait to see his head smashed out over the ground.

'Then in 1915, my country said, "son, it's time you stop rambling there's work to be done."'

The wolf took down his prey. He was on top. It was time to see the final blow. He leaned forward.

'So, they gave me a tin hat and they gave me a gun. And they marched me away to the war.'

It never came. He waited longer and it still didn't come. He slammed his fist into his knee and then rubbed at the spot where the pain had shot up his leg. He watched in disbelief as his champion lowered his fist and stood up. Then he heard it, finally heard it.

'And the band played Waltzing Matilda.'

He turned and glared at Michael. 'Stop it, Stop it! You've ruined everything.' He leapt from his chair, grabbed Michael by the scruff of his collar, and struck him.

His face was twisted with anger, more or less the first time he had shown his true expression since he had arrived at Tamworth. His hate for the people that walked the streets flowed out of him.

'These country idiots, have come here for a show. And you want to fuck everything I've done?' he snarled at Michael through gritted teeth as he held his face only an inch from his own. 'I should've thrown you away like one of those used-up whores.' His temper had completely snapped. All he wanted was to throw the little bastard off the edge of the podium. 'Everything I have worked for. So many weeks, months of planning for this night and you ruin it!' He pushed the boy hard against the railing; his head hung out over the edge. 'I'll fucking send you down…' Something hard hit him in the side of the head and he stumbled. His face throbbed with pain and when he held his cheek, it felt wet. He let go of Michael as soon as it hit and steadied himself on the railing. As he opened his eyes, he saw a can of XXXX beer roll and hit his foot. Foam bubbled from a large dent on the side.

Shepherd looked up and saw the eyes of the entire arena stare right back at him. He looked down to the fighters and saw that both his champion and the bastard he captured in the hotel standing side by side. A moment of silence held the arena as Shepherd settled himself and felt his smile spread over his face again. He moved to the microphone and brought Michael with him.

'Now sorry for the disruption to t-t-tonight's entertainment,' he managed as he patted Michael's shoulder gently. He looked over the faces of the men and women in the stands closest to him. He didn't see admiration, nor respect. A cool shiver ran up his spine and he felt like he knew how the Mayor felt, all that time ago. 'That was just a small outburst on my part.' He laughed and looked down to Michael. 'He's alright, aren't you son?'

Michael broke free of his grasp and stepped away.

People murmured in the crowds now and Shepherd felt small, so very small.

'He's raped a lot of girls in his hotel!' the boy called out. He was away from the microphone, yet Shepherd heard it reverberate through the speakers and his heart sunk.

'Lies. All Lies,' he retorted, but his smile faltered.

'He sends me down to the jail to pick new ones for him,' Michael called again, a look of defiance on his face. 'He's not what you think.'

'Shut up, you little shit!' he roared, and he heard his own voice echo back at him, again and again. The crowd stirred, more bottles and cans started to fly through the air.

'No!' he called. 'Stop!' Shepherd looked down at the fighters;

they still watched him. He saw the dark brown eyes of his champion locked on him and he felt alone. 'Start fighting!' he called to them but they didn't move.

Then a man, one of the spectators that had been happy to watch along with everyone else, climbed onto his podium and approached him. Shepherd held out his hands to shield himself as the farmer came down on him, while everyone watched and growled from their seats. He saw the anger in the man's eyes, even the dirt embedded on the skin of his hands. Shepherd closed his eyes.

A shot rang out. Part of the blast was caught by the microphone and it echoed and reverberated again and again. The man in front of him stopped. He leaned on the rail, then fell beneath it and was gone.

There was a brief moment where the entire arena was quiet. Shepherd looked over his shoulder and saw Billy, a smoking revolver in his hand. His eyes were still swollen and his nose black, but through it all Shepherd could see the realisation in his eyes at what he had done.

The crowd erupted in a violent wave. Shepherd looked long enough to watch one of his guards below be overpowered by a swarm of angry people. He grabbed Michael by the shoulder, turned and ran.

RANKIN

*'But they don't know
There can be no show.
And if there's a hell down below,
We're all gonna go.'*

Curtis Mayfield – *If There's a Hell Down Below* (1970)

The shot rung through the bleachers, and seemed to echo off every flat surface. Every nut, bolt and screw held fast, as if holding its breath. The entire arena stood in silence as the body fell from the podium. They watched as the brave man's lifeless form tumbled through the air and crashed into the stands below. The tension in the air was suffocating, so thick that nothing was able to push through it. When it snapped, the earth trembled with the roar of anger and injustice from every being in the stands and Rankin watched as Shepherd's dream world tear itself apart.

More shots rang out as the guards that were spaced every few feet on the wall of the pit were overwhelmed. Some were crushed by the multitude of feet that trampled over them, others were just torn apart by mothers, fathers, sons and daughters. People that had just started their days as farmers, clerks, or even servicemen. Everyday Australians.

Rankin turned his head and saw Chris slowly climb to his feet and shake his head softly. Rankin moved to go to Chris' side but a large hand slapped gently against his chest and stopped him. He looked up and saw the brown eyes of the large man who moments before had tried to kill him.

'I need you to help me,' he said again as he lowered his eyes to the ground, as if ashamed. 'I can't let him…'

'Your brother,' Rankin said knowingly. The eyes shot back in an instant, anger loomed deep within them, 'I know. He came to me while I was locked up.'

The hand on his chest fell away, and they turned and watched as Shepherd latched his hands on the monster's brother and fled. Rankin watched as the scarred and scabbed face of the giant twisted into a snarl of rage. Rankin placed a hand on his meaty shoulder.

'You get the kid, but I get Shepherd.'

When they locked eyes again, Rankin felt the fear that had consumed him minutes before. The eyes weren't the shade they had been. Yet they weren't the black orbs that he had seen at the beginning. The brown was traced with black and the surface of the colours changed as the surface of his eyes moved. They rolled over each other like a boiling pot of oil and tar. His lips parted, to show teeth smeared with blood and Rankin realised that all he had managed to do with his flurry of brass ended blows, was to split the man's lip.

'We'll see.'

Chris had managed to stand and had gone straight for the gaping hole where the LandCruiser's door had once been. There was a click as the fuel pump engaged and then a dull whir. The LandCruiser fired up and there was rattle of metal on concrete as the broken front bar jostled against the face of the pillar.

'Rankin, we're leaving!' he called out from the driver's seat and Rankin left to join his friend.

As Rankin closed the passenger door, the rear door behind the driver opened and Chris looked about. The suspension sagged as their new ally heaved himself in. Chris looked at Rankin, a worried expression on his face.

'Don't worry, just get us the fuck out of here,' Rankin said.

The arena was in as much chaos as the stands; men had surged over the edges and had swamped the remainder of the Chinese. Others had thrown the guards that remained down there and watched as the Chinese soldiers set upon them like a pack of wild dogs.

Metal screamed as the LandCruiser backed away from the pillar it was nosed into and there was a great crunch as the rear bar connected with the pillar behind them. The transmission clunked and tyres spun as Chris urged the large Toyota forward and ground the passenger side down the first pillar as they went past. Then they were in the open.

People surged to them. One man leapt onto the sill of the driver's side and tried to pull Chris out of the gaping hole. Chris yelled and fought back, his concentration left the windscreen and he drove over a group of people that ran across in front of them. The LandCruiser bounced heavily and tilted dramatically to one side and Rankin was sure they were going to tip, but at the last second Chris turned the wheel into the tilt and hammered the gas. They remained upright but not unscathed, the man on the sill remained and now held the steering wheel as he fought Chris for control.

Rankin tried to move forward, across his friend to strike at the attacker, but just as he moved, a large hand clamped down on the attacker's face. He uttered a short scream of surprise before he vanished from sight.

Rankin laughed. 'Should keep you around.'

Their passenger sat there, his eyes focused out the window as if he was on a Sunday drive. He grunted, and Rankin turned back to leave him in peace. He did so in enough time to see the closed container doors rush towards them as the LandCruiser's engine wound up. 'Oh, fuck not again.' Rankin groaned as he braced himself against the dashboard.

The world went dark as the large Toyota entered the small tunnel and then, with an explosion of twisted steel and groaning suspension, they were free.

There weren't as many people outside of the arena as he would've thought. Perhaps the exits weren't designed to handle such an outflow of bodies. Mostly, everything was dark in the night. There were no street lamps this far out of town. Most of the people he could see hurried toward a line of trucks and cars that filled a field a few hundred feet away. All except three.

Chris didn't need any directions; as soon as he saw the familiar lines of Pestilence and the three people that clambered into the cab, he turned the LandCruiser toward them.

SHEPHERD

'Behold a pale horse
And he who sat upon him was Death
And Hell followed with him.'

Revelations 6:8

The V8 roared into life as Shepherd slammed his door shut. His hands were still clenched into Michael's shoulders like the talons of an eagle in the lamb that was its feast. He turned to Billy, who had started to get the Holden rolling. 'Any time Billy,' he said in a high quiver as he urged his last Lieutenant on.

He would have loved to have known where Lewis had decided to run off to. Ever since power had been restored to the bulking green tank, he had stocked it with fuel, supplies and had vanished. It was probably for the best, in a situation like this, it was people like Lewis that were the worst to have around. They would be the first to support you, yet the first to drive their dagger into your back as they smiled into your face and said 'hail Caesar.'

The Holden's body rattled as the V8 surged them forward. They bounced onto the highway and settled at speed, somewhere above forty. The child who lay across him kicked and squirmed as he tried to get free and Shepherd struggled to hold onto him. The boy's foot kicked out and jammed Billy in the ribs. Billy yelped in surprise and took his eyes off the road to lay into the boy.

A car had begun to pull up beside them. Shepherd could hear the engine whirring over the droll tone of the Holden. He didn't care too much for cars and didn't pay too much attention. He was still as focused on his efforts to restrain the child as Billy beat on him. Billy drove a fist down and wailed on Michael's leg, who screamed as all the fight went out of him. Billy raised his head and looked back out the windscreen, finally to concentrate on the road. He looked to his left at the car that had started to move up on their side and looked away. Shepherd didn't care.

'Just take me back to the hotel, Billy. I need to collect a trophy of mine.'

Billy snapped his head back to look over his shoulder at the car that had gained on them.

'Oh shit. That's Jonathan's.'

Shepherd turned to look as the red LandCruiser pulled alongside them while they hurtled down the highway toward Tamworth's town centre. The driver's door was gone, and a skinny man with a grey, ragged beard sat in the cabin and glared out at them.

'Run him off the road!' Shepherd roared, and Billy swung the Holden so that it slammed into the Toyota's side. There was a crunch of metal and the cars rocked against each other. Only the lights of the Holden cut through the night, the LandCruiser beside them lurked in the darkness.

Billy swung the wheel in again and the Holden rocketed towards the red hull. As they came close, Shepherd saw the face in the backseat. He saw the scarred twist of a snarl, he saw darkness where the eyes were and the mauler's hand that reached out for him. The window at his side shattered and he was sprayed with small shards of glass.

Michael cried out, then he looked up and saw his brother. All the fight in the world came back into the boy at that point, as he surged to get to the window, while Shepherd struggled to hold him back.

'For Christ's sake, Billy, run them off the road!' he called as he strained to hold Michael back. The Holden shot to the left and slammed into the hull again. This time, the driver of the Toyota lost control and the back end washed out over the dirt shoulder. Shepherd saw a glimpse of a hateful look from the backseat and then they vanished into the darkness behind them.

Shepherd rested his head back on the seat and sighed, then he began to laugh. 'You didn't think I was going to let go of you that easily?' He looked at the boy and continued to laugh, the high pitch quivered at its peak. 'Oh no, you're staying with me for some time, my son. You're the only insurance I have,' he paused and considered. 'Well, almost.'

MICHAEL

'No more Waltzing Matilda,
For me.'

Eric Bogle – *And the Band Played Waltzing Matilda* (1971)

The Holden came to a screaming halt outside of the Tamworth Hotel. Billy killed the power and Michael was dragged from the cabin. Shepherd's fingers dug into his shoulder and the pain was tremendous. His legs ached from Billy's blows and his head swam with the events of the past hour.

Shepherd no longer smiled, a line of sweat had run down from his hair line across his cheek and had begun to form a ball on his chin. His feet dragged along the pavement and then the hardwood floor of the hotel's porch. He saw the door coming and closed his eyes before Shepherd slammed his face into the ornate carved timber to open it. Lights danced in front of his face as the world spun from the impact and tears started to form at the corners of his eyes. He blinked them back. He wouldn't allow himself to cry, not now. Not after everything he had been through, everything he had seen. If anyone was going to be a man right now, it was going to be him.

There were people in the bar, the barman who had started to ready his establishment for the rush he expected after the show. Prison guards that weren't required at the arena and Ryan, who leaned against the bar top, a look of shock on his face.

'Anyone comes through that door, you fucking shoot them!'

Shepherd roared to them as he climbed the stairs to his room. Michael tried to climb as well, but the pace in which Shepherd dragged him was too fast and the toes of his boots merely kicked against the timber edges as they went. Those people didn't know what had happened at the arena. The rioting had not reached town, neither had the killing. They had no idea what was coming for them.

Once more, Michael's face was slammed into the timber door as Shepherd burst through. Shepherd threw him down and the boy fell to the floor, though the carpet softened the blow on his cheek. The man that had once been so collected and controlled in every ounce of his manner, was now lost in a world of panic. He swore and spat as he threw the free-standing mirror out of his way, the glass shattered as the heavy frame crashed to the ground and Michael sighed as he saw the plain slats of board that lay behind the broken glass.

Downstairs, people yelled in a panic. He heard Billy shout that he didn't mean to do it. He heard the sound of a glass break and then it was drowned out by Shepherd's fists as they crunched through the plasterboard. Michael's vision had doubled, then tripled, and then settled back into the darkness of the room.

Shepherd stood where his mirror once did, a look of fear on his face as he broke section after section of plaster away. White dust filled the air and sifted to the ground as the plaster crumbled before it broke. He finally understood. 'He tried to hide it,' he said in a soft voice but Shepherd never answered him, he just continued to break more and more of the wall away.

Outside he heard the sound of an engine, its pitch high and the warble of tyres as if something heavy tried to turn sharp and fast. There was a shout downstairs and then it sounded as if the world had caved in below them. He heard timber boards snap, metal screamed as it twisted and crumbled. Below it all, he heard the screams of the people that had been in the bar, he heard Billy swear and then a gunshot.

Shepherd didn't stop, he only became more frantic as the sounds echoed up. Someone downstairs howled with such pain that the blood in Michael's veins curdled. It went on and on until the end it became full of tears and sobs. Then he heard his brothers' voice.

'Where is he?'

It was deep boom that he remembered and he recalled the time his brother had helped him with the Trackers, his face pressed up to Kel's as he demanded to know where the keys to the Fairlane were.

'Upstairs....' came Billy's broken voice. 'Up.... Stairs....' Then there was a muffled gurgle and the sound of a heavy weight crashing to the timber floor. Shepherd finally stopped and turned as the first heavy footfall was heard on the stairs.

He swore as he rummaged on his desk, the centrepiece of the room. Thud. He pulled a long slender blade that glistened silver in the darkness. Thud. Once more, Michael felt the strong fingers dig into his shoulder as he was lifted from the ground. Thud. He felt the coolness of the metal at his throat, his breath caught in his chest as he sucked air in and tried to pull his neck back away from the blade.

Thud. Thud. Thud.

The door burst open, Jack's body filled the entire doorway. The light that tried to work its way into the room was buffeted by his sheer mass. Michael felt the fear in the man behind him as Jack ducked his head to enter the room.

'You stay back!' Shepherd roared, as he pressed the letter opener closer. The icy bite wore off as the metal warmed against Michael's flesh. 'You fuckin' stay back, I swear to God.' His voice trembled with each word.

Jack looked around the room and took it all in. Michael heard the air rush as his brother took in a deep breath and exhaled. He saw his heavy chest rise and fall with the motion. Then he turned, his eyes drawn to the corner, the hole in the wall. To Michael's horror, he walked away.

Shepherd continued to tremble. He shuddered as his feet edged closer to the open door that Jack had left as he dragged Michael with him.

'Don't,' Jack said, his back turned. 'It won't do you any good.'

Shepherd stopped his advance to the door and instead backed himself further into the corner. The tip of the blade hovered a hair's breadth from the boy's throat. Michael watched as his brother plunged his fist into the wall and in a cloud of white dust and powder, he pulled the rifle from the wall.

He walked back to the centre of the room. The dull, grey steel frame didn't reflect any light. Michael doubted that it ever could. Jack seemed to surge with it in his hands and his eyes locked on Shepherd's once more. His face twisted into a snarl as he leaned his rifle up against the desk and clenched his giant fists.

Jack advanced slowly. The light had now entered the room from the hallway and Michael could see his brown eyes. 'Do you remember what he said to you?' he growled as he approached. 'As you left?'

'You stay back. I fucking swear to God.'

Michael felt the tip of the blade dig into his neck and the warm sensation that began to trickle down his throat. Jack didn't stop. With each step, he felt the knife's point dig deeper and deeper. He wanted to cry out, he wanted to tell his brother to stop but Jack didn't even look at him. He opened his mouth, but nothing came out.

'No God will save you.' Jack raised a hand.

But it was all too late and too slow. Michael felt warmth on his back as Shepherd pissed himself in his fear. He felt the hot kiss of steel to his throat. He felt the warmth run over his body and down his chest. The speed in which it ran from him was only matched by the haste in which it was replaced by the chill. He still felt the fingers dig deep into his shoulder, and he watched as Jack looked down at him. An expression on his face he had never seen before.

He felt cold, so cold. As his body twitched and the vision began to fade. He saw his brother's face turn to hot rage as his eyes swam with darkness. Black veins spread out from the scab on his cheek. They ran down his throat and stood out from his flesh. Then his vision failed him, and just before his final sense left him and the sounds of the world went to static, he heard a horrifying scream.

He felt himself begin to fall and fade. His body hit the ground, but he didn't even feel it. He thought of his Mother and Susan, maybe he could stand with them now by the lake, beyond the maze. Maybe.

CHRIS

'When you think about death,
do you lose your breath or do you keep your cool?
Would you like to see the Pope on the end of a rope?
Do you think he's a fool?'

Black Sabbath – *After Forever* (1971)

Dust continued to list down from the ceiling. The pub's structure groaned all around them while the stalled LandCruiser ticked softly. Chris was exhausted, yet his arms twitched with power as the adrenaline continued to pump through his veins. Once this was all over, he would sleep, for now he continued to fight.

Before he had rammed the front doors of the Tamworth Hotel, he had allowed the LandCruiser to come to a stop partway up the street. His eyes were wide with anticipation and the tip of his tongue lapped gently at the cracks on his lips. His eyes washed over the rear quarters of Pestilence, like those of a man who had seen the face of a long-forgotten lover. The taste of the memory hovered inches above the watery tongue, the feel of her partly faded hull. Only the faint recollection of a smell held strong, but of what he couldn't remember. He just wanted to be in her again, to let it all wash over him and then he would be safe once more.

Rankin shot him a concerned look as he slipped from the LandCruiser's gaping driver's side, while the large wagon sat in the darkness. Chris waved at Rankin to wait for him, then turned his back on his friend and the maniac in the back seat. Slowly and silently, he crept toward his old friend. His heart thumped in his throat as he slunk across the bitumen; his eyes darted from the curtains in the windows of the hotel back to his Holden once more. The closer he came to the hotel the more it shed its secrets to him. He heard shouts from the lower floor, panicked and stricken voices while heavy footsteps paced back and forth. At first, the fear shot through him that he had been spotted, but with each step the words became clearer and clearer.

'He was going to lay hands on him. What else was I supposed to do?'

The owner of the voice was lost to panic. His voice trembled as he spoke and even from the distance, Chris imagined that he could hear the short breaths of a man whose chest was tight from fear.

He had no time. He needed to get what he had come for and leave again. His hand ran down the flank of the Holden and his arm erupted in goose flesh. When his hand felt the chrome handle, a shiver ran up his spine. He sighed as the latch popped and the steel door swung outward. The interior had been cleaned to some extent, the stained carpet and vinyl that hard started the night with a clean slate was now covered in the small marbled shards of the shattered passenger window. His eyes focused on a single point. A small bead of blood stood proud on the bench seat. For the moment, the fabric still held strong against the flood. As he slipped his hand behind the seat, he wondered if the owner of that drop of blood even knew they had lost it. So much had been spilled this night, he felt stupid to linger on a single droplet. Nonetheless he was fixated.

Chris felt the coolness of a jack handle, the grit of an old rag. His eyes burned into the blood speck and he almost saw each strand of fabric swell as it absorbed the foreign liquid. Then his knuckle brushed cold steel and beneath it he felt the old grips. He blinked and moved his eyes to his hand as he pulled his old bayonet from its home. All seventeen inches of flat, dark steel glinted softly in the moonlight. It was time to end this.

The further the night had progressed, the stranger time had felt to him. Although each moment, each step and breath seemed to sap at the minutes and hours, only seconds had passed since he had left the LandCruiser. Rankin hadn't even looked impatient when he had hoisted himself back into the seat and threw the wagon into gear. The interior was quiet. All of them silent. Then as he dumped the clutch and hammered the throttle, the world was thrown into chaos once more.

Timber splintered and metal crunched as the wagon burst through the main doors. The passenger side tore an enormous chunk out of the frame and timber splinters were thrown like daggers through the air. As the vision cleared and before he was thrown forward, he saw a split image of the shock on a man's face. The fact that this man was the one who had pistol whipped him earlier hadn't even crossed his thoughts. Just the plain and simple 'Oh fuck me,' plastered across his dial would be something that he remembered till his death.

There were more people in the bar than he had thought, five or six, but already there were less. He watched as one man slumped over the bar, he didn't even get a chance to look at the commotion before a large splinter of timber drove through his back and sprouted out of his chest. The barman threw his hands over his face as he disappeared behind the safety of his well-oiled bar; a couple even turned to run. Still, the pale-faced, double denim wanker stood there with his revolver by his side. The circles of his eyes were only matched by the ring of his lips.

In the cabin of the wagon, he felt the hull shudder and with one final burst of steam from its cracked radiator the LandCruiser died beneath him. To Chris' surprise, it wasn't Rankin that had moved first, it was their passenger. Once more, he felt sick at the speed in which the bastard moved as his shadow fell over the stunned inhabitants.

He heard the passenger door pop open and from the corner of his eye he saw Rankin leave the LandCruiser, yet Chris' eyes were fixed on their passenger. He watched as a sleeve of the denim jacket rose on the man's arm as he tried to raise the revolver. The gunshot roared through the room as the panicked shot went wild. The report rolled off the remaining walls of the hotel and pounded at Chris' head. However, it lasted no more than a second before it was replaced by the sickening screams of the revolver's wielder.

While the fight for the ground floor of the Tamworth Hotel exploded in front of him, Chris was helpless but to watch in horror once more as the madman's hands went to work. With each horrific blow of hatred, power and rage, he was left wondering how he and Rankin had managed to leave that pit alive. He watched as bones were broken, his armour of worn denim did little to soften the impact. He watched as dark blue turned a sick brown and an ever-increasing pool of blood formed beneath them.

Then he looked to Rankin, his friend and protector, as he did his part. He had felled one burly man with a brass clad strike to his throat. The would-be attacker lay to his right and clutched at his collapsed airway while Rankin continued to grapple with another man who was near wider than he was tall. It was then he saw the barman again, as he slunk out from behind his well-oiled top. Chris watched as the barman moved to Rankin's side and lunged forward, the blade of the knife in his hand dazzled in the light.

Rankin and Chris moved at the same time. Rankin pushed the man he grappled with back with one hand while with the other he latched onto the wrist of the barman's knife hand. The colossal bastard threw the battered remains of the denim man hard into the wall as the barman pushed Rankin back onto a table. The two struggled for purchase on the blade. The only other attacker left free to assault was the broad son of a bitch who Rankin had pushed back. His attention was still on the two that struggled over the kitchen knife and when Chris drove his shoulder into his side, the sound of surprise as air rushed from his body filled Chris' ears. They crashed to ground and knocked more bar tables aside as they fell. When they landed, they did so atop of the body of the poor bastard who had lost his struggle for breath after Rankin had hit him. The two rolled over him, face to face, as they punched and spat at each other.

Chris clamped his left hand on his collar and drove his right fist into his fat face. They were so close he smelt the beer on his breath and saw the hairs between his eyebrows that tried to bridge the gap. The first hit broke his nose and blood covered his mouth, then Chris saw his bayonet, still in his hand and raised it.

'Where is he?' the booming roar echoed through the room. Yet the four men continued their struggle. Rankin fought to keep the kitchen blade from driving into his eyes, while Chris strained against the broader man's outstretched arm. The bayonets blade was so long that even while the man below him held his wrist at its furthest point, the tip of its blade caressed his chest. Chris saw the look in his foe's eyes, the desperation as he tried to push his arms further forward, all Chris needed was one more inch and the blade would taste his flesh.

'Upstairs…' The broken voice of the denim draped sack of shit. 'Up… Stairs….' He had tried to say more, but the sound of a blood-filled gurgle filled the room. Then came the sound as a wet, heavy mass hit the floor and then beneath the struggles of the four men and the two blades, heavy footsteps echoed throughout the bar.

Chris turned his head as he watched the maniac climb the stairs, his face turned upward to the landing. He couldn't see his eyes, only the darkness of the wound to his cheek. The man below him roared and when Chris looked back down, he had shifted his grip lower on

Chris' arm with one hand and with the other he had grabbed the dull blade of the bayonet. Chris leaned all of his weight forward. In his strain, his mouth spread wide in a grin and through his teeth he let out a low cry that became louder the more he pushed. He shrieked his cry of death while he pushed and slowly the grip of his foe began to fail. The howl continued to rip from his throat as a door above him exploded inward. Eventually, the tip of his bayonet touched the man's flesh and began to push through.

Each fraction of an inch felt like a mile. He saw the look of renewed determination on his foe's face turn to panic and then despair. He started to plead for his life, to beg for the endless progress of the steel to stop. That they could work it out and that he didn't even care for the wanker upstairs. The strained grin on Chris' face widened and his low roar continued to rise in his throat.

The pleas turned to cries and then gurgled sobs as the blade pushed deeper and deeper into him. Chris saw the bulge in his eyes and thought that he could almost see the point where the blade's tip penetrated his heart and nicked his lung. The strength of the man below him waned and with one final push, he ended it. The man's grip on his arm loosened then thudded to the ground. Blood ran from the corners of his mouth as he tried to breathe and he choked. It spattered across Chris' face from the last cough he uttered, and then he was gone.

'You stay back, I fucking swear to God!' A voice came from upstairs; the fear carried along with it, almost fluid. Defeat echoed with every syllable while the sheer terror rolled on his tongue.

Chris turned to Rankin. His friend was now on the ground; his fight had become desperate. With one hand he held the blade of the barman. Blood ran from his hand that had been torn to ribbons by the steel that he clung to. The other hand was wrapped around the barman's throat. Chris didn't hesitate this time. He saw the look of pain on his friend's face and thought he saw fear somewhere below. The bayonet pulled free with little effort. Blood ran down its fullers and as he walked, it left a spatter behind him, as if he were a careless painter that had forgotten to remove the excess from his brush.

The fight went out of the barman, more from surprise than from injury. He felt the struggle for the blade die below him when he sunk his fingers into the mop of hair on his head and reefed his head back. They held eye contact for the moment before the blade of the bayonet slid into the notch at the base of his throat and down into his chest. The motion was smooth and slick, and the blade felt no resistance. The barman stiffened, his eyes fixed on Chris' and a single tear formed in the well of his eye and ran up over his brow. When Chris pulled the blade, blood spurted up out of the hole and from the barman's mouth. A smell filled the room of acid and rot, and Chris knew the blade had punctured his gut.

The barman collapsed onto his side. His life fled his body before it had hit the ground. Rankin remained on his back, his left hand clenched in tight ball above his heart while he panted. As Chris bent down to help his friend to his feet, he heard a roar of pain, anger and suffering from the rooms above.

They both raised their heads as the hairs on Chris's neck stood on end. The roar was thunderous, the already weakened structure of the pub seemed to rattle on its braces and dust continued to list down from the cracked ceiling.

He didn't just hear the roar, he felt it, he felt it inside of his head, in his bones and his stomach, which now wanted to purge itself. Below it all, he could hear the screams for help and the constant repetition of the lord's name. Then the ceiling began to tremor while dust and chunks of plaster and timber began to shake loose and tumble down on them. The screams of pain and death cut through them while the roar of sorrow and anger drove into their minds.

Rankin clambered to his feet and began to back up, his eyes remaining transfixed on the murder above. Chris, likewise, had begun to move without realising it and soon he felt the smashed front end of the LandCruiser at his back. With a final sickening thud, the hotel fell into silence. The two remaining men glanced at each other, both of them shaken and unsure of what to do.

A door to the rear of the hotel slammed inward and they heard the pounding footsteps as men rushed toward them. Rankin grabbed Chris by the arm.

'Time to leave.' His voice was low, but it carried the stress they both felt. Chris nodded and began to turn when the newcomers burst into the room.

Four, well-armed men faced them, their rifles trained on them. They glanced at the bodies that littered the floor and expression of hate washed over their faces. They muttered to each other names of the men that had fallen as they looked from themselves to the men before them and their faces twisted with their rage. Chris stood frozen, sure that this was going to be his end. He didn't know if the men had followed them from the chaos at the arena or whether they had no idea what had happened in their town. He waited for the walls of lead to rush towards him and was resigned to death when a mangled heap of flesh and cloth fell to the ground between them.

Everyone jumped. The sound the corpse made when it hit the ground was that of a wet two-hundred-pound sack. Blood spattered upward from the impact and rained down on them. The room fell back into silence, all the eyes were on the mess that lay between them. One man took a step forward. Cautiously, he raised his rifle to the stairs and followed their path upward with his iron sights. Each man concentrated on the short, exasperated breath of the advancing rifleman and the short scuffs of his boots on the boards.

Further and further, he advanced. The barrel of his rifle climbed with each shuffle. Chris' eyes had begun to water, in all the excitement he felt as though he had not blinked the entire time he had been in this damned place. Chris closed his eyes. The exact moment he did, a large weight crashed to the ground in front of him and he leapt backward. He gasped as the LandCruiser's buckled and creased bonnet cut into his back. As his eyes opened, Chris saw what remained of the rifleman. The body was crushed beneath the soles of two enormous work boots. As his gaze lifted, Chris saw the face of the giant that had tried to kill them not even half an hour before.

In his hands he held a large rifle. A straight yet short magazine sprouted from its frame. His pockets bulged out from his thighs; the square shape of more magazines pushed through the denim. His eyes were black orbs, dark veins ran from the wound on his cheek and carved crevasses down his neck and across his shoulders. Long, dark tendrils worked their way across his skin and with each deep bull's breath he took they seemed to advance across his flesh. Wordlessly, the black orbs scoured Rankin and Chris. Its mouth was twisted in a horrendous scowl. It raised the rifle toward them.

'On your knees!' a man from the back of room commanded. Behind the giant came the sound of rifles being cocked. The giant froze. Between the legs of the big man, Chris could see those of the rifleman who had advanced. He stood right behind him, close enough to place the muzzle of his rifle to the larger man's flesh. Chris edged closer to the side of the LandCruiser. His heart pounded in his throat. The tension in the air was suffocating, and he felt a trickle of sweat run down his spine.

If anyone had told him that a man could have turned faster than another could have pulled a trigger, Chris would not have believed them. To say that a man that was the size of the one before him could do this, seemed laughable. Chris did not even see him turn. One second, he faced him, the next Chris was looking at his back.

Chris had seen enough. He turned and made for the side of the LandCruiser.

Behind him there was a gasp as air left someone's body. Chris ran past Rankin and grabbed him by the collar of his Chinese service uniform and dragged him. Automatic rifle fire filled the room and pounded heavily in his ears. The frame of the front door was shattered, leaving only the thin gap between the destroyed hull of the Toyota and the remains of the hotel's front wall, as an exit. Chris, as malnourished as he was, slipped through easily. Rankin, on the other hand, became wedged.

Chris turned and grabbed his torn hand. Rankin strained as he tried to squeeze through. Beyond his friend's face, Chris saw the flashes of gunshots while the reports pounded into his head. Timber cracked and splintered under the withering fire from the men left standing, and the LandCruiser's windscreen blew in. Men screamed and swore below it all, but they may as well have been whispers for the sound of the rifle in the giant's hands.

'Come on!' Chris groaned as he put all of his strength into his efforts to pull his friend through the small gap. With a brass clad hand, Rankin grasped the Toyota's B pillar and pulled as well. With the sounds of death behind them and the smell of gunpowder filling their heads, Rankin slipped free. The roars continued to chase them as they ran for Pestilence; the look of her had never seemed so sweet to Chris. He fumbled with the handle and finally reefed the door open when the gunshots stopped.

Chris and Rankin piled into the Holden and a sickening thought came over Chris. He had not checked to see if the keys were in the ignition when he had taken the bayonet. As if afraid to check, Chris sat there, while his hand hovered halfway between his knee and the ignition.

'Oh fuck, get moving man!' Rankin whimpered beside him and

Chris looked to the rear-view mirror. The LandCruiser had started to edge backwards. Closer and closer, he moved his hand towards the ignition, as he prayed that the key was there. The closer his hand moved, the further the LandCruiser backed out. The face of the giant was visible over the bonnet, the black eyes scoured the street in search of them.

There was click and Pestilence whirred beneath him. The black eyes fell on them and with a roar of hate, the LandCruiser shot back into the street. He pumped the gas.

'Come on girl.'

Whir, whir, whir. The black eyes were closer, the butt of the rifle hung out from over his shoulder as he closed the distance between them.

'Fuck man, go!'

The engine fired and once more the power of Pestilence's Chevrolet plant filled the air. Fire spat out from under her hull, which illuminated the face of the beast behind them. Chris slammed the Holden into gear.

He knew Rankin wasn't ready. He knew it before he did it, but he had no choice. Rankin flew out of his chair and once more, the back of his head connected with the windscreen as Pestilence shot backward. The distance was not far, yet the speed at which she took off was remarkable. The black eyes filled the rear-view, nothing but hate and death in them. There was a crunch and the rear hitched and shuddered and to Chris' horror, the engine stalled.

RANKIN

*'I met one man who was wounded in love
I met another man who was wounded with hatred
And it's a hard, it's a hard, it's a hard, it's a hard
It's a hard rain's a-gonna fall.'*

Bob Dylan – *A Hard Rains a-Gonna Fall* (1963)

Lights danced before his eyes. The newly christened baptism of fire that had exploded in the back of his head had stretched its knife point around the side of his face to meet his left ear. The blow that the psychopath had dealt him in the pit seemed like it was an eternity ago. Yet the remnants of the throbbing pain that shot up from his lower jaw to somewhere deep inside his inner ear still persisted. Now that the two had joined together in one grand symphony of fire and blood, he felt as though his head was about to explode. He collapsed into the footwell once more and for a single moment, he groped for his SLR.

Some part of him deep down, thought this whole Tamworth nightmare had been a dream. They had never made it out of Brisbane. The atrocities he had seen in the river, the bus, and the butchered civilians. The child at the bars of his prison cell and finally the pit of the arena. All of it had been a dream of his subconscious that had started its sketchy playback the moment his head had first kissed the scarred and pitted glass of the Holden's windscreen in the streets of Brisbane. Of course, it had to have been a dream, a nightmare. The black orbs that swallowed half of the giant's face, the veins that tracked down his cheeks to his throat. All those horrific features that had been there one minute, only to have disappeared the second before the final crushing blow.

They had disappeared, along with the hate, the lust of blood. The blackened flesh of his torn cheek had remained, but the brown eyes that were soft in comparison to the black pits they had replaced had thrown him.

'Help me.' That was what he had said. If nothing else was believable, the fact that he had gotten to his feet and agreed to help the man that had almost slain himself and his last friend was the sticking point. None of it made sense.

His eyes were closed as his head rocked with agony. He heard Chris swearing as he struggled to fire the Holden's plant. He would open his eyes and see the barrel of his SLR as it rested against the bench seat. He would raise himself and see the Chinese approaching through the hole in the brick wall they had created. Yet, if that was the case, why did his left ear scream with agony? Why did his ribs continue to pain him each time he moved his right arm? And why could he feel the coolness of the brass knuckles that were wrapped around his own?

The starter motor whirred and the smell of fuel filled the cabin.

'You've flooded it,' he said dreamily as he slapped his left hand to the seat, as he felt for his rifle. His palm hit the fabric with a wet slap and slowly the needles of fire began to pierce his palm and course their way up his wrist. He swore aloud and finally opened his eyes.

He stared in amazement at the ribbons of flesh that had once been his palm. The fingers that coursed with his blood, the flesh that seemed to distort under its flow. In his dream, he had held the wrong end of a kitchen knife, while a barman had tried to drive it into his chest. It had been a dream, it had to have been a dream, he constantly clung to the thought in his mind.

The frame of the Holden hitched and metal groaned. Chris swore again as the starter motor whirred. Each gut-wrenching attempt to fire the plant became slower and futile as the battery began to drain. While the stress grew behind the frantic pleas and curses that Chris uttered with each attempt, Rankin continued to stare dumbfounded at his hand. If he was where he thought they were, the front bar had become caught in the LandCruiser that was parked on the streets of Brisbane. That was where they had to be. They had to be there.

The frame's groans turned to screams as the sound of metal tearing filled the air. Rankin heard rivets pop as hinges were torn loose and then there was silence. Through his bloodied fingers, he saw the tailgate pull away from the rear of the Holden's tray and the rear end seemed to rock with the movement, then he saw his face. The black orbs, the veins that coursed down across his face now, the hatred, the malice. The metal of the tailgate twisted in its hands as it roared and finally laid eyes on its prey.

The starter motor whirred again. The smell of fuel had mixed with the coolness of the night's air that rushed in through the broken passenger window, Rankin felt as though he wanted to be sick. Yet this time the sound was different; there was a low rumble and gurgle as if it had phlegm stuck somewhere in its throat. Then the suck of air rushed around them as Chris held his foot flat to the board and the huge four barrels of the Holley carb began to suck.

The engine roared to life below them and the giant lunged. Rubber churned and howled as the transmission hurled them forward, but it didn't matter. It didn't matter how fast or how hard Chris' pale ute could propel them, he could still see the hateful black eyes staring at him through the rear window. With each movement the big man took in the tray, the Holden shifted on its suspension. Rankin still looked through the mess of blood and flesh on his hands while Chris propelled them through the streets. The peaks of buildings and the glowing amber of street lamps whistled past them, to cast odd shadows through the cabin.

The V8 surged with power and they gained more speed. Everything outside became a blur, but there was nothing he could do but watch the slow advance of their hitchhiker. Every ounce of fight that was in him had fled, his body was exhausted and every breath was a labour. It had taken everything he had to stay alive against this monster in the pit. That was due to the room he had to move and the others that had thrown themselves into the fight, only to lose their lives. Now, he sat like a stray dog in a trap, not even the strength to bare its teeth as death came down on it.

The Holden hitched slightly and the brakes locked up. Rankin felt himself get pushed back into the broken dashboard once more as the overweight nose of the utility scraped the ground. In the tray, the big man lost his feet and came rushing forward. The rear window exploded in a brilliant spray of glass as the giant's face crashed through. Each fragment caught the pale amber of the outside light and sent it in every direction. Blood ran small streams over the black veins from a hundred minor lacerations, yet still the giant did not falter.

A horrible sight filled his vision, as the blackened flesh curled up from his mouth in a triumphant sneer. One massive arm pushed through the weakened glass and reached for him. He watched as large shards of glass that still sat strong in its frame, gouged the skin on the beast's arms and shoulders and blood rushed forth. It fell upon the fabric of the seat and pooled in the giant's palm as it formed a bloody glove around his outstretched hand.

The V8 surged again and the tyres howled, yet they didn't shoot forward. Rankin's body slid toward Chris. Without thinking, he clamped his brass clad hand down on the sill of the passenger door. The giant's face still burned only inches away from him now and for the first time, he felt the heat that came from him. It was like he had pushed his face against the hot body of an exhaust; he felt like his skin wanted to blister, his eyes wanted to burst. Two fingers dragged down his cheek and he let out a scream. Then the Holden's back end whirled with the power of the V8's roar; the last of the glass in the sill of the rear window cracked as it let go, and the burning face was gone.

Part of Rankin wanted to climb to the seat and watch as its body tumbled across the bitumen. He wanted to see how it fell and he wished to God that it hurt the son of a bitch. But the fear was still inside of him. The possibility that it had already risen and chased them clung to his throat. While the power of the V8 surged them forward, he was driven back into the seat and his legs became caught up under him. He couldn't see the outside. He didn't know where they were headed or what was behind them. If they didn't turn soon, only one thing would follow.

As if in answer to this last thought, Chris roared beside him, 'Heads down!' and hunched himself low in the driver seat. Under the road noise, the V8 and his hammering heart, Rankin heard the thunder of automatic fire, and although he had little to space to cower in, he pressed himself lower to the floor pan.

Chris turned the wheel hard in an attempt to make the Holden track across the road. Despite his efforts, the horrific sound as bullets slammed through the Holden's body soon filled his ears. The fabric of the bench seat in front of Rankin exploded outward and he felt something rush past his head and into the dashboard. He heard rattling beneath them as bullets glanced the transmission casing. The windscreen that had been replaced was racked once more with holes and cracks ran outward from their centre.

Chris hissed as blood flew from a gash that appeared on his arm and once more Rankin watched the flow it took. He was sick of blood.

He'd had enough of death and suffering. He needed it all to be over, he was finished. Holding his hands to his face, he screamed again, as if he was insane. His own blood covered his cheek from the slash to his palm and he felt ill as the warm stickiness covered him.

With a final clink of broken glass, the only side mirror shattered, and the barrage ended. Rankin's howls of horror ended shortly after. He'd let his hands fall to the floor and his body was all twisted up as he lay in a heap in the footwell. He had no energy left to move. He lay there, for some time in silence, only the rasps of his breath to signal that he was alive. His eyes remained open but unfocused and with each bounce of the suspension, his eyes washed over the interior. Glass lined the floor and the seat; dirt covered the Chinese uniform he still wore; blood tracked its way down Chris' arm to drip from his bent elbow.

He didn't know how long they had driven, nor the direction, and he didn't care. Sometimes, beneath the blatt of the Holden's exhaust, he could hear people on the streets. There were roars of anger and cries of pain. In one instance, a man had emitted such a shrill pitch that Rankin couldn't decide on whether its owner had laughed or cried.

Soon the sky turned red and he had thought that dawn had arrived. The smell of smoke touched his senses and he heard Chris mutter, 'Good God.' Rankin never lifted his head to see what they had passed, yet still he felt the heat and saw the fire dance in Chris' eyes.

It took what seemed like hours for the sky to return to darkness and for the sounds of death and pain to finally leave his mind. For once, he was thankful that sleep had taken him. He didn't even feel it coming for him when it did. Perhaps that was what death would feel like when it eventually claimed his soul. He doubted people felt it, or knew. He just needed to either die or sleep, the way he felt, he wouldn't have cared if it was the former.

When he woke, his neck screamed in agony at the angle he had succumbed to. His legs had gone numb, and every part of him had at least one complaint or another. When he looked up at Chris who had shaken him from his slumber, he threw every insult he could muster toward him. Part of it was the fact that he had woken him, the other part was probably due to the fact Chris had let him sleep in that position in the first place. When he finally clambered from the cabin and into the late afternoon sun, his body shook from his lack of energy, his stomach groaned as cramps struck him and he determined that his outburst was due to hunger.

At first thought, the service station had been abandoned. The front door to the small shop area was unlocked, yet still someone had seen the sense to smash the plate glass window that marked its frontage. The store had been ransacked, items which once sat proudly displayed on their shelves had been cast to ground in careless swipes. A lot had been taken, but enough lay around the store for them.

Rankin let his back slide down the end of a shelving bay while he tore open a cardboard package of crackers. Wordlessly, he devoured the box. His lips smacked while he shovelled handful after handful of the dried biscuits into his mouth. When he was about halfway through the packet, he coughed when a large soggy clump had become stuck in his throat.

As if in panic once more for his life, he crawled across the ground and left large splotches of blood from his still bleeding hand. His eyes caught on what he looked for and he moved for it. Still, he coughed as he yearned for the air which had struggled to move past the glob of shit in his windpipe. He fumbled with his ruined hand and ripped the top from the glass bottle and, as if he had never had a drop in his life, he took a large swig.

The hot fire touched his lips; his tongue drowned in the memories of years that had passed. Like a band of savages that burned their way through town after town, the whiskey burned its way down his throat and sat in his stomach. He took the bottle from his mouth and sighed. How many nights had it been? Weeks, months even, since he'd even thought about whiskey. He laughed. That was a lie. When something had a hold on you that bad, its nails sunk that far into your flesh that when you removed it, your body and mind were left scarred. To look at a scar on your body and think of the blade that made it was the likeness in which he dreamt about whiskey. There were people that existed that felt only ecstasy when they let blood flow from their veins. They knew it was bad to cut themselves, but they still did it. For them it might feel good, but now, even as he raised the bottle to his mouth again, he felt like shit.

The bottle was only small, half of its contents now swilled around in his stomach. It was enough. He could already feel his head begin to swim; the few handfuls of crackers he had crammed into his mouth had done nothing to stem his hunger. He needed to find something better, but first he needed to tend to his hand. He sat up once more. In anticipation of the pain, his hands had begun to tremble and he wanted to drain the rest of the golden liquid. His self-medication had always worked for any ailment in the past, but he didn't, he couldn't. He held out his palm and splashed the whiskey over it.

He roared and tears swelled in his eyes. He clenched both his hands, his eyes closed, and his body stiffened, as the wave of pain shot up his arm. Finally, the pain passed enough for him to stop. He opened his eyes, the word swam beyond the tears and blurred his vision.

Chris stood over him and frowned. He held a bottle of spirits in his hand.

'Great minds,' Chris said as he knelt down next to him. 'Let me see it.'

Resigned, Rankin held out his hand again. The shakes had tripled and his palm throbbed with each heartbeat. Chris hissed when he saw the shredded flesh and shook his head. He placed the bottle of spirits on the ground and stood again.

Rankin clamped his hand shut and held it close to his chest as he rocked back and forth. He tried to fight the throb, while he listened to Chris rummage through the shop. He didn't hear him return, but he smelled the spirits as Chris doused a rag with them. He opened his eyes as his hand was pulled from his chest. Without even knowing what was happening, he had begun to scream again and fight as Chris dabbed the spirit-soaked rag into his wounds.

'We need to clean the shit out of it,' Chris said impatiently. Rankin was deafened by his own agony as he fought with each movement of rag on flesh. At one point, he assumed he had passed out as the world swam with darkness and his screams seemed distant, as if they weren't even from his own lungs. In the next moment, it all rushed forward and the pain with it. He walked the fine line between which lay between the conscious state and darkness for some time.

Chris slapped him on the shoulder, 'If I was a doctor, I'd give you a lolly, but I thought doctors only gave good girls treats.' Rankin looked up at him, consumed by his pain. His heart still hammered hard in his chest. 'And you, my friend, have been a downright cunt.'

'Fuck off, idiot,' Rankin muttered as he held his now bandaged hand close to his chest. The throbs remained, but they were nothing compared to the feeling of an untrained hand dragging a rough spun rag soaked with methylated spirits through an open wound. Chris laughed to himself as he left Rankin to his misery.

Rankin's eyes opened, as a new sense of purpose washed over him.

'Time for me to return the favour, man.' He slowly and shakily gained his feet.

The laughter died in Chris' throat. He stopped and turned slowly. 'What?'

'Your arm.' Rankin sneered as he watched his friend's eyes drop to the gash on his arm.

'Nah, it'll be—'

'Nah nothing, mate, we need to look after it,' he said as his sneer stretched to full grin. 'Wouldn't want my mate to get an infection.'

Despite his friend's refusal, Rankin got his way. He laughed each time Chris jerked or hissed with pain. Undoubtedly the gash on Chris' arm was nowhere near the severity of Rankin's hand, still, Rankin took little enjoyment from the lack of screams and moans. When he finished, he wrapped the white cloth around Chris' arm and threw the spirt soaked rag into his face. 'Now who's the cunt?'

Chris grumbled something but Rankin didn't hear it. He had returned to his search for food. As he scoured the shop, he held the half-eaten box of crackers close to his chest with his bandaged hand while he sporadically rammed his free hand to his mouth. He came across a few untainted packets of jerky, five more boxes of crackers and a few packets of chips. Nothing fantastic if one considered their figure, but in the circumstance they would do.

Once his hunger had been fulfilled, he turned to his next desire: cigarettes. His stash had been confiscated when they were captured in Tamworth. From time to time while he sat there in his cell, the fat bastard Ryan had flicked him a packet. Not the smooth Benson and Hedges he had brought into town but filter-less Camels. Part of him had wanted to quit the smokes as well, either that or smoke his own shit, which still would have been better. Now he stood and looked at a fully stocked shelf of Winfield, Benson and Hedges, Marlboro and even Log Cabin Pipe Tobacco. He felt like a child at a confectionery store. He emptied the shelf and threw them all into a box that he later stowed in the back of the Holden.

Tired, the two men agreed to stay in the store a while longer while they both caught up on some sleep. Chris would sleep first, while Rankin happily sat back and devoured crackers and smoked cigarettes while the time passed, then after a few hours they would switch. The Holden was parked out of sight, around the back of the store. No doubt while Rankin slept Chris would venture out the back to look his 'girl' over.

Before the first shift of sleep, however, the two decided to sit back. Chris had stumbled across another couple of sample bottles of whiskey and had asked Rankin to join him. As he had already fallen off the wagon once in the day, Rankin took him up on his offer. They sat in the morning sun, shared a packet of Twisties, and sipped at their sample bottles of Jack Daniel's.

The warmth of the sun on his skin made Rankin tired. Yet the more he wanted to yawn, the more he ate and the more he drank. The familiar wash of the whiskey ran over him and settled him. The stresses of the past days, weeks and months seemed to drain out of him, and he looked at the bottle in his hand. Why had he ever decided to walk away?

'Tell me something,' Chris spoke up after a while. Rankin looked over at him, his eyebrows raised. 'Why did you decide to help that big bastard?'

Rankin downed the rest of his bottle and clambered to his feet. 'If I'm going to think about that big fucker, I'm going to need another drink. Was there anymore in there?'

'Yeah, shitloads, in the office.'

Rankin nodded and took his leave. The small town was quiet. It was eerie to an extent, but both of them were happy to be alone for the most part. They'd had their fill of other people, foreign and domestic. Rankin still had no idea how far they had travelled from Tamworth. Not that if he had heard the name of the town they were in, it would mean anything to him.

As with most people in Australia, he knew the bigger cities but not the towns that lay in-between.

He entered the office and immediately found the box that contained the liquor. It sat on the office desk directly to the right as soon as he entered the small room. His friend's footprints were in the dust on the floor, a single over tracked course led from the door to the desk and out again. Chris had not searched the rest of the office. Rankin took a quick look around while he popped the top off another bottle of Jack.

A small doorway was cut into the wall directly in front of him, one of those crappy plastic dividers was pulled across it. He took a swig as he approached it and curiosity took a hold of him. He poked a finger through the small plastic handle and the plastic clattered as it slid back on its track. The smell hit him instantly. He took a quick look into the room and then backed away as he swore. He held the bottle to his nose and took in a deep breath. The whiskey burned his nostrils but it was all for the better. He downed the rest of the bottle in one large swig and shuddered.

Behind him, he heard footsteps and Chris entered the room, the remainder of the bag of Twisties still in his hand. 'A man would die of thirst,' he grumbled as he entered the office. He looked at Rankin and frowned. 'What's wrong?' He took a breath. 'What the fuck is that smell?'

Rankin pointed to the small adjoining room as he took another bottle for himself and passed one to Chris. The two men walked back and looked inside together.

A man's body was hung by his feet from a loop in the ceiling. A rope ran from his legs, through the loop, and off to an oversized hook mounted on the wall. His body was black with rot, his stomach had been opened and his innards lay in a mess on the floor below him. His hands lay open, with intestines looped through his fingers. Black mess ran up his arms and his face from where he had tried to push them back in. His eyes were sunken and his mouth hung open.

'Christ,' Rankin said as he downed his bottle.

'Don't pray to him,' Chris groaned, 'This was done in his name.' He pointed to the wall to his left. Large red letters were painted on the plaster, the paint had run from the heavy slather they had been cast in.

'"He who believes in Him is not judged. He who does not believe has been judged already,"' Rankin read aloud. 'Fuck that.' He groaned as he turned his head and left the office, taking the box of liquor with him. The two men left the hanging man and returned to their spot in the sun. After what they had seen, they sat in silence again for a long time. Finally, Rankin spoke up.

'Not Christ.'

Chris looked at him. 'What?'

'Not Christ,' he repeated. 'It was done in the name of that Shepherd guy in Tamworth.'

'Who?'

'You didn't meet him, you were knocked out. The guy that was doing the speaking in the pit.'

Chris nodded like he knew what he meant. Then he looked back to him and changed the subject. 'You going to answer my question now?' At Rankin's confused look he clarified, 'Why did you want to help that guy?'

Rankin looked down at the dirt between his legs and lit another cigarette. 'Why do you think I helped you?'

CHRIS

*'And I am you and what I see is me
And do I take you by the hand
And lead you through the land
And help me understand
The best I can.'*

Pink Floyd – *Echoes* (1971)

The shadows crept over the land while they watched. Even though their eyes were open they didn't see the progress of the dark. Chris' mind would wonder back to her as if it had come home from a long day's work. His body was safe and his hunger was assuaged, nothing left to do but to hang up the proverbial hat, coat and bayonet. Throw the keys to Pestilence into the bowl that sat by the front door and sit back to read his favourite book.

In his head, the book never contained any words. One day, he imagined he would hear something so beautiful, a phrase, a sentence or stanza, something so perfect that it would embody what she was. Until that day came, every time he thought of her, it was only of her hair and her eyes, all else was lost to him. He couldn't remember the feel of her, her taste. Even as he looked up into the sky to search for the constellation that lay in her eyes, he doubted that he would know it if he saw it.

He blinked. The world had taken further steps along the shade scale to black. He looked towards a gum that stretched fifty feet into the air some distance away in the rolling paddocks. Only moments before, he had been able to see each branch clear against the sky. He had seen the rosellas settle in for the night, their feathers all puffed out as they cleaned the day from themselves. Yet now all he saw was a blob of something that loomed just behind the light. He laughed to himself, one so sad that it verged on the edge of sobs and tears. He let the sampler bottle clatter to the ground at his side and its contents glugged to the earth, unfinished, unwanted, undeserved.

He closed his eyes once more and focused on her as the smell of the liquor swept over him. His mind burned with the labour, the attempt to draw the files from some distant location in the back of his head. He wanted to remember every line, every curve, but it was no good. Somewhere, at some point, those features had become lost to him. Faded like the photograph in his wallet. The saddest part was that he couldn't even remember when it had happened. The veil had fallen over her face just as the shadows had crept along the earth during the late afternoon embers. No matter how long he looked, searched or focused on a point, the dark crept over the world and no flame could hold it back.

Beside him, Rankin tipped back another swig of whiskey. The collection of empty glass bottles had grown, no thanks to his own efforts. Not having the taste for hard liquor, Chris had downed two of small sampler bottles, even that had started to make his stomach roll end over end. On the other hand, Rankin had thrown them back like they were water. In the time that Chris had struggled the last sip down of his second bottle, Rankin had downed six and showed no signs of slowing.

The last words that either of them had spoken still rung in his ears. 'Why do you think I helped you?' Rankin had asked through bloodshot eyes and Chris had never answered him. He had sat and watched the earth disappear before his eyes while beside him his friend drank and smoked. He pondered the question, but to no avail. They had met in that busted up apartment block in Brisbane, then they had escaped the ruins together. Chris had told him about his journey after they had seen the bodies of the people in the river. Rankin had said that he would help, but why?

Chris had a car which was a good option to tag along and in the same token, since the time they had left Brisbane they had accomplished no searching for her. In fact, with each mile they had driven away from Brisbane, the more he had regretted the decision to take the western road. It was the path of least resistance. He knew she would be south and she would be with *them*, but when the road came to a fork and there was only one car, he supposed that one either rode or died, maybe both.

The Chinese that remained wouldn't stay in Brisbane, this much he knew. The west was lost to them. Their only line now was to stay on the east coast and to head south. Town by town, bay by bay. That is where he would find her, but would Rankin help him? They had kept each other alive, that much was certain, but when it came down to driving back into the fight, would he follow?

'I don't know,' Chris said. Rankin jerked beside him as if he had woken up. Slowly his head rolled on his shoulders so that he could look at the man beside him.

Rankin grunted as if in acknowledgement, then after he blinked a few times, he straightened himself and yawned. 'What?'

'I don't know why you helped me or that big bastard.'

Rankin's head thudded back to the wall of the service station as he rolled his eyes. He rubbed at his face with his one hand that wasn't bandaged. 'Does it matter?'

'Well, the more I think of it, the more it does,' Chris came back.

'Stop thinking about it then. I'm too drunk to talk about this shit now.'

'Nah mate, that big fucker nearly killed us in the pit. Some kid starts singing a song and you bring him along. Where he nearly kills us again.'

Rankin's head snapped toward him, anger visible in his eyes. 'Alright for you to judge, mate, you were unconscious the entire time we were in that fucking place. I thought you were going to die on me.'

'Yet here I stand,' Chris said.

'Yet here you stand,' Rankin growled. 'The man that's driven half the countryside in search of his wife that he reckons the Chinese has taken from him.' He stood and lit a cigarette. 'All this distance! Tell me, man, how many people have you seen dead along the way?' His voice had become a roar.

'Hundreds, maybe.'

'Thousands!' he scoffed. 'Don't give me hundreds, fucking thousands!' Spittle flew from his mouth as he roared the words.

Chris fell silent. Despite what he had seen personally, which wasn't much seeing as though he hadn't walked through every town, house by house. He thought Rankin's prediction to be low balled, tens of thousands seemed more accurate, maybe even more. It was hard to think how many civilians had fallen in the Darwin massacre. Rabbits, his friend, just in his death, there had been more than a handful taken with him. What about the soldiers who were bombed at the base? The lone pilot that had managed to get his plane into the air. How many? He just didn't know.

'That boy who was singing in the pit was that big bastard's brother,' Rankin went on, quieter now, but rage lingered in his voice. 'He came to us while you were knocked out. Both of them were prisoners there. I didn't give a shit about that big bastard. I was trying to help the kid!'

'I never even saw the kid at the hotel, but I saw a kid in Pestilence,' Chris replied.

'Ahh, I don't know.' Rankin took a few steps away and blew plumes of smoke into the air as he chuffed angrily. 'The way that bastard came down stairs again, I doubt he's alive. Poor little shit. To be honest, I forgot all about him once I saw that fuckers' eyes again.'

Chris looked at him. He didn't think he had ever seen Rankin show fear before, but what he was seeing now had to be something close. 'His eyes.' he repeated. Chris had been involved in the fight, but he was still weary from his concussion. The closest he had come to the big man was when he had tried to choke the life out of him but he had never seen his face. The interior of the LandCruiser was dark and he'd had only had eyes for Pestilence. He watched as Rankin shuddered and lit another cigarette from the embers of the original.

'They…' he took a deep drag on the cigarette. 'Change.' He spoke the word in his exhale, smoke whisped from his mouth and lingered around his face. 'When we spoke, he was normal. He had eyes like the kid that we tried to help, they were the same.' He shivered again. 'But when he drove his face through the back of the car…'

'They were black,' Chris spoke softly. He remembered now the eyes he had seen in the bar of the hotel. 'Those I saw. I didn't see him any other way, I thought he had something wrong with him?'

Rankin slid himself back down the wall of the station and he thudded softly to the ground. 'I think he does. If you had seen the man that was behind those eyes that I saw.' He paused. 'If you had seen the kid. Then you would've helped him.' He spoke the last words as a whisper, his anger diminished. Chris watched as he flicked the butt of his cigarette into the night and saw the trail of its fire fly into the darkness. Small embers danced from its body as it bounced along the dirt and grass. As the dew overcame it, the glow lessened and it vanished from sight.

'Okay,' Chris said as he nodded. He didn't know why he had asked the question. He couldn't remember whether he had been concerned for the decision, or just plain curious. Nevertheless, it had started his mind working and he wanted to know more about the man that sat next to him. 'Okay. So why did you help me?'

Rankin looked at him.

'You said why do I think that you helped me? I get why we helped that guy. I just wanted my ute back, but I still don't get why you're helping me.'

There was the faint sound as plastic crunched and Rankin twisted the top off another Jack Daniel's bottle. He lifted it to his mouth and even in the darkness Chris saw its contents drain. 'I don't think I have.'

Chris scoffed a soft laugh through his nose. 'Why did you come with me? After Brisbane.'

Rankin tossed the empty glass into the darkness and reached for another. After a quick mental count, Chris was sure this would have to be his eleventh. 'No better option, I suppose. Man, I don't know. You said you wanted help finding your wife, I needed to get the fuck out of where I was. You help me, I help you.'

They both fell into a broody silence after this. Chris had noticed that Rankin's breathing had become heavy with drink. The ends of his words slurred into the beginnings of the next. Chris knew he was stupid for pushing conversation when Rankin was this way. They hadn't known each other for long, but a man drunk is not himself. He watched as the next bottle was hurled into the air and Rankin reached for another.

'Christ, don't you think you've had enough? Anyone would think you're an alcoholic or something.' He didn't know why he said it, the moment he did, he realised his error.

'Yeah, and anyone would think your Missus was dead.' Rankin said it low and cold.

It hit Chris like a freight train. The coldness in the way he said it stuck into his heart. Anger burned in his head and for a split second, all he wanted to do was to pound Rankin's head into the ground. To see the blood spill from his broken nose and to push his teeth out through the back of his throat. Then in the same way as his memory had faded and the shadows had crept forward of the tree line, his anger subsided and he climbed to his feet.

He turned his back on Rankin and walked away. The man behind him, the supposed friend, didn't move. As Chris rounded the corner, he heard the tell-tale noise of another bottle seal being broken. Not a word of apology, nor that of anger, came from either of them as Chris approached Pestilence.

Her battered lines sat shrouded in darkness, now somewhat incomplete from the lack of tailgate where the ferocity of the one who they had helped backfired. He didn't run a loving hand up her side. He didn't even offer her the look of a wayside lover. He reefed open the driver's door, piled himself inside and slammed the door shut behind him.

The engine fired and projected its driver's mood as unburned fuel spattered the ground beneath the blackened hole of its exhaust. The transmission clacked three times and the back end squatted with the power that exploded beneath it. The Holden shot out from its position of cover; its live rear end swayed ferociously on the loose dirt below as Chris hammered the car in his distress. Its body bumped and ground its way onto the highway. Once back on the road where it was king and nothing could touch it, it echoed its power and might throughout the country side for all the world to hear.

He pushed her hard and the headlamps cut through the shadows. Whether they had crept up on the road or descended from the night's sky did not matter to him anymore. All darkness bowed before her and parted like the Red Sea. She bore down the highway as she headed south and continued to lay rubber. Angie may be to his east, but for now he would head south and come around on them and hit them hard. There was no place where Pestilence could not reach, no road he could not master. He would find her. No matter what the drunk fucker thought, she was alive.

The Holden mastered its tyres; they rolled smooth over the dirt then the tarmac. Her growl softened and the speed began to ease. There was no need to run, nothing chased her or her driver. He carried his burden with him on his shoulders, his hands, and most of all in his mind. His head had become weary from the carnage of the day. He had re-entered the world of the living, only to find himself in that damned pit and had not rested until the service station, which now lay behind him.

He cut through a town and didn't even apply the brakes as he passed the burned houses. Some cars were scattered in the street, but still the road was wide enough for Pestilence to power through. Only one wreck had almost pulled him unstuck, the frame had been flattened and the crushed roof of the vehicle lay below the height of the Holden's bonnet. Only in the last seconds had Chris seen its shattered shape and had adjusted Pestilence's course to its left. It came within a hair's breadth of the battered utility and Chris never gave it another thought or look. He just continued south, away from his problems.

By the time 'Willow Tree' had flashed before his eyes, he was almost asleep. No matter how hard he pushed her, no matter the speeds they reached together, he could not outrun exhaustion, nor could he forgo sleep any longer. He allowed her to slow to a crawl, as if powerless to control her any further. He let her coast, while his eyes strained to remain open and he leaned over the steering wheel in an attempt to see through the water in his eyes. He had a faint recollection of pulling into the driveway of a house. The engine died below him and then he collapsed. He sunk deeper to his side as the engine ticked under the hot weight of its bonnet and his eyes succumbed to the weight of their lids.

When he opened his eyes, he felt the stone beneath him again. He knew he was in his courtyard, but darkness shrouded it and for the life of him he couldn't see the steel fence that surrounded it. His skin erupted with gooseflesh as the cold of the night cut through him. However, somewhere in front, he could feel heat and he knew he needed to move toward it. He lifted himself from the stone and he heard a sound come from the gloom in front. He listened, Tick, Tick.

He took a step forward, as he strained his ears to hear the next tick when he was blinded by two circular beams of sheer, brilliant light. He turned his head and closed his eyes while he lifted his hands to shield them.

Tick, Tick.

He moved forward, as he still shielded himself from the brilliance. Tick, Tick. The high beams seemed to cut through his fingers and eye lids, nothing could stop them. He kept moving, almost there. Tick.

He placed his hand on her bonnet and felt the warmth that lay beneath. The beams continued to burn to either side of him as he placed his other hand flat to her warmth. At his complete touch the starter motor rolled, she fired into life and shuddered, as if excited by him. Her motor idled, then surged. The warmth turned to heat, almost unbearable in its burn. The paint at either side of his hands began to bubble and he snatched his hands back in fear. There were three quick clunks of the transmission, and her body lurched toward him. He took a step back, the look on his face turned from love to fear as his second most cherished thing in the world stalked toward him. Slowly it tracked him, then the engine gave a short blatt and the beast lunged for a moment, only to resume its slow crawl as the heavy cam lumped then lumped after him.

Chris continued to back up across the stone courtyard. It would not be long before he ran out of room and was stuck between the steel of the border and the iron of Pestilence front bar. He continued to back up, his eyes still blinded by the accusing light and his hands still failed to shield him. Then the back of his heel connected with something and he began to fall backwards. Pestilence roared in anticipation, but she didn't lunge forward. Instead, she came to a halt directly over his feet as his back fell against a set of stairs. Chris sat there while he propped his back off the painful angle with his elbows. He looked at the hammered front end, the railway track that had created so much carnage yet had received little damage itself. He thought back to the beginning; of the Chinese soldier she had crushed against the cinderblock wall in his shed and thought that he could see the remnants of his journey, pitted into the old iron rail.

He looked over his shoulder. His breath caught in his throat as first he saw the muddy footprints on the steps he now recognised. He traced them up the porch and in through the front door of his house in Darwin. As if mesmerised by the vision he saw through the headlights of the Holden, he rolled himself over and climbed to his feet, his mouth slightly ajar.

Climbing the stairs, he headed toward the door. Pestilence's horn sounded and he stopped and looked back to her. The headlights still burned, yet his eyes had adjusted and he continued to stare at the windscreen. The driver's door opened, its hinges screamed as it swung open by itself. He took another longing look inside of his house, which seemed perfect in this glance and headed back to the gaping door of the Holden.

He was almost surprised to see the cabin empty when he rounded the door. The whole cabin sat in darkness. He saw the stained carpet and the slight tear in the bench seat from where his screwdriver had punched through his pocket all that time ago. To his amazement, the lever down by the edge of the sill began to move by itself. There was a pop as the lever engaged and the bench seat collapsed forward. Chris stood there, his mouth still ajar at what was happening. In the darkness, a glint of steel caught his eye and his hand went for it. He felt the coolness of the metal under his skin and the wetness of the sweating timber grips as he pulled his bayonet from the cab.

Everything seemed to fall into place as he climbed the steps of his porch once more. He had remembered almost all of it when he entered his house and saw the carnage again. He saw Angie's book on the floor, the mud splattered footprint slathered over its pages. Over the lush surface of the hall runner, he saw the glint of broken glass from the frames that had held the photographs of her. He saw the underside of their clamshell armchair as the base slowly rocked on its curved back. Then the hallway cabinet, its leg snapped under an impact that he would never know and it lay collapsed in his path.

He took a step down the hall; the glass crunched under his feet. He thought that he could see scratches running down the wall, towards their bedroom door. The hallway was dark, yet the light that shone in the room beyond, peered out from beneath the door that remained closed to him. He took another step then lifted himself to clear the hall cabinet. His bedroom door began to tremble and shake in its frame. He adjusted his grip on the bayonet and raised its tip to eye height. He took another step. The ferocity of the door's trembles doubled, then tripled with his next movement. Not even a foot away from the hall's end now and the entire structure seemed to shake. Beneath it, he heard a metallic grind as everything seemed to quiver harder and harder. He reached out his hands to touch the door.

He sprung awake. His eyes opened wide and his hand moved for the bayonet he thought he had at his side. It was daylight; the sun kissed his skin with an intensified heat through the Holden's remaining glass. It took him a moment to realise that the world still trembled. The Holden seem to shake on its suspension and through the broken windows he heard the tell-tale sound of the grind of tank tracks.

RANKIN

*'I ain't got me nobody,
I don't carry me no load
Ain't no changes in the weather
Ain't no changes in me.'*

Lynyrd Skynyrd – *Call Me the Breeze* (1974)

Rankin's head swam with the mistakes of the night before. As he lay there and his mind struggled to regain consciousness, the morning sunlight came over him. The warmth lapped at his face while he continued to swim through the thickened sludge of his thoughts and dreams. If years of waking up hungover had taught him anything, it was that a man's mind is a lake. When a man fell asleep it was like he had submerged himself in that lake, whether to sink or swim depended on how much he drank. When sober, the water was crystal – he woke at the end of each slumber refreshed as if he had just had a shower.

Yet when he drank, the lake turned dark. The water that was once refreshing became thick like a slurry of concrete and mortar, threatening to cling to the swimmer's arms and drag him down to the depths of its dark belly. Not only this, but creatures lurked below the depths. Monsters with claws like the blade of Chris' bayonet and teeth of steel that once they latched on, they tore away at you. They reminded you of all your mistakes and ill-gotten fortunes. They relished on the fear, the pain of regret and the sorrow that came after.

Only when the swimmer had finally freed himself from their grasp and crawled exhausted and bleeding on the far side of the bank would the vessel wake and remember everything they had told him.

He stirred in the low light. His eyes opened, then slammed shut again as the sunlight pierced their hide. He moved his hand up to rub at his eyes and fabric pressed against his face. A shot of pain ran down the crest of his head and dribbled down his spine. He opened his eyes once more and stared blankly at the bandaged hand for some time.

He blinked; his eye sockets felt like sand over the rough stone of his eyes. His tongue was stuck to the roof of his mouth and he felt like he either needed to spit or vomit. Moving his lips over his gums in an attempt to moisten them, he tasted the foul remnants of some bit of jerky or packeted morsel from the night. Propping himself up, he felt the ache in his muscles that lingered from his slumber on the concrete path outside of the service station.

He tried to spit. A glob of green, sinewy shit splattered against the brick of the structure and clung to it. In his semi-conscious state, he became fixated on it. Would it hold its position or succumb to the gravity that pulled at it and crash to the concrete below?

'If it was Australian, it would fall,' he grumbled to himself as he lowered his eyes and clambered to his feet. As he gained them, he kicked a small glass bottle and sent it skittering across the concrete, where it fell from the path and nestled into the soft grass. His eyes were drawn to the sound, then to the rest of the fallen soldiers, as he had always called them, that lay around him. He didn't have to be a betting man to figure that he had drunk the place dry. Each bottle he laid his eyes on was another blow to him.

'Fuckwit!' he swore. He stamped down hard on a cluster of empty bottles. The glass shattered under his boot and clinked as more were set spiralling outward from the impact. 'How could you be so weak!'

he roared to everyone and no one as he bent down and scooped up a handful of the little bottles with his unbandaged hand and hurled them into the air.

The anger was hot in him, the disappointment in how he could come so far, make so many milestones, only to let it all go in one foul swoop. His breath was hot, his head pounded and the world was streaked with light from the tears that lined his bleary eyes.

'Each fucking time,' he growled as he bent down to pick up a jagged shard of glass. He placed his bandaged hand against the wall of the station. Remnants of whiskey still lined the edges of the glass shard and it seemed only fitting. 'You look at this, and remember.'

He sunk the jagged point into the flesh of his forearm. The pain ran up his arm while the blood trickled down and soaked into the bandages that covered his palm. With gritted teeth, he ran the glass up his arm. His hand shook as he carved flesh along its path. With each inch it travelled his eyes became clearer, his mind fell out of the drinking swell and rang with the clarity of the new day. A low growl issued from his throat as he pulled the glass along his skin. He traced all the way from the back of his wrist to his elbow, then he stopped and let the shard fall bloody from his shaking hand.

He panted as he looked at what he had done to himself, the torn flesh and the blood that trickled down his arm. 'Each time, look at it,' he growled again. 'Never, again.'

His head fell forward to touch the brick of the wall. Lightly, he began to tap his skull against its structure while he continued to swear at himself and his stupidity under his own breath. The part that really irked him, was how could Chris sit there and let him do this to himself? A new sense of anger shot through him; disappointment in himself leaked out over the rim of its cup and began to contaminate the one person left to him. 'And where is he now?' Rankin roared as he lifted his head and looked around. He was alone. Lighting a cigarette, he looked down to the ground to see the littered remnants of perhaps forty or fifty butts that surrounded his perch of the night before. He took the butt from his mouth and went to throw it. His mouth tasted like the entire Chinese army had taken turns shitting down his throat. He cocked his wrist and prepared to flick. Then he relaxed and placed the butt back into his mouth again. 'Let's not throw the baby out with the bathwater...'

He entered the service station and looked for any sign of his friend. The more he looked, the less he found and his brow furrowed at the inexplicable disappearance of Chris. He called out a time or two and then thought of the car. With a new sense of hope he set back outside and rounded the corner of the station at a jog, with a full expectation to see Chris asleep inside the battered cabin of his Holden.

He came to a stop and let the smouldering butt of his smoke fall to the ground. There was nothing. He was truly alone. Without a thought, his hand went to the pouch on his hip and a part of him relaxed as he felt the metal beneath the leather. He had no weapon apart from Max's dusters, and his only remaining friend had abandoned him. He lit another cigarette and looked down to the gash in his arm.

He had cut his arm as a reminder to his future self to why he shouldn't drink, but to what had happened last night, he had no clue. He looked to the earth where the Holden had sat the night before. A small patch of oil stained the earth where the engine had hung. Tracked along either side were sets of tyre tracks that lead back out onto the highway. Rankin followed them, the concern that lay in his gut moulded further into resentment with each step. Finally, he reached the black top of the highway and saw the burned rubber which etched the Holden's path further south.

Rankin stood there for a while as he continued to rack his brain. Somewhere deep down, he remembered the sound of the exhaust cut through the night and how he'd bellowed after it. 'Good riddance,' he mumbled. He began to walk the highway and left everything else behind him. His arm still bled as he paced, and as his mind rolled over and over, his heart began to race. As his pace turned slowly into a jog, he remembered the hurt expression on his friend's face. He remembered the shot of anger that shone in his eyes the moment before he stood up to walk away. He recalled that he had actually wanted Chris to hit him. He'd craved it and even thought about further insults to sling at him and...

His gut rolled and he moaned as the words he'd spoken to Chris came back to him. 'You low shit.' He groaned as he began to pick up his pace. His body ached and his gut was empty, but none of that held a candle to the hole that was torn in his chest. As he ran, the blood that lined his left arm spattered along the ground. Now that he remembered most of what had happened the night before, he thought he deserved more than a cut on the arm. Neither of the two men knew what lay beyond the walls of the service station. The reach of the Shepherd had been long enough from what he understood, who knew how far they could've reached and what may lay ahead. Now because of stupid, damned words, he had lost his only ally.

His feet pounded the black top and a pain sunk into his gut. The stitch pulled at the scar on his side and he clapped his hand over it but kept up his pace, while the alcohol in his system made him cramp. Ahead, he saw a small town with cars lining the streets. Perhaps he would find one to take him the rest of the way. He continued to run, his lungs became hot then screamed with burning fire as he pushed himself on and on. He never bothered to look at windows or listen out for the sound of other men. He rushed to the first vehicle he could find and leapt into it.

The Leyland P76 sat crooked alongside the curb. Rankin reached for the ignition and found nothing. He swore as he searched the cabin.

Leaning across the centre console and opening the glove box, he found nothing but a hundred crumpled receipts and the service manual. He slammed the compartment shut and then rummaged through the centre console but found nothing but a woman's lifetime collection of makeup and assorted brands of tampons. He searched each door pocket and folded down both sun visors to no avail. Finally, he sat and looked out at the world through the windscreen.

The town had been abandoned. A chill crept up his spine as he looked from quiet house to empty general store. No more than twenty structures lined the one street town. There would have to be ten to twenty vehicles parked throughout the street, but how many would actually have the keys in their ignition? He didn't think the cars had been abandoned, just the people had been taken or evacuated? Because of this he doubted if there would be any keys left in ignitions at all. He thought back to his days as a mechanic and the very limited experience he had with twelve-volt electrics. He sighed, he was more apt to butcher the Leyland than to get it running and the way his heart hammered in his chest he didn't want to take his time in doing a good job.

As he swung himself back out of the dormant P76, he imagined he had some idea of how his friend must feel. Rankin had only known Chris for a short portion of his life, yet for the moment his world revolved around his search for the older man. And the redemption that might come at their reunion. All he needed to do, all he wanted, was to find his friend.

Rankin thought of the nights that Chris had spent running his thumb across the face of the photo he held in his wallet. The tears he had fought back on so many occasions. He felt like he had an understanding of what the poor man was going through, the love he felt for that woman. Then a part of him thought back to Mary and what had happened, the way his life had spiralled into its downward dive. He could never understand the way his friend felt, he doubted that he could ever love someone the way that Chris obviously loved his Angie.

He continued to run down the street, glancing in the windows of the silent hulks he passed. He hoped for a break but none ever came. There were so many options and so little time. He could break into a house and turn the whole of its contents upside down in search of a key. If he was lucky enough to find one, but where would he start? He looked around helplessly from houses to cars. Desperation bit at the heels of his conscious, he needed to act and now.

As he laid his eyes on a fifties Land Rover. If anything was apt to be easy enough for him to steal, it would be that. He rushed over to its side and slammed his elbow into the window, shattering the glass under his force. Then, as he reached in, he struggled to find the door lock, so he decided to pull the exterior handle and see what happened. The door clicked and rusted hinges groaned as he sheepishly swung the door open. He quickly brushed most of the broken glass off the seat and leapt into it.

The Land Rover faced the road out of town, which remained basically flat for the most part but crawled into a hill at its exit. He rummaged around the spartan interior and was relieved to find a flat-bladed screwdriver. He rammed the blade into the Rover's ignition barrel and pounded on its base with his palm. With one bandaged hand, he turned while the other belted the back of the screwdriver, then he felt the internals let go and the barrel rotate. To his joy, a soft, red, gleaming light shone from the dash. He cranked it over again and heard relays click into action in the engine bay in front of him.

'Come on, girl.' He closed his eyes as he readjusted his grip on the shaft of the screwdriver and worked it over again. The starter motor sounded weak, the rotations were slow and strained. He pumped the accelerator for dear life but nothing happened. 'Fuck it,' he swore and pounded the steel dash. As if swearing at the Rover was going to help it start, nonetheless he turned the shaft again and heard the death clacks of the starter motors solenoid. Although he couldn't call himself an expert about cars electrics, nevertheless he knew that the sounds he just heard meant that the battery was dead.

He pushed the clutch and took the Rover out of gear, he opened the door and clambered out. As he began to push the heavy four-wheel drive, he shook his head. Of all the cars on the street to push toward a hill, of course he had to pick an old Land Rover. He lowered his head and arched his back as he put all of his strength into it. The Rover started to roll and it went easy enough, but it was headed for the curb. He adjusted his grip and reached a hand through the broken window and pulled down hard on the steering wheel. The slow speed and the lack of power steering made it hard to steer, but after a few tugs the heavy frame came about and picked up speed as it headed toward the base of the hill.

He put everything into it; the pace moved up to quick steps and then a jog as his shoulders burned and his back ached. He gave one final push as he tore the door open, leapt inside, slammed the shifter into first and popped the clutch. The nose dipped savagely as the old Rover's engine turned over. He trumped the throttle and heard the exhaust cough and wheeze behind him. He pushed down hard on the clutch and gave it more juice. The body rocked and rolled as it lost speed, but the engine caught and chuffed as it struggled to hold onto its life.

He eased his foot off the throttle and the engine seemed to do better. He thanked any God above him for a chance to drive and not to walk while the Rover came to a stop at the bottom of the hill. The engine ticked over, the tappets rattled, and the shaky idle was not something that instilled a rock-solid confidence in Rankin.

Nonetheless, he would drive faster in any piece of shit than he could walk or run. For ten minutes he sat in the cabin and smoked while he listened to the tappets rattle and clank, and the belts slip and groan. While he smoked, he tested himself with attempts to diagnose faults with only his ears, as his old boss had in the past. When he was finally satisfied that the Rover was warm enough to move and not stall, he threw the shifter into first once more, urging it up the hill and out of the lonely town.

As the view of the one street town that he hadn't bothered to learn the name of disappeared in the side mirror, he thought about how no one had tried to stop him. Where was the owner of the Rover now? Had he been forced to go to Tamworth? Had he fled South, away from the threat of the invasion, or away from the tightening grasp of Shepherd? Either way, no one stood in that town that cared for Rankin. If people existed back there, they didn't want to meet him, they didn't want to help or hinder. He was used to that from his life as a veteran. Yet somehow, he preferred the thought of people that chose not to reveal themselves to those who met with his gaze and then turned their heads to look away in disgust.

He frowned as he drove on. Each movement of the gearshift was sloppy as it ground into gear. Each turn of the wheel was over compensated for and had to be corrected. He had never owned a car, nor had a driver's licence, but that had not stopped him from learning in his time as a mechanic's hand.

Rankin had no clue where to start to look for his friend, so he kept the Rover to a low speed. It trundled and groaned its way along the dusty, lonely road with nothing but the thoughts of the past and the pain in his arm and bandaged hand to keep him company.

As turn after turn fell behind him, he felt more at home behind the wheel. His confidence soared and for a time he even forgot to search the shoulders for signs of the Holden. He continued to push the Rover forward as he listened and fell in love with how the old hull reacted to his controls. Once more, he felt like he understood his friend a little more. The old Rover failed to react to him in the way which he saw the Holden move to Chris' commands. One day he hoped that he would sit in it again and perhaps even have the chance to drive it – if Chris would talk to him, that was.

Over the slight twist in the road and through the spacings of some trees, he saw the hint of another town and he let the Rover slow itself. Tilting his head slightly out the window, he strained to listen for any sign of the Holden's V8, but he heard nothing over the clatter of the Rover's tired engine. He turned his head to read a sign as he passed, just another label of a town with an odd name that he doubted he would remember by the time he passed through. The Rover followed the road around the corner to face the entry of the main street.

His heart stopped in his chest. Without a thought, he slammed his foot hard on the brakes and the Rover came to sloppy halt. He fumbled for the door handle and swore as he tried to free himself from what was soon to be his tomb. Frantically, he hung his arm out of the window and pulled up hard on the exterior handle. He rushed as he pushed the door open and heard the rusted hinges groan for their last time.

Then he leapt from the cabin as he heard the thunder of cannon fire. He heard the scream of steel and a horrible groan as the Rover was torn to shreds behind him and thrown from the road.

JACK

*'But I'm strong.
Strong enough to carry him.'*

The Hollies – *He Ain't Heavy* (1969)

Nothingness. He felt not a thing. He couldn't see, couldn't hear nor did he want to. Time meant nothing to him, nor had it for the past weeks that he had spent in his semi-conscious state. Every time he came forward and took control, all he felt was pain, suffering and confusion. Since he had lost consciousness in the streets of Kootingal, he had seldom had control of his own body or mind. The last proper memory he had of that time was of that slick bastard driving the butt of his pistol into his head. He had seen the concerned expression on his broken face and then there had been nothing.

He had awoken in a prison cell for a short time. He remembered the heat that had radiated from his body, the smell of sweat and rot. Then as his level of awareness had risen, the pain that had come with it was unbearable and he was forced to yield once more. He knew that the 'other' had control of him each time he stepped away, but he didn't care. With the loss of control came a numbness that Jack found to be refreshing. The burning sensation that seemed to boil through his veins disappeared as did the migraine and the weakness. However, these benefits were merely the sides to a main course meal. The centrepiece for Jack was that along with everything else he forfeited when he handed over control, he lost the feeling of regret of his own mistakes.

He didn't know how long he had remained in this state; seconds seemed like decades. The only sense he had of what happened around him in the world outside, were the small snippets that were allowed to him. For the most, he felt as if he was in the Fairlane with a blanket thrown over the top. Images whirred and fluttered beyond the threshold, yet to him they were no more than pages of a photo album being flicked through across the other side of a room. Muffled sounds accompanied them and at times, single words or phrases rang out but nothing more. Then all of a sudden, the veil that blinded him would be lifted and maybe for a second, he would see, he would hear and he would feel.

The first time this happened, where he had been aware yet not in control, had been in the prison cell. The veil had lifted and Jack was helpless but to succumb to his own curiosity and look. The meat of his hand had clasped the iron bars and squeezed. He saw the flakes of rusty metal sift down from the bending bars. Beyond, was the face of a man. His face was solemn and stern as he tried his best to keep a calm demeanour, but even Jack could see the fear in his eyes as he pressed his body back against the stone wall behind him. The breath of his own body rang in his ears, but it sounded wrong. It sounded primal, like the grunts of a wild animal that laboured in a hunt. Each exhalation sent a shiver up his spine and even in his cell of solitude he began to feel hot and weary once more. It became louder and louder and it was to the point of becoming unbearable, when it stopped.

As swift as the image had been revealed, he was thrown back into darkness and silence as the veil came back down around the hull of the Fairlane. Jack resigned to his solitude and tried to relax. The heat washed away and with it went his stress.

Then through the speakers of the Fairlane, a voice that was not his own rasped the words that had stuck with him: 'Remember what you saw today. And if I get my hands on you, no God will save you.'

Beyond that, he had remained in his solitude for a long time. As if he was a man in an iron lung, blinded, deafened, armless and legless; he had no life left to him. If he spoke, he didn't think anyone could hear him, except for the other. Instead of feeling relief in his solitude he began to feel like a prisoner in his own mind. Thoughts of Michael and what he needed to do to help him began to flood through him. Yet he hadn't even seen him since his fall in Kootingal. He needed to know. Needed to gain control of himself once more.

In his solitude, he reached for the handle of the Fairlane. As he touched it, the lock snapped down and the handle moved freely. Jack went for the lock and pulled it up, but he felt resistance as he went. The lock strained against him. He fought with his mind as much as his might and slowly the tab began to rise. With each fraction of an inch the tab rose, he felt the heat enter the cab. The pain started in his cheek and rose through the nape of his neck to the crest of his skull. Then finally, it raised enough for him to open the handle and push the door open.

When he opened his eyes, he stood in a field. Lights burned down on him and the sound of thirty thousand people washed over him. He panted, as the pain of everything came back over him. Sweat ran down his face and his spine. He looked throughout the crowd and saw a podium built outwards.

There stood the man.

Even from this distance Jack recognised his face but he didn't care for him. The most important thing was that he saw Michael by his side. He snarled as his gaze returned to the man in the suit. He went to take a step forward and collapsed. Catching himself on one knee, he rested there for a second as he lifted his head to take another look at the podium. He was vaguely aware that someone advanced on him. He could hear the light, rapid footfalls as they approached and he thought he could hear screams. Then the world plunged into darkness as the arena lights switched off and he felt something hard slam into his face. Just like that, he lost his footing and his control.

The speed with which he was sucked backward alarmed him. His vision of the world whisked away like the screen of a television that's had the plug pulled. All sounds became muffled. The air rushed out of him, the door to the Fairlane slammed shut behind him and the locks clicked home while the veil fell over the Fairlane once more. In his darkness and silence, Jack knew something was happening, something bad, in the world around him. The Fairlane rocked violently and the veil began to slip.

Jack caught a glimpse of a small Asian man as he squirmed in his own hands. He saw his fingers clench through the flesh and he began to pull and tear. He saw the Asian's face clench with pain and then explode in horror as his body began to tear apart down the line of his sternum. Blood flowed from the widening wound that began on his left shoulder and gushed over everything to almost conceal the fact that his body was being torn in two. Then that one was gone and he watched his hands mutilate another foreigner and another. Then it turned to another man, this one was larger, built like a fighter. Jack watched as his body approached him like a buffalo determined to squash an intruder.

Jack saw his limbs lash out at the fighter, faster than he thought he could move, yet not fast enough. The fighter ducked and weaved and lashed out with strikes of his own, but Jack's body didn't slow. Finally, he glimpsed his face and saw that this man was Caucasian. His blonde hair hung in messy rags over his face as he threw his body from side to side in attempts to escape the inevitable. Below the hair, he saw piercing blue eyes and a mouth twisted into a sneer.

The world was thrown into darkness again as his view was cut off.

The heavy body of the Fairlane still shook from time to time but the veil remained fastened over the glass. Jack tried the handle but the lock was securely fastened. He tried to pull the lock up but it wouldn't move, he slammed his elbow into the glass but it wouldn't break. He roared to himself as he continued to fight, then the radio crackled and a soft voice came through the speakers of the car.

'Then in nineteen fifteen my country said, "son…"' The voice was familiar to Jack. Although he had never heard Michael sing, he knew it to be the voice of his brother. He paused, for a moment as the radio's sweet tones turned to garbled static. As if in response to the voice, the Fairlane seemed to fight it. The hull shuddered and twisted. The locks snapped up then slammed home once more.

'They gave me a tin hat and they gave me a gun.'

The whole frame trembled, the dials on the radio spun while the heater vents snapped closed, then opened again. Jack put all of his effort into lifting the lock. If Michael fought for him, then he needed to give everything he had to open the damned car. He needed to gain control of his body, he needed to save him.

'And they shipped us away to the war.'

The lock popped open and Jack reefed the door handle open, then all of a sudden, he was back in the arena. The fighter was under him; Jack's massive left hand had him pinned to the ground and his right hand was a fist of iron cocked next to his head. He looked down at the fighter below and their eyes met for the first time.

'Help me,' Jack had said. What he meant to say was help Michael, the last one left to him. The one he had tried to protect his entire life from either his father, the Trackers, even himself. Even then, he could feel the rage of the other inside of him, as it burned him away. He felt a shudder in his mind as his vision pulled back and it took everything he had to hold himself forward. His vision went dark, then came back brighter than ever.

The heat was upon him again and fierce. The wound on his face seared while his side was a dull throb. Nevertheless, he was in control again and strong. He felt as he had in the Tracker's yard. He felt like a freight train that couldn't be stopped and nothing would ever hold him back again. He stood in the arena and glared up at the man from the prison cell who now held Michael in his hands and threatened him. He took a step forward and the voice in the back of his mind called to him.

'Kill them, kill them. Let me kill them, you're too weak.'

Jack didn't reply in speech. He thought back to his demon, 'Never again.' There was a brooding silence, then a cackle.

'You can't fight me. I'm more you than you are yourself now.' The cackle boiled through his mind again, in a reverberation from ear to ear. *'You feel your temper rising? That's me. You lose your cool and I'm there. One wrong move, Jacky boy, and I'll own you again.'*

I'd like to see you try, Jack thought to his demon. He felt so much in control that he doubted anything could ever shake his grasp on reality. He had won for the time being and for the next fifteen minutes, he held his mind.

He held it while the trio escaped the arena. He held his temper while he drove his fist through the pale Holden ute's window as they fled before him.

He even held his wits as they burst through the doors of the hotel and he broke the man in the denim jacket. He never cared for anyone's names, although the two in the car offered theirs to him, he couldn't remember them. All he could think of was Michael, his rock. The one who gave him something to hang onto and allowed him to keep his sanity.

But when he entered the upstairs room and he saw Michael again, he saw the blade at his throat. His first reaction was not to protect him, it was to go for the rifle. Every part of his body wanted to hold

Michael in his arms like he had in the mountains, but something made him turn his back and break through the wall like he had done in the Tracker's house. Like he had done in his own bedroom the night he had killed his father. Something about that rifle made him whole like nothing else in the world did, not even Michael. Michael gave him the rock to cling to, but with the rifle he could protect his rock and everything else.

The Browning Automatic Rifle burst through the dry wall, clutched in his hand and for a second, nothing else mattered to him. He took his time as he walked back to where he needed to be. He took too much damned time and when he got there, he felt confident in his strength, in his size, that no matter who or what stood before him, they would bow down before his might and do as he commanded them.

However, he had tried this at the Trackers yard and even the fat slug Kel hadn't backed away. It wasn't until he demonstrated his strength by crushing the skull of his brother with his bare hands that any type of fear came into that fat bastard's eyes. He had already seen the fear in this man's eyes. Had seen it in the prison cell, and he could see it now. He advanced on the pair in the corner and it reminded him what the other had said in the prison cell. 'No God can save you.' He saw the fear explode within the man and for a second, he thought he had won again.

'Is he afraid of you, or is it fear of me?'

All at once his confident evaporated. He reached for the man who held his brother hostage, but too slow. As his hand dragged through the air, he saw the blade slide across Michael's throat and the blood ran in one red, rushing torrent down his brother's front.

For a moment he just stood there in shock; he couldn't believe what he had just witnessed. Every emotion in his body fell out of him, as if he was incapable of expressing anything ever again.

Then, as if a wall of fire rose from the gaping mouth of a volcano, he felt the rage come over him. He felt the tug of the other trying to pull him backward, and he let it take him. The screen of the outside world fell away, as his body uttered a scream that was horrifying even to him, a roar from another world, and then he was plunged back into the Fairlane.

The numbness washed over him and he was relieved. His brother had died due to his failures. If he didn't need that damned rifle like a child needed a blanket, then perhaps he would still be alive. He had lost his family. He had lost the only thing that he wanted to live for, and now he had lost control of his body again. This time, Michael would not be there to get him out. This time, he had lost.

The Fairlane shook and shuddered with the events of the outside world, but Jack didn't care anymore. He heard muffled screams as if the Fairlane had driven past a crowd of dying people. They came and they went. Visions and flashes of light tried to burst through the veil but this time it held tight. Men screamed and died as if they were miles away and the hull of the Fairlane shuddered. Jack just sat in the passenger's seat, emotionless. His head rocked heavily on his shoulders with each bounce and jolt of the car.

He stared blankly at the windscreen and the blackened cover that shrouded it. Even when the cover slipped at one point and the face of the fighter was revealed to him again, Jack didn't react. However, he did take in what he saw. He saw the fighter curled up in the footwell of a ute. From the perspective that Jack looked down at him, his body must have been in the tray. In his peripherals he saw the blurred outlines of houses and street poles flash by, so he assumed the ute travelled at a decent speed. The fighter looked defeated, he held his hands to his face and blood seemed to run from them. Yet, he saw the piercing blue eyes glaring at him through the bloody red fingers. Then the Fairlane shuddered and jolted once more and the fighter was gone. The vision now showed him the tail lights of the battered utility as it hurtled away from his body. Then the world was dazzled by the familiar muzzle flashes of the Browning and the veil crept back over the windscreen.

Jack sat uninterested, through the whole display. Still emotionless, he leaned forward placed his face in his hands. He wanted to cry, but no tears came. He wanted to do something but there was nothing he could do. Nothing would change what had happened, nothing he did could change the past. There was only one thing he could do to make up for everything he had done. Only one last deed would redeem his actions, yet even then he was helpless. To kill himself, a man needed to be in control of his body.

The veil slipped slightly and through the thin slither of windscreen he could see that his body sat at the controls of a vehicle. Headlights illuminated a dirt winding road with lines of trees on either side. He saw an image of his hands, bloodied and dirty, clasped around a notched steering wheel.

Jack scowled and swore. Clenching his fists and grinding his teeth together, he sat and stared at the windscreen. He was sick of being violated, of being a passenger in his own body. It was because of this intruder that everything had happened and now he needed to act to take his final revenge.

He slammed his elbow into the window. The glass barely even made a sound. He drove his fist into the windscreen again and again and nothing happened. He grabbed the door lock and heaved with all of his might and the tab didn't even shift a hairs breadth. He spat and thrashed his body around. He kicked his boots into the glass of the driver's window and headbutted the passenger side for good measure but nothing happened.

It had become stronger. Each time it took control, it was harder for Jack to step back forward.

'Only Michael got me out of the damned car last time and now he's dead!' he roared. As if he had only just realised it, he knew he had seen it. He had seen the life slip from him. 'He's dead,' he repeated. Jack's face twisted into a horrible mix of despair and rage.

He jammed his fingers into the rubber of the door seal. His thick fingers were much too large to fit in the small gap, but he pushed harder and harder. He headbutted the glass window and drove his knee into the door card, all the while he pushed hard with his fingers to pry into the space. One finally slipped in and he felt the rubber press around his flesh as the other fingers slowly wormed their way in. He swore and raged as tears escaped his eyes while he continued to fight his cell for his freedom.

Then finally they were through and his arms bulged with the effort as he pulled downward on the top of the door. Downward and away from himself, he pushed as he strained, while the heat began to flow over him again. Then finally, the glass shattered under the strain and the metal peeled away as the door gave way and opened.

Jack found himself behind the wheel of a Ford truck. He blinked as awareness came back to him and the rage of the other washed away. His hands fell off the steering wheel as he blinked and looked around the cab. He saw the Browning on the bench seat next to him. The Browning's magazines were spread everywhere, most of them empty. The truck's engine whirred and Jack sat there, his hands at his side as his chest heaved breath into himself. The truck bounced and Jack turned his head to look out the windscreen, still unsure if the truck was even in motion. His eyes widened and his hands gripped for the wheel as through the windscreen the road vanished into nothing.

CHRIS

'When will those dark clouds disappear?'

The Rolling Stones – *Angie* (1973)

The rear-view mirror vibrated with such ferocity on its bracket. The entire world that could be seen through its small yet clear face, became a mere blur of its former self. Lines melted into curves, colours washed over each other to form a conglomeration of shades. As the rumble of the diesel moved further up the road and closer to his position, more of Pestilence's parts began to succumb to the rattle. As if the car itself dreaded the weight of the monster that ground itself toward her, her driver's mirror began to tremble.

Barely even a shard remained of the flat circular pane, Chris watched, helpless, as the last remaining morsel of mirror jostled its way free and fell to the earth where it shattered upon impact. The centre ash tray, still perfect and unused, began to rattle in its tracks, and slowly worked its way out toward him. The driver's window which sat low in the skin of the door, rattled against the walls of its cell, like a maddened prisoner on death row trying to escape the final and inevitable darkness.

Finally, the gear shifter itself began to shiver in its socket. Only slightly at first, as if it suffered from the small shiver that ran up one's spine in the first real cold of the year. A frown came over his face and his eyes became blank. There was no real cold in Darwin, nor would any of the people he once knew have the chance of feeling that again.

The tremors in the broken street, the grind of steel on bitumen. The pale blue Freightliner and the fires that engulfed his friend and that damned tank. His hand closed into a fist and he closed his eyes.

In Africa, the German Panzers had near driven them to insanity. The sound of their engines, the roar of their cannons, but more so it was the waiting. While a soldier lay in wait in the foxhole he had dug amongst the sand and stone, they continued to come. They never stopped, continuing to crawl and shudder their way along the sunburnt landscape. The sand that jostled and lost its grip as the rolling death came near was a sight he could never forget. The way it shivered. The way the large clumps would give way to tumble down on the man below and threaten to bury them in the hot sand that hid them.

He opened his eyes. They had destroyed the Panzers in Africa. One by one, the giant hulks fell silent only to be swallowed by the sand that had once terrified him. The fires of Rabbit's road train had swallowed the Chinese iron in Darwin and although it emerged a flaming beacon, those that were inside were cooked. Although they instilled the fear into every man, he would not succumb to it.

He shuffled his position and lifted his head to peer out through the broken glass of the rear windscreen. The green hull of the tank had worked its way up the road toward him. The top flap was open and a Caucasian man's upper torso sat squat against the horizon. Chris strained his eyes to focus on the man. His shoulders were square blocks, a red and black plaid jacket covered a barrel chest. His facial hair was jet black and from what Chris could see there was more of the black iron curls on his jaw than on his head. Chris' view of his scalp was covered by an Akubra, while his jaw lay hidden behind the large beard that hung down at chest level. With each bristled movement of the tank, a heavy machine gun bounced gently in its cradle to his side.

As Chris watched the progress of the tank, he noticed for the first time the state of the town. The place looked as though a bomb had been dropped that had selectively destroyed three houses in a row, then skipped one, only to move on and ravage another four. His eyes scanned over broken roof tiles and collapsed sections of wall which exposed living areas that had mostly been emptied of their contents by looters. Even from his hidden position, he saw lounges overturned and cabinets with doors hung open, their contents spilled over the floor and shelves that remained. Front ornate windows had been blown inward, the curtains that had once sheltered the interior from the harsh rays of the sun, now bristled in the soft breeze.

He noticed movement further up the street toward him and he lowered himself. There was another man dressed in jeans and a work shirt; he had one of the Chinese AK-47s slung over one shoulder. The butt of the rifle clattered against the steel bumper of the Ford he leaned over. As Chris watched, he threw garments over his shoulder, then a woman's purse. With another movement, he pulled a small white slip and was about to discard it when he paused, pressed the fabric to his face and inhaled. With a look of satisfaction, he rammed the slip down the front of his shirt and continued his ransack of the Ford.

The man who sat on the tank surveyed the street as its hull rumbled along. He raised a hand and barked an order as another man appeared from behind the tank. This one carried an Enfield similar to the one Chris had carried throughout Africa. He walked through the front yard of a house across the street from Chris' position and kicked the front door wide open. As the tank moved forward and blocked Chris' view, he disappeared into the house.

Chris swore to himself underneath his breath. How stupid could he be to have put himself into this situation? All over drunken words that in the end meant nothing. He needed to get out of Pestilence and hide; soon enough the men's search would put them right on top of him. He stole another glance. Only four houses lay between him and the tank, even less for the men that searched the houses.

He heard a shout, then a gun shot. Chris lifted his head slightly and saw the man on patrol stumble backwards as a filthy wretch of a person leapt out of the bush directly in front of him. The armed man clutched a hand to his jaw, the other holding the Enfield that he waved wildly in the air.

'Runner! Bring him down!' The bearded tank rider roared over the rumble of the beast below him.

There was a tumult of shouts and sporadic fire in answer. Chris stole a last glance at the runner, at the desperation in his eyes. Filth covered his face and arms, shit lined the front of his shirt, and the one thing that seemed to stick into Chris' mind long after the image of him had left: he was barefoot. He heard the thuds as stray rounds slammed into the structures and he saw the runner's unnaturally skinny body duck down between two houses. Chris had found his chance.

The driver's door of Pestilence popped and he slowly pushed it outward. His plan was to move from the car to the inside of the house whose drive he had parked in. As he dragged himself out of the cabin, the hairs on the back of his neck stood on end. He felt horribly exposed, yet he kept moving. Sliding his hand behind the bench seat as he went, he felt the cool steel touch his palm. He dragged his bayonet with him as he left the cabin.

So far, all the eyes were on the space where the runner had vanished. He still heard the slap of boots on bitumen as men rushed toward the position. Chris swore again as he dropped to his stomach and slid himself under the still open door toward the Holden's front end. The place where the runner had vanished was beyond his own. If one of the pursuers happened to glance his way it would be 'Goodnight, John-Boy. Goodnight, Elizabeth.'

As he scuttled backward, he felt the sill of the door bite into his upper back and heard the blade of the bayonet grind against the concrete. Underneath the belly of Pestilence, he saw the flitter of the chaser's boots as they moved in and out of his window of vision. He shuffled his legs behind the front tyre and had just pulled his torso around when he saw the first pursuer come into sight. Chris let out a sigh of relief as all he could see of him was his back as the newcomer moved away, his eyes trained down the sights of his rifle.

From his position of safety at Pestilence's front end, he peered out of the driver's side. Two men had made their way between the two houses; he saw the dark blue of the first man's work shirt disappear and he turned to look at his next course of path. The distance between his position and the front door of the house was twenty feet of open landscape. The house itself looked to be untouched by the ravaging that had burned through the town. He shook his head; it was too far. He ran his scarred hands through the barbed wire of his beard and racked his brain. His eyes fell on the closed garage door directly in front of him. It would make noise as he forced it open, but he stood a better chance than being caught out in the open.

As he moved to the garage door, he heard more shouts. He forced his fingers below the lip of the rolled corrugation. He held his breath and began to lift. Clunk, clunk, clunk, the door began to lift. The sound as each level of corrugation folded in sounded like artillery in his ears. He looked over his shoulder at the tank's spotter. His eyes were still trained on his men's progress, his hand now rested on the grip of the machine gun to his side. Clunk, clunk, then there was a soft metal scream and the roller door jammed.

Chris swore softly to himself. The door had only raised five inches, not enough for him to slip under, yet he didn't want to make any more noise. The rumble of the tank in his head slowly drove him insane with its incessant grinding and chirping. He held his breath as he put more and more force onto the door. He felt a short, sharp movement and then heard a loud screech as the door became free. The speed in which it rose almost put Chris off his balance. The base of the door shot up past his face and he lost his grip.

The base screamed toward the ceiling and he tried to grab it, but he was too slow. It slammed against its stops and began to rapidly descend. Without a second thought of the tank, Chris pushed himself forward. He heard a shout behind him, but it was incoherent over the rattle of the tracks. He plunged himself forward into darkness, felt himself crash into a timber ladder which went sprawling at the impact. As the roller door crashed down behind him, he heard the rattle of machine gun fire.

Light burst through small holes cut through the corrugated steel. The sound of the automatic fire was drowned out by the rapping of bullets as they cut through the roller door and hammered into brick walls, timber shelves, and whatever lay upon them.

He kept low as he rushed toward the back of the garage. Shrapnel tore through the air around him as he went. The only saving grace to his situation was that the more holes that were punched through the door, the more light was let in and the better he could see. Still, he clutched his bayonet and he moved to the rear door of the garage and pushed it open.

When he was through, he found himself in a fairly modern house which had been well kept. Small signs of what had happened to the outside world were evident in the tossed cupboard doors of the kitchen and the wide thrown bay of the pantry. Otherwise, it looked as though someone had moved house.

Chris moved into the kitchen and surveyed the rest of the house as he went. The dwelling's interior was open plan. From his position behind the kitchen bench, he could see the front door. A beautiful, glossy hardwood that had been inlayed with stained glass that cast shadows of blues and reds over the living room. The living area and a dining table, which had been overturned, still seemed neat to him apart from the shattered glass and discarded belongings which had been scattered and trampled into the shagpile rug.

To his right, a corridor led down beyond the garage door, which Chris assumed would lead to the bedrooms and bathroom. Finally, the near wall seemed to be made entirely of highly glossed, glass centred French doors, through the centres of which he saw the untidy mess of the back yard and boundary fences.

He moved quickly now, with the garage door and brick wall in-between himself and the tank he felt a little more at ease, even just to be out of open view. Outside, the machine gun had fallen silent and he heard the black bearded tank rider resume his barking commands.

How many of these bastards are there? The thought had never crossed his mind while he was in Pestilence. Now that he tightened his grip on his bayonet, he wondered how many would come through that door to capture him or to kill him.

The shouting outside intensified as the tank's engine dropped its low drawl to an idle. In the distance he heard gunshots, more of the ragged pop, pop, pop of the Chinese AKs. He scanned the kitchen, desperate for anything, while outside he heard the slaps of boots running up the drive. As he laid his hands on the only thing of any use that was left to the kitchen, a dusty old glass, he saw the silhouettes of two men approach the front door.

Chris crouched behind the kitchen counter and took a deep breath to settle the rumble in his chest. The front door burst open and the living room was filled with the idle of the tank's diesel and the thud of men's boots as they rushed through the door. In his right hand he clasped the handle of his bayonet and in the other, he death-gripped the glass. He could hear the breath of the men, the sounds of one man's boots slide gently across the hardwood floor and the swish as the other made contact with the large, plush rug. He estimated only two, for now.

'Where the fuck is he?' a man whispered.

'Lewis said he saw one come in through the garage.' At this, the other man strode through the house and Chris heard the soft rattle of the action of his rifle as it was swung around quickly. 'Check there. I'll check the bedrooms.'

The slow pace of the footsteps began to approach him, Chris slowly shuffled himself backwards toward the wall of French doors. The tip of his bayonet scraped softly against the hardwood boards, but no man seemed to notice. Further and further, he shifted himself. He moved so slowly so not to make any noise, while the footsteps came closer and closer.

As he slid himself around the counter, he felt even further exposed to the man that remained in the living area. Thankfully, his attention was on the garage door. Chris waited while he listened to the footsteps move past the countertop. He kept himself below the level, Chris moved to the living room side. He worked his way forward, being careful to avoid the shattered glass and the crunch that would come if his feet were even to gently press on a single shard. There was a bang and a rush of footsteps as the second man burst into the garage, then the sound of his boots stepping down onto the concrete base. Chris moved to the hallway. He briefly caught the glimpse of the back of his first target as the garage doorway whisked by.

He settled himself against the wall and repositioned his grip on his bayonet. Further down the hallway, he saw the shadows of the second man, as he slinked across the walls. Chris moved into the doorway and placed the glass in its centre as he moved through. The man was propped in the centre of the garage floor, fixated on a pile of rags that lay next to a box. He moved his head from side to side as he tried to see exactly what it was, while he edged ever so closer to it.

Chris' boots slipped down onto the concrete silently. Being careful to avoid anything kicking anything on the littered ground, and he closed the ground quickly.

In the last moment, he stood and held the bayonet in a direct stabbing motion. He clapped one hand over the mouth of the man in front. There was a short exhale of surprise and even in the darkness, Chris could see the whites of his eyes as they shot open in giant circles. With a sharp movement, he rammed the bayonet forward and watched as its tip burst through the flesh of the man's chest and the soft fabric of his shirt. His eyes widened even further as he coughed and Chris felt the blood spray against his palm. The life left him as fast as the blood soaked through the linen of his shirt. Chris lowered him slowly and dragged his blade from his chest.

'See anything?' A voice rang out from the hall.

Chris stood and moved to the far wall of the garage. He kept his eye on the open doorway and strained himself to hear for the sounds of his approach.

'Danny, have you seen anything?' he called again and soon after heavy paced footsteps echoed down the hall.

Outside on the road, he heard a man yell frantically, 'Car. We got a car coming.' This aroused a further volley of shouts and a sound Chris never wanted to hear again in his life. The hydraulic whine as the tank's turret began to pivot on its base.

'Jesus Christ,' the man in the hall muttered to himself as he approached the doorway. 'If it's not runners in the streets, its escapees from...' There was a soft thunk and then the shatter of glass as the newcomer kicked the cup from the doorway. His head came into view along with the confused expression on his face as he looked down at what he had kicked and then he saw his companion.

Chris watched his expression change a multitude of times in that short moment before he brought the blade of his bayonet around in a long arc. He watched as the second man's mouth opened in surprise and then the blade caught him across the bridge of his nose.

There was a hollow thwap and the soft sound of a crunch, and the man fell backward. The blade rolled in Chris' hand and already he doubted the effectiveness of his blow when outside there came a tremendous roar. The building seemed to shake with the concussion. Chris rocked slightly on his feet but moved forward into the doorway his arm raised for another swing.

The second man was on his back in the hallway, blood streaked over his face from the gash in his mangled nose. His rifle lay on the floor next to him and he fumbled at his waist. Chris advanced on him, his arm raised. The whites of his victim's eyes shone through the red streams that flowed over him. Chris began to bring the blade down, when he saw what his target had fumbled with. He adjusted his swing and aimed for the man's wrist.

The slap of the dull blade hammering the man's wrist was only drowned by the report of the pistol he had pulled from his belt. With the blow, the pistol skittered across the floor and its owner screamed in pain. Chris fell onto him, still disorientated by the concussion of the tank's main cannon, his boot caught on the step. His bayonet was still low from the swipe and he decided to discard it, its blade being too long for the close struggle.

Even with his wrist broken, the wounded man still fought him. Blows were exchanged at short range and offered little effect. They rolled across the floor, blood covering them both from the gash across the man's face. As he forced him to the ground once more, Chris saw the whites of his eyes again. He saw the blue iris at their centre as he closed his hands around his throat. He slammed his head into the floorboards as he clenched his grip.

The broken wrist slapped uselessly at his arms, while the other pushed up on his chin. He felt the man's legs, as they kicked under him.

Either the bayonet or the pistol slid once more, propelled by the dying man's struggling feet. Chris pushed harder and squeezed, his forearms straining with the force. The pressure under his jaw relaxed somewhat and he lowered his gaze. The man's face had turned red and his eyes seemed to bulge from their sockets. His mouth opened, then closed, then opened once more. He gave a shudder and then his arm fell, lifeless, to the floor.

Chris staggered to his feet as he panted. He felt old. Somewhere in all of it, a pain in his side had started to throb, almost like a stitch. He took ragged breaths as he bent to retrieve his bayonet. He placed the blade flat on the shirt of the dead at his feet and ran it across to clean the blood from the steel. As he stood, his head reeled and he steadied himself on the wall as he continued to suck air. He eyed the pistol which lay up the hall. The low light made the metal look dull and the blood from its owner's face covered the walnut grips. He retrieved it; the beaver tail of the Colt dug into the webbing between his thumb and forefinger. He had lost his revolver in Tamworth, at least he now had something else.

'Where is he?' he heard from out on the streets, muffled under the exhaust of the Tank.

'He's moved to the back of the first houses,' said another voice, further away.

Chris didn't know whom they referred to, but he needed to get out. With the Colt nestled in his right hand and as the bayonet hung loosely in his left, he moved to the French doors and peered out into the yard.

RANKIN

'All I see turns to brown
As the sun burns the ground
And my eyes fill with sand
As I scan this wasted land'

Led Zeppelin – *Kashmir* (1975)

The roar of fire and twisting steel filled Rankin's head. The extreme heat of the flames that had engulfed the Rover washed over him. As he hit the ground, he couldn't help but awe at the power in that heat. It was as if he had just walked from a cool room into the heat of the day. It felt as though a man had been set on fire before him and then walked right through him. The heat seemed to push him, lift him from the ground. Then it hammered him downward and clawed at his throat, as if trying to take his last breath for its own.

He thought back to the images he had seen of the monk in the streets of the Silver City. The man who had calmly positioned himself in the middle of a busy Saigon street, poured gasoline all over himself and then lit a match. The act was nothing to Rankin. It didn't swell up the need for change or urgency in which it was intended. It wasn't until he was on his way to Vietnam almost a decade later that it had had its effect on him. He was older, he was perhaps a little wiser, but more importantly, he was now about to engage in open combat with these 'people.' If that elderly man could sit in sheer silence while the fires of hell consumed him, then what were the rest of them capable of?

That was all behind him now, as was the heat. The jungles of Vietnam had not claimed him. The darkness of the tunnel had allowed him to escape. He had clawed his way out of his sandstone grave and pushed through the forge of Brisbane. He had even escaped the most horrific of all of these when that damned Holden had whisked him away from the Wolf of Tamworth. None of it ever mattered. He reckoned, either a man survived or he died. His time was now or never. Like the burning monk, he would walk willingly into the fires again and welcome them with open arms as if he were to greet Max, Gary and Will.

Everything happened so fast. The Rover burst into flames almost the instant before it was thrown to the shoulder in a twisted, mangled heap. Rankin hit the earth hard. His hand screamed as the bandaged pads dragged and clung to the black top as his body rolled over it. His head swam with contrasting visions of green fields and frightened, fleeing horses to fire and blackened steel. His body felt slick and he realised he had already begun to sweat profusely.

As he rolled from the road and down onto the dirt shoulder, he heard the coarse shout of men from the town. Calls of 'He made it out' and 'Move up, move up' made his heart hammer harder. He rolled onto his back as he continued to slide off the shoulder and out of sight of the town. Down and down, he slid, surprised at just how steep the land fell away from the shoulder.

As he went, his eyes widened. Before him was a mess of at least fifty cars and trucks all mangled into each other. Some lay on their roofs, their underbellies already turned to rust where the metal had been torn fresh by the descending roll or by the impact of another wreck. Some of the hulls were blackened by fire, while others looked as new as the day they'd rolled off the factory line.

His ass bounced off a rock that jutted out of the slope and he felt the impact go up his spine. The bump lifted him from the ground and he fell forward. As he went end over end, the sight of a man's head crested the shoulder. Rankin was only ten to fifteen feet from the first wreck, but he was helpless to move any faster than the uncontrollable tangle he was in. Each roll and twist seemed to push more and more air from him. Dirt had gotten into his eyes and his mouth. He wanted to scream as if it would pull him out of this never-ending cycle. Then there were shouts from above and rifle fire. He heard the pops from muzzles above him, and the heavy thuds as the bullets peppered the ground around him.

The blue fender of an upended sedan get closer and closer. A bullet hissed and whined as it ricocheted off the hard surface of a rock and groaned off into the distance. Then he slammed into the fender. Both metal and body gave way at the impact as he was brought to an immediate halt. Whatever breath that remained in his lungs shot out in a surprised shout. He fell to the ground as the thuds of bullets into dirt were replaced by the heavy pongs and screeches as they tore through steel. Winded, he crawled under the raised rear end. He crawled through the dirt, mud and broken glass and found himself inside the sedan.

The men up on the shoulder ceased fire as soon as they lost sight of him. Rankin heard them shout commands to each other and underneath it all, the rumble of the tank.

'Fucking tanks,' he grumbled as he struggled to suck air. It was harder for him to move inside of the car; his bandaged hand and his boots slid across the vinyl roof lining as if it were ice. He rolled onto his back as outside he heard the shooters begin their descent down the shoulder. He clutched the head rest, then the steering wheel, and dragged himself forward.

Through the cracked windscreen of the overturned wreck, the world seemed dark. Shadows were cast over dead grass and mud puddles by the twisted frames of the vehicles. Still, he needed to move and get out of the car that he was seen crawling into.

Surprisingly, the car had taken little damage in its tumble off the edge and the front windscreen and side windows were still mostly intact. Rankin shifted himself to the passenger's side, which felt odd as it was upside down. He propped his boot against the 'C' pillar and pushed himself closer. He reached up and clasped the winder and began to turn. The window shifted and jammed.

He swore as he repositioned his body. Outside, he heard the dirt shift as the voices of the shooters came closer. He turned the knob the other way and of course, the window began to retract. He forgave himself his panicked error and continued to wind the handle, as he pushed the glass upward in its frame with his other hand. Then, as he strained with his legs and pulled with his hands, he dragged himself out into the gloominess.

Back out on the ground, he moved quicker. His chest still ached from the impact and he had a royal pain in the ass from the rock. Otherwise, he breathed easily again and he felt strong. He moved beyond a brown Brougham, which lay on its side and rested his back against its bonnet. He heard more dirt shift and finally the sound of another body impacted on the metal fenders of the car he just escaped.

'He's gone,' one of the shooters called, the disappointment of a loss rung out in his voice.

'He'll be in there somewhere, start looking,' another one growled, but his voice seemed further away.

Rankin rested his head against the Brougham as he positioned himself into a crouch. He looked around as he hoped for an escape. The early morning sun still had not beaten the entirety of the morning's fog away and a low cloud seemed to hang amongst the wrecks. Yet, through the mist, he saw that the mess of mangled cars stretched for two hundred feet.

The further they stretched, the less mangled they became, as they spaced out into neat rows. Rankin was surprised to see the canvas canopies of a few army trucks in the mess, but his heart lifted as he looked beyond where he saw a steep rise from the paddock he was in. At the top of the rise, he saw the peak of the roof of a house and the line of a metal wire fence that marked its border. This is where he needed to move to. If he could make it into the town, his chances would be higher.

He slunk his way forward and slid through the narrow gap between the Brougham and a burned-out Volkswagen. He kept himself low, only moved in short shifts and slides to allow himself to hear the progress of his pursuers. However, he began to get curious. Rankin wanted to know exactly where they were and whether he could see the paths they took. Pulling himself alongside the blackened Volkswagen, he peered over the hood. He saw one man, draped in a long overcoat. The armed man held his rifle in a ready position as he neared the backend of a utility he was focused on. He moved in short, sharp steps and finally leapt around the ute's edge as he held his rifle up ready to fire. Rankin watched as his shoulders slumped and quickly ducked his head as the shooter whipped his head around for any hope of seeing his prey.

'Fuck this.' Rankin heard him say. Then a short blast rang into his ears as the shooter placed two fingers into his mouth and whistled. The pitch became higher the longer it rang out. 'We need a couple more men down here!' The shooter bellowed before he let out another shrill blast.

Rankin bit into the side of his lip as his brow furrowed. He clutched at the earth with his good hand and felt the dirt grind between his fingers. He looked back toward his planned exit. Another man's head appeared over the fence, bouncing as he jogged toward the boundary.

Rankin's heart stopped as he saw him. From the position the newcomer approached, Rankin was widely exposed. He rushed and headed toward the open backdoor of a Datsun. Before he pushed himself inside the car, he felt there was a moment when the two of them locked eyes. He felt sure that in a minute either a shout would ring out or another whistle blast would cut through the air and then rifle fire would rain down on him from every direction. Instead, the newcomer simply vaulted the fence and went into a slide down the embankment, where he vanished from sight.

Rankin moved through the Datsun and pushed himself across the back seat. As he moved to the middle of the car, he looked over and saw a man's face.

He leapt back into the cushion, bringing his bandaged arm across to shield himself from the blow he thought was imminent. Then he relaxed, letting his arm fall down to his side.

The occupant of the Datsun was mostly rotted away. Rankin was surprised he hadn't smelled him before he saw him. The corpse's head was turned at an odd angle so that he looked into the back seat over his right shoulder. He had been strapped into the passenger seat after he had been shot in the forehead.

Even as Rankin turned and moved through to the other side of the Datsun and out again, the image of the pallid skin that hung in loose sheets over the frame of the man's skull clung to his mind.

There were other bodies. In one car he found a woman who had either been large or her body had severely bloated during the days she had spent in the cabin of the Ford pickup. The deeper he went, the smell started to overcome him. It was as if it came from the earth that he crept along.

He moved beyond an EH Holden wagon, where the mutilated body of a young man sat in the driver's seat. He thought back to the streets of Brisbane and the EH Holden they had pried from the edge of the crater. The model was right, but he had remembered a woman and child with the young man. A part of him inside shrugged as he moved on. 'They never even said thanks.'

With each second, the canvas canopies of the two army trucks seemed to get closer. Yet, as they did, the smell seemed to worsen. Car by car and ute by ute, he moved on, until finally he rested against the large walls of the truck's tyres.

His eyes watered at the smell; the air had become thick and stale. He rummaged through his pockets for the hope of a handkerchief that he never had, or anything he could clap over his mouth to breathe through.

In the end, he moved around the back of the International. A blackened hand lay over the edge of the tailgate. Rankin paused when he saw it. He saw the dark skin, shrunken from the days in the exposure. The golden gleam of the ring around his third finger stood a stark contrast to the sick black of his flesh. Rankin had to look. He quickly flashed his eyes around the line of other cars that surrounded him. None of the shooters were nearby, two had taken the far left whereas the other had circled back around to where he had begun. There would be at least twenty car bodies between him and his closest pursuer.

He stood up and peered over the tailgate. The sight was horrific. The bodies had been left as they were, then driven down to the truck's final resting point. The Australian soldiers had been shot from the back of the canvas opening. Some had tried to make it out through the left side, but had become entangled in the canvas curtains. Others had tried to charge their killers and had been shot down before they cleared the truck's body. Young men and older veterans lay as one combined heap of limbs and swollen black faces. Even in the cold they were alive with flies and insects that swarmed over their corpses, that made it look as if the whole mass was one breathing being.

He fought the urge to vomit and lowered himself to the ground. Tears leaked from his eyes and ran down his cheeks. Emotions broke through him like the waves on a cliff face. Anger, sorrow and worst of all, the fear for Chris. If this is what these animals had done to their own country's servicemen, then what would they do to him?

There was the sound as metal compacted and ahead of him, Rankin saw a man leap onto the bonnet of a car. The man scoured the mass of wrecks, his eyes darting from shadow to shadow. The butt of his rifle rested on his hip. Rankin moved around the side of the truck to conceal himself behind the large tyres. He took his time to glance around; if this rifleman had appeared, then more could have come up on his position. His gut had turned to stone, as if to embrace the anger that had swum up inside of him. It wasn't far to the embankment now, only this man stood in front of him and his escape into the town.

He moved up, from the bulking front end of the first International to the next. He heard the rifleman muttering as he urged the escapee to show himself. Rankin moved closer. Only a few cars lay between them.

A shot rang out above the embankment, it was muffled in comparison to rifle cracks that had been aimed at him. The man on the bonnet turned his head to its sound. He shrugged. 'Looks like they've bagged the other ratbag!' he called out to his companions. This brought laughter from across the paddock.

Anger boiled deep inside of Rankin. He clenched his fists, and didn't even feel the pain that shot up his wrist from his damaged left. The rifleman stepped down from the bonnet, the suspension of the car he stood on groaned as his weight was alleviated. He moved toward Rankin and headed across the far side of the vehicles that were neatly spaced. Two cars between them, now only one. Rankin lowered himself below the squared bonnet of the Valiant that concealed him. He gripped at its bumper and closed his eyes as he listened to the crunch of the rifleman's footsteps. Closer, closer. Rankin slipped his fingers through the brass of his dusters, braced himself, then lunged.

Rankin wrapped his arm around the man's throat and reefed him back behind the Valiant. He brought him down hard and Rankin heard the air rush out of him as he slammed to the ground. Their eyes met. The man's mouth was open, ready to give away Rankin's position as he brought down the entire weight of his body in a brass ended blow to his throat. There was a horrible, sickly wet sound as the man's airways collapsed. Rankin remained there by his side as the short struggle for life ran its course before him. There was a final gurgle and gasp and the man's body went limp.

Rankin watched him for a few moments longer, then took the man's rifle, an army SLR. Had it belonged to one of the poor souls that still lay in the back of the International? Rankin shook his head as he discarded the fleeting thought, he turned to the embankment and moved on.

The embankment in this section was mostly lined with thick grass. He would be able to move up it easily enough. However, he would still be left exposed for twenty feet or more until he cleared the fence and then, he didn't know. He took a quick last look behind him; he couldn't see any of the pursuers. He had nothing to gain by waiting. So, he started up the slope.

The grass was slicker than he had first thought. His boots slid on it and many a time he fell forward and lost momentum altogether, if not a foot or two in a slide backward. He clung to the grass with his good hand while he dragged the SLR up in his bandaged mitt. He was halfway to the top and had started to make better ground, only ten feet of steep slope remained.

Behind and below him, he heard a sharp whistle cut through the air and his heart stopped.

'On the slope, far side!' a voice called out.

A hiss cut through the air and a lump of dirt exploded in his face. The surprise of the shot made him loose his grip but he continued his momentum. He needed to get up the slope, if he turned to shoot, he would be killed on the spot. He needed to continue. Only a few more feet to the top now. More shots from behind, and the thuds as bullets hitting dirt. There was another hiss and the stock of the SLR splintered in his hand. A pain shot up his arm and he let the rifle go and never looked back once.

He cleared the fence easily. Pain still shot up his arm as he moved through the yard. The grass was knee high and the drag on his boots, as they cut through the grass made him feel tired and old.

'Where is he?' a voice called out.

'He's moved to the back of the first houses,' another voice much closer.

Rankin swore low to himself as he kept moving, the breath hot in his chest. He reached the second boundary fence and cleared it. The sound of the tank's engine rose to a pitch and he heard the screech of metal on bitumen as it began to move. He needed to get past it, needed to clear the bastards on his heels. He ran for the next boundary fence, another low metal frame. He placed his hand on its edge and began to hoist over when something heavy crashed into him.

He tumbled over the fence and felt the air rush out of him again. The man that had crash-tackled him was larger than himself. Big labourers' arms pinned his face to the ground and he felt a knee ram into his lower back. Rankin grunted in pain. He placed both hands flat on the earth and gave everything he had. Rising from the ground, he swung himself over as he threw his right in a wild hammer fist. His fist connected with the face of the big bastard on top of him, sending him sprawling. Rankin seized his opportunity;

he shot up and leapt onto him. He sunk his knees into his guts and slammed his fist down into his face. Over and over, he pummelled the man's head, the blood shooting out of his busted nose.

Then he was tackled again, and another man dragged him to the ground. Again, his head was slammed into the earth and this other man was on top of him. A rifle butt sank into his guts and Rankin doubled over as the rifleman stood.

The one with labourer's arms had gained his feet and headed towards him. Rankin shot a kick out into the knee of the one with the rifle, who screamed as he fell over. A boot sunk into Rankin's back and again he grunted with pain. The big armed prick was above, lining up for another kick. Rankin grabbed his crotch with his right hand and squeezed. The power went out of the kick instantly and the man went down in a screaming heap.

Then something hit him hard in the back of the head and he went down. He must have lost consciousness for a second or two, as in the next instant the big bastard was back on top of him bringing his big labourers arms down in wild swings of fury.

Rankin squirmed and lashed his head from side to side as he tried to get out from under the man. The wild swings, grazed his face at first, too crazed and untrained to match Rankin's movements, but soon enough, there were solid connections. Again, his consciousness started to wane and the world began to reel, then snap back to attention. The one with the rifle now stood behind them and laughed as he looked down. Through his vision that doubled and tripled as he thrashed about, Rankin saw the rifleman look up and his smile vanished.

The man raised the rifle. As it rose, his face twisted and his mouth opened. A shot rang through the air and the rifleman collapsed backward. The big bastard on top of him raised his face, his fist still cocked, ready to give Rankin another one. Rankin saw his face collapse inward, his nose disappeared, his jaw distorted and his brow bulged as his features were replaced by a bloody mess. Rankin pushed him off and went to climb to his feet when he saw another figure above him.

Tired and aged, Chris held out a hand to him.

'People are going to start talking about you and me if we keep meeting like this.'

JACK

'And, It's all over.
The war is over.'

The Doors – *The Unknown Soldier* (1968)

Jack slammed his foot down on the brake while he worked to swing the large steering wheel. The road vanished around a shaley rock face and the truck travelled at too greater speed to be able to make the turn on the graded dirt. The tyres locked and the steering went vague. A horrible feeling seeped into his spine through the vinyl of the bench seat as the rear end began to drift outward. Still, Jack fought the slide as he struggled to turn the heavy front end into the rock face. He released the brake pedal and stomped on the throttle and the motor surged. The steering lightened again as the horrible feeling in the back end washed away with the power that churned through it. The front end bounced, and the truck picked up speed. He felt like the captain of a large ship as he tried to escape the treacherous touch of an iceberg, except he imagined a ship would react faster than what the old truck had.

Slowly, the front end came about as the tired motor waned. He just wanted to plant the bumper into the rock face to stop himself. It was his only hope to hold the road. The engine surged, yet he heard below the baffle of the leaking exhaust a knock and clunk.

Jack furrowed his brow as he buried his foot further into the floor and he gripped the wheel. The engine stalled with a furious clatter as its internals mashed against each other. The front end of the old truck dipped furiously as the power that drove it died beneath him. There was a scream of metal as the drive shaft sheared under the strain and the truck rolled freely once more.

Jack jammed his foot down hard on the brake pedal, but it pressed to the floor in a soggy mess. He saw what was coming and pushed himself into the seat and grasped the steering wheel with two white-knuckled fists. The back tyres skittered as they teetered on the drop-off; the front glided aimlessly for the very edge of the rock face. Jack closed his eyes and waited.

The rear wheels gained the dirt road once more and for a moment, he thought he had made it. Then the metal bumper screamed as it ground against sandstone. The front seemed to drop for a moment as the grating sound intensified, then it completely stopped. The front end dipped savagely and the rear lifted in a groan of old steel and worn bushes.

Jack opened his eyes and saw the pockmarked dirt road come forward at a great rate to meet with the windscreen. The glass exploded inward; the roof caved in. Jack felt himself want to fall, but he held on tighter than ever. Then the truck rolled again and he felt it pick up speed as it slipped off the embankment and began to roll sideways.

Trees and brush smashed into the hull of the truck. Claws of timber and bark reached through the ever-increasing wounds in the steel to tear at him. All Jack could do was to continue to brace himself and shrug his head down away from the ever-lowering roof. Over and over, the hull rolled, as it clattered and dismantled itself with every turn. With one turn the roof buckled even further and slammed Jack in the crest of his skull. Stars danced before his eyes and he felt a searing pain down his neck. He scowled as he relinquished his grip on the wheel with one hand and pressed it to the buckled steel of the roof.

He roared as he pushed. Every part of his body was in its own fight while the cabin of the truck twisted under his strength as the roof tried to come downward against his force. Beside him in the cabin, the Browning clattered against the dash and buried its muzzle in through the material of the seat. Jack was helpless but to struggle as the battered truck fell down another embankment. The feeling of weightlessness came over him and his stomach sank.

The truck slammed back down to the earth with such force. The steering wheel snapped free from its shaft and Jack's arm shot back with the release of pressure. Quickly, he tried to hold himself down as he strengthened his efforts up on the roof with both hands, then he felt himself slip. With a crash, the chassis of the truck slammed into the trunk of a great gum and the battered cabin broke free. Down he tumbled in his metal cage. Over and over again he went and it seemed the more he tumbled, the faster the rolls became.

When the trucks cabin finally came to a stop, it was no more than a mangled piece of iron. None of the doors opened; the roof had collapsed to the point that the hole where the windscreen had once been was now reduced to a six-inch gap, whereas the slot for the rear window had doubled in size. Craters had formed in the metal, shaped around his hands, which pressed outward.

Jack crawled out of the cabin on his hands and knees. The Browning lay in the dirt. Jack had lost sight of it somewhere on the hill. His heart thudded in his chest with relief as he scooped it back up into his hands. The rifle felt at home in his grasp, like it had the first time he had touched it. Although he was broken inside, the weight of the Browning nearly completed him. There was only one thing he needed to do now to put himself to rest. He needed to see his brother one last time and then all of this heartache could end.

He looked around. Behind him, a trail of carnage marked the

trucks path down the embankment to lead to the point where the twisted cabin remained. The forest petered out before him. Below another short fall, he saw lights in the twilight of the dawn. Structures and peaks of roofs could be seen emerging from the darkness and Jack scowled as he looked over them. He returned to the cabin briefly and recovered what magazines and ammunition he could find. Burdened with his rifle and his pockets full to the brim with the large magazines, he headed down the embankment to the town.

As he walked, he thought of Michael and his small body lying lifeless on the ground where he had left him. He stopped in his tracks. Where had he left him? He knew he was in a hotel when it happened, in a town he had never seen before, but when was that? Ever since his fall back into his own mind, he had lost his sense of time and direction. And now he stood in some forest that bordered some town he didn't know.

'Where am I?' he growled, expecting an answer from his mind. Expecting the cackle of the demon that fought for control of his body. 'Where have you brought us?' he roared.

His mind was silent. Not a single murmur echoed from the depths, not even a single laugh.

Jack's face twisted into a snarl; the old scabs on his face pulled at the flesh beneath. 'Like I need your shit anyway,' he grumbled as he continued down the slope.

Eventually, he found the track where he would've driven the old truck had it not taken its leap of faith. It felt good to be back on the road as he stepped down the bank to stand in its centre. With each step he took, his heart pulled at him to turn around. He knew that each step in this direction took him further from Michael and where he wanted to be, but he needed to get his bearings.

The dirt ground under his boots as the light broke through the lessening canopy and illuminated the rocks and the trees. Shadows cast in all directions, as if not even the plants or the stones knew what time of day it was or where they should cast their shade.

Still, he walked on, his head upright and his back straight. The wounds that had ailed him the last time he walked with his brother seemed a distant memory, only the scabs remained. The flesh beneath had reknitted itself and soon there would only be scars. As he followed the fire trail, he eventually felt the ground level out and the forest ended before him.

He stepped out into the open like a man who had spent a year of his life locked in a prison cell. He looked to the sky, then spat as he continued to trudge down the track. The smell of cow shit filled his nostrils and he could now see farms in the distance to either side. He didn't change his course, he only cared for the town he had seen. Eventually the dirt track led him to bitumen, a main road that streaked onward in either direction.

He thought back to the town that he had visited with Michael. He'd been half dead by then. Jack held onto that moment; it was the last time he had felt like himself. However, the further he walked, the less he thought that was so, and once more he spat to the earth as if to expel the thought from his body altogether.

Before him, the steel back of a sign appeared from the gloom. He paused slightly and then hurried towards it. His hope was to find his way back to Michael, but if he could work out where he was first, then that was a start. The sign was one that marked the distance to the next towns, it read:

FORSTER – 3

COOLONGOLOOK – 12

BULAHDELAH – 30

NEWCASTLE – 103

SYDNEY – 190

At the very top of the sign, smaller black letters read: PACIFIC HIGHWAY.

The words meant nothing to him. 'Forster,' he growled. This had to be the town he had seen from the forest. Nonetheless, it meant nothing to where he had come from. Sydney was the only name on the sign that he recognised, yet he had no reason at all to go there.

He let the rifle fall to the ground. It clattered as it did. His shoulders slumped and his hands hung open.

'Where is he?' he asked.

Softly, as if it came from a man that stood behind him, he heard the familiar rasp, the voice of his demon. *'Who the fuck cares?'*

'Where is he?' Jack roared this time, as he clenched his fists.

The cackle came instead of a reply this time. Jack could feel his anger boil over. He could feel himself on the verge of a snap. He took a breath and took a step towards the sign. His whole body shook with rage.

'Where…' he shouted as he stood before the sign, 'The fuck…' he bellowed as he raised his fists, 'Is he?' He brought his fist down and into the metal sign. The sheet metal buckled under the force of his blows, but he didn't stop, he couldn't. He pummelled the sign over and over again in his frustration, each time the metal twisted and crumpled under the force of his anger. Jack bent and grasped one of the poles that sunk into the earth and he roared as he ripped it from its foundations. The sheet metal screamed as rivets popped under the strain and he tore the pole from its brackets. Then he raised the pole and hammered the remains of the metal downward. It shrieked in his hands with each tearing swipe he made and with each swing, his rage worsened in his frustration.

Then, as if he was suddenly consumed by something, Jack felt his conscious slip. He felt the urge of a power, pull him backward, pull him deep inside of himself. He staggered and fell to a knee. His head seared with pain from the internal struggle, his vision doubled, then tripled. The world spun before him and he put his face into his hands and screamed. The force that pulled him back intensified and, in his mind, he saw the Fairlane that lay in wait for him. His internal prison that waited to bar him inside.

He doubled over, his hands ploughed themselves into the dirt as he tried to hold on to something. He felt the veins bulge on his neck and the world seemed to darken around him, even though the sun sat above the horizon. Taking a deep breath to calm himself, he felt slightly better. He took another and another. Finally, he felt the grip of his demon relax on him and he collapsed to the earth.

The cackle sounded again from the depths of his mind. *'How does it feel?'* The voice echoed in his mind as his vision continued to swirl. *'A man like yourself, you put everything into your rage. You put everything into your violence and your brutality.'* Jack rolled onto his back. His chest heaved. *'But now that's just me.'* The cackle sounded again, long as it trailed and bounced from ear to ear. *'Each time you get mad, I'll be here. Each time you lose your temper, I'll come forward.'* The laugh continued in stereo while the raspy voice ranted over the top. *'You won't be able to help it forever. It's in your nature to be cruel.'*

Jack held his hands above him and he looked at them. For the first time in the light, he saw them, saw the blood that caked his skin. Saw the chips of bone and matter caked in-between them, the flesh under his finger nails. He wanted to be sick. He could even taste it now, as if the old, stale flesh and bone stuck in his throat. Cutting off the air way, stopping him from breathing.

'And when you do. I'll have control.' The laughter stopped and everything went quiet. *'And I'll be free.'*

Jack let his hands fall to the earth, then just laid there on his back for some time. 'Michael,' he whispered. He had started to come to terms with the fact that he would never lay eyes on his brother again. He didn't even have a photograph, he didn't even have the damned book that the boy had loved. Slowly, as if he had the rest of his life to do it, he turned his head and saw the Browning laying on its side.

'Michael,' he said once more as he reached for the rifle. 'I'm sorry.'

He dragged the rifle over to himself, as his mind fell into an eerie silence, as if the demon watched and waited to see what he did. The cool metal didn't even touch the surface of the heat in his body, as he laid the rifle on his chest and slid the cocking handle back to expose the chamber, the hungry mouth.

Letting the rifle fall down to his waist, he pulled the barrel upward and nestled the muzzle under his chin. He thought about his mother. Grace had always cared for him; she didn't deserve what had happened. He thought about the Darcys and how Paul had stupidly tried to talk him down. They should have run. He wasn't blind to his actions then, although he had already begun to lose control. His body had just moved like someone had guided his hands and he'd just let it happen. Just like he had let the old lawman die. None of them deserved what they had gotten.

He pushed his chin down hard against the muzzle and felt the steel press a ring into his throat. His hand moved down to the trigger and it shook as it did. Still, his mind was silent. The demon had not uttered a single sound. His hand closed on the grip and tightened; he felt the coolness of the metal on his index finger.

He took a breath. Just as he was about to squeeze, he felt the power of the demon pull him back again. The suddenness took him by surprise and he almost slipped. His hands spasmed as if they were under their own commands. The bolt began to slide forward, driven by the hunger of the chamber. It was all over now; the sequence had started and no one could end it. Jack closed his eyes; it wouldn't matter now if the demon came forward. They would die together.

Click.

Jack's body jumped at the sound. His eyes opened and he sat up.

The bolt had slammed shut, but the rifle hadn't fired. Then he looked to his side and saw that the magazine lay on the ground next to him and scrawled into the dirt by his own hands were five words.

The letters were rough and little lumps of flesh, blood and bone had fallen from in-between his digits as his hand wrote the words: Not yet.

RANKIN

'Forward, always forward...
Onward, always up....
Catching every drop of hope,
In my empty cup.'

Duncan Browne – *Journey* (1973)

Rankin looked up at Chris. A smile was partially hidden below his scraggly beard and his hand that wavered slightly before Rankin's face. Crow's feet were etched in the corners of his eyes as his face smiled along with his mouth, yet his eyes couldn't shed their sorrow.

For a moment, Rankin lay there with the bodies as Chris stood over him, almost frozen. Then he raised his own hand to meet his friend's gesture. His body groaned as Chris dragged him to his feet. Even his head throbbed, but he couldn't remember if it was from the whiskey or the blows the two idiots had landed. His eyes were clamped shut as if he tried to stop his brain from pouring out through his tear ducts.

A grumble escaped Chris's lips as Rankin finally gained his feet and opened his eyes. He cocked his head in interest as he saw the pain wrought across Chris' face as he strained to lift him. The partially hidden smile had now totally vanished and nothing in his friend's face embodied anything that came close to joy or humour. Rankin furrowed his brow in concern at the sound of the short, sharp, ragged breaths and he placed a hand on his shoulder.

'Man, are you alright?'

At first Chris wouldn't even meet his gaze. He just panted while he stared at the bodies at their feet.

'Just... Getting old,' he replied between gasps.

Rankin looked at him for some time. Then he clapped his friend on the back and embraced him. At first, Chris' body was rigid and Rankin felt him tense under his arms. Then he felt the tension go out of his shoulders and a hand patted lightly against his back. The embrace was short, barely even a second. When the sound of shouts from behind them rang up the hill and were answered by more from the street, Rankin let his friend go. 'Come on, old man. We're not out of this yet.'

Chris led him into the adjacent yard. They moved quickly and kept low as they vaulted another fence. The yard they landed in was beautifully sculpted, although overgrown, and as Rankin boots thudded into the ground, he felt himself sink into the soft topsoil. Chris ushered him onward and led him into the back of a stunning house.

The glass folding doors were mostly closed, pushed ajar just enough for the men to slip through, which left them criss-crossed on their rail down the length of the brick wall. Once through the doors, Chris took a sharp right and led Rankin into the kitchen. As he moved, he turned his head and peered out of the front door, which swung gently on its hinges but he didn't see a single soul.

They paused behind a large counter that separated the kitchen from the lounge. Chris spun on the balls of his feet and placed a hand on the side of the counter he leaned behind. He looked Rankin in the eye and put a finger to his lip.

Rankin strained his ears, but all he heard was the rattle of the tank's engine as it idled somewhere on the street. The sound of it seemed to rattle through the walls more than it drifted in through the open front door. Then his ears pricked up. For a second, he'd thought he'd heard something far off and distant, below the clatter of the tank. He lowered his head and butted it softly into the counter. He strained even more to hear it, but there was nothing.

Chris moved, and Rankin followed obediently. They moved from the kitchen into a long hallway. Rankin paused as he saw a body crumpled up one end, yet he moved along after he saw that Chris didn't offer it a second look. They moved into the garage, a room that would've been plunged into pitch darkness if not for the many beams of light that penetrated through its roller door, like the fingers of a dream weaving their way through a nightmare. Another body lay crumpled in its centre, a pool of blood had worked its way across the filthy concrete floor. In one section broken glass was scattered. The shards breached the surface of the blood that surrounded it like the jagged bluffs of a rocky cliff section, waiting to tear the bow out a passing ship.

Once more Chris didn't offer the body a second glance as he moved wide, and distanced himself from the blood pooled on the ground and the scatterings of glass. Rankin followed, while on the street there was clunk of a transmission and the screech as the tank began to roll again. The two men placed their hands against the cool metal of the roller door as they placed their eyes to the ragged holes that were punched through.

Immediately, Rankin saw what Chris' motive was. The Holden was parked directly on the other side. He saw the pale white paint, the scarred railway iron. Even with his limited view, he couldn't mistake Pestilence for any other.

He shifted himself and looked further up the street. The tank ground its way along the bitumen and Rankin caught the tail end of its green bulk as it disappeared from his view. His brow furrowed once more and he turned to Chris.

'It's moving off the street, it's moving into the yards.' He whispered.

Chris nodded. 'Let it, we will be gone by the time it swings back around.'

Over the grind of the tank, far behind them, he heard a shout. 'Over here!'

'Can you see any more on the street?' Chris whispered as he slid his fingers under the lip of the door.

'Fuck, they're both dead,' once more the distant voice carried.

'Where is he?' came a reply.

'Search the fucking houses!' At this, the tank's engine roared and its scrambled screeches picked up pace.

Rankin's heart hammered his chest and he placed his eye to another hole in the door as he continued to scan the streets. His eyes watered and the bleary, streaky image he saw through the jagged metal showed him only cars and houses. 'No, I can't see anything.'

The tank's engine dropped to deep drone as it laboured with something and then they heard the cracks of timber and crumble of stone. The sound of destruction rolled up like a wave as it broke on the sandy beaches. He heard glass break and roof tiles splinter as somewhere a house was being driven through.

'It's now or never, man. We can't wait here anymore.'

Chris nodded, and together they lifted the roller door slowly. They moved it slightly above their knees and Rankin held it. 'Move, go on.'

Chris dropped to his stomach and rolled out. Rankin heard the sound of Chris's boots sliding, then gripping, the concrete drive. The weight lifted from his hands.

'Okay, come on.'

Rankin dropped and rolled out. As he did, he saw a smear of blood on the concrete where Chris had rolled out. He thought to himself, how did he manage to get that blood on himself when he walked wide of the puddle? He shook his head and thought about mechanics and their proneness to become covered in filth just by walking past a car.

The roller door clattered gently as Chris placed it down. Rankin rolled over and sat up. Pestilence's heavy iron bar was directly in front of his face. Over it, he saw the scarred grille and the sealed beams. For a moment, his heart skipped a beat as if he sat face to face with a tiger and all he could do was sit and pray while it sniffed at his flesh and decided whether it wanted to sink its teeth into his face.

Chris moved around to the passenger's side, pausing only to peer over the bonnet of the Holden in the direction of the crumbling house. Behind him, Rankin heard a shout of a man directly in the house behind him.

'Fuck! Danny! Another one in here. Simon, Brendan, get the fuck in here.'

His heart took another skip in his chest as he moved to look at Chris. The passenger door popped as Chris worked the handle, and the door yawned as it opened. Rankin moved around to the open door. He didn't want to show any part of his body, so he crawled on his hands and knees. As he went, he questioned the angle the Holden sat on and once more his brow furrowed as he looked down to the end of the drive and his heart sunk.

In the cab, he heard the click of a solenoid as Chris turned the ignition to 'On'. Rankin shot a hand up and grabbed his leg. As Chris laid across the bench seat, he craned his neck to look back at Rankin. 'Don't waste your time.'

'What do you mean don't waste your time?' he hissed as he glared back.

Rankin pointed toward the rear end of the Holden as his shoulders slumped. 'Your back tyre is shot out.'

'Fuck! Fuck!' Chris slammed his hand into the Holden's dash. The look in his eyes was more of a father's disappointment in a misbehaving child than of a man who had just lost his ticket of escape.

In the garage, he heard the sound of glass crunching under foot. 'Oh Jesus Christ. What the fuck is going on here?' A whisper from beyond the roller door.

Rankin shot Chris a look, his eyes wide and his eyebrows raised. Chris fiddled with his belt and passed Rankin out his bayonet and then curled his legs up as if to hide himself. Rankin took the blade. The timber was warm in the palm of his hand while the metal spine kissed his flesh. Rankin slunk back to the front end of the Holden and paused. He placed his right hand on the tyre while the other clung to the haft of the blade.

'Oh, fucking Jesus. Fuck.' He heard the man on the other side of the door whimper over his dead comrade. The roller door shuffled, then began to roll up fiercely. Rankin moved.

'He—' The start of the word was all the man in the garage was able to get out before Rankin drove the blade into his stomach. His clenched fist slapped into the man's gut, then he held his enemy closer to him with his right while he pulled back and slammed it forward again. The man's hands were raised to lift the door to the ceiling and he had no way to defend himself. His eyes were wide with shock and each time Rankin slammed his fist into his stomach, his mouth twitched and his eyes widened then closed. The man's stomach had become wet and now his fist slapped horribly against flesh as he drove the blade in up to its hilt for the final time. The smell of gut hit him instantly and he felt his own stomach want to roll.

Over the dying man's shoulder, he saw another man step into the doorway of the garage. His eyes widened and his mouth hung open. Rankin pushed the corpse back into the garage and he fell lifelessly, his arms almost weightless as he fell back.

'They're here!' the newcomer yelled as he raised his rifle. Rankin reached up and grabbed the roller door and brought it down hard as he threw himself downward to escape the fire that was about to hit him. The door clattered in an ungodly racket as it lowered and bounced out of its runners. Gunfire exploded inside the garage and more holes punched through the metal. One stray bullet hit the iron bar and ricocheted off into the air, whizzing and whirring as it sailed off into the distance.

Rankin gained his feet and moved to the side of the Holden. Chris had already started to clamber out of the car, groaning and bitching to himself as he went.

'Time to move, old timer,' Rankin growled as he grabbed a hold of Chris and pulled him from the cabin. Both of them ran for the street.

Rankin turned back and saw that two houses down, the building was destroyed. A large cut had been torn through its centre, chunks of structure were visible from the crumbled surface of the houses collapsing edges. A rifleman ran onto the street. He looked around bewildered and his eyes narrowed as he saw the two on the street.

Chris raised his pistol and fired two shots in his direction. The rifleman ducked as if something had just whirred over his head and moved off the street as he shouted something incoherent.

'Keep moving!' Rankin yelled as his boots hammered the pavement. Each impact drove a nail into his head and he wanted to scream as if it would release the tension in his brain. Then he heard something. The pain didn't seem to matter so much as the sound he was sure that he had heard. His eyes opened and he looked to the sky, his head darted left and right in time with each pounding foot slap, as he scoured the clouds and the deep blue for the slightest speck.

The worn-down, dilapidated building to his right exploded in a shower of splintered timber and shattered brick. Rankin raised his arms to shield his face while he continued to run down the street. The tank bore down on them as it churned over stairway banisters, lounges and other furniture. Everything was lost now to the sound of the screaming steel tracks and the drone of the labouring tank's engine. Chris and Rankin ran for their lives, while rifle shots ricocheted off the black top around them. They worked with everything they had just to get another step in and then another.

The tank cleared the houses and roared after them. Rankin turned and saw the top hatch fly open. A dark figure rose from the iron shell and glared down at them, and instantly Rankin remembered him. The pale skin was now lined with grease, yet the bushy black curls of his beard were unmistakable even from this distance.

Rankin turned back to the road and pushed himself harder while Chris had matched him step for step, but slowly he had begun to fall behind. Rankin turned to him, he saw the sweat run down his friend's face and the exhaustion in his eyes. Chris turned and fired three times at the figure perched up high on his throne of steel.

At least one round hit the armour, but the rest went wild. Rankin turned to Lewis, he saw the bloodshot eyes and the beginnings of a grin. As the tank edged closer and closer, it chewed up the gap between them while the clattering and incessant rattle worked through their bodies. Inch by inch, the tank gained on them and with each step, Chris became weaker and his speed waned. Rankin looked around. He needed to do something but what could he do against a tank? All he had was Chris's bayonet.

The breath in his lungs was hot, but still he ran. Beside him, Chris's gasps had turned to a ragged suck.

'Come on, man. Just keep running.' Rankin tried to encourage him, but Chris' head was down and he didn't even acknowledge him. Rankin knew that any second Chris would fall, and the tank would roll right over him. Behind him, he heard the hydraulic whine as the turret began to move and he thought, this is it.

He looked back and expected to see the shit-eating grin, but it was gone. Lewis' eyes were not on him, nor had the turret spun to meet him. Lewis looked to the sky and his face was twisted in what could have either been hate or fear.

A shadow fell over Rankin and for a second he was in shade, then the sun continued to beat down on him. He looked up while he continued to run. Meanwhile behind him, the tank had begun to verge off to his right. Rankin slowed and grabbed Chris, who collapsed in his arms.

'What….' – he coughed long and hard – 'what the fuck are they doing?' he croaked as he fought to catch his breath.

Rankin looked up and saw nothing. He looked to the street and saw the rear of the tank move between two houses. The rattling sensation in his bones had subsided and the constant drone of the tank's engine faded to a dull roar. As it moved between the houses, the sound of its exhaust baffled then was briefly blocked by one of the structures as it moved and Rankin finally heard it.

Whup, whup, whup, whup.

There was no mistaking it. He looked up as the black hull of a Huey flew low over the houses. The rotors cut through the air effortlessly as its powerful engine roared above him. Its hull banked as it continued on its path, and Rankin saw the M134 barrels jut from its side, while the gunner sat squat and expressionless.

Then hell opened up and fire burst from its side as the barrels began to spin. The world seemed to tear in half as the street was torn to shreds under its power. Rankin looked down the road and saw the men that had chased them, torn to pieces. There was nothing that could protect them. Some tried to flee but were cut in half by the saw blades of lead that rushed over them. Brass casings fell from the sky and showered over Rankin, hundreds, thousands even. Then as quickly as it had begun, it finished and under the thump of the rotors, Rankin heard the whirring of the barrels as they slowed.

'We need to get off the street,' Rankin said as he stood and brought

Chris with him. 'We need to get the fuck out of here.'

'No arguments here.' Chris groaned and they hobbled together to the opposite side of the street. The Huey behind them banked and the pitch of its turbine rose as the rotors beat down on the earth. Rankin turned and saw it climb and bank hard so that the gunner looked directly down at them.

Then the earth shook and a shock wave rolled over them as the tank's main gun fired into the air.

'Missed, you fuckin' bastard,' Rankin swore as he and Chris stumbled up a house's porch.

'Come on,' Chris croaked, but Rankin was frozen. He wanted to watch this. He wanted to watch the cavalry of the air burn the steel fucker to the ground, he needed to see it.

The Huey pulled out of its bank, the sound of its rotors rolled over the earth once more as it pelted toward them again. Rankin watched in awe while behind him he heard the front door of the house open. Chris lumbered inside.

'Come on baby, burn the bitch,' Rankin chanted as he clutched the balustrade. The earth shook again as the tank's main cannon roared once more. The saw the Huey lift slightly in the air as if a surge of wind had rushed underneath it and pushed it in the air, but it kept on coming. 'Come on, baby.'

Beyond the house directly in front of him, he heard the rise of the tank's engine and once more he heard the grind and splinter of timber as the tank began to move again. He watched the frame of the house bulge and shudder as the iron beast moved through it, all the while the Huey bore down on it. A rushing sound filled the air. A jet stream flew from under the hull of the chopper and rushed to the earth. The back of the house exploded in fire and the clatter of the tank's tracks turned instantly to grinding steel.

The frame of the house collapsed inward and fire engulfed it.

The Huey roared overhead and he heard the whup, whup, whup as it banked off in the distance. The remains of the house across the street shifted and stirred, all the while the steel ground against itself beneath it. Then the rubble shifted and the tank emerged ablaze. It shuddered as it crawled. The right track was jammed, then it turned freely once more to propel the iron hull to the front lawn, then it jammed again. The left side continued to turn, the engine laboured and coughed a sickly wheeze as the beast turned, crippled.

As it came about, Rankin saw its rear torn to shreds by the blast of the rocket. Flames clawed out of its broken armour and blackened the steel that it touched. The right side freed up for a second and then the engine stalled.

'Yes!' Rankin roared. 'Take that, you son of a bitch!'

The Huey passed over head once more and Rankin ran out to the street and held the bayonet high in the air. 'You beautiful bastards.' He called almost in a cry. In the jungles, the sound of the Dread always brought him safety and now he thought that even the Dread itself would fade in his memory in place of this Huey.

He strained his eyes as the Huey banked above him. 'Titan.' The words where white and drawn by hand to emulate drops of blood down the side of its nose. The side gunner raised the barrels of the M134 and for a split second Rankin thought he was about to mow him down. His hands froze, his heart stopped. Then the gunner lowered the barrels and gave a thumbs up as the pilot took the Huey off on another pass of the town.

Whup, whup, whup.

Rankin turned back to the porch, where he had witnessed the battle between the air and land. He trotted back to the door to find Chris. He didn't have to look far; his friend was lying in the hallway. At first sight, Rankin thought he had passed but as he took a step into the hall Chris rolled and raised the pistol. He saw bleary eyes and a pale face. The pistol in Chris' hand shuddered and then it fell to the ground as his eyes shone with recognition.

'Ahh fuck, I'm getting old.' He groaned.

'You and me both.' Rankin laughed, his headache completely dissolved. He thought nothing could break his mood after what he had just witnessed. He hoisted Chris up and once more the two men groaned. Rankin put Chris's arm over his shoulders and he limped his friend back through the front door.

Together they ambled down the porch steps and to the street, while the tank continued to smoulder in the yard across from them. Chris looked up and whistled at the sight of it.

'Takes me back to Africa,' he said solemnly.

'Yeah...' Rankin started, but the smile vanished from his face. 'Hey look, I just wanted to apologise.'

'Don't worry about it,' Chris said softly, his eyes still on the tank.

'Nah mate, I was wrong. I—'

Chris squinted his eyes and he looked forward. 'Wait. Something's not—'

A shriek of anger came from their side and something hit Rankin hard and low. He buckled under the impact. He went down and took Chris with him. The two men sprawled on the black top in shock at the surprise. Rankin rolled over and saw a horrible figure stand above them.

Lewis had been burned within an inch of his life. The hair on his head and his beard had been singed back to the flesh, which had mostly melted from the intensity of the heat. His shirt was indistinguishable from the meat on his chest and his arms were raw and red muscley sinew. The flesh that surrounded his lips were gone and his yellowed and black teeth stood out from his jaw. Red from irritation, his eyes bulged from their sockets, no longer shielded by their lids that had retreated from the heat up into the mess that was his forehead. He raised his arm in which he held a warped machete and he roared a horrible, throaty gurgle of rage.

Chris brought up his pistol at the same time that Lewis brought the machete down. The report echoed throughout the street and Lewis staggered back as he clutched at his side, his swing was broken by the shot. He roared and came again. This time, he lashed out with his foot in a vicious kick which sent the pistol to skate across the bitumen. Rankin moved and dug the tip of the bayonet deep into Lewis' leg.

Again, he roared and lashed out at Rankin with the charred machete. Rankin ducked and rolled to the side, he heard the steel skim the bitumen and then he was on his feet. He held the bayonet low to his side and he stood squat and steady. Lewis climbed to his feet and turned to him. Behind him, Chris had started a slow crawl toward the pistol.

'Come here, beautiful,' Rankin sneered and raised the tip of the bayonet. Lewis gnashed his teeth and gurgled something inaudible. The flesh around his throat and face wept puss as the muscles tried to move for him to speak. Lewis brought the machete down in a slash. Rankin stepped back and felt the blade pass an inch from his face.

Rankin lunged forward and pushed the tip of the bayonet toward Lewis' face, but he sidestepped. Next, he brought the bayonet around in a slicing motion across his chest and outwards. Lewis brought the machete up just in time and the two blades crashed together.

They moved apart and began to circle. In the distance, Rankin could still hear the Titan in the skies as it circled the town. He heard the M134 spool up and deliver a short, powerful burst into an unknown target. The rotors continued their whup, whup, whup as the two men continued to circle.

This time Rankin moved first. He feigned with a stab before he readjusted and swung the blade downward at Lewis' face. Once more, he brought the machete up in time and this time when the blades crashed together Rankin saw scaley flecks fall from the spine of the machete.

The steel is burned, he thought. It will break if I keep hitting it.

Lewis swung the machete in a counter which Rankin ducked. He rolled to his right and regained his feet in time to block a wild, overhead chop. The blades crashed together again and more scale exploded from the spine. Rankin kicked out and took Lewis' left leg out from under him, sending him to his knees. He brought the bayonet down in a chop again and again. Each time Lewis blocked and the steel rung out, more and more of the machetes spine eroded from the impact. Rankin roared and brought the seventeen inches of cold steel down and this time he heard the snap.

The machete splintered an inch from the handle and the blade clattered to the ground. In the pass through, the bayonet sliced down through the melted flesh of Lewis' face and burst one of his eyes. He roared in pain and lashed out with the broken steel in his hand. All Rankin had to do was lift the blade; Lewis did all the work himself. In his blind charge, he impaled himself.

Lewis stopped as blood trickled out between his teeth. Rankin pushed further and then twisted the steel as blood exploded out of his guts. Both of Lewis' burned hands went to the blade in him and clenched around Rankin's hands.

There was some strength left in the disfigured body, but not much. Rankin placed a hand on his shoulder and as he pulled him close, he forced the blade out and brought its tip up with all of his force. The bayonets tip punctured the flesh under Lewis' chin and drove through to break through the roof of his mouth. There was a short gasp of pain as the blade continued to drive through flesh and bone. Then Rankin saw the life leave his eyes and the whole weight of the man rested on his outstretched arm.

The Depths Within: Part 2

He let him fall, and the bayonet slipped from his skull as he did. The burned, bloody mess lay in a heap at his feet, and Rankin continued to look down at him with a sneer. Behind him, Chris had retrieved his pistol and had regained his feet. He limped over to Rankin and leaned on him.

'Don't know about you, mate,' Chris groaned as Rankin raised his head to look at him, 'But fuck Tamworth.'

CHRS

'Where will it lead us from here?'
The Rolling Stones – *Angie* (1973)

The more his body ached, the older Chris felt. His mouth was dry, his stomach was an empty knot of fire and stone. Sweat coursed down his face and stained the pits of his shirt while every part of him screamed for water. Yet the sight of the burning tank across the street and the remains of the man at their feet sent a cold chill running up his spine.

'Come on,' Rankin growled softly. His young friend supported his weight. 'Take a rest over here, old timer.'

Rankin led him back to the porch and eased him down. Chris tried with all his might to hold the burst of pain from escaping his lips, but as he finally let the stairs take his weight, he groaned. He closed his eyes for a moment and just concentrated on his breathing while his head started to spin.

'Seriously, are you alright?'

The words seemed distant, almost as if he had heard the conversation from the lips of another pair of survivors. At first, he didn't respond, just continued to breathe with his eyes tightly shut. Finally, he slowly opened his eyes, the tears that had formed blurred his vision. He saw the outline of a figure standing over him. The air shimmered around him, pushed into waves of faint swirls by the heat that emanated from the hull of the burning tank. His eyes slowly began to clear and he saw the look of concern on his friend's face. The usual sneer of defiance was now replaced by a furrowed brow and a frown.

'I'd like to see you at my age,' Chris groaned as he shifted himself on the porch. 'Should have seen me when I was your age…' He began to laugh, then coughed. 'Made you… look like…. A bitch.'

Each cough felt like daggers in his gut and he was forced to double over. Saliva ran from his mouth and snot drooped from his nostrils. He spat onto the ground and stared at the blackened, bloody mess that splattered as his feet. Overhead, the helicopter had started its approach once more and as he slowly raised his head to look at Rankin, he half expected to see the look of concern on his face once more. Instead, Rankin's head was raised as he watched the oncoming course of the helicopter. Chris didn't think Rankin had seen and he quickly ground his foot over the bloody clot.

The rotors beat down on them as the chopper hovered momentarily overhead. Dust flew from the earth and shot up in all angles. Chris felt a burn in his eyes and the taste of grit in his mouth. He shifted himself again and lowered his head into the porch. Rankin had now turned his back on Chris and stood with his hands on his hips as he watched as the black hull lowered itself to the ground in front of them.

The wind buffeted his clothes and the power of the chopper's engine hammered his ears. It had all become too much for him to handle. Then, as the skids touched down, the power went away. The roar tapered down and he heard the engine wind off and shut down. The rotors continued to whirl and sent sediment flying away in fear of the wind. Just as he thought it would never end, the pilot finally stopped them and the hull shuddered with the force.

The street was plunged into a depth of silence that seemed surreal. No one in the chopper spoke, nor did Rankin. Chris raised his head to see the side gunner stare at them over the tops of his sunglasses. The demeanour in how he sat behind the machine gun was as if he was on a joy ride. He slumped casually over the bulk of its rear end, a cigarette hanging unlit from his lip.

On the far side of them, the cabin door reefed open and a tall lanky man, draped in military greens, stepped out. He took a moment to look at the two survivors over the short nose of the chopper before he removed his helmet and tossed it back onto the seat. Each one of his strides seemed like two of Chris'. With the rotors now motionless, he stood over six foot tall. His face was stern and his back was as straight as a die. He closed the ground between them quickly his semi-march/stride. Chris watched Rankin take two steps forward to meet him.

'Thanks for the help, man,' Rankin said with a smile as he extended his hand for a handshake. The military man shook his hand and a large smile spread over his face. 'You really got us out of a bind there.'

'Thank the two back there,' The soldier said, as his smile continued to widen. 'I was just a spectator. I'm Captain Caitlin. We've been trying to weed out a defector come dictator in these parts, you boys were lucky we came across you when we did.' He gestured to the tank behind him. 'These suckers have been raiding towns like this all through these parts, taking...'

Rankin didn't let him finish. 'Yeah, we know, we were coming south from Tamworth ourselves. The fuckers picked us up a week or so ago.'

Caitlin gave Rankin a funny look, the smile faltering on his face. Chris didn't know if he was surprised that they had escaped Tamworth or was pissed that he had been interrupted.

'Shepherd?' Rankin continued

'That's right.' Caitlin interjected. He placed his hands on his hips and tilted his head slightly as if in demand of a report.

'I reckon you boys finished off what was left of his guys just then. Tamworth was in full riot when we left last night. Shepherd is dead.'

They stood in silence for some time. Chris just watched them from his position on the porch only ten feet away.

'And I suppose we owe you our thanks for this service, Mister—?' Caitlin proposed.

'Bartlett. Corporal Rankin Bartlett,' he said. Although his back was to Chris, he could imagine the sneer spread over his face as he saw his head tilt toward the Captain. There was no salute. 'And no, you don't owe us any thanks. A small boy called Michael brought it about but I suppose he is dead now as well. I don't think he could have survived what happened.'

'A child killed him?'

'Not the boy. You could say it was his brother, but from the last we saw of him there wasn't much of him left.'

Caitlin nodded at Rankin's words, then he turned his head to look at Chris. He walked past Rankin and approached him, extending his hand once more.

'And who are you, my poor friend?'

'Ch... Chris Lowe,' he spoke. 'Thanks again.'

Chris watched Caitlin's eye scour him. They went up and down his body, took in his stance, the words that came out of his mouth. Then he nodded and turned his back on him and returned to Rankin. Something didn't feel right.

'Corporal, you said.'

'That's right.' Rankin sneered as he spoke to what would be a superior officer. Having served in his day, Chris noticed the lack of protocol in his friend's actions. The feeling of unease swelled in his guts.

'Where is your unit?'

'Lying dead on the streets of Brisbane. I was part of the returned servicemen that left from Richmond.'

'Ahh.' Caitlin nodded again as he walked around Rankin and pretended to be fascinated by the wreck of the tank once more. 'And I'm sure you served your part well.'

Rankin didn't follow the Captain as he walked past him once more. He continued to face Chris. Chris saw the anger on his friend's face. He saw his hands move down to his hips, brushing past a pouch that lay on his belt while the fingers on the other hand caressed the blade of his own bayonet, which rested through one of his belt loops.

'Fuckin' court martial me if you don't believe me, mate, but everyone was dead when I left.' Rankin's eyes burned with anger and he looked directly at Chris. Then he blinked and turned his eyes to look at the ground at his feet. 'If it wasn't for Chris, I wouldn't have made it out at all.'

'No doubt,' Caitlin said indifferently. 'We've been picking up boys here and there along the coast with similar stories of their heroics.' Caitlin continued to walk around, kicking loose stones on the ground as he did, his hands fastened to his hips. 'But that's all by the wayside now. We need all the men we can get so we aren't asking questions. Just happy to have you home, Bartlett.'

Chris laughed. There was something off with this slick bastard. He looked at Rankin once more. His face had turned a bright red.

'Home?' He began to advance. 'I'm done with you lying bunch of fuckwits.'

The speed in which everyone moved was heart stopping. The gunner in the side of the chopper snapped the back of the machine gun around and spat his unlit cigarette to the ground. Caitlin spun around. He now had a pistol in his hand which he held out in front of him. Rankin had pulled the bayonet and brandished it like a short sword.

'Stand down, soldier,' Caitlin said. The smile on his face was gone as was the buttery tone of his voice. 'This is all beyond you and I. Headquarters needs men to hold Sydney before the reinforcements arrive from Melbourne. We cannot afford to let these little invading fucks gain another foothold.'

'Bullshit!' Rankin roared, 'the Chinese force is already falling apart, I saw it in Tamworth.'

Caitlin lowered his pistol slightly 'What you saw was their Western contingent. They sent a small force West, down through the hills to Tamworth to cover their flanks and dispel any militia forces. I suppose we can thank Shepherd and his army of misfits for their demise, but the main leg of the force is making its way down the coast of New South Wales as we speak. They're resupplied often by sea and we don't have the forces just yet to repel them.'

'This all sounds like the same shit I was fed before I was sent to Brisbane.'

Caitlin laughed. He lowered his pistol completely and let it hang by his side. The gunner on the side of the chopper did not relinquish his aim. 'I'm not a politician,' the Captain said. 'I'm a soldier like you, following orders.'

'I'm not following orders.' Rankin barked and once more, Chris imagined the sneer on his face as his shoulders squared as he readied himself for a fight.

'We all do, whether we like it or not,' Caitlin said once more. He slotted the pistol back into its holster. 'New Zealand forces have landed in Melbourne, along with the American remnants that left Vietnam.' He turned to the helicopter. 'Where do you think this came from? All of ours that were left over from lend lease burned in Brisbane.'

Chris watched the discussion he knew he wasn't a part of. He knew it in the way the Captain looked him over. The officer saw it when Rankin hadn't. There was little to no fight left in Chris, but Rankin on the other hand was a warrior. They would take him and he would fight for them again.

'Rankin,' Chris called out. Both of the men stopped and looked over to him. 'Go with him.'

His young friend looked like a child torn between the decision of which parent to side with in a divorce. Rankin looked from Chris to Caitlin, then Chris again. The expression on his face changed from sadness to anger, then back to sadness once more. Slowly, he walked over to him and knelt in front of him. 'I don't want to leave you alone.' His voice was soft, as if he didn't want the military men to hear him.

'It doesn't matter.' Chris replied. 'One: they're not going to give you a choice. If you don't go with them, they'll call it desertion and either arrest you or shoot you. Two: I need to find her. She's not your wife, she's mine. I'll find her by myself.'

The two men looked at each other in silence. There was little else to say.

Rankin stood. He held the old bayonet that Chris had stored for years by the blade and held it out to him. 'This is yours. Thanks for lending it to me.' Chris took it. The linseed oil soaked timber felt comfortable in his hand. He ran his eyes up the blade; there were a few new chips in its steel from the beating Rankin had given it, but nothing terrible. Chris smiled and put the blade down on the step beside him. He held his hand out and Rankin shook it.

'Help me up.' He said softly and Rankin did. When he stood again, he put both hands on his younger friend's shoulders and looked at him. 'You stay alive.'

Rankin smiled. 'You find her, man.'

They embraced. They pounded each other's backs briefly, then broke apart. Rankin took one last brief look at Chris, then turned and went with Caitlin. They spoke briefly before they returned to the helicopter. Both men looked back at Chris before they left and neither spoke. Chris stood there and watched as he leaned on the banister rail to his side for support.

Rankin was ushered into the cargo area of the chopper. He climbed into the back as if he was an old cavalryman climbing onto the back of a horse. The chopper's rotors slowly began to turn and its turbine began to whine. Whup, whup. Slowly at first. Then, with each passing second, the rotors picked up speed and dust began to fill the air again. Even the flames that still spurted from the busted tank struggled to fight the winds. The pitch of the turbine continued to climb while the exhaust roared and the helicopter began to rise.

Chris held eye contact with Rankin for the most part as they began their ascent. 'It's for the best,' he said with full knowledge Rankin would never hear him. He raised his right hand to the air and waved a final time while he continued to hold his left to the ache at his side.

Whup, whup, whup. The helicopter rose further and Chris finally lost sight of his friend. All he could see now was the underside of the black hull as it began to move away.

He watched it off, like a father watching a ship carry his son off to war. It grew smaller into the horizon and finally vanished. Chris smiled and turned up the street.

Slowly, he dragged his feet with each step as he made his way past the bodies and wrecked cars that succumbed to the hell fire of the helicopters side gun. The bitumen was broken beneath him and at one point he almost fell as he lost his balance in a large pot hole. Still, he continued. His bayonet hung low at his side; his pistol jammed down the back of his pants.

Pestilence still sat where he'd left her. She wore more scars now from the tank's machine gun that peppered the roller door in front of her, but they were only cosmetic. She was his rock now. In the end she always had been. He leaned up on her side and felt the coolness of her steel. He ran his left hand down her side as he moved to her open door. He reached behind her seat and retrieved his tyre iron and tools. Long lines of red etched the paint where his fingers traced and, on her side, where he leaned was a mess of his blood.

'It's okay, honey,' he spoke softly to her as he began to go about the repairs to her tyre. 'It's okay.'

Once he had finished, he felt as though he was about to die. The energy had left him and all he could bring himself to do was to sit in her to think. He took the pistol from his belt once he was finished and held it in his hand while he looked down at it. Then he looked at the burns on his hands and his arms and he thought about that day. He thought about the invasion. The paratroopers and his escape from Darwin. About the mud he'd seen on his porch when he'd climbed the steps. Tears began to roll down his cheeks as he remembered the state of the lounge room. The pictures of her on the ground, the frames broken under the boots of the men that had entered the house.

He had a lot to think about, and it seemed that he had the rest of his life to do it.

JACK

'Guess I've got that old travelin' bone
'Cause this feeling won't leave me alone
But I won't, won't
Be losing my way.'

Creedence Clearwater Revival – *As Long as I can see the Light* (1970)

With each inch that the sun edged its way into the sky, Jack lost sense of his direction. A man who had something to live for clung to it; a man that had a goal of any kind had something to strive toward; a man that had given up on everything had his own life to take. Jack had none of these things. The only things left to him were his strength and his anger. Yet with each dragging step he took, he surmised that he didn't even have these.

Tell a carpenter to build a house without his hammer. Tell a tree feller to lay down a ghost gum with no axe or saw. How could he walk through this world without the only things he had relied on his entire life?

The Browning's butt dragged along the earth as he walked. The rifle still held something for him, almost like a candle in a window on a long, dark, lonely night, but even that was tainted. Even that was linked directly to the parasite that lived inside of him. Every turn of his mind, every flash of anger, it was there, ready to take it all from him in a heartbeat.

Since he had attempted to take his own life, the demon had been quiet.

At least Jack had that much. For the pasty twenty minutes, he had rolled his life over in his head, as he searched for some sort of hope to continue. He needed something, anything. If the demon wouldn't let Jack physically use his body to end his own life, then he needed to think of something else.

He stopped on the road and looked to the horizon for some sort of ledge he could hurl himself off, but there was nothing. Holding his breath, he listened for any sound of an oncoming vehicle that he could throw himself in front of, but there was only silence.

In the distance, he could hear the ocean. Jack had never learned to swim and that option was viable, but the ocean terrified him. He could imagine that in his own fear he would not be able to maintain control while he drowned. Realistically, the biggest problem with drowning was whether the demon could swim. Whatever it was, it needed to be quick and needed to deal so much damage to his own body that it didn't matter who was in control of it.

Jack spat to the earth, a bad taste had been in his mouth ever since the truck, and he couldn't shake it. He would give anything for a cigarette. A cigarette would wash away the foul taste and leave one of its own for him to cherish.

As he walked, a familiar scent struck his nostrils. He stopped, sniffed and shook his head. Jack had never thought addiction to be a reality, but it was odd the way the brain worked. Not a second had passed since he'd thought about having a cigarette and now he could smell the smoke. Jack tried to think about the last time he had a cigarette; he couldn't even remember when it was. Had he even had any left when he left the house in Chinchilla? He sure as shit didn't stop at the station to buy any.

He took another breath and this time he felt it in his throat, the way that second hand smoke annoys others smokers. The feeling stopped him once more. The road before him wound off to the right, trees blocked his view beyond the bank. He took a knee and listened, for some time. He heard nothing. Then there was the soft clink of metal bouncing off bitumen and someone laughed. Jack scowled, spat once more onto the road, and his jaw muscle began to work. Slowly, he left the road, dropping down off the bank into the trees and making his way to the source of the sound.

He made his way slowly through the trees. At one point, the gaps between the trunks were too small for him. Rather than pick another route, he pushed them apart to make his way through. When he did this, the upper branches swayed and brushed against the limbs of its neighbours. A family of starling's broke from their cover and screamed at the injustice. Jack froze and raised his head to the sky. The branches continued to sway back and forth. He returned his attention to the road beyond the tree line; the men that were there had not taken any notice.

He continued to make his way through the trees and paused at every twig that snapped under his weight. Eventually, he was able to see through the foliage enough to make out what lay beyond. Six men stood around an International truck. The front end of the heavy machine was jacked into the air and the front passengers tyre had been pulled. The men that stood there with hands on their hips were dressed in tan uniforms. Jack's brow furrowed as he continued to watch on. They looked like soldiers to him, but from where he crouched. He couldn't see any rifles. He saw a puff of white smoke emit from one of the soldier's mouth and realised that he had indeed smelt cigarette smoke.

The group laughed as they watched one of the smaller men struggle to roll a large inflated truck tyre to the front end. Each time he pushed it, the tyre would roll itself at odd angles and push itself and the man wielding it, into the truck's frame. Jack saw the frustration in the younger man's eyes as his elders stood around him and laughed without lending a helping hand.

The man struggled again to make the tyre roll the way he wanted it to. He became further unbalanced with every step, then finally he fell and the tyre rolled away from him. The other soldiers laughed and slapped their thighs as the truck tyre bounced past them. A few of them turned to watch as the tread bounced over the small embankment and made its way down the hill toward Jack and the tree line.

It bounced as it came, then lost its balance and flipped end over end. Each time the side wall slapped the earth, speed was ebbed from its motion. It came to rest only five feet from where Jack waited, hidden from the soldier's eyes by the shrubs in front of him. He snarled as he watched it come to rest.

'Fucking soldiers.'

Up on the bank, the men continued to laugh as the young man made his way over the bank.

The smoker followed him. 'It's alright Morgan,' he said as he choked back his laughter. 'I'll give you a hand getting it back up.'

They headed directly toward Jack. He was stuck. If he moved now, they would see him. If he stayed where he was, they might see him. There wasn't much he could do, so he sat down behind a large bush and tried his best to conceal himself and his rifle.

'You guys are being cocks,' the younger man said as he walked down the slight slope to the tyre. Jack could see the redness in his face and the embarrassment was clear in his voice.

'Like I said,' The smoker replied, still chuckling, 'don't worry about it. We're just having fun.'

The younger man stopped at the tyre while the smoker kept up his pace. Jack lowered his head, the smoker headed right for him.

'I thought you said you were going to help me?' The young man cried, his hands out in front of him.

'Yeah, I will,' the smoker replied, 'I just need to take a piss first.'

Jack didn't move. He closed his eyes and tried not to worry about the soldiers only feet away from him now. Up on the hill, the remainder of the soldiers continued to snicker and slap each other on the backs.

Then one of them said, clear as day, 'I'm fucking starving. Next roo we see I'm going to shoot it for us.'

Jack opened his eyes. They were armed.

While the men up on the bank bitched to one another about whether they liked the taste of Roo meat, Jack's mind ticked over. He wanted to end himself. He had tried and failed, but if others could kill him, then he had the answer to his question.

In his mind, loud and clear, he said to himself: They can kill me. They can kill us. He didn't know why he did that or whether he expected an answer from his thought but he never received one. The demon inside of him had vanished. For now, it was only him.

Something trickled against his arm. Jack snapped back to reality. Water had begun to run down from something and splattered against him. He turned his head and saw the smoker, standing on the other side of the bush to him, his cock out as he sprayed him down. Jack stood up.

It took longer than he thought it would for the smoker to see him. It wasn't until Jack's head was level with the smoker's chin that the colour began to run out of his cheeks. At his full height, Jack stood easily two foot taller than the man before him. As he continued to rise in his stance, the smoker's gaze followed him up and up, while the smouldering cigarette hung from his lip. Jack reached out and plucked the cigarette from his gaping mouth and took a drag.

As the smoke filled his lungs, Jack felt a soft tingle run up his spine and settle in his head. He exhaled in the smoker's face and grinned. The smoker fell back over himself and started to scramble away, his cock still hanging out the front of his pants. Jack advanced on him and left the Browning to hang low at his side. The young man turned to look at his comrade scramble away and then saw Jack. A shout of surprise escaped him as he turned to run back up the hill.

'Oh fuck, oh fuck,' the smoker cried as he rolled to his hands and knees and tried to get up.

Jack lifted a boot and kicked him square in the ass. The smoker sprawled over and cried out in pain as he slid along the dirt.

'What the fuck?' he heard from the truck.

'Quick, get the rifles.'

The smoker tried to gain his feet again but Jack placed a heavy boot in-between his shoulder blades and pressed him to the ground. He lifted the Browning and placed its muzzle to the back of his head.

Above Jack, the other men were in a scramble, and he heard the familiar sound of rifles being racked. He did the same. The Browning's charging handle ripped back with a totally different sound. Jack looked up, the grin still plastered across his face. The five men that remained on the embankment all had their rifles trained on him. He could see the whites of their eyes over their iron sights. He could see the fear.

'Give it up, man,' one of them called down. 'There's no good way out of this.'

'Not from where I'm standing!' Jack boomed back at them.

'Put it down!' another man yelled.

'You'll have to come down here and take it from me!'

None of them fired.

'Come on man, please,' the smoker cried beneath his foot. 'We're on the same side here.'

'No one is on my side!' Jack growled back at him. 'If your pussy brothers up there don't fucking end me, then I'll end the fucking lot of you.' He roared the last part for their benefit and raised the butt of the Browning to his shoulder.

'Put it down! Now!' the same soldier repeated.

Jack fired the Browning into the earth next to the smokers' head; the man screamed. Above, one of the rifles cracked and Jack felt a sear of pain in his right arm. He looked down at it, a line of blood ran from a cut in his bicep. Jack scowled and raised his head.

'Finish it!' he roared up to them. He spun the Browning around and smacked the butt down into the smoker's ass. He groaned in pain.

'Hold your fire.' This new voice was calm, and somewhat older than the rest.

Jack turned his head to the sound and saw an older man, dressed in the same uniform as the soldiers. The middle-aged soldier walked in front of the five riflemen. He held his hand up to them as he did so, and they lowered their rifles.

'Son, why are you doing this?' he said, his hands on his hips.

Jack continued to look up at him. He didn't say a word, he just continued to scowl.

'I can see what you're doing, and frankly, my boys aren't the killers you're after.'

'They'll kill if they want to stay alive.' Jack sneered up at him.

'Yes, they will,' the older man replied, still calm. 'But you won't be the one they will be defending themselves against.'

'Then they'll die!' Jack roared. His breath was hot in his chest. He stood there and snarled up at his would-be killers, the muzzle of the Browning now resting on the smokers' neck.

The officer looked down at him for some time, then he turned to his men. 'Come on, get that wheel back on the truck. We've wasted enough time here.'

Jack's shoulders slumped. 'You can't ignore me,' he growled up at the soldiers and shouldered the Browning once more. 'I'll split this fucker in two.'

The older man turned to him with an expression on his face as if he was about to deal with a spoilt child. 'Son, I don't know what rock you've been living under these past weeks, but we have a hundred thousand screaming Chinamen hot on our asses. I know these men carry on like children and you wouldn't dare think they would be soldiers in the Australian Defence Force' – He shot back a disapproving look to the men crowded behind the truck – 'but we are getting out of dodge and time is of the essence.'

The young man came back down the hill in a sulk and went to grab the tyre. Jack turned the muzzle of the Browning in his direction, half-heartedly. The young man eyed it, but continued his task.

'So, you can either stand there and wait for those sons of bitches to come down on you, who'll be sure to oblige your wish. Or you can get your ass in the back of this truck. Either way I don't care, just get your damned boot off my man's back and stop wasting my fucking time!' he screamed the last few words.

Jack stood there in shock. In his whole life, nearly every man that he had faced had feared him. Either that or he could bend them like they were an insignificant stick. Yet, this old man had him. He had read Jack like one of Michael's open books. Jack had wanted them to shoot him, he had no real intention of hurting them. Deep in his own mind, he heard the cackle roll against the walls of his skull.

He looked down at the smoker who still squirmed under his boot. The man tried to get up, Jack pushed him back down. His face turned to a scowl once more. 'I didn't say you could get up.' The smoker looked up at him, a dumbfounded look on his face. 'I'll get what I want from you lot,' he growled. 'One way or another.'

Jack raised the Browning in the air and was about to bring the butt down hard, when the first rifle shot cracked. Jack stood there as if waiting for the hail of bullets to overwhelm him, but nothing came. No pain, no blood, no darkness. Only the echoes as rifles cracked, they fired in bursts, not singular. Then the screams came from the truck. He looked up at the truck and saw the soldiers amassed behind its heavy frame. Their rifles were in hand and he could see the bullet holes form in the canvas back. Beneath him, the smoker had started to squirm once more, as he struggled to get free. Jack lifted his boot.

The smoker ran up the embankment and leapt behind one of the rear tyres, while the canopy was torn apart by the automatic fire. Jack watched in amazement. Some of the Australians had returned fire, but their shots weren't aimed and Jack doubted that any of their shots even came close to their targets. Jack squatted as a wild round whirred past his head. Who would shoot at Australian soldiers?

'A hundred thousand screaming Chinamen.' He repeated the old man's words to himself. He thought back to the arena where he had awoken, where Michael had saved him for the last time. He had seen small Asian men there, but they couldn't be from the Chinese army. 'Bull-fucking-shit.'

He got to his feet and stormed up the hill. He listened intently to the clatter of the automatic fire as he went. Four, maybe five separate rifles. 'A hundred thousand my ass,' he growled. Halfway up the hill, he came to the young man, who cowered behind the spare tyre. He bent as he passed and lifted the tyre up easily with one hand. He came to the truck and stood behind the cowering Australians. Some of them turned and looked up to him; the fear was still in their eyes but he didn't think it was due to him. They feared for their lives.

Beyond the back of the truck, he saw a man's legs sprawled; the owner didn't move. Jack stepped to the side and saw the body of the older man who had just scalded him. The front of his shirt was stained red and a part of his arm had been blown off. He stared at the body. Anger swelled inside of him and the cackle echoed, *'He was a waste of air.'*

Jack scowled at the insult.

Beyond the truck, he heard some of the attacker's advance. Two of the rifle's cracks sounded much closer, while the other two were close, but still back from the road. Jack lifted the Browning in one hand and looked into the breech. The brass was stacked, ready to feed, ready to fire. He started to walk around the back of the truck and something grabbed at his leg. It was the smoker that held him.

'You'll get killed,' he said, raising his voice over the gunfire.

'You pussies couldn't man up,' Jack growled. 'Maybe they can.'

Jack came around the side of the truck and bellowed as he hurled the truck tyre with all of his might in a back handed swing. It sailed through the air like a discus. Above it, he saw a small soldier in a lighter tan uniform with red crested epaulettes climb the embankment. In his hand he held an assault rifle, it was pointed at the ground across his belly as he ran.

The tyre caught him full in the chest. Jack heard the air rush out of him as he was violently thrown to the ground. As if nothing had stood before it, the tyre continued on its course through the air, undisturbed.

Jack continued around the back of the truck, the Browning now semi-raised as he walked. The second soldier shielded his face from the course of the tyre and slowly came back into a ready stance. Jack placed a heavy boot across the rifle on the downed attacker's chest and trained the Browning on the second of the vanguard; the heavy bolt slid forward.

The Browning bucked in his arms, heavy and powerful. With the first shot, Jack saw the Asian's guts tear open and a spray of mist and shit fly from the back of him. He turned his eyes up the slope and saw another Asian who had taken aim.

The Browning belched death a further two times before Jack snapped the rifle around. Again, the rifle bucked into his shoulder.

Four consecutive shots came from the muzzle and fire filled the air. Up on the slope, the third attacker was hit high on the right shoulder, the assault rifle in his hands dipped as it began to fire in a fully automatic spray before the other rounds from the volley caught him in the body and drove him down.

Jack knew there was at least one attacker remaining He brought the rifle back over to the left and saw a man run back into the tree line. He was small and fast as his figure darted between trees as he went. Jack squinted and held the Browning steady. The world was enveloped once more in the fire and lead of the Browning's roar. It churned and hammered with each round fired. Bark flew from trees; branches were blown clean off in the volley. Somewhere in the carnage he saw a spray as the Chinaman was torn apart, he watched him fall as he continued to fire. Jack knew he had gotten him, but he couldn't stop.

The demon pulled at him again. *'Good, kill them. Kill them all. Get angry.'* Jack felt himself start to slip; he had begun to lose control.

The bolt slammed forward and stopped. Jack gasped for air, as if he had emerged from the depths of the sea. He felt himself come back. He took another breath and looked down. The first Asian soldier was still beneath his foot and he squirmed to get the rifle out from under Jack's boot. Jack stared at him while he writhed beneath him; their eyes never parted as he brought the steel pad of the Browning's butt down on the man's skull in one swift movement.

The Australians began to emerge from behind the International. Some of them scratched their heads. Others moved up the hill, their rifles in hand as if in an act they had done something. Someone slapped him on the back. Jack turned slowly and glared down at the smoker. He wore a smile, but he backed away slightly at the look on Jack's face.

'You saved our lives,' he said quietly to him. 'Th-Thank you.'

Jack's facial expression didn't change. He pushed past the smoker and laid the Browning in the back of the International. As he walked beyond the body of the old man, he pointed down at it. 'Thank him, he was the only thing keeping you pussies alive.'

Jack turned around and saw the smoker squat next to the old man's body. There was a look of sadness in his eyes. Jack strode over to him and grabbed the smoker by the shoulder and stood him up.

The smoker didn't look up at him, but he held a hand up and said, 'It's okay. I'm okay.'

Jack cocked his head. 'I don't give a fuck about you. Give me your fucking cigarettes.'

RANKIN

*'Well I'm looking out at an overcast sky in the morning
I can't hear the warning as it calls to you.
As the birds migrate and the wind is raised
I can see the eagle soaring.
Although I'm just a pawn in natures game like you.'*

Russell Morris – *Wings of an Eagle* (1973)

As the Titan powered through the air, Rankin leaned his head back on the cabin wall and closed his eyes. He was exhausted. The world swam in his head, voices of people long gone mixed with the muffled words of Caitlin as he spoke to the pilot via the headset he wore. Wounds long since scarred over ached alongside his still throbbing hand and his worn-out limbs. Amongst all of it, the sickening crank of his hangover continued to roll over and over like the lumpy cam in Chris's Holden. He tried to sleep but the longer he listened to the Whup, Whup of the Titans rotors, the more he wanted to be sick. He thought about Vietnam, the damned heat, the damned rashes and the screaming. His body relaxed, however, the screams became louder.

He dreamt he was back in the Jungle. Sweat poured from him. His ammunition was low, almost out altogether. The Black Dread was nearing his position, he could hear its powerful rotors beating down on the jungle. The constant thud of the fifty rocked through everything.

He was going to get out, he needed to get out, but the damned screams were killing him. He couldn't handle it anymore, he needed them to stop. As he moved through the jungle, he felt the vines wrap around his arms and his throat as he tried to move beyond them, while the screaming became louder the more he pushed through. His SLR became snagged on the vines and he tugged and pulled on the slimy surface of the stock in an attempt to pull it loose. The vines broke up above him and began to fall around him as the rifle finally pulled free. Yet as he turned and started to move, crashing sounded from above him. He looked up and fell backward as he raised his arms to shield himself from what he saw.

The vines snapped taut and the lifeless body of Rixon bounced slightly on its tether. He swung gently back and forth as his eyes kept their lock on Rankin's. Rixon's body was black with rot. The flesh on his hands was mostly gone, leaving only the dull white of the bones beneath. His chest was torn open, exposing his shattered rib cage. Behind the cage he saw his heart, which continued to beat despite its armour of mud and grime. Rixon's mouth opened and two millipedes escaped his craw and ran down his neck as his body uttered a horrible groan. Then the smell hit Rankin and he turned away.

He heard the screams once more just beyond the vines and he passed Rixon's body; his feet brushed against Rankin's shoulder as he went. Once more Rankin pushed through the vines and fought his way through, as the incessant screaming fought to be heard over the hellfire of the Black Dread behind him. Rankin stepped into a clearing and wanted to break down and cry.

Where he had stepped out, the jungle seemed to end. Torn apart and dug out, root and stem by the Vietcong. As far as he could see, the field was chopped and rutted to make the ground uneven and difficult to traverse. Worse yet, were the Punji stakes. It seemed as if every square foot of the field was filled with stakes that jutted outward and upward at inconsistent angles. Flies buzzed around the faeces that covered each and every stake, which gave the whole field the impression that it was alive.

In the field, Rankin saw Will. He screamed in agony as he tried to move forward. His guts had been torn open and trailed out behind him to where they had caught. Blood ran down from his mouth and from his ears. When Will opened his eyes, Rankin saw that the sockets were crammed full of the same shit that had been rubbed all over the bamboo stakes.

Will screamed again and held his hand outward as he crawled forward another foot. With each movement, the punji tore more away from him and Will's screams intensified with every further tear in his flesh. Rankin watched in horror as his old friend tried to stand, and failed, falling forward onto another stake. The sound as flesh parted and the lifeblood splattered out of Will joined the fight to be heard over the screams and the power of the Dread, and lost the split moment after it had won.

Will held his hand outward as his body slowly slid further down the shaft it was impaled upon. 'Kill me!' he screamed as he tried to pull himself forward. 'Kill me, man. It never ends, it never ends!'

Rankin looked down at the SLR in his hand then raised it to his shoulder.

'They put you through the same thing all over again. Let you feel the pain of how you died in war. It never ends.' Will spat through blood and snot. 'Fucking kill me!' His friend began to cry through eyes that were no more.

Rankin levelled the sights and fired.

He sat upright in the cabin of the Titan, his breath heavy in his chest. He looked around. Caitlin sat calmly across from him and watched with a soft smile on his face. Rankin pulled a packet of cigarettes from his pocket and dropped them. The wind from the open cargo bay doors caught the packet and sucked them straight out the side. Rankin didn't even watch them go. The moment they left his grip, he had reached for another packet that he knew he had in his other pocket. The wrapping was crumpled severely and his fingers shook as he tried to pull out a bent smoke. He put the butt in his mouth and tried to light the end, but no matter how hard he sucked, the cherry wouldn't light. He held the cigarette in front of him and saw the tear in the paper right at the filter.

'Fuck it!' Rankin swore as he threw the ruined packet out of the window after the good.

Caitlin laughed and slapped his knee. Under the power of the Titan's turbine Rankin couldn't hear any of it. He just saw the officer's amusement and the anger in his stomach started to burn. Caitlin settled himself and reached into a breast pocket. He pulled a brand-new packet and held them out. Rankin looked down at them, saw the perfect corners on each side of the cardboard wrapper, and seized them. He chain-smoked three before he looked back at Caitlin again.

It was apparent Caitlin had never looked away. He sat with a slumped back; his elbows leaned across his knees as he watched Rankin smoke, his eyes mostly hidden by the dark lenses of his aviators. He pointed to a section of the cabin beyond Rankin's head and he turned to follow.

A headset rocked gently with the motion of the Titan from its hooked position on the cabin wall. Rankin unhooked them and placed them over his head. Immediately, the overwhelming noise of the rotor was cut down. Caitlin reached down beside his seat and the sound changed in the speakers on Rankin's ear.

'You look as though you've seen a ghost,' the captain remarked with a fatherly look on his face.

Rankin shrugged as he lit another cigarette. 'Something tells me after this is all over, I'm going to see a lot more.'

The captain shook his head and reached down to his side again. 'Move to your left, there's a small button on the side of the hull, press that if you want to talk.'

Rankin did so. 'Thanks for the smokes.'

'Thank our good friend, Uncle Sam,' Caitlin remarked as he settled back into his chair.

Rankin looked down at the packaging again. Lucky Stripes was the brand. Part of Rankin wanted to throw the cigarettes out of the cargo bay door again. He hated the Americans; thinking about them now was the last thing he wanted to do.

'Why cigarettes? They couldn't give us men?'

'They've given us that and—' Caitlin began

'Yeah, like you said.' Rankin cut him off. 'The ram rooters and the Yanks have landed in Melbourne. Why? Sounds like the fighting is going to be in Sydney, not Melbourne.'

'That's because the fighting in Sydney has already begun.' Caitlin said without hesitation. 'The harbour's blockaded and supplies can only come from air or by truck.' Caitlin pulled out another packet of cigarettes and tore them open. 'We've backed out of the city mostly, there was no way to protect ourselves from the naval guns.'

'And what about our navy?'

Caitlin shook his head as he exhaled a whisp of cigarette smoke that was sucked out into the open.

'I'm not going to lie to you,' Caitlin said, yet Rankin thought that was a lie in itself, 'the situation is not a good one. We scattered most of our sticks into the wind at Brisbane. We have no air power apart from a few of these the yanks brought over from Nam.' He gestured to the Huey they sat in. 'We have no armour and only a band of misfit survivors from a bunch of lost causes remain to us.' He sighed. 'We are holding a base that has been set up in Western Sydney. It is the key to Melbourne.' He said the last words like they meant everything to him. He held his hand up and emphasised at different points as he spoke. 'The Chinese will need to come through Western Sydney to get to Melbourne. The city doesn't mean anything to them, from what we can tell. It's mostly abandoned now anyway.'

Rankin shook his head; this was a joke. 'You conscripted men to fight overseas, yet you're not doing that now?'

Caitlin smiled. 'They are, but now most of the civilian population is well south of Sydney.'

'You guys are useless,' Rankin scoffed as he shook his head.

'Write a letter to the Prime Minister, I'm only doing what I need to do.'

'And what's that? Flying about acting all high and mighty?' Rankin had grown tired of this wanker already.

'Doing what I can to secure our flanks before the main threat gets here,' he said. 'And where we can, find more men that are able to fight and re-enlisting them. You already know all this.' The annoyance spilled out in his voice.

'Then why did you just take me? Why didn't you take my friend back there?'

Caitlin offered him an odd look, as if the answer to that was obvious. 'Our field hospital is overflowing as it is. Soldiers only now, we can't afford to treat anyone else. Anyway, I doubt your companion would have survived the trip.'

Rankin screwed his face up. 'Bullshit... He wouldn't make the trip?' he said in question, then shook his head. 'There was nothing wrong with him.'

Caitlin shrugged as if in dismissal of the conversation and looked away. 'From where I was standing, it looked like he had a gunshot wound to the stomach. If he didn't get immediate help, it was over for him. As we couldn't help him immediately, his life was beyond help.'

Rankin didn't believe it. He would have seen, he would have known, it couldn't be true. So many thoughts ran around in his head. Part of him wanted to go back to Chris while the other half of him knew it was too late for that. Would he ever see his friend again? The chances were slim, he knew that much at least. Even if what the captain had told him was a lie, Chris had been on a suicide mission from the beginning.

'When this is all over,' he said to himself. 'I'll find you man.'

'You need to press the button to talk,' Caitlin interjected.

'I wasn't talking to you,' Rankin shot back angrily as he depressed the button.

Caitlin held his hands up in a calming gesture and turned his head once more to look out the cargo doors. He pointed with one hand while the other moved down to the side of his seat.

'Welcome to Sydney.'

Rankin followed Caitlin's gaze out of the side door of the Huey as the Titan banked. The suburban sprawl below them looked almost abandoned. When Rankin had left Sydney, the streets had been alive with bustling traffic and the footpaths had been scattered with people as they went about their lives. Even though the invasion had already begun, it had seemed as though the fighting was in another country all together. The people of Sydney seemed untouchable.

In hindsight, Rankin thought they seemed ignorant. Now the streets of Western Sydney were mostly quiet. He saw only one or two vehicles that traversed the streets and those were green and tan Military Internationals.

Rankin found the main road; a few military trucks were parked along it and men moved around below them. Some of them had stopped to look up at the Huey as it powered above them. Rankin had to laugh when he saw one of the men wave. Black smoke trailed up into the air from a house that smouldered in the middle of one street, while a few men stood around it and watched.

'They've started,' Caitlin said over the speaker.

Rankin looked at him funny, then looked back out the door. The main road joined another at a 'Y' intersection. Two main roads turned into one, one main highway that headed south.

'The key to Melbourne,' Caitlin said again.

Rankin followed the trail etched out below him of the great southern road. He thought to himself and figured this could only be what he knew as the Northern Road that would eventually link up the Hume Highway.

'The key to Melbourne indeed,' he mumbled, not bothering with the radio switch.

Along the western side of the Northern Road, just on the south side of the intersection, a large field had been cleared. It looked to Rankin as though at one point it would have been a football field or two easily. Now it was filled with trucks, the odd jeep and another Huey. Rankin could see from where he sat that some of the trucks had been destroyed by the fighting, wherever it had been. Some had tyres missing, while the large cabs of others leaned forward, exposing their engines.

Beyond the field was a courtyard, a U-shaped brick structure surrounded it. The stone work in the courtyard was made out to be the sign of the cross. The pitch in the Titan's turbine lowered slightly and Rankin felt the hull begin to sink in the air. As they went down, it seemed pretty clear to him that they were going to land in the courtyard.

Rankin leaned over and pressed the switch. 'What did you say they've started?'

Caitlin didn't look at Rankin. He just stared downward, out the side of the Huey. 'They started preparing the defences. The brass that remains here have been trying to nut it out for the last week.'

Once more, Rankin screwed up his face. 'Defences? If all our military power is in Melbourne, shouldn't we retreat? Shouldn't we lead them on further and stretch their supplies even thinner?'

Caitlin smiled as he continued to look down. Slowly, he turned his head. 'The last of the Australian army is here in Sydney,' he said, unblinking. 'Sydney won't fall. We will hold this intersection until the reinforcements arrive.'

Rankin didn't bother with a reply. He lit another cigarette as the Huey lowered itself down into the courtyard and he shook his head. The intersection was a choke point. One hundred thousand Chinese soldiers against what remained here.

He should've stayed with Chris.

RANKIN

*'As the days roll on and the nights get long,
The changing of the seasons
And the falling autumn leaves, they bring me down,
They bring me down.'*

Russell Morris – *Wings of an Eagle* (1973)

Rankin sat in the middle of the road; the cloth of his shirt stuck to his body from the sweat that poured out of him. Although the air that kissed his skin was cool in the early morning darkness, the work throughout the night had been arduous and taxing. He leaned his head back and felt the chill in his scalp as his wet hair touched the steel fender of the car behind him. He lit a cigarette and took a deep drag. His eyes darted from the dazzling flame of his lighter to the skewed shadows it cast along the outskirts of the street. Dawn was yet to grace the day and the horizon was as dark as the depths of his dreams. Yet around him the sounds of grunts rose and fell as men shifted the lifeless weight of cars about the street.

He'd had little trouble working throughout the night, his eyes had adjusted fine and he was able to guide the hulls of the vehicles as he and two other men pushed them about. However, as dawn approached, every last touch of light seemed to suck out of the earth, until it seemed that even the stars in the sky lost their will to go on. The world seemed to sink into shade the way it did when a cloud drifted aimlessly across the power of the sun, as if to sacrifice itself for those below.

It became harder and harder to judge correctly. Steel bumpers hissed as they ground across the guards of another car, or crunched as they crumpled against the brick structures. At first Rankin thought that it would be impossible to not see a building in any light. He didn't understand how something so large could be so hard to see. Yet as the fatigue settled in and the light was sucked from the air, walls and ledges that they had not even thought to manoeuvre about in the earlier hours seemed to leap out at them from the darkness.

In the few days he had been back in Sydney, this was the first night he had worked with no light. The three other nights they had been in preparation, they had at least had the warm halogen glow of the International's headlights, while they worked to the methodical thud of its engine. However, as the days went on and the threat from the north loomed closer, things began to change. Work lights were taken away and most movement was restricted to night. The brass that remained feared the Chinese scouts would realise their numbers.

From what Rankin could tell, there were arguments about whether they should hide their numbers and make the Chinese believe the threat was minimal or to make them think the numbers were more than what they were. On one side, an easy target could seem like a pushover, and would entice the enemy to rush in with little thought due to their overwhelming numbers. Whereas on the other hand, beliefs of a main battle force would lead to an all-out, planned assault. No matter which way they looked at it, there was no way out of a fight.

Work had already begun on the defence strategy when he had arrived. Cars, buses, trucks or whatever they could find, had been pulled from the main road. Stacked fender to fender across side streets, and in some places blocking any exit from the main road. They were attempting to create a funnel; they wanted the enemy force to be directed down the main street which was being robbed of any form of cover that could be removed. Free from cars, the middle of the road was a dead zone, not an inch of cover to be had. The yards that lined either side of the main road offered little more, apart from the odd brick letter box or corrugated iron fences. Those that could be removed, were.

Rankin wasn't stupid, however, he felt somewhat like a mushroom as the days passed on. He had not seen Caitlin since they had landed and had fallen into the dull routine from the get go. He had not been given a rifle, but he had been fed and a packet of Lucky stripes had been slapped into his hand while they told him not to worry, their American friends would be there soon.

On the second day of manual labour, the soldiers had been told from that point on there was to be no movement in the street during daylight hours, no exception. As a reward, they were told they were to work all through that night. The men that surrounded him bitched that not only had they worked the last five previous nights but all the days as well. Fatigue had worn them away. With the loss of the work lights at night, tempers had run thin, and small jokes were taken personally. Rankin alone had broken up four fights in the first two nights. Afterwards, he had laughed at the fact that he was the one who had broken the fights up and not the one who had instigated them.

Rankin saw their plan unfold before him. He had never been told the grand picture, just the usual, "do this, do it faster and have it done five minutes ago." While the team Rankin worked with continued to push cars (that more than likely ran, they just weren't allowed to start them) into position, another team had begun to chop up the main road. Six fox holes, four feet deep and six feet wide were carved into the road in staggered plots.

The doors to houses were fixed shut, windows boarded up, the side entrances to yards blocked at the front ends of houses with all the contents that could be pulled. Everything was done in the dark, everything was done by hand. Rankin's job was to move and position cars and heave them onto their sides. He hated it.

As he and his team pushed a small Datsun along the street with ease, they stopped to watch another squad struggle to remove a couch from a house. The two soldiers constantly argued as one pushed while the other tried to lift and tilt the couch to pull it out of the narrow door. Rankin and the two men he worked with laughed and smoked as they watched the struggling soldiers. Finally, the one on the outside of the house snapped, he flapped his arms in the air as he swore and walked away. The men laughed as they watched the soldier who was left supporting the other end of the couch as he called out to him. 'Alex, Alex.' They heckled Alex as he walked off, and howled as he flipped them the bird. 'Alex,' the remaining soldier called again. 'Yeah, good idea, go and get some help.'

The two men Rankin worked with were the best part of his situation. Travers was a larger man with a balding red pate. A man in his early forties, his face was freckled, along with every other person with red hair in the world. He was a fit man but always had the habit of hitting the spot of his pants where his cigarettes lay. Every night, he would arrive for the work with a fresh pack of Lucky Stripes, 'Thank you, Uncle Sam,' and every night he would get two out of it before he slipped and squashed the rest against a car's body.

Caycho had the darkest complexion out of the three. He was a squat man with large shoulders and was a great asset when it came to manhandling vehicles. Rankin and Travers continuously just referred to him as Gringo due to his poor excuse of a moustache. The three of them spent most of their time together, and Rankin felt like he was in a group of friends again. He often thought about Gary, Max and Will and the time they spent at "Fuck Me's." Then he thought about Chris and their adventures. He thought about the Holden, the big bastard in Tamworth, the dark eyes, the brutality of the man.

Rankin shook his head and jumped slightly as the cigarette in his hand began to burn him. He flicked it away and watched the remains of the cherry smoulder in the shallows of the filter. All it had given him was a single drag in the time that it had burned all the way down to singe his fingers. He rubbed his face with both hands. The scabs from the knife wound scratched at his brow and cheeks. With gnarled knuckles, he kneaded his eyes and yawned.

'God.' He shook his head again and stood up. 'I'm getting too old for this shit.'

'You're half my age and do half the work,' Travers bitched at him.

'Is this where you tell me back in your day you had to walk twenty-seven miles to school bare foot and with a hundred-pound pack?' Rankin retorted as he lit another cigarette. 'Rain, hail, or shine?'

Travers laughed. 'You're forgetting cyclone, earthquake or blizzard.' He pulled out his packet of cigarettes and pulled a particularly squashed and bent smoke from the rumpled package.

Rankin shook his head again. 'Finish these and we'll move this last car into position. Dawn's not far off.'

Travers was now on his fifth attempt to light the cigarette. He stopped to look at the sky and nodded. The horizon was now visible; red and orange had begun to streak into the air in long strips.

Rankin walked over and kicked Caycho's boots. He snored loudly as he jumped and blinked up at Rankin. In the early dawn, his friend looked hilarious as he spluttered awake. 'Come on, wetback.' Rankin laughed. 'You want to get paid, don't you?'

They finished their cigarettes. Of course Caycho had to mooch one and they returned to their task of moving the heavy Ford they had found in the drive of a house. It had been some time since this car had been moved, the brakes seemed to engage intermittently, like some wanker sat in the cabin and jammed the pedal on.

The three men strained, Rankin and Travers were toward the back while the wetback remained up at the A pillar to steer with one arm when required.

In front of them, they heard the rumble of a diesel and they paused slightly to look up. Two large spotted beams burned their eyes in the morning dullness. All three of them ducked their heads and continued to push as the International came up on them.

'Caitlin's going to rip these guys a new asshole,' Travers muttered as he strained.

Rankin grunted in acknowledgement as he continued to heave. His head was low and he saw the light dance across the ground beneath him. The international rolled up beside them and the brakes howled as it pulled to a stop.

'Need a jump, boys?' A voice called from the back of the truck. The remark was followed by the sniggers of the other men under the canopy.

'Yeah, good one, smart ass,' Caycho called back.

'Get pushing that car now, boy,' a man said in a mock drill sergeant voice. 'Double time.' More laughter came.

'Hey Morgan,' another voice now. 'These guys remind me of you struggling with that tyre, poor old son.'

Rankin gave up his struggle with the Ford; he stopped and rested his ass on the bumper. As he lit another cigarette, he looked to the back of the truck and saw four men lean over each other to look out. They all looked young, stupid and cock sure. 'Where have you lot been?' he asked. 'You just get here?'

One of the younger men answered him. 'We're just in from the north coast, think we were some of the last to get out. We've had the Chinese on our backs most of the way down.'

Travers grunted as he gave the Ford one last push, then realised his two friends had stopped. He offered Rankin a sheepish look and tried to light another broken cigarette.

'So, they're not far behind?' Rankin asked the younger soldier.

'Wouldn't say so. They stopped harassing us once we got close to Sydney, but otherwise it's been a nightmare. Couple of times we thought we were goners.'

Rankin nodded. 'Yeah, have heard a few horror stories.' He started around to the side of the Ford. 'You boys better jump out here, the roads been chopped up in front and the truck won't get you any further. Tell your driver to kill his lights or the Captain will have his foot up his ass shortly after he's finished reaming mine.'

The men turned to each other and began to gather their gear. Rankin watched as he leaned up on the Ford and smoked. The tailgate of the truck swung down and the men started to pile out, SLRs in hand and packs on their back. They were all young. One of the first men out was the youngest. He came over to Rankin while another man who also smoked went to the truck's cabin to let the driver know what Rankin had told them.

'What's your name, kid?' Rankin asked him as he approached.

'Morgan.' The kid shifted the pack on his back and swapped his SLR to his other hand. He extended out his hand and Rankin shook it.

'Rankin Bartlett. Did you guys fight in Brisbane?'

The kid nodded. 'Deception Bay. It was a mess.'

Rankin looked at him, his eyebrows raised. He remembered that name from when they had divided up the returned servicemen at the air base. Half went to Enoggera, while the rest went to Deception Bay.

'Shit, really?' Rankin asked. 'I was in Enoggera. We got our asses handed to us.'

'Oh, it was the same on our end. They smashed us with naval fire. I just hope we're far enough away from the harbour out here.'

Rankin slapped him on the back and continued to talk as he looked over his shoulder at the others that still clambered out of the truck. 'With that we should be fine. I just hope the fuckers are starting to run out of tanks—' He stopped halfway through his sentence.

He froze as he watched the gargantuan shape emerge from the back of the truck. The Internationals suspension groaned slightly as his weight left the tray. In the early morning light, it was hard to see his face, but his size struck him. Then the big man turned and pulled a strange looking old rifle from the back and Rankin snapped.

His face twisted in fear and anger as he clutched the SLR in Morgan's hands. The kid was shocked by the outburst in anger, but held onto his rifle.

'Give it to me!' Rankin snarled as he lashed out and struck Morgan in the jaw. The kid went down and Rankin snatched the SLR. He brought it up and trained the sights on his target. 'You motherfucker.' He swore as he tensed on the trigger. The silhouette of the Wolf of Tamworth turned to him, but the old rifle did not come up to meet him. Rankin felt something hit him on his right and the SLR in his hands bucked as the shot echoed through the quiet morning.

Morgan had regained his feet and had tried to take the SLR back. 'Don't! What are you doing?' The other men from the back of the truck turned and saw the commotion and there was a clatter as actions were racked and then Rankin had five other SLRs trained on him.

'What the...' He heard Travers say and out of his peripherals he saw his friend duck behind the Ford.

'Fuck off!' Rankin snarled as he threw Morgan off him again and brought the SLR up once more.

'Stop, don't shoot!' someone called.

'Put it down!' another shrieked.

Rankin felt a hand on his shoulder and heard Caycho say into his ear. 'Man, what the fuck are you doing?'

'He can't be here!' Rankin yelled as he brandished the rifle at the giant. 'He'll kill all of us.'

'Bullshit,' one of the newcomers yelled.

'He saved all of us!' Morgan shrieked as he tried to get to his feet once more.

'We couldn't stop him!' Rankin yelled hysterically. 'Me, my friend and fifty fucking Chinese couldn't stop him!'

'This bastard's insane,' another newcomer remarked.

'He's fine now but if he clicks, if…' Rankin shook his head as he remembered the eyes change from the lifeless black pits to the sad brown. He remembered the dark lines that etched his veins as they ran down his face and his neck. 'If his eyes go black then that's it, you can't stop him. We have to kill him now, otherwise we'll all die!'

The whole time, the giant stood in the shadows, motionless. Rankin knew his eyes were fixed on him but he didn't speak, he didn't move. He didn't try to defend himself or run, he just stood there.

'We went to help you get your brother, man!' Rankin yelled at him. 'The little boy I saw in the jail, Michael! Then you tried to fucking kill us again.'

The light grew around them. As things became more visible, he saw the features in Morgan's face better, saw how young he really was. The kid was lucky to be sixteen and he went to Deception Bay? This country was going to shit. Rankin could now see part of the giant's face, he saw the scarred side of his face, the distortion in his flesh. The dull grey metal of the rifle in his hands, the weapon that looked like it was from another time. He could see all of this, but he couldn't see his eyes.

'I've got to do it, man. I've got to,' Rankin murmured almost in tears.

'Put it down. Last warning!'

'Come on man, please, we don't want to do this.'

'You don't understand.' Rankin's finger tightened on the trigger.

'What the fuck is going on!' The voice ripped through the air. 'Turn those fucking lights off? What is everyone shouting over? If there's been another fight over some trivial bullshit, I swear I'll shoot the fucker who started it!' Caitlin stormed into sight and stopped when he saw the situation. 'You put those rifles down right now,' he growled. The anger seemed to swell inside of him. 'You lower them right now or I'll throw you all in the back of this piece of shit,' he kicked the tyre of the truck 'and send you to the fucking Chinese with bows on your head and handcuffed.'

The look in the newcomer's eyes said it all. They didn't want to get into trouble, but they didn't want to lower their rifles while Rankin still held his high. Some of the barrels dipped then returned.

'I'll put signs on your asses saying insert coins here for a good time. I'll fucking shoot you where you stand.' Caitlin brought out his own pistol.

No one moved. Not a barrel dropped, not a word was spoken. Rankin's eyes remained fixed on the Wolf's face. With the growing light, more and more of his face was visible. He felt the muzzle of Caitlin's pistol touch his head. 'Son, I didn't save you from that tank to shoot you, but I will if you don't lower your weapon, so help me God.'

Rankin's face screwed up. He was out of options, not that he'd ever had many. He lowered the SLR and gave it back to Morgan. There was an almost audible sound of relief in the air as everyone lowered their weapons and shifted on the spot.

'What the fuck, man?' one of them said. 'We're supposed to be on the same side.'

The looks they all gave him were of disgust and mistrust. In all honesty, he couldn't blame them. He looked at the giant and brown eyes stared back at him. He couldn't say for sure the mix of emotions that lay behind their surface, but there was no anger, that much he knew.

'All you newcomers, go down the end of the road and rest up. You've had a long journey to get here and the shit's about to hit the fan,' Caitlin said, then he turned back to Rankin. 'You three, get that Ford off the road and then do the same for yourselves. The sun's almost up, we don't need to let these fuckers see more than they have to.'

With that, the captain turned and stormed off down the road, stopping only to yell at the International's driver again. The newcomers turned and followed suit. Each of them shot Rankin another mistrustful look as they went. Then only the Wolf remained. He still hadn't moved. For some time, the two men stood there and eyed each other as if in wait for one or the other to move. As if Rankin had a fighting chance, the Wolf was armed and Rankin was not.

Rankin heard Travers and Caycho move behind him.

Caycho said, 'Come on man, let's move this piece of shit.'

Rankin didn't break his eye contact. 'Yeah,' he said, 'let's do that.' He turned his back on the giant.

The three men returned to pushing the car. Rankin was sure the brakes had seized now because one wheel at least dragged rather than rolled across the earth. They heaved and strained. 'Fuckin' piece of shit!' Rankin muttered.

Suddenly, it was as if the car had become a third of the weight of what it was. The tyre still dragged, but it was like it was under its own power. Rankin looked up and paused halfway through mid-push. Travers was gone and next to him the man he'd almost shot pushed the Ford with him.

Rankin opened his mouth to say something.

'Push the fucking car,' the Wolf said to him. 'I'm not going to do it all for you.'

JACK

*'Hangman, hangman, hold it a little while.
I think I can see my brother coming.'*

Led Zeppelin – *Gallows Pole* (1970)

The wavering flame of the lighter flickered before his face. Lines of darkness swirled through the shades that were cast upon the walls to his sides. Jack let the tip of his cigarette waver dangerously yet tantalisingly close to the heat. Even in the darkness he could see the very end of the paper begin to singe and wrinkle under the heat. Flame was the end of everything, it left nothing behind but the wasted ash of remains. Yet for the cigarette that was pressed between his lips it was the beginning. Its sole purpose in its own creation was to be lit and burned, worth nothing more at the end of its course than shit on the ground.

He snapped the lighter closed as he took his first drag. The shades' dancing patterns were cut from the walls in an instant. Exhaling, he watched as the smoke listed its way through the air in the remains of the house. Was his life bound to follow the same course? The 'other' was like a fire running through the scrub, the more it burned, the less remained. Yet each time Jack felt him come forward was like the first drag of a cigarette. He felt strong, he felt untouchable, until he felt nothing at all. As he flicked the butt and he watched a stem of ash crash to the floor below him, he thought about the parts of himself that he had already lost. His home, his work and parents. His brother.

He went to take another drag and paused. His eyes strained in the darkness as he concentrated on the tip of the cigarette and saw that his hand had picked up the slightest of trembles. Jack continued to watch the jagged line of smoke at its base. A scowl spread over his face and he clenched his fist. The cigarette twisted and broke under his power and the cherry bit at his flesh as if it was dying bite from a mortally wounded animal. He discarded the broken remains and rose to his feet.

Around him, people raised their heads to look at him. The men that had first raised their rifles to defend themselves from him, had raised them in his defence. They hung about him like a small dog. They told him jokes, they asked him questions, the one who smoked continuously offered him cigarettes. Apart from Morgan, who hung around him like a bad smell, Jack didn't know any of their names, nor did he care for them. They spoke to him and looked up to him as if he was their friend, while Jack barely even noticed that they existed.

He walked through the room they had been tasked to demolish, his foot falls echoing through the cavernous hole in the rear of the structure. The furniture had been cast through the hole they had created through to the back yard, then other men had come along to collect it. In ten minutes, there was to be a briefing, where the men that thought they were in charge, told them the way it was. In the low light of the early evening, he could already see men from other work zones as they moved to the courtyard. Jack reached into his pocket and brought out his packet of cigarettes. He pulled one from the packet and examined it. As he finally placed the butt in his mouth and lit it, he thought to himself that in the end, if nothing but ash remained of his body, it would be for the best.

His tag along buddies followed him all the way to the courtyard. A few of them asked him more questions, some of them about the Browning, others asked about who he was and where he came from.

Jack never answered them.

The Browning was what it was. It hung at his side and seemed older than the earth itself. No word that Jack spoke could describe it or the burden that had come with it. The questions about himself only brought pain and with each further prod and poke they gave him, he felt the anger swell inside of him.

To see the remnants of what was supposed to be the Australian army was pathetic. Dirty men stood around the courtyard as they smoked, none of them were armed. Dirt covered the flesh that was exposed. The whites of their eyes stood out from the darkness. Their demeanour was reflected in how they looked; the men did not move with vigour or purpose, they milled about like a child that had been bullied into a corner.

Then there was the one who had tried to kill him. Jack picked him easily from a group that stood some twenty feet from the rear brick steps. Jack saw him through his cigarette smoke. The man's eyes never left him while he smoked. His head was leaned forward as he looked up at Jack while he sneered. Jack held the eye contact for some time until a voice from the top of the brick steps drew everyone's attention.

'Men,' the officer who had broken up the stand-off called. 'You have been working your hands to the bone for as many nights now and for what you might ask?' He took a pause. 'A Dingo is described as a cowardly predator. They will run from men on sight, they will never stand to face men in the open. I'm sure right now the Chinese that have beaten us back mile by mile, inch by inch, have that same impression of us.' He began to descend the steps as he looked out at the battered remains of the men that stood in the courtyard.

'But have any of you ever seen a Dingo when he is cornered?' He asked as he held his hands out in question. 'They become ferocious when forced into a corner. Their back hackles, they bare their teeth and they will fight to the death if they need to. Right now, we are that Dingo. We are what remains of the Australian Defence Force. Sure, there aren't as many of us as there once was.' He placed a hand on the shoulder of a man who knelt with his head down. 'We have all lost friends to these mongrels, but we fight for all of them now. From all reports, our foreign adversaries will be in our sights at dawn.' The men's ears pricked at this like dogs. Jack scowled as he saw men begin to talk amongst each other.

'Now, now hear me out.' The officer quelled the crowd before him. 'I know it's a daunting prospect, but I assure you our reinforcements have already left Melbourne.'

'Bullshit!' a voice called from the crowd.

Jack saw a flash of anger cross the officer's face, then as soon as it appeared, it vanished.

'I swear on my life,' the officer placed a hand over his heart. 'The New Zealand army with American support from those who were already in the Pacific are whisking their way towards us as we speak.'

'And what's going to stop the tanks from rolling right over us before they get here?' another man cried out.

'You are!' the officer yelled back. The irritation poured out through his voice now. 'Each one of you has a job to do and by Christ, if you do it, then we will hold these bastards. You've all seen the gauntlet we have been creating, have you not? You've all seen that my... *our* plan is coming to fruition. Now you need to play your part.'

Jack's brow furrowed at this. As he looked around, he saw men nod their heads. Clear recognition was in their eyes about what this officer was talking about. Jack had no sense of plan; he had been told to clear that house with his small band of followers and tear a hole in the back of it. He looked at his followers. From the looks on their faces, they had little idea as well. Jack returned his eyes to the young fighter, but he was gone, as were his two friends.

'There are only a few seeds left to sow in this whole situation, so keep your heads.' The officer continued, 'We all know our place in the gauntlet and now I need twenty volunteers. These men will be the make or break of this whole operation.' Men began to step forward.

'Stop,' he commanded as he held out his hands. 'You'll want to hear what you are volunteering for.' The men fell back in line, sheepish expressions plastered across their faces.

'These twenty men will be the bait. We have the gauntlet, we have the murder holes, the fox holes, we have even blocked all the exits from the street. Now we need to ensure that their men come down that street. The twenty that volunteer will ambush the Chinese before their lines hit our street. You will draw them down to our position and fall back into line. If you get into trouble, we will not be able to help you.'

'What if they have tanks again?' another man called.

The officer looked out at them. 'The force concerning us has three remaining tanks. Of that, I am sure.' Men began to murmur amongst themselves again and the officer held up his hands to silence them. 'We need the tanks to come down the gauntlet as well.'

The crowd erupted in a mass of swears, hollers, and shouts of the soldiers dissent. The officer once more held his hands up but this time his actions did not quell the uproar.

'Okay. Okay,' he tried, but still nothing cut them out.

'We're all going to die!' one man cried.

'He's trying to kill us!' another shouted. Men began to get to their feet. The anger in their eyes rested on their foundation of fear.

A shot rang out. It echoed through the evening air as the shouts and grumbles diminished.

'I... *We*,' The officer corrected himself again while smoke listed from the pistol in his hand, 'have a plan for the tanks. The entire invasion has been based around their use of tanks, so did you think

I would forget them?'

Jack noticed that he didn't correct his referral to himself this time. He wondered if this low-ranking officer was the last of the officers to remain.

'You all need to calm down,' the officer continued. 'You all have your duties; you know your places. Those of you on the flanks hold them at all cost. Those of you who are bravely volunteering assemble at the gates to the highway.' He pointed to a steel cyclone fence that allowed access to a road that wound off into the distance. 'The rest of you head straight to arm up and then finish your jobs and get ready.'

Men started to head off and Jack turned to his followers. They all looked up to him, confusion and fear in their eyes.

'The men who arrived yesterday from the north coast, I need to see you,' the officer called out over the commotion of men moving.

'That's us, isn't it?' the smoker remarked to the others.

'Who else could it be?' Morgan replied.

They moved towards where they had last seen the officer through the sea of dirty men. Jack, standing two feet taller than the next tallest man, could see easily. As he pushed through the crowd, he saw men begin to assemble over at the cyclone fence. One of the men that stood there was his nemesis. Once more, their eyes locked and once more the other man stared at him through the smoke of his cigarette.

Jack spat and continued. The officer nodded when he saw them approach him.

'Good, you're here. I have a job for you.'

'Job?' Morgan enquired.

'Everyone else has theirs, except for you lot.' The officer checked some notes on a piece of paper, he spoke as if he wasn't paying attention to them. He looked back up, as if he was seeing them for the first time and then said, 'Follow me.'

The officer led them out of the courtyard through the bustling men. Many stopped to ask the officer a question, but he quickly sent them on their way with a brisk, 'Do what you're told and you'll be fine.'

'We need you boys for a special job. To tell you the truth, I picked you lot due to the size of your friend here.' He gestured at Jack.

The officer led them amongst the few trucks that remained from the blockade construction and as he rounded the front of one, he held his hands up and said, 'Here she is.'

Jack rounded the corner and took a back step. His height meant his line of sight was aligned straight down the barrel of a large artillery piece. The cannon sat on rubber wheels, one of which was flat. Specks of rust coated the barrel in odd spots that lead up to the large muzzle brake.

'Isn't she a beauty?' the officer remarked as he ran his fingers down the long barrel. 'It's an L118 light cannon. I think she will do fine against the enemy tanks.'

'That's all well and good sir,' The smoker remarked. 'I'm sure it would and all, but we aren't trained on those pieces. We couldn't aim it.'

The officer smiled at him. 'Son, aiming isn't going to be a large part of it. I'm sure you won't miss at twenty feet.'

The men looked at each other, even Jack was taken aback by this remark. He stepped forward. 'Twenty feet? Listen, I'm not part of your assholes' army here, so don't just volunteer me for anything you wish.'

The officer didn't flinch, he just looked up at him and continued to smile. 'You know the hole I had you tear in that house?' He asked them as he looked from Jack to the rest of them and then back again. He seemed to ignore Jack's statement altogether. 'You boys are going to haul this old girl right through there and pop those tanks like balloons as they trundle past.' As he spoke the word *pop*, he plucked at the air in front of his face as if he had a needle in his hand.

Jack squinted at him; he was unsure of the mental stability of the officer altogether. He shook his head as the officer continued and felt the anger inside of him at how everyone just seemed to ignore him as of late.

The officer slapped his hand on the barrel as he continued to smile and said, 'Now follow me and I'll show you where the shells are. We don't have many, so as I said, you won't miss, will you?' At this, he turned back and looked at them with a stern look.

'No... No sir,' Morgan remarked.

'That's what I like to hear.'

He led them to a tent across the courtyard. Men still bustled all around as they collected their rifles and stuffed magazines into their pockets. Jack shifted the Browning on his shoulder, his mouth started to run dry. When he had awoken in the truck, he had only a few magazines of ammunition left to him. All of his supply was lost to him. Instead, the empty metal shells of the magazines he had rattled in his pockets as he walked. Perhaps when he ran out of ammunition, he would discard it. Perhaps he would be free of his burden. He wasn't an expert on firearms, but he knew the casings that the Browning took were almost a half-inch longer than those of the army's rifles.

He pulled a magazine from his pocket and popped one of the long cases free. He held it in his hand as he continued into the tent and followed as the men parted to make way for the officer. The captain led them to the rear of the tent, where he kicked a crate.

'There you go boys, there's your arsenal.'

Jack peered into the crate. Amongst bundles of straw that stuck out at odd angles were two enormous artillery shells. He looked at the officer. 'I thought you said there were three tanks.'

Once more the officer smiled up at him; Jack hated the look in his eyes. The officer looked straight through him. 'Two burning tanks are better than three rolling.'

The only thing Jack could do was scowl.

'Okay!' The officer clapped his hands. 'You, my large friend, take the shells to the house and come back. While you're doing that, I'll teach these fine young men how to work the fine lady.'

Jack held the Browning's shell casing in front of the officer's eyes. 'I need these as well.'

The smile vanished from the officer's face and his brow furrowed as he took the shell from Jacks finger's and rolled it about in his hands.

'American?' he asked. Jack didn't reply. 'Yeah, American alright.' He looked at the Browning that hung on Jack's shoulder. 'No doubt they all take the same?' Once more Jack did not reply to him, just snatched the round back out of the officer's hand and reinserted it into its magazine.

The officer scratched his chin and pointed to a corner of the tent. 'Look over there, in our final supply drop they sent us some old shit that the Americans took back of the South Vietnamese. You may be lucky.' He slapped Jack on the shoulder and the odd smile returned to his face. 'Now don't take too long. We needed that cannon in that house five minutes ago.'

His followers exited the tent along with the officer, and left Jack alone. Outside of the tent, he heard the soldier who handed out rifles, repeat himself over and over again. 'SLR, five mags. SLR, five mags.'

Jack leaned the Browning against a shelf that was crammed with food rations and walked over to the dusty crates that the officer had pointed out.

Property of U.S. Govt.: The words were painted across the tops of all the crates. Jack broke them open with his hands, the timber and the nails that clamped them down giving way under his strength. He pulled old rifles from the crate, all of which he was sure told their own story, and threw them to the side. Crate after crate contained only the same full stocked rifles until finally, he found a smaller crate. Already badly damaged, he broke into it easily enough and finally he found what he was after. Two green tins, strapped with metal bracing. The familiar words printed on their side: U.S. 30 CAL. M1 BALL.

Jack paused when he saw it, then rushed to open them. He was so engrossed as he ran his hands through the sea of the brightly shining brass casings that he didn't hear the footsteps behind him.

'I need to talk to you.'

Jack snapped his head around. Even though he was crouched over the metal tin, he was still the same height as the man he had once fought in the arena.

'Fuck off,' he grumbled as he returned to the tin.

'Fuck off nothing. You've got to fill me in on what the fuck is going on with you. You owe me that much.'

Jack's temper snapped, he whirled around and grabbed the smaller man by the throat. 'I don't owe you a damned thing!' he roared in his face.

The fighter squirmed in his grip. 'You fucker!' he groaned as he struggled to breathe. 'I should've shot you.'

'You should have,' Jack growled. 'You would have done me a favour, but you didn't.' Jack lifted him from the ground as his legs flailed. 'Look at my eyes!' He roared again into his face as he shook him.

Bloodshot as they were, Jack saw the man open his eyes as he struggled. They made eye contact and held it.

'You can see that it's me. If it wasn't, you would already be dead. So, either kill me or don't, I couldn't give a shit, but you know what happens if 'he' comes forward. So, do us both a favour and stay out of my fucking way until you pony up the balls to do something.' Jack let him go and he collapsed at his feet.

Jack turned back to the tins of ammunition, he picked it up and placed it in the crate next to the two artillery shells. He hoisted the Browning onto his shoulder and heaved up the crate and went to leave the tent. Just as he reached the exit, a hand grasped his ankle. Jack stopped and turned back to the soldier who still struggled to regain his breath.

'If you feel... yourself going...' he gasped. 'If you think it's going to happen. Leave,' he said to him. 'I can't stop you, I couldn't stop you in Tamworth and I can't stop you now but you can't kill those men out there.' He let go of Jack's ankle and sat up. 'If you do, then we're all fucked. Do it for your brother, man.'

Jack wanted to get angry at his mention of Michael. He wanted to feel like he had been provoked into killing him, but he felt nothing. Even the other's voice that egged him on, which now had seemed to mould itself into his own thoughts, didn't do anything to him. The man at his feet was just another broken soldier, sitting there in defeat. Jack walked away.

He spent the time it took him to drop the artillery shells in thought. What would happen if he left? He thought about surviving and what it meant. He didn't know what he wanted anymore. It had barely been a week since he had tried to kill himself. Now he had travelled south with a band of soldiers, that fled an army and he was a part of it. Time flowed over him like the drops of rain into an overflowing cup. He figured he would fight, figured he would stay. If he died in the fighting, then so be it. If he didn't, then he would think about it then and only then.

He worked his way through the backyards of houses and dropped the artillery shells on the floor of the structure they had partially demolished. The Browning clunked heavily as he let it fall to the ground. He had carried the damn thing so far, if only he had never found it. For the first time since he had found the rifle, he left it behind, unprotected. There was no wall to hide it in, there was no blanket to wrap it in. He needed his whole body and it couldn't come with him. As he walked away from it, he shuddered at the emptiness it left inside of him, at how odd it felt not to have its weight at his side.

When he arrived at the compound, his followers were in practise of the operation of the cannon's breech. The officer paced back and forth impatiently as he watched them, correcting them when he felt they had made a mistake. When he saw Jack, he held his hands in the air. The smile was now gone from his face.

'About time.' He urged Jack to hurry up and continued to rant. 'Get the cannon into that house and boys remember what I told you. Not a shot is to come from that house until the first tank drives past the living room window. Then you let them have it.' He turned to Jack and pointed at him. 'Did you find ammunition for your rifle?'

Jack nodded.

'Good,' he snapped. 'Don't use it until that cannon has fired, you hear me? Not a single damned shot.' He looked around and lowered his voice so that no one else could hear him. 'If we lose that cannon, then we're all fucked. So, listen to me when I tell you this.'

He emphasised every word: 'Do. Not. Fire. A damned shot!'

CHRIS

*'Everywhere I look, I see your eyes.
There ain't a woman who comes close to you.
Come on baby, dry your eyes.'*

The Rolling Stones – *Angie* (1973)

All the lies overcame him. Everything he had worked for and hoped for, meant nothing. Every damned dream that he had, every hint of her. His ambitions and his resolve, poured out in front of his eyes like a glass of water to a man dying of thirst.

He had nothing left, nothing to spew, yet still his pain sat in his throat, to choke and suffocate him. The more he tried to move past it, the more it drained his strength, the more he faded. He had tried for two days to move out of that town, he had driven Pestilence, now as she rolled on her spare, to the boundary and back and had found himself sitting only to stare at the smouldering remains of the tank that had almost taken his life. Something about this town didn't want him to leave and he found that all he could do was remember.

It is said that remembering is the hardest thing that someone can ever do, and for Chris this was an understatement. He had brought himself to the bedroom door countless times, had put his damned hands on the gleaming knob. So many times, he had tried to see what had happened in that room, but now as he sat there and his life flowed out from the hole in his side, he remembered.

His hands shook as he brought the pistol up and rested its muzzle against his temple. He closed his eyes and sobbed as in his memory he walked to the bedroom door and the pressure of the pistol's muzzle pressed harder into his temple. His eyes opened, but they were already dead to the world. The colour they had once shown was gone, the vibrant blue replaced by the grey and lifeless. The bristles of his beard were now completely white and he was tired, just so tired of the lies. His finger tensed as he squeezed and he waited for the end as he remembered.

His breath was hot in his chest. It felt like an eternity that he had stood at this bedroom door as he dug for the strength within him just to turn the gleaming brass knob. From the other side of the threshold, he heard movement. The swish of a foot over the shag pile rug, the sound of fabric on floorboards but no voices. The brass warmed in his hands and he knew that when he took his palm away the residue of its print would stand out from his sweat.

Once more, he took another breath, as if to prepare himself. He thought about the silence, the calm stillness of the house. Although it had been plunged into chaos at some point before, the state it was in now was like the calm before the storm. It was too quiet; nothing felt right. There was more movement from beyond the threshold and the sound of a voice, a low whisper. He couldn't tell if it was from a man or a woman. Chris furrowed his brow, took a deep breath and turned the gleaming brass door knob.

The door swung open silently on its well-oiled hinges. Every inch it travelled revealed more of the room and with each inch his stomach tore and twisted. The room that was once inviting, warm and comfortable, now felt cold and hostile as he took his first step. He moved slowly and quietly, yet it wouldn't have mattered as the men that stood before him were preoccupied. Two men stood at the foot of his bed. One stood proud with his arms crossed while the other leaned on the timber frame with an elbow. Both looked down at the ground. Chris tried to see past them, but whatever it was that held their attention was behind the bed. He heard the swish again of movement over the shagpile and a soft grunt.

He continued into their room. Every fibre of his being burned with the feeling of violation. He repositioned his grip on the bayonet and continued. Slowly, softly, he advanced. His chest felt tight with the shallowness of his breath. Still, he moved on, still he neared the backs of the two men that stood before him. Soon they would feel the heat of his breath on the backs of their necks.

The further he penetrated into the room; a figure began to appear behind the bed. A shoulder at first, then an arched back. The jet black hair of a man that was on his hands and knees, as he moved in odd sharp movements. Chris moved closer; he saw the sweat stained olive drab of the man's shirt.

Another step closer. The white skin of his bare ass shone out in the dark room in stark contrast.

Another step. The Chinese soldier to his right now blocked his view and something had spilled over the floor as each step he took his feet seemed to bind and grab with a stickiness.

He took another step, the half-naked soldier on the floor moved his ass back and forth, the breath caught in Chris' throat and he took a final step forward to stand almost between the two waiting soldiers.

Angie's face was pale. Her blouse had been torn down and with each movement from the soldier who had mounted her, her bare breasts jiggled. Red streaks of blood lined her chest and were spread across her.

Still, Chris saw the burning red hand print that was emblazoned on her flesh. Although her skin had always been pale (she was never one to tan), now it seemed wrong. There was a greyness in her, her usual beauty was gone. Her red lips were slightly parted and Chris saw that a strand of her long golden hair was caught in her gape. Her eyes were open and unblinking.

It felt like an eternity that he stood there. Each second that passed, the paler she seemed to get, the more the slash at her throat stood out to him. Finally, Chris broke.

Wordlessly, he rammed the bayonet through the back of the man to his left. He didn't make a sound and over the commotion at their feet, the sound as steel pushed through flesh, didn't draw attention. Chris still stared at her as he did it. Slowly, he turned his head to look away, but it was hard. In his peripheral, he saw the impaled soldier look down to the steel that had sprouted from his chest. Chris blinked and turned to him. The skewered soldier's mouth was open in disbelief while a thin line of blood trickled down from his lips. Chris felt the weight of the man come through the blade as his legs started to give out. He moved slightly and the soldier to his right turned his head.

Chris watched as the soldier casually turned to look at his comrade. He glanced, then began to turn away when he jumped. His spasm caused his leg to shoot out and he kicked the third soldier who grunted something guttural at the intrusion. By now, the life had left the soldier Chris had skewered and he fully supported his weight with the small handle of the sword bayonet. Slowly, he tilted the blade downward and as the cries of surprise filled the room, the lifeless body slid from the blade and collapsed to the ground.

The soldier to his right began to back away as he screamed, his eyes pleaded as he held his hands out in front of his face. Chris brought the blade across in a wild slash as he himself began to scream. There was a loud slap as steel bit into bone and flesh and the soldier fell backwards over the back of the man on the floor. Chris continued to scream as he moved forward. The look of horror and surprise on the final soldier's face as he turned to look over his shoulder burned in his mind.

Again and again he brought the blade down, as he slashed and hacked, while he screamed a bloody fury with each strike.

He stabbed into one of their guts, and the smell of shit filled the room. Flashes of flesh torn and ripped from bone flashed in his mind. In his rage and his frustration, he screamed in their faces as he pushed the steel into them. He stood up and kicked down on their faces as he spat insults at them. Then he fell on them again to punch, stab and tear.

The one who still had his pants around his ankles crawled for the door. There was no breath left in him to scream and only Chris could be heard in the small unforgiving room.

Their blood mixed with hers intertwining in the soft fabric of the shag pile rug and that enraged him even further. What was their blood to mix with that as pure as hers? Chris rushed forward and drove the blade up his ass. The half-naked soldier arched his back as he gasped in pain. His face was contorted as he stared up at the ceiling and his body spasmed. Chris climbed to his feet and drove his foot into the back of the man's head, and sent his face crashing to the floor boards. He straddled him, the blade of the bayonet still wedged deep up inside his abdomen, and brought his fists down into the back of his head.

His voice broke and his hands were white-hot. Still, he pounded and broke the being under him. He sat up, reached behind him and tore the blade from his asshole. He brought the lug of its pummel down in the centre of his spine and the body spasmed underneath him. He brought it down again on the back of his skull and he heard a loud crack, but it still wasn't enough. Howling, he forced the tip of the blade through the crack in the man's skull with one hand while he punched the side of his face with the other. He slammed his knee down on his neck and bent the blade back on itself. The steel bent, then twanged, as the shattered skull burst open and flesh and brain were splattered over the drywall and floor.

It still wasn't enough. Chris stood and slammed the sole of his foot down on the gaping hole in the back of his head again, and again. Each time the sounds as bone cracked and splintered filled his head, but it was never going to be enough, never.

Somewhere in his head, he heard the sound of rushed footfalls as they pounded the boards in the living room. He didn't care. He continued to scream, fight, kill, and tear until he saw the soldier burst into the room.

Chris looked up at him. He saw the horror in the newcomer's face as he looked from the blood and brain splattered Australian to the destroyed bodies of his brothers in arms. Then he turned and ran.

Chris followed him, panting as his boots slapped the floorboards in pursuit. The newcomer cried as he ran and he stumbled over most everything as he tried to escape Chris. They made it to the front porch before Chris slammed into the back of him and they tumbled down the stairs together. They landed in a hot mess on the gravel and Chris felt the small stones bite into his face and his arms, but he didn't care. He moved on top of the newcomer, who still screamed and reached for something on his chest. Chris raised the blade and prepared to bring it down.

'Beautiful…. Family…'

Something made him pause in his strike as the soldier beneath him held a photograph up to him.

'Beautiful…'

Chris saw the innocent faces of the four children. All of them looked the same, apart from their hair. One child had her jet black hair tied into pigtails which shot out at either side of her head as she smiled a grin of mostly missing baby teeth. The rest were boys who stood with stiff backs and beaming faces. A slender woman stood to the left, draped in a silk gown. Her expressionless face was beautiful.

'Family...'

Chris looked back down at the newcomer, the blade of his bayonet still positioned above his chest. Again, the soldier on his back tried to push the photo into Chris' face and he pushed it away in anger. He raised the blade again and roared as he brought his fist down to slam into the soldier's forehead. There was a solid clap as his head rocked back into the gravel and he lay there unconscious.

The air seemed so heavy in his lungs that he thought it was going to suffocate him as he regained his feet. His body was exhausted and tears cut clean rivers through the grime on his face. The bayonet fell from his hands as he crunched his way across the gravel. Pestilence sat there, her eyes washed accusingly over him. It was all his fault. A groan escaped his mouth as he walked into his shed, his shoulders slumped while his back waned. He reached under the rim of his work bench and grabbed the two-gallon fuel container; the fuel sloshed around as he briskly brought it out from the darkness.

The smell of fuel cut through the air. His nose ran, encouraged by the rivulets that his eyes produced. He carried the open container back into the house. As he staggered, fuel slopped over the brim of its spout and spattered over the floorboards. As he went, something clung annoyingly to his foot and slapped the hardwood boards with each second step.

He stopped. The photograph of the soldier's family was stuck to the blood and gravel that caked the soles of his boots. He plucked it and briefly looked at the faces again. Most of them now were covered by the blood and dirt, he looked at the expressionless face of the lady, then he screwed up his face in anger and scrunched the photo in his hand and continued to his bedroom. The photograph fell to ground behind him and slowly began to unravel.

Chris broke down again when he entered his bedroom. The fuel cannister fell from his hands and clattered to the ground, its contents lapped out and mixed with the blood and guts that covered the floor. He fell to his knees at her side and wept. Sobs escaped his mouth as he dragged her weight up onto him and pulled at her torn blouse to cover her chest. He howled as he wept for her and held her close to him. He pulled his handkerchief from his pocket and dabbed at the blood spots on her face. The tears continued to wet his cheeks and hers as they dripped from his face as he sat there with her for a long time. Cradling her body as he told her it would be okay. His fingers ran along the slash of her throat as his tears were renewed. Then he ran his fingers through her long golden locks but his dirty, grimy hands caught in the knots.

His old body strained as he lifted her from the ground. As he placed her on their bed, his tears dampened what remained of her clothes. He settled her in the beds centre and took care in positioning the pillows under her hair. Then he ran his fingers down her face for the last time and closed her beautiful eyes. As he pulled the comforter over her, he paused before he covered her face.

'I...' he sobbed, 'I can't do this by myself...'

He slid the comforter over her face and then he broke down for the last time at her bedside. He clutched at her arm and held it to his face.

'Wait for me.' He cried, then he stood and left the room.

He was faint and struggled to stand as he staggered down the corridor. The smell of fuel washed through his head and the world spun around. He collapsed in the lounge room and lay there for some time. When he tried to stand, he fell again and his hand touched something. Through the tears that blurred his vision he saw it was the book she was reading: Of Mice and Men. He clutched at it and held it to his chest as he slowly gained his feet. He stumbled into the kitchen and violently opened drawers, spilling most of their contents onto the ground.

Finally, he found a box of matches and together with the book, he headed back into the hallway. He stood there, and looked at the door to his bedroom, the doorway to broken dreams. He struck a match, but his hands shook too much and he snapped the stem instead. His whole body trembled as he struck another.

The smell of sulphur suffocated him as he held the flame to the pages of her book. The pages curled at first, then blackened. He lightly fluttered the pages open and they finally caught alight. He let the match fall to the floor and lobbed the burning book through the doorway. The petrol ignited before the book even hit the ground with a mighty flump. The flames shot to the ceiling and cast yellow light down the hall as its flames flickered.

'I love you,' he whimpered, 'I'll always love you.' He turned and left his house, the house he had loved her in. He stumbled down the porch stairs and finally collapsed on the gravel and succumbed to his emotional and physical exhaustion.

The air in Pestilence was stifling. The wound at his side was a cancer that ate away at him. The final memory of her as she lay on their bed was too much. He closed his eyes and his hand began to tremble as he started to squeeze harder on the trigger. Harder and harder.

He screamed in anger, sorrow and pain as he slammed the butt of the pistol down on the steering wheel. It fired in the impact and the shot cut through the windscreen. It sent a spiral of cracks outward from its point of origin and he almost felt her react beneath him. He paused, then slammed the pistol down again and again on the dash while he screamed and cried out.

'What was it all for?' he shrieked through his tears. 'I couldn't fucking save her. I couldn't ever find her through any of this shit!' He held the pistol up in front of him and looked at the damage he had created on the dashboard of his second love. He threw it to the floor of the passenger footwell as he continued to cry. 'I couldn't even take my own life.'

He slumped over the steering wheel and sobbed. The dash felt warm under him, almost like it attempted to comfort him. Everything he had ever had was gone. Everything he had ever wanted from his life was finished. Nothing mattered now, he supposed it never had.

The bayonet sat bloody on the bench seat next to him. Pestilence's cab lay in tatters from the journey. Chris looked at his burned hands and wept. All of these wounds and all of these things that he had brought with him along the way, all of them may as well be packed up and swept away. For no matter how many times he swung the bayonet in anger or in sorrow, he could never cut the curtain that lay before her.

No matter how hard he drove Pestilence or how far she carried him, she could not drive the road that would take him to her. No matter how much pain he felt in his hands or his whole body, or how much he fought, he would never feel Angie's touch again.

He looked at the pistol once more as it lay still cocked on the floor of the cab. Why didn't he shoot himself? There was nothing left for him now. None of it could ever come to any good. Something made him look higher and he saw Pestilence's dashboard. Something had caved it in on the passenger side and he frowned. He knew it was there, but how did it happen?

'Rankin,' he muttered as he looked at the damage his friends body had created when they had rammed the personnel carrier all that time ago. 'Rankin,' he said the name again.

He had been his last friend. The one who had seen the truth, but had kept it to himself. He'd known she was gone but still he followed and had helped. Chris thought about his actions, he thought about everything he had done in his search for her. He had been through everything all to find her and for the hardest parts, Rankin had been by his side.

The starter motor whirred, the engine fired, coughed, then stalled. There was a pause as the fuel pumped whined and then bound up as the pressure built.

'Come on, baby,' he said to her as he turned the key. 'How about we have one more ride?'

The starter motor whirred, the engine caught and roared.

RANKIN

'Living is easy with eyes closed.
Misunderstanding all you see.
It's getting hard to be someone but it all works out.
It doesn't matter much to me.'

The Beatles – *Strawberry Fields Forever* (1967)

His head swirled in the commotion that surrounded him. Men struggled to his left as they pushed a vehicle to its desired position while others hurriedly shovelled road base and chunks of tar from a half complete fox hole dug in the main street.

When he had first seen this place from the air, it looked as though everyone had just gotten up and left it. Now it looked as though the war had already rolled through it. Cars lay crumpled together in some odd conglomerate that blocked avenues between houses. The road was torn to pieces, holes large enough to swallow six men across, cratered its midsection. The gloom of the night seemed to fill them as if it were drops of rain that formed a puddle. Darkness brimmed over and swelled, as if trying to swallow anything that fell beneath its depths. The houses were robbed of all their previous charm, windows either boarded up or covered by the furniture that once lay within. Murder holes were chipped through cladding, timber and brick, which made it look as though the structures were already shot to hell.

As he stood and waited for the rest of the voluntary squad, he watched the progress of the 'grand plan.' Caitlin spoke about this as if it was a plan that was conjured by a team of crack military strategists, but Rankin wasn't sure. Caitlin had constantly corrected himself from 'I' to 'we' and as each night turned into day and the captain called an end to the night's work, there seemed to be less of the man than the night before. The look in his eyes became more desperate; he laughed too loud at jokes that weren't remotely funny, and then overreacted at the slightest infringement. The pistol he had held to Rankin's head on two previous occasions, now seemed to live in his hand. He wielded it like the power of God, and Rankin figured it was only a matter of time before he either took his own life or that of one of his men.

Rankin watched as six men worked well together, shifting the powerless bulk of the Huey along four wooden logs. Almost Egyptian in their industriousness, the men rolled the Helicopter along its skids. When one log rolled out from under the skids, a man grabbed it and threw it back under the front. The M134 jostled on its mounts as the black hull rolled toward its final destination. The plan regarding the Huey had brought about some dissent. It was to remain grounded and when the situation became dire, the M134 would expel the remnants of its ammunition down the street, to allow enough time for the men who were pinned down to retreat.

The men, of course, wanted the bird in the air, to rain fire down on the Chinese as they approached. Rankin, who only ever felt safe back in Vietnam when he heard the rotors of 'The Back Dread,' likewise wished this could be so. However, Caitlin was adamant. Every ounce of fuel that was available to them was to be used in petrol bombs. Whatever round of 7.62 the M134 Gatling held within the helicopter would remain, while the rest of the reserves were to be used in the foot soldiers' SLRs and the few M60 machine guns. Although the power of the M134 could not be matched, it wasted far too many rounds and supply was low. The estimated five hundred rounds that still lay within its belt would allow roughly seven seconds of constant fire before the barrels would run dry. Seven seconds of blind chaotic hellfire that would fill the world with fire and metal. Seven seconds for the men to get back to the courtyard.

Rankin looked at the sky and his stomach sunk as he saw the first signs of dawn. Automatically with that anticipation, he needed to take a piss. He lit a cigarette and looked around at the other men; they all waited for Caitlin but he was nowhere to be seen.

'Fuck it,' Rankin mumbled as he lit a cigarette. 'We know what we're doing boys?' The others looked at him with doughy eyes. 'Come on. Let's go wind these fuckers up.' Rankin turned and began to walk up their gauntlet. He walked past the machine gun nests, the fox holes and countless turned over cars. Behind him, the others followed. Twenty men would walk out beyond the first defences and try to drag the enemy down the line of hell. Rankin doubted if any of them would return.

As they neared the first fox hole, he looked to his right. In the gloom of the early morning, it was hard to see the barrel of the cannon. The glass of the living room window remained intact and the curtains were partially drawn. Yet beyond the dust and the darkness, Rankin saw the outline of the enormous muzzle brake, pointing slightly downward to the street. Beside it, and almost as large, sat the Wolf of Tamworth. They made eye contact one last time before Rankin moved out of the street.

Rankin was left feeling that he would give anything to know what was going through the giant's mind at that point. He sat motionless as he stared out of the window, the barrel of his rifle raised up beside him. His eyes cut straight through Rankin's and bored holes into the earth behind him. He looked as though he was in a trance, yet no darkness surrounded his eyes.

As they neared the last few feet of what they knew to be safe land, men stood to watch them leave. Rankin felt as though he wanted to stop. Everything in his body screamed in warning about the danger that was to come, yet he continued to smoke as he took a final step over the threshold and into the land beyond the gauntlet.

JACK

*'I think you're gonna like it
I think you're gonna feel like you belong
A nocturnal vacation
Unnecessary sedation
You want to feel at home 'cause you belong.'*

Alice Cooper – *Welcome to my Nightmare* (1975)

'Do. Not. Fire. A damned shot!'

The words cut through Jack like a white-hot piece of steel. He didn't know why or what it was that ate away at him or more specifically the other that lay inside of him, but the words had affected him somehow. He felt as though he was living a nightmare, everything that happened in the past up to that point came forward and haunted him like the spirits of ghosts long past. Not even the Browning could comfort him, as no matter how many he saw, no matter how many came into the street, he couldn't do a damned thing.

The demon inside of him rolled around like a restless dreamer. Incoherent words and screams of pain drifted forward to Jack's consciousness. He felt the urge of need, as if he had to do something, but there was nothing to do. The more he thought about it, the more he realised that was the problem.

The artillery piece was positioned inside the living room. The weight of it and the strain that it had caused him were only aches below the flesh. Jack couldn't even remember moving the cannon into place, yet there it sat beside him. Like the rest of them, it lay in wait. It hoped, craved, needed someone to step up so that it could lay them down.

The words of the demon's mind rattled through to him again and again. More shouts and grunts of pain among the single words that rang clear. His irritation grew as the itching inside of his head reaching a boiling point and then surpassed it. The smoker came over to him and offered him a cigarette and it took everything that Jack had inside of him not to tear the man to pieces. Instead, he took the cigarette with a trembling hand and lit it.

He sat there for what seemed to him like decades; he smoked a cigarette that never ended while the demon inside of him rolled over and over in its own torment. Part of Jack wanted to know what was happening, the other part wished that whatever it was would kill it so he could be free of its wrath. Then a set of words came through as clear as if they were spoken straight into his ears.

'Do not fire a damned shot.' Those were exact words that the captain had spoken to him, yet another man's voice echoed them. Jack did not know who it was or why he heard those words again. He felt the sickness inside of him swell and even a drag on the cigarette made him want to hurl up everything. He stared down at his free hand and clenched his fist hard; he concentrated solely on that task, yet the feeling didn't diminish.

His chest grew tight, his vision swirled as with each moment he grew more anxious. His breaths became shallow and he started to fidget. Sweat ran down his face and his arms. The wound to his cheek and his chest, which was now little more than a partial scab, burned like the infection had come back all at once. Finally, he couldn't take it anymore. Inside of himself, he reached out to the demon that struggled inside and he felt the claws latch onto him. Not like before. They didn't pull or try to drag him from consciousness, but they clutched onto him the way a fearful child clutches to their parent during their first thunder storm.

He wanted to know. He wanted to learn why this had happened to him. Why it had fought for control of him the moment he racked back the cocking handle on that rifle. He needed to know. Although his eyes were open, he could no longer see what happened beyond their glassy gaze. He stood face to face with a man in his thirties. His chest was broad and his shoulders square. The uniform he wore was a dark green like those of men he had seen in his previous visions. His hair was short like his father's and his eyes were sunk back into their sockets. A single dog tag hung around his neck, the identifier taken along with his life long gone.

Jack felt the hate inside of him grow at the sight of the one who had done everything to him. What angered him more was that he looked too human. For what he did and the control that he had, he couldn't be. He looked like anyone else. Jack wanted to throttle him, he wanted to tear him limb from limb, but he couldn't move. All he could do was watch.

They were back in the jungle. The Americans that surrounded him looked as though they were protecting him. The formation of the men held lines against all angles, yet the dense trees shadowed everything beyond them. The Browning was eager in his hands, yet he couldn't use it. He was not allowed for some reason. Something was stopping him. Jack strained his thoughts to try and understand as more Americans moved up beside him. Slowly he started to understand things; they started to come to him like he had always known it.

Visions snapped in his mind like he had forgotten them and had all come flooding back at once. The man's name was Oscar Weir.

He was born in 1913. He was raised in Boston and enlisted after Pearl Harbour. Jack saw visions of all of this. He saw a child playing in the street, he saw the house he had grown up in, he saw the girl he had first kissed.

He saw a vision as he boarded a ship named Phoenix and he knew that was headed to the South Pacific. He saw the Browning, the first time it had ever touched the man's hands, it looked as new as the day it was made. Then he saw the death, the men emit screams of pain in their death throes. The Browning fired over and over, while the heat of it swallowed everything. The roar of its power deafened those that faced it. Then the fighting was over. They rebuilt and survived and kept moving.

Then it happened. An American officer sat with his hands folded in his lap. The jungle surrounded them and they whispered as they spoke. Jack had the feeling that this man was Weir's commanding officer.

'The Japanese are targeting BAR gunners all throughout the Pacific theatre,' he said in his whispered tones. 'They're probing our lines and waiting to hear them fire. When they pinpoint the location, they throw everything they have at that position until the gunner is taken out and the BAR disabled.'

'So, what are you saying?' Jack heard Oscar Weir's voice for the first time. It sounded normal, not the cackle of the demon that lived inside of his head. Just the voice of a young man.

'I'm saying that we can't afford to lose you or that rifle. That's the only thirty calibre, automatic weapon we have with us and we need it if they charge.'

'Don't worry you won't.' Oscar tried to leave, but the officer grabbed him by the arm.

'You're not understanding me, soldier.' His face became stern. 'You don't fire that damned bitch unless you absolutely have to, I don't give a hot damn if there are Japanese crawling all over us, you don't shoot that rifle unless you know one hundred and twenty percent that they are in full charge. Because if they pinpoint you and they take you and the BAR out we're all dead anyway. So, you need to let us and the other men around you do the heavy lifting. Not only is it for your safety, but it's for ours.'

'This is garbage, sir.'

The officer grabbed him by the collar and shook him.

'You listen to me, you goddamn son of a bitch. Do. Not. Fire. A damned shot!'

The words coursed through him and burned as they sailed through his skull. Then the night was dark. The Americans surrounded him as if in an attempt to protect him. He heard the cracks of sticks as they snapped like gunfire beyond the tree line and leaves broke free from their branches to list to the ground. The men were all on edge; the tension was so thick in the air he could barely breathe.

Then a rifle shot ripped through the air and an American fell screaming to the ground. The two on either side of him rushed to him to save him and other men began firing into the tree line. Their M1 Garands popped fast accurate shots and then came the spring of metal once they expelled their empty clip.

'Cease fire. Cease fire,' the officer called to his men. 'Conserve ammunition!'

But the stress of it was too much for them. More rifles began to fire in blindness. Three Japanese men appeared from some bushes. They were covered in leaves and sticks and at first, it looked as though it was the trees themselves that descended on them in the dark. They were cut down almost immediately by the other Americans. More shots rang out, everywhere now. Confusion and breakdown were only inches from them. Then explosions ripped through them, as Japanese grenades seem to fly at them from all directions.

Many men went down, some of them continued to scream. Somehow, a fire had started and men were burning. The enemy came out of the jungle disguised as the trees themselves, and they screamed while they ran the Americans down. Oscar raised the Browning but hesitated. His finger hovered above the trigger.

Then a sharp jerk pulled the rifle down and the officer stood over him. 'What did I say to you?' he screamed in his face. 'Do not—'

He never got the rest of the words out as a Japanese bullet tore most of his face off. The officer collapsed on top of Oscar, and the two men fell to the ground. Quickly Oscar regained his feet and once more he raised the Browning. The Japanese were in full charge, then they feigned back, then another charge would happen in another location and they would follow through. Some men were engaged in hand-to-hand combat, others still fired into the tree line while the rest either screamed or lay silent in death.

He had all the power in the world in his hands. He had the most powerful rifle in the Pacific theatre. The rifle the Japanese soldiers feared enough that they would throw everything they had, just to disable it. Yet he couldn't use it. Panic rose in his throat as he watched his friends die around him, he wanted to help them but he didn't know how. Everywhere he turned the rifle Americans were partially in his sights. He watched another group of men emerge from the trees and surprise the Americans that were too busy firing in another direction. Expressions of agony spread over their faces as the shrub covered soldiers plunged their bayonets into their backs. They went down and squirmed in pain as the Japanese impaled them again.

They were being overrun. He needed to do something. He stood and lifted the rifle in his hands, determined to let the power be known, be damned whether they targeted him or not. At least they would stop killing his friends.

A searing pain spread across his shoulder and upper back. He fell down and slid himself backwards. A small, slender man stood above him, a face as solemn as the officer's yet with zero compassion in his eyes. He raised his sword above his head and brought it down. Oscar was able to get the Browning up in time the first time, but the second time, the steel plunged into his stomach.

Not yet defeated, Oscar pulled himself upward and beat the Samurai officer to death with his bare hands before he removed the blade from his guts and retrieving his Browning once more. There were no more lines of defence. Men fought everywhere, some with rifles, others with bayonets or their hands. Destroyed and desperate to do something in the last of his consciousness, he shot them all. Americans and Japanese. Friends and enemies, he killed them all, in his desperation to use the power that was in his hands.

Tears ran down his face as he fired into the men that lay on the ground. Blood shot up in the air with each shot that hammered into the bodies that were crumpled over each other. He screamed, a sound that seemed to come from another world as his mental state completely broke. He roared along with the Browning until he finally collapsed and fainted.

Everything went dark for Jack. Everything went silent. The figure of Oscar Weir was no longer beside him. It was as if he stood in a large hall that let in no light. Then, as if the walls of the hall were the lids of Oscar's eyes, they opened and Jack was shown one more thing: Robyn Tracker, thirty years younger than he was the day that Jack Baker walked through his office door.

Robyn leaned over Weir's body with a sneer on his face as he rummaged through his pockets. Jack remembered the photograph that hung on the stairwell of the Trackers' house. Photographs back then didn't paint people in true light, they rounded edges, they hid the true features. Yet still he knew the man that leaned over the body and those damned eyes. Behind Robyn, he saw other Australian soldiers as they moved about and sorted the bodies.

Robyn stood up and with him, he took the Browning. One of Weir's strong hands reached up and grabbed the stock. Robyn turned back and paused for a second. Then the sneer spread back over his face as he leaned back down and lodged his knee onto Weir's throat.

'This will be worth some money back home bubba,' Robyn whispered. 'Now be a good Yankee and die.'

Jack felt the struggle in Weir, he felt the hate. He felt the last thought that went through his mind as he cursed Robyn and the rifle that would lead to so much death.

The vision ended abruptly, and Jack came back to his senses. He didn't know how much time had passed, but the sun was up and light poured through the living room window. He saw men on the street. His hands moved as if they weren't his own. He acted as if it wasn't him in control. He felt the weight of the Browning in his hands, felt it buck as it fired.

RANKIN

*'And castles made of sand
Fall in the sea eventually.'*

The Jimi Hendrix Experience – *Castles Made of Sand* (1967)

Rankin sat with men whose names he did not know. Travers and Caycho waited back in the gauntlet, neither of them detached enough from their own lives to offer it up so freely. What made it so unusually cruel was the waiting. When a man knew the moment that he was likely to die, each moment beforehand became a profound torture. He had seen it back in the camp with the way the men fought amongst each other; he had seen it in the way they drank and smoked and now he saw it again. Each man sat by themselves. None of them had spoken a word to each other the entire walk out, short enough as it was. They maintained their silence as they found positions to hide in. They had simply walked up the road a few hundred feet and had sat down to wait.

Rankin wasn't sure about what the others had decided, but he had walked up and down in the early morning sub-twilight to look for a position that offered him enough cover with a shred of hope for a retreat. Eventually, he had decided on what was left of a retaining wall. The wall lay on the side of the road where the intersection of the gauntlet lay. It was two hundred feet of stone letterboxes, burnt-out car bodies and trees which led him back to the safety. It wasn't what anyone would call ideal, but it was good enough. Ten men lay in wait in front while the remainder were either at his side or to the rear. Some fiddled with the stones at their feet, while they stole glances down the road to watch for the oncoming assault. Rankin on the other hand, hadn't bothered to look. He figured he would hear them before he saw them.

The hardest part of the morning for him was not smoking. Several times he had put a cigarette in his mouth and had almost lit before he had thought better of it and placed the smoke back in its packet. The wind was to his rear, he felt its cool caress on the back of his neck and the last thing any of them needed was for the vanguard of the Chinese to be alerted to their position by a face full of second hand smoke. Instead, he sat and watched the sun rise, illuminating the ground before him while he rolled a grenade around in his hand. It would be any moment. The moment just could not come fast enough.

The sun had barely risen above the horizon when he felt the first tremor in the earth. At first he had almost missed it, consumed as he was with fiddling with his cigarette lighter. He paused mid-movement, then shuffled himself down lower to the road. With one hand flat on the concrete of the driveway, he lowered his ear to the surface. He couldn't hear a damned thing but every now and then he thought he felt something. He strained his ears to hear for the sounds of heavy rumble of the tank's tracks, but nothing. He raised himself slowly and froze.

Three Chinese soldiers were only mere feet from the first men of the ambush force. One of the Australians, a larger fellow who had decided it would be wise to hide in the tub of a utility, had laid down with his hands under his head. Rankin almost panicked. He wanted to do something, to throw a rock or something to warn the soldier. He looked around for something, anything. Then he heard the Chinese speak to each other.

The soldier in the bed of the truck rolled slowly to his side. He drew his knife and looked back at another soldier who signalled to him, three fingers for three enemies. Rankin peered out around the retaining wall and saw the soldier in the back of the ute nod. In front and to his right, another Australian soldier moved into position with his knife.

Only seconds remained between calm and chaos. Rankin readied his SLR and waited. The Chinese soldier on the far left walked alongside the utility now, while the one on the far right neared the other soldier who likewise planned to attack with a knife. That left the middle Chinese scout. Rankin didn't know if anyone had a plan for him. He held his breath.

All at once, the two Australian soldiers moved.

The one on the right leapt out from behind the car while the one in the back of the utility sat up and lunged at the soldier closest to him. The Chinese soldier on the right tried to react but only had his rifle up part way when the steel of the Australian's knife plunged into his chest. The first Chinese scout was dealt with. The Australian on the right kept moving for the one in the middle.

None of it mattered. Rankin watched helplessly, as all of Caitlin's plan fell to shit before him.

The enemy closest to the utility saw the Australian sit up. He took two steps back, avoided his poor attempt to grab him and fired a volley of three shots into the man's chest. Dead where he sat, the Australian fell back into the utility and didn't move again. Chaos consumed the street, the Australian who had stabbed the first Chinese soldier was gunned down by the one in the middle. The two remaining Chinese began to yell as they retreated. Rankin leaned out and fired two shots at the soldier closest to the utility, at the same time nearly every one of the Australians in hiding opened up. The street was filled with gunfire and the screams of the Chinese soldiers who although had no chance themselves, had given everything away.

Men began to move out from cover and Rankin waved at them to get back down, but he was behind them and they didn't even see him. The remaining eight in front moved up to fallen soldiers and tried to revive the Australians that no longer moved.

A man to Rankin's right went to move out from cover and Rankin caught his eye.

'Get back into cover!' he hissed at him, loud enough to be heard over the short distance. The man obeyed and settled himself in a ready position. Rankin shuffled, and pushed the butt of the SLR into his shoulder and did his best to cover the men that were foolishly out in the open.

Beyond the eight men, Rankin could barely see anything. The Australian's now tried to drag their fallen back. He tried again to wave at them, to get their attention, to try to stop them and get them out of the open. There was dull thud way beyond them and an instant later the road at their feet exploded in a shower of rubble, shrapnel and fire. Bodies flew everywhere and came down among the rubble in a mess of blood, limbs and screams that cut through the ringing in Rankin's ears.

Rankin ducked back into cover at the explosion and lowered his head to the shower of rubble. He heard the crunch of metal and a glass pane shatter as a body landed on a nearby vehicle. When he looked back out, he saw one man scream as he dragged himself back to their position. His legs were gone and a pile of guts and shit dragged behind as he went. He continued to scream as he pulled himself back to safety.

Another man was alive, but on his back. He held his stomach while blood poured out of his ears and his mouth as he gurgled for help that would never come.

The ground below Rankin's feet began to tremble, the loose soil that had showered down onto the lip of the retaining wall jostled. He looked beyond the carnage and saw the first tank. It approached at full speed, its hull bouncing with the small inconsistencies of the road beneath. Infantry advanced behind it. They ran at full pace to cover the ground before a counter could be established.

The ambush they had planned was finished. They needed to get back. Rankin leaned out from behind his cover and fired at the men who ran beside the tank. They ducked their heads as his first rounds ricocheted off the heavy steel of the tank's frontal armour.

'We need to move!' Rankin yelled, as he fired another two shots. 'They're trying to rush us!'

He turned to look at the soldier who was at his side, but he was gone. Rankin saw him run down the road back to the gauntlet. He turned back to the front, the tank had cleared easily over a hundred feet of ground, it was now fifty feet beyond the utility and was closing fast. He fired another two shots as men spread out in front of him again. Then he turned and ran.

His feet pounded the pavement and his heart hammered in his chest. They had fucked the whole thing up. Most of the men that were in position behind him had fled. He saw them disappear down the opening of the gauntlet as he threw himself behind a stone letter box. He crashed into another Australian who was still in position and they both swore as they crashed into the ground. Confusion had started to set into them. They needed to get back under control before they were all killed.

Rankin grabbed the soldier he knocked over by the collar and dragged him to his feet as the first shots from the Chinese began to ricochet around them. He pointed to the base of a heavy gum twenty feet to their rear.

'You move there, then stop and cover me!' he screamed at him. 'I'll cover you but you need to stop to cover me. Okay?' The Australian nodded and Rankin moved into position. 'Go!'

He leaned out as he heard the soldier's feet pound the pavement behind him. The SLR bucked rapidly in an attempt to get the Chinese to lower their heads. One man was hit in the chest and collapsed, the two around him ducked behind cover. He swung about and saw a Chinese shoot the legless screamer in the back of the head as he still tried to drag himself forward. Rankin shot him in the stomach twice, then moved on. The tank had slowed its pace to a crawl now as it moved beyond their forward position. Enemy soldiers followed close behind it and Rankin hammered the armour toward the rear to keep them behind the tank.

He turned to see where the soldier was who was covering him was, and watch the soldier take up a firing position behind the tree ready to fire. Rankin ran. He kept his head low as the Australian fired to either side of him. Rankin ran past the firing position and threw himself behind the wreck of a burned-out car. Again, he was surprised to find more Australians behind the wreck. They exchanged quick glances as they all cowered behind the blackened steel. Rankin spat into the street and raised himself out of cover. Training his SLR on the mass of Chinese, he fired.

'Now!' he screamed back. His comrade broke cover, bursting into a sprint. Rankin knew there was no cover now until the gauntlet. Thankfully, the other two that were crammed behind the car had likewise started to return fire as the Chinese broke cover shortly after his comrade and charged while they fired in a fully automatic spray. Rounds skittered off the blacktop and hammered into the burned steel of the car frame. The Tanks coaxial machine gun peppered houses and the road as if it was blind and had no idea where the Australians were. Rankin unloaded his magazine on the advancing Chinese and then pulled then pulled a grenade from his belt. He saw his comrade run past in his peripherals as he fumbled with the pin, when a hand fell on his own.

'We'll take it, you go back,' one of the two behind the car yelled at him.

'You be right on my ass!' Rankin bellowed, as he retrieved his SLR and ran for his life.

He heard the thud as the grenade exploded in the street, but he had no idea as to the success of the charge. The tank's machine gun rattled behind them and concrete chipped at their feet. Twenty feet to the intersection, sounds of mixed fire from Australian SLRs and Chinese AK knock offs. He was out of breath and found the only thing he wanted to do was to have a cigarette. As he ran, he dropped the magazine out of his SLR and rammed a new one home. He racked the slide for good measure. He needed to do something while he ran without cover.

Ten feet to the intersection.

He ran alongside his comrade, the first one who had stayed to cover him. Rankin looked over to him as they neared the end of the street, both men ran flat out. He was only a boy, Rankin thought. Then a loud slap sounded next to him, and his comrade fell in a mess of blood and lung. Rankin didn't stop. He left him to die while he threw himself behind the only cover he could find, so he could do his best to support the two that were behind him.

The mail box was small and offered him nothing in terms of protection, but when a person was scared, anything between them and the almighty was worth its weight in gold. The two remaining ambushing Australians were in full retreat. They must have left only seconds after Rankin. They fired wildly from the hip as they ran, while behind them the tank bore down ever so closer.

'Go! Go!' the one who had taken his grenade bellowed at Rankin as he waved his arm. Rankin once more turned his back and ran.

As soon as he placed his first step into the gauntlet, he felt safer, but not safe enough. He didn't stop running, there was forty feet still remaining before he would reach the first fox hole. He pushed himself harder and harder. He didn't dare to look behind; the sounds of the gunfire were bad enough. The tops of helmets shuffled in the foxholes, he saw the eye of every man in the street on him. The barrels of their rifles pointed in his direction. He kept running, and finally threw himself down into the first foxhole.

He panted and coughed as he tried to catch his breath. One man grabbed him and shook him, 'What happened? How many?'

Rankin pushed him. 'Get the fuck off me.' He glared at the soldier, and then instantly felt bad, it was Caycho. The look of concern was plastered across his face.

He held out his hand to Rankin. 'It's okay man, you're safe now.'

Rankin shook his head and pointed back. 'Get ready, it's just beginning.'

They threw themselves to forward slope of the foxhole and rested the tips of their barrels over the edge as they looked down their sights. One of the two had powered ahead of the other as one came into the street in a full sprint. Seconds later, the last Australian stepped into the gauntlet. He hopped as he stumbled and tried to run. His SLR was gone and he clutched at a large red spot that blossomed on his right leg.

'Come on!' The leader of the two yelled as he hesitated and stopped running. He held out his hand and it wavered in the urgency that coursed through his body as the wounded soldier hobbled towards him. The two men joined hands as the tank came tearing into the street behind them. They had time to turn, and Rankin saw the arm of the leader go around the wounded man's shoulders as the hull of the steel beast turned toward them.

Rankin ducked his head as the coaxial ripped up the road, he didn't need to see what had happened to them. He saw everything he needed to in the faces of the men in the foxhole beside him. The faces of those who had successfully lured the beast into their trap.

Rankin turned and slowly raised his eyes above the level of cover. Thankfully, he couldn't see the remains of the men that had fallen, but the tank sat motionless at the mouth of the intersection. Its nose was pointed directly at them.

'Come on, you big bitch,' Rankin muttered. 'Come and get me.'

They heard the rumble of the diesel, the clunk of the transmission, and then the engine roared as the tank continued down the street. Rankin felt a mixed feeling of dread and joy as the heavy machine lurched toward him. The men behind the tank shuffled to get back into cover, three lines of men, over ten in each line. More of them assembled at each side of the intersection. They were like a swarm; they seemed to come from nowhere.

The tank rumbled down the street at a snail's pace. At the level he was at, he saw the feet of the men behind it beneath the undercarriage. The tracks ate up the road, the diesel pounded in his ears.

'Come on baby, come on, big girl,' Rankin muttered. They were to wait until the cannon took out the first tank and then all hell would break loose once more.

He watched as a team of Chinese moved down the left side of the road. A few of them tried to find holes in the walls of cars they had made. A team of forty slowly made their way down the right, ten of them disappeared down the side of a house and didn't re-emerge.

'Fuck,' Rankin growled to Caycho, 'they've gotten through.'

His friend looked at him over the receiver of his rifle. 'They always would. It was a deterrent.'

At the beginning of the street, they saw the barrel of another tank come into view. Behind it was another large group of men, they walked semi-hunched, their rifles low as they felt safe. The tank continued on. It didn't follow the first.

'Fuck,' Rankin repeated. The plan hadn't even kicked off and already it was up the shit.

Twenty feet remained until the first tank was on their position, it wouldn't be long now until the cannon hit it. Rankin took a deep breath to settle himself. He needed to keep his head, he couldn't allow himself to panic.

Suddenly, the street was flooded with the sound of automatic fire and the sharp sound of shattering glass. Rankin dipped his head as he saw streams of blood fill the air behind the tank that approached them. Beneath the undercarriage he saw men lifted from their feet and thrown as the rifle fire hammered into them. Rankin turned and saw the giant, his eyes were glassed out as before, as he fired his old rifle through the living room window at the oncoming soldiers.

'Now we're fucked,' Rankin gasped as he saw some of the other cannon operators grab the giant and struggle to pull him back. The Chinese soldiers all opened up on the house and in turn, every soldier in the street began to fire their weapon.

The machine gun positions behind Rankin began their heavy thud, the positions focused on the enemy soldiers on the opposite sides of the street, which created a cross fire somewhere above Rankin's position. He lowered his head once more as he saw men torn to pieces by the unrelenting fire of the M60 positions. He watched as they tried to clamber onto porches, only to be cut down as they tried to force their way inside houses which had already been sealed off.

Rankin joined the fray and shot one man in the back as he tried to climb over a car wall. Another he felled as he tried to break through a boarded window. He shot the foot off a man who cowered behind the still advancing tank and then shot him in the face as he fell. The hydraulic whine of the tank's turret cut through all the noise. Rankin stopped firing to change magazines. He watched the turret come about and over his head, it continued and stopped directly at the living room window where the cannon was hidden, only fifteen feet from his position. He turned and threw himself onto Caycho and the world shook as the main gun roared. Dust filled the street and got into Rankin's lungs as he felt Caycho thrash beneath him.

'Get off me, man!' Caycho yelled as he pushed. Then the whine of the hydraulics came again and the motor thundered as the tank began to roll forward through the dust once more.

The machine guns behind continued to shoot through the dust to spatter houses and men alike. Rankin pulled himself up and saw the tank close in on their position. Other Australian's had already moved to foxholes behind them. 'Come on!' He yelled to Caycho as he grabbed him and started to pull him up. 'We need to get back. The artillery is gone.'

He pulled him up the rearward slope. As Chinese infantry rushed out of the dust, Australian men in the rear fox holes lit them up, as did the machine guns. The air was heavy with lead, Rankin saw two men fall in fox holes in the second row, unlucky as they were caught by the inaccurate spray of the Chinese. He pushed Caycho forward and threw himself forward into the second row.

The tank was five feet from the first foxhole now, Chinese soldiers miraculously flooded into the first line of fox holes already. Most of them were wounded or already dead by the time they made it there. Rankin watched as Australian soldiers pulled pins on grenades and lobbed them into the forward foxholes and lowered their heads. The roar was tremendous as several grenades exploded at the same time. Bodies were thrown into the air from the frontal cover and fell lifelessly back to earth with the dirt and soot.

The machine guns continued to hammer the Chinese as they flooded into the streets and continued to try and break through the fortifications between the houses. He heard gunfire on the flanks, which meant that some of them had gotten through. The tanks hull groaned as the front of its tracks came over the lip of the first fox hole and screams of the Chinese soldiers that were still alive below it filled Rankin's ears.

'We need to move back again!' he roared as he pulled Caycho with him, but he was too heavy. Rankin stumbled with the extra unexpected weight of his friend. He turned back to him and saw that he had been shot. The back of his head was caved in and his helmet hung loose on its strap. Rankin looked at him for a moment in shock, as the tank dipped down into the frontal foxhole and skidded on the loose dirt.

Rankin let go of Caycho and his body fell to the bottom of the foxhole, while the other Australians began to vacate back into the rearward rows. The tank's treads continued to churn and the walls between holes began to collapse under the weight. Rankin turned and tried to roll himself out as the walls collapsed.

Caycho's lifeless face disappeared beneath the dirt as he was buried. He caught one last glimpse of his friend as his open eyes were slowly covered by the dirt that fell over him. Rankin tried to pull himself up but he slid back. He pushed hard with his hands and tried to dig the butt of the SLR in to pull himself but he continued to slide back.

Machine gun fire continued to rip through the street, bullets ricocheted heavily off the tank's armour while the diesel thudded monotonously behind Rankin. The earth shifted below it which slowed the tank's progress but it had already burst through the frontal wall of the second fox hole. Rankin watched as it came. He tried to push himself back but the soil was too loose for him to grab a foothold. The diesel thudded and the tracks ground away at the earth only feet away from him.

'Oh God!' he yelled as panic swept over him but he couldn't hear his own words for the roar of the diesel. 'I don't want to die. I don't want to die like this.'

The earth shifted below him and the tank blotted out the sun. The world fell into darkness.

JACK

'Hope you got your things together,
Hope you are quite prepared to die.
Looks like we're in for nasty weather,
One eye is taken for an eye'

Creedence Clearwater Revival – *Bad Moon Rising* (1969)

Dust filled the house like a curtain of thick smoke. Jack's head pounded and his body ached as he lay face down. He thought he could feel the Browning underneath him as something was stuck into his ribs. He started to lift himself and he felt the strain as rubble fell from him as he moved. To his side lay the smoker, his face a bloody ruin from the explosion that tore through the house. Jack clambered to his feet and retrieved the Browning from the rubble. He expelled the magazine, put the empty into one of his huge pockets and rammed a fresh one home. He cycled the action and felt the power in his hands come back to him.

The house had half collapsed around them. The shell from the tank had hit the brick structure on the junction end of the street side section, the entire wall had collapsed. The roof sagged down on that side and raised three foot higher above his head, the entire thing separated from its joists.

On the street only feet away the fighting raged on, men were dying everywhere and the tanks exhaust fumes had started to fill the house. The cannon had survived the explosion but its axle had sheared off, which left it collapsed half on the ground to its right side. The only inflated wheel that had remained to it when they had moved it into position was now gone.

Jack moved to the rear of the cannon and brought the Browning with him. Through the gaping hole they had created in the rear of the house, he saw a young man sit with his back to the cannon. It was Morgan. Jack moved to him and grabbed him roughly by the shoulder and dragged him.

'They taught you to use this thing?' he barked at the boy as he threw him down in front of the breech. Morgan looked up at him and nodded slowly.

Behind him he heard the guttural language of the Chinese and he spun in time to see three soldiers run up the ramp to the hole they had created. He raised the Browning without a second thought and lit them up. The heavy calibre rounds turned the men into unrecognisable, mutilated shells of what they used to be. The rifle from wars long-forgotten tore limbs from the men it hit, bones shattered under its power and life left them slowly as they groaned and suffered.

Jack reloaded the Browning and turned to Morgan. 'Load it!' he roared, jerking his head toward the cannon as he moved to the front window to check that no one was forcing entry behind them. Chinese now tried to escape the massacre on the street and he shot one man in face as he pulled himself through the shattered living room window. Jack saw the Chinese pile into the first of foxholes and began to raise the Browning to tear through them, when the tank came over the top of them and they began to scream before the front of it came down and crushed them.

'It's... It's loaded,' Morgan called out.

'Shoot the fucking tank!' he roared back at him as he shot four more men who tried to climb the porch. The faces of the men he shot were not determined. They were afraid, they just wanted to survive, yet man after man that climbed the porch he shot down.

'Shoot!' he roared again as he loaded another magazine.

'I can't,' Morgan cried back. 'The sighting is all out.'

Jack glanced back. The kid was right. Since the axle had broken, the barrel was now angled through the roof.

He growled as he let the Browning fall to the ground. 'You watch and fire when it's ready,' he barked again to Morgan as he leaned down and grasped the remains of the cannons mount with both hands. His arms swelled, his back straightened. He pushed hard with his legs and slowly the cannon began to rise. Jack roared with the strain, and held the mount steady. Slowly the barrel began to fall.

'Ready?' Morgan asked as more men began to pile onto the porch.

'Shoot the fu—' Was all Jack got out.

The cannon bucked viciously in his hands and a tremendous pain shot up his arm from the palm of his left hand. The men on the porch were thrown violently from it, and Jack never saw them again. The barrel recoiled down, and the blast shot sideways out of the muzzle brake.

His head swam from the concussion and he dropped the cannon as he stumbled backwards. The room filled with the smell of burned powder, timber and plaster. More of the roof collapsed around them as his lungs filled with powder residue and dust. He crawled to the window and peered out over the lip of its destroyed frame. The tank was hit hard in the joint between the turret and the hull; a great hole was torn through it and smoke billowed out from its belly. He saw the turret fold open and smoke gushed out as a man tried to escape from the top. He was shot before he could get out and he fell slowly back into the depths.

He couldn't hear a thing. The world had receded into silence apart from the constant ringing that pounded his brain. His heart hammered in his chest, and he coughed viciously as he tried to expel the rubbish in his lungs. Morgan ran up to him and tried to pull him up. The boy shouted something at him and pointed. All Jack could see was the boy's mouth move, but he followed the direction of his gesture.

Chinese men flooded over the fence of the backyard. More than he thought was possible. He retrieved the Browning and hissed as he felt the pain in the palm of his hand. He fired long bursts into them as they ran across the yard. Many of them fell. Blood splattered the grass beneath them as they collapsed from their wounds. Those that made it past didn't even give Jack a second glance, they just continued to run.

His left hand screamed in agony with each magazine change as bone ground against bone. With the second to last loaded magazine now inserted into the Browning, he reached into his pocket and pulled all the empties that he had. He shoved them into Morgan's chest and then pointed to the green tin in the corner of the room, that was covered in dust. The white writing still barely visible.

Morgan understood what was asked of him and set about his task, while Jack continued to hammer the Chinese as they poured into the yard. The world was still silent apart from the ringing. The thud of the Browning was felt more than it was heard and it sounded as if he was underwater.

Beneath all of it, he could hear his breath and the voice of the demon Oscar Weir as he cried, *'Kill them, kill them. Kill them all!'*

RANKIN

*'There'll be no one to save, with a world in a grave.
Take a look around you boy, it's bound to scare you boy.'*

Barry McGuire – *Eve of Destruction* (1965)

The force of the cannon fire pushed him back into the soil. Dust and silt filled the air, which created a wall that was impossible to see through. The tank's hull groaned and cluttered as the internals were destroyed. The tracks hitched and tried to continue their motion, but the loose soil beneath only churned in place. Finally, with a tremendous scream of metal, the tank shuddered, then became silent. Smoke listed from the side the cannon destroyed and inside he heard sobs of suffering, the coughs and pleas of the dying crewmen that echoed against the walls of armour that had once protected them. Rankin heard their hands scramble against the metal that would soon become their tomb as they tried desperately to escape.

Rankin turned his back on the tank and scrambled once more up the slope of the second foxhole. Miraculously, he still had his SLR and he pressed it close to his chest as he forced himself through the third foxhole and into the fourth. The machine guns still laced the street with peppered bursts. Although the dust hindered their aim, it also slowed the Chinese advance. Rankin heard metal clang behind him and as he dropped into the fourth foxhole, he saw the top hatch open on the tank. The man who tried to escape barely caught a breath of fresh air before he was shot from multiple angles and disappeared back down below.

Rankin checked the breach on his SLR and blew dirt and grime from its chamber. He lifted his head above the rim of safety and saw a wall of Chinese scramble over and around the tank, as they pushed forward and tried to find cover. On the sides of the streets men swarmed the porches to find their way into houses. Rankin saw Chinese soldiers push relentlessly on the wall of cars that blocked the access the backyard of the house that held the cannon. Slowly, the cars began to move under their collective strength, all the while the screams of the desperate and dying filled the Australian's ears.

He raised his SLR and fired into the men. He shot three of them in the back before a round hissed of the dirt just to the left of him and he took cover once more.

'Molotovs!' He heard a man scream from the foxhole behind. Rankin looked up. Yellow streaks of flame cut through the air above him as the men to his rear launched their supply of fuel filled bottles. Below the gunfire, the screaming and the dying, Rankin heard the sharp crack of glass and then a soft flump. The world became brighter and the screams beyond his line tripled in their intensity.

He raised his head above the rim of safety once more. The flames had encapsulated the entire front of the tank, a large section to its right and most of a house to its left. Chinese walked blindly as they burned, their faces black dishes of agony while their limbs flailed helplessly. Rankin shot three burning men and watched as they fell. The fires continued to eat away at them even though their life had already left them. An Australian soldier pushed him on the back of his helmet and Rankin turned to look at him; it was a man he didn't even know.

'Let them fuckin' burn,' he growled at Rankin as he lit another cocktail and hurled it through the air.

The walls of soot, dust and fire slowed the advance only by a little.

It wasn't long before walls of men pushed through and the machine gun's sporadic rhythm was foregone for long streams of fire. Rankin turned to his left and saw through a murder hole, men engaged in hand-to-hand combat within the house. The flank was at risk of failure.

Rankin turned to who had hit him in the back of the head and repeated the action to grab his attention. The soldier turned slowly as if ready to start a fight of their own in the safety of their foxhole.

'Left flank is falling! Get the men to hold the line here. I'll go reinforce them!' he screamed to be heard over the carnage.

The soldier nodded at him, then turned to the two men on his left. 'Cover fire!' he roared and the three of them raised their rifles above cover and began to pepper the street.

Rankin left the safety of the foxholes.

The air was hot and heavy with gunfire as he ran as fast and as low as he could. Bullets hissed as they threw up dirt all around him as he made his way across the front yards and had begun to make his way onto the porch of the house under attack, when he paused. The bodies of all the Chinese that had been shot as they tried to make their way through the barricaded front doors littered the porch, if he tried the same he would join them. He feigned right and shot left, breathing easier as he placed the corner of the house between him and the fighting. Extending himself to his full height, he ran at the wall of cars that Travers, Caycho and himself had made and clambered over it. Screams came from inside the house as Rankin rushed down the side of its exterior, pausing only as automatic fire ripped through walls just above his head.

He stopped at the edge of the building, readied his SLR, and then came around the side with his rifle raised. He shot two Chinese as they tried to come over the boundary fence, while he saw another who had climbed the back porch, raised his rifle. Rankin ducked back as the porch climber fired a spray in his direction. The automatic fire was relentless; Rankin did not want to break cover. He held his rifle in the direction he knew the soldier was and emptied his magazine into the side of the porch. The SLR bucked savagely in his hand as metal tore through timber, cane furniture and then the man they were intended for.

He reloaded as he rounded the porch and ascended the worn mission brown steps. The scene was just as abhorrent as the one on the street. Chinese corpses littered the porch, some had made it inside unscathed and had engaged in hand-to-hand combat with the machine gunner and crew. Three Australians were dead from either gunshot wounds or knife wounds. Only the machine gunner was left. He turned to look at Rankin with a desperate plea in his eyes.

'Hold the flank. We are almost out of ammunition, then we can fall back.' He paused the firing stream of the M60 to say those words and continued the thunderous fire. Rankin replenished his magazines from the dead at his feet, then he moved back to the rear of the house and took a knee under a portrait which hung on the wall. The people within the frame were obviously the family that had used to live there.

All the lives that have been displaced, he thought, as he racked the SLR and prepared to hold the flank.

JACK

*'My bloods so mad, feels like coagulating.
I'm sitting here, just contemplating.'*

Barry McGuire – *Eve of Destruction* (1965)

The pounding in his head thudded in rhythm with the Browning. With each magazine he threw into the old rifle, he became more and more consumed by the hate and the rage inside of it. It moved seemingly by itself, its bolt fell forward, although he didn't even think he had pulled the trigger. Each time he emptied a magazine, he slid it to Morgan and each time he reached for a fresh mag, it was there.

The barrel had gone from an earthy grey to red and the heat sent waves of distorted air through his sight picture. Yet as each soldier rounded the house through the breach they had made in the wall of cars, he sent them crumbling to the ground. Bodies littered the yard everywhere, some of the men were only wounded and they crawled over their fallen brothers as they tried to get to cover. Then the next wave of men desperate to get off the street would storm over the top of them and then fall themselves, under the Browning's withering fire.

Magazine after magazine, wave after wave, the Browning thudded its monotonous beat. He could feel himself being lost; he could feel Weir drag him back. The urge to take control of his body, the urge to kill for himself, it was overwhelming.

As though it came from underwater, he heard Morgan scream to his right. Jack turned and saw that Chinese had poured through the shattered window and had come about the cannon. He swung the Browning as Morgan cowered away from the advancing soldiers. It rocked in his hand as the bolt did its work. The wall to Morgan's right was splattered with blood as the closest two soldiers were dismantled where they stood.

Jack was mesmerised by the carnage that took place before him. He found he couldn't stop; he needed to injure and maim. He needed to kill. A soldier lunged and grabbed hold of the Browning as he destroyed the others in the house. The soldier fought and screamed like a banshee as Jack overpowered him and pushed him against one of the remaining walls. The enemy's hands were still on the Browning's receiver and Jack slowly pushed against him; he never broke eye contact. He bathed in the screams as he pressed the white-hot barrel into the flesh on his face. He watched as features melted against the steel, skin blistered and burst under the heat that was pressed into it. One of the man's eyes turned a milky white and then, with a pop, liquid poured out onto the now smoking steel and boiled on contact. He held it there, against the soldier's weakened struggles, until he finally gave in. Then Jack raised the Browning and shot him.

The street was on fire and Jack could see soldiers burning alive as they tried to douse the flames. They moved too slow, as if they were blinded and confused. Three of them became lifeless where they stood and fell to the earth. Morgan screamed again and Jack turned to the rear of the building. He leaned outside as the building shuddered, three houses up another tank churned its way through the yards with a line of infantry to its rear. There were at least forty men behind the tank. He would not be able to hold them.

He reloaded the Browning as his mind whirled with options, while Weir screamed at him to let him forward, to let him kill. His eyes fell upon a large brass cylinder. There was one remaining shell for the cannon, but its barrel faced the wrong direction. To his right, he saw the rifle that the smoker carried and he seized it. He dragged the smoker partially with him until his stiffened hand fell from the grip. He forced the rifle onto Morgan and boomed at him as he moved. 'Keep them off me.' He spoke slowly and emphasised each word, as he struggled to speak over the constant screams of Weir.

The Browning clattered to the floor as he returned to the broken axle of the cannon. A snarl spread over his face as pain shot up his arm from his injured hand. He roared as he lifted the immense weight and pushed into it. The cannon balanced against his strength on the flattened tyre. Slowly, with his efforts, the cannon began to swing about.

In the yard he could see soldiers' storm through, they didn't even offer them a single glance while Morgan sat there and watched them. The barrel swung about as he struggled to move the weight and then it stopped. He pushed and pushed, each time he felt a knock against his strain. He looked to his left and saw the barrel touch the last supportive beam on that side of the roof. Jack scowled as he took two steps back, the veins bulged in his neck and on his arms. He roared as he moved the cannon harder than he had ever pushed and the timber joist shattered under his strength.

With a horrible groan, the roof collapsed on what remained of the house and exposed the grey sky above them. The gaping hole in the side of the structure was reduced to no more than a four foot chasm and Jack positioned the barrel to its line.

'Load!' he boomed at Morgan as the main gun of the tank came into view. He forced air into his lungs as his arms waned under the weight. Morgan disappeared to the rear of the cannon and he heard the tell-tale thud as the breech slammed home.

'It's too high!' Morgan screamed at him and Jack swore.

He dropped the axle and allowed the cannon to crash to the floor. He walked to the front and grasped the barrel with two looped hands over his head. The Chinese in the yard had seen them. He roared as he dragged the barrel down to shoulder level and then he fell to his knees. The tank came into view, while the Chinese fired at them. He felt a hot sting in his side and felt the patter of the bullets hit the cannon's surface.

In a blinding flash and a thunderous roar, the cannon fired. It recoiled out of his hand and sent him sprawling to the ground. The smoke that it generated blinded him to the yard, and once more his ears had retreated to offer only their high-pitched squall. He coughed as he dragged himself to his Browning. All the fight in him was spent. His arms weighed a tonne each and his legs had had enough. He moved himself forward, the Browning lay there in the silt. Forward. Forward, as the war raged on around him.

He was only two feet from the rifle's grasp when he saw the Chinese come through the smoke.

RANKIN

*'The pounding of the drums, the pride and disgrace.
You can bury your dead, but don't leave a trace.'*

Barry McGuire – *Eve of Destruction* (1965)

While the M60 rained metal fire down on the street behind him, the SLR in his hand contested to be heard. It seemed that no sooner had he reset the charging handle he had to count down the rounds until he was forced to reload. They just kept coming. The yard below the porch was littered with dying men, holes punched through them the size of a man's fist, yet still some of them didn't die straight away. He didn't want to stop his fire. He didn't want a lull in the shots because above it all, the gunfire blocked out the groans of the mortally wounded.

He reloaded again. Six men came around the porch and held tight to the house. The first one that came into view jumped at the sight of Rankin and fell back. The three behind him charged. Rankin managed to fire three shots before they crashed through the doorway and bowled him over, the SLR fell from his hands. He screamed as he fought, punched and kicked, while he swore to himself that he wouldn't succumb to panic. More men came through the doorway and two of them piled a top of him, one of them drew their knife.

'Flank, flank!' Rankin roared to the M60 gunner. He didn't know what else to say. He pushed up hard under his attacker's chins, and tried to get them away from him. The blade hovered above his face, the SLR was too far away.

'Fuck. Flank!' he roared again, his arm buckled slightly under the weight of the men then snapped straight once more. A scream escaped him as he hooked his foot under the stomach of one of them. He pushed with everything he had and the soldier tumbled backward to block the doorway. Rankin rolled slightly as the blade came down, he caught it beneath him as it thumped into the floor boards. He rolled on top of it and caught his attacker's wrist as he brought his fist up to slam into the Chinaman's face. He too went crashing to the ground, and then the entire back of the house erupted in point-blank machine gun fire.

Holes punched through the wall, glass shattered, men broke and blood filled the air. Rankin stayed low, as he scrambled for his SLR while the M60 gunner continued to destroy everything at the back of the house. The six men and more lay dead either in the house or on the porch. Rankin regained his rifle, checked the chamber and returned to his position.

'This flank is going to fold, we need to get out of here!' He called to the gunner.

'Last belt. Fall back.' The gunner replied as he slammed the dust cover back down on the M60.

Rankin covered the machine gunner's retreat from his position at the back door. Men continued to flood into the yard, but none managed to surprise him again. He knew it was his time to move when the next man he went to shoot was cut down by the M60 before Rankin even had a chance to gain the soldier in his sights. He ran while the machine gun thudded its metallic rhythm. It burned his ears as it barked almost directly in his face. Rankin ran past him and vaulted the next boundary fence.

As he moved between houses, he saw the chaos on the street. Fire had spread along the grasses of the lawns, men crawled, either burned within an inch of their life or were shot down as they ran. Rankin heard grenades explode somewhere to his left and then something that could only be the cannon, as it fired once more. The ground shook beneath him from the concussion of the gun. He heard metal screech in the distance and metallic clunks but he continued to run. He pulled himself up behind a brick barbeque mount and called for the M60 gunner. He waited with his rifle trained on the fence, in wait for his man to come over.

Rankin watched as a hand appeared atop the timber posts. Then his head bobbed up as he tried to leap the boundary, but the M60 weighed him down.

'Come on, throw it over,' Rankin called out to him and the gunner did. The heavy stamped metal of the gun didn't even make a noise as it landed on the soft grass. The operator joined it shortly after. He picked up his weapon and ran for Rankin.

Automatic rifle fire rapped through the timber of the fence and Rankin ducked his head as the yard was filled with a cross fire. The gunner dropped, the M60 fell from his hands and he screamed as he clutched his lower back with one hand and reached out to Rankin with the other.

'I can't move my fucking legs!' he screamed, his words full of agony as he tried to claw his way to his weapon.

Rankin lifted himself out of cover and fired the SLR wildly into the timber. He didn't even bother to aim, he just needed as much lead to go through that fence as possible. He moved forward, desperate to repay the favour that he owed the gunner. The slide slammed home and rifle clicked. Automatically he dumped the empty mag and rammed a new one home as he walked and racked the charging the handle. Then he fired again, the butt of the rifle low on his hip. The receiver bucked with each shot. He continued to move forward as he fired, each step meant another shot. More enemy fire rattled through the timber boards, but it was half hearted and not aimed.

He reached the gunner and kicked the M60 to him. The gunner grasped it while Rankin sat him up and began to drag him back. The M60 chuffed as it fired. It left spent links and shells that glistened with the blood of the man that fired them as they made their way back to cover.

As they were almost back to the safety of the barbeque mount, Australian soldiers hustled into the yard from the house. One of them carried another M60 while the other two held SLRs. They looked shocked to see the two men in the backyard of the house they defended and at first they didn't help. Then the two riflemen slung their SLRs and took over the recovery of the now waning machine gunner while Rankin took control of his SLR once more.

'Move back,' the new machine gunner barked at them. 'They've already moved past us. We need to get back to the courtyard.'

JACK

*'Though I'm going, going.
I'll be coming home soon.'*

Creedence Clearwater Revival – *Long as I can see the Light* (1970)

Jack Baker urged himself forward into the smoke. His eyes darted from the stock of his Browning to the men that approached him. At first, they didn't see him, yet as his enormous figure shifted in the silt, they turned their heads and paused. His arms were covered in grime, blood and sweat. The violent recoil of the cannon had stripped the flesh from his shoulder, and now the pain he felt was blinding. Weir fed on his pain and used it against him. Jack felt as his fingers clutched the back of his hair and tried to pry him away from the control but still, he did not yield. All he needed to do was reach the Browning.

The Chinese advanced on the house, the rifles of two men were trained on Jack while the others scoured the walls of the structure's remains. His giant hand slapped the floorboards and dust clouded around his palm. No matter how hard he pushed himself, he was not going to make it to the rifle before they were on him.

Behind them, in the backyard of the house, the second tank limped its way forward. Jack saw the hole that was torn through the forward section of its side armour. He heard the steel tracks grind against the warped frame as it clattered on. Even the second tank had defied them, just another failure to add to his long list. Jack stopped moving and rested his head on the dusty boards. He had wanted the Australians to kill him in Forster; he had tried to take his own life. All of these things didn't matter a damn anymore. He was not alive for a purpose.

A rifle shot cut through the house and Jack flinched. He marvelled at how he didn't feel pain, as he imagined he had just been shot. Then another shot and another in quick succession. He opened his eyes and raised his head. The two forward Chinese were down, another had his rifle raised, but it wasn't pointed at Jack.

To his left, a rifle fired twice more and the third Chinaman fell. He saw Morgan move to the hole in the back wall, his rifle raised. Outside, a rifle shot cracked and blood ripped from the back of Morgan's shirt. His battle rifle fired as he fell back and he began to gurgle as he tried to breath.

Jack began to move once more. He felt his rage take control. His vision was darkening and he knew he had to keep his head. Inch by inch, he dragged himself while Morgan raised himself on one elbow. Forward again with waning force as the lone Chinaman walked through the hole. He finally laid his hands on the stock of the Browning as the Chinese soldier shot Morgan at point-blank range and silenced his gurgles.

Jack growled as he clambered to his feet, the Browning trained on Morgan's killer. His vision broke, then returned. He saw double, then triple, and then it snapped back to the purest of clarity. The roar inside of his head came in waves as if someone clapped their hands over his ears. Somewhere, he heard the scream from another world, the same tremendous roar he remembered when Michael had died. Then he realised it was him and he moved forward.

He saw everything he did to that man. There was no escaping it. The shadow had fallen over the Chinese soldier faster than he could swing his rifle. He swatted it from his hands and threw his entire weight on him. The fear in the Chinaman's eyes consumed everything as his first fist fall landed square on his face, shattering his nose. Confusion replaced the fear as his fist rose again and then he broke the man's jaw with the second.

The third time, the eyes didn't open, nor did they for the fourth, fifth or sixth. Jack picked him up and threw him across the room. His head slapped against the steel of the cannon's barrel and his body flipped like a ragdoll. Then Jack was on him again. Blow after blow he laid into that man as he roared and spat. When his eyes finally opened again, Jack saw his own reflection in them. He saw the hatred in his own face, saw the rage and most frightening of all, he saw his own eyes.

Weir cackled in the back of his head as Jack finally gave up on his prey. His chest heaved with the exertion and his heart pounded in his throat. Out on the street a machinegun fired, a stream so fast it sounded as if it would tear the sky itself open. The sound of it drowned out every other rifle in the whole battle. Jack heard the incessant pattering of the bullets as they slammed into the ground and houses so fluid that it reminded him of summer's rain. It churned for a few seconds and then it fell silent as the fighting resumed.

Jack picked himself up and collected his magazines that were spread across the floor while the battle continued around him. He exited the house and felt the coolness of the breeze in the air as he approached the side of the crippled tank. It shuddered as its tracks bound up against the damaged armour. It trembled as if it knew he was coming for it, coming to end its life. There seemed to be no one around him now; the fighting had moved on. He heard rifles and machine guns fire down toward the courtyard and still the crippled tank struggled to make it there.

From the torn hole, he heard the remaining crew's guttural language and he heard their surprise as he pushed his arm through the torn metal and he felt his fist close down on flesh and fabric. He roared as he pulled his arm from the twisted steel and the flesh on his arm was dragged along its jagged edges. Further and further his arm came and whomever he held in his grasp with it. He felt the structure of the being in his grasp shift as he forced it through the gap in the steel. Bone by bone, joint by joint, they all succumbed to his strength like dominoes in a chain until finally he dragged the sorry mess through the hole. He threw it down on the ground and it hit like a wet towel as blood smeared the side of the tank and ran red rivers down its flank.

He heard Weir's cries once more for Jack to step aside and let him take over. But that could never happen, that wouldn't happen. Not at least until he was done with this fucking thing. The screams continued inside as he climbed the hull, he heard reports muffled by the remaining armour as he tore the top hatch free with his bare hands. Rage consumed him, but still he resisted his demon. He reached inside and latched onto the first man he could find.

He had expected a fight, or a struggle to some extent. Instead, what he found was the man's weight was heavy and lifeless. Still, he pulled him from the depths and he heard the metallic clank as something weighty fell from his grasp. The man had shot himself in his own fear. His eyes were wide and expressionless, his jaw was slack. The bullet from his pistol had blown the back of his head outward and Jack felt the matter fall over his hands. The anger seemed to run out of him as if air had left its tyres. He let the dead soldier fall back inside and he dismounted the tank's hull and he stood there by its side for a moment, contemplating.

He thought about Weir's words, that if he ever came forward again, that would mean his end. Never again would he see the light of day. Then he thought about the man from the arena, the man in the tent that had almost killed him when he first arrived in this shithole. How he had pleaded with him to leave if he ever felt like he was going to lose control. He said that they didn't deserve it, what *he* would do to them. But how had he deserved what had happened to him? How had Michael deserved his fate?

He hung his head and looked at the Browning in his hands. A snarl creased the corners of his lips. Then he turned and walked away, leaving the fighting and the conflict to his rear.

RANKIN

*'I heard the sound of a thunder, it roared out a warning.
Heard the roar of a wave that could drown the whole world.'*

Bob Dylan – *A Hard Rains Gonna Fall* (1962)

The small group of Australian soldiers that remained of the left flank burst into the street. As the flank folded behind them, they fled in retreat and ran straight into the broken chaos of the gauntlet. Lines were non-existent. Some men that had once occupied the foxholes had remained and were engaged in firefights in the open. The lack of cover that had caused the carnage of the Chinese forces now left the Australian soldiers with nowhere to hide. Rankin saw one Australian fall to the ground as six Chinese soldiers clubbed him to death. Bodies of Chinese and Australian alike covered the remnants of the tarmac. Some managed to make it out of the foxholes, others did not. Rankin saw the hands of men whose lives were cut short as they scrambled to climb the soft soil, as he had only moments before.

The five soldiers from the right flank did not engage with the enemy. The two that supported the wounded M60 gunner scurried ahead, while Rankin and the remaining gunner covered them from the rear. They skirted the edge of the street and emerged only yards from the final foxhole. Rankin couldn't believe how many Chinese stood before him. With all the lives that had been lost to gain the two hundred feet behind him, he couldn't understand how so many could still be left alive.

They needed to get through. They needed to get the courtyard. The M60 opened up to his left, and Rankin sporadically fired his SLR. He only shot at those that had looked in their direction. Otherwise, there were just too many.

'At this rate we'll never make it!' the gunner roared at him.

'Fuck the courtyard!' Rankin yelled back as he rammed home a fresh magazine. 'Head for the Titan. We'll use the Gatling.'

The gunner looked at him and nodded. Rankin ran up to the two that carried the wounded man. 'Come on, stay on my ass. Beeline for the Huey!'

Rankin took off and left the men to follow behind him as he headed for the grounded helicopter. He tried to count the enemy as he ran, maybe a hundred, maybe more. All he knew was that their attention was drawn to the courtyard. He could already hear rifle fire from the direction; what remained of the Australian's had already retreated, their foxholes mostly abandoned in the chaos. Shots fired behind him and a man screamed. The Australians left on the street were gone, swallowed by the swarm. One of the two that had carried the gunner had fallen and the other gunner took his place.

They weren't going to make it. Rankin knew they were all done for.

He slowed his pace, almost defeated before he had even reached the Huey. But he wasn't far from the safety of its hull. He turned back to look at the grounded chopper and the M134 bolted to its side and he almost screamed when he saw it.

Captain Caitlin, either laughing or crying, sat behind the M134.

'No, no, no!' Rankin yelled, holding his hands out in a passive gesture. 'Not yet, just wait.' He saw the barrels jolt into motion as they spooled up and all he had time to do was fall to his stomach as the world turned to fire and metal above him.

The sound of metal churning bore through his skull as he watched the wall of lead rip through the Chinese horde. Bodies were torn in half, heads exploded. The air was filled with a red mist as men who had nowhere to run or hide were torn apart. Each bullet tore through a man to reach another and continued on its path. There was no distinction between gunshots, just one horrible shattering roar as around sixty rounds per second tore from its multiple barrels.

Red mist followed the stream of fire as Caitlin raked it across his foes. The men that saw it had no time to react. Nor did the three remaining Australians behind Rankin. He watched in horror as Caitlin tore through them, still hysterical in his wailing. Then the ear-splitting shred of metal stopped and all that remained was the sound as the bearings reeled away as the M134's barrels continued to churn.

Of the hundred or so men that stood before Rankin, only twenty remained. Each man was red with the blood of their brothers and their eyes shone white. They stopped, as if afraid of another burst of fire, stunned at the carnage they had witnessed. Rankin lay there, still stunned in his own right and stared at the remaining Chinese.

A shot ripped through the air and blood spurted from the chest of one the Chinese soldiers. Caitlin continued to wail as he left the hull of the Huey. With his pistol in hand, he fired into the stunned Chinese who stood there and looked at him. Then Rankin joined him and together they felled the rest.

Once the last man had fallen, Rankin turned his SLR on Caitlin, with tears in his eyes while the fight for the courtyard continued.

'You fucker,' he said to him. 'You shot your own men.'

Caitlin panted and swayed in place. He pointed the pistol at Rankin and pulled the trigger.

'You're out, shithead,' Rankin sneered at him, as he trained the barrel of his SLR on the Captain's face and he started to squeeze the trigger.

He was suddenly hit by a savage force from behind. The SLR fired, but the shot went wild as he was thrown by an explosion. He hit the ground and felt a wave of agony come over him. The Huey had burst into flames and it smouldered like the captured tank it had destroyed so many days ago.

Rankin's eyes blinked rapidly as he tried to get to his feet, when he saw that Caitlin stood above him. His hand wavered as he held his pistol in Rankin's direction. In the time that the explosion had given him, Rankin saw that the slide of the Captain's Hi-Power had returned into battery and he had no doubt that the pistol was loaded this time.

'Do you think I care about them?' Caitlin cried as he placed a boot on Rankin's chest and pushed him into the dirt. 'Do you think I care whether I live or die?' he snarled as he placed the muzzle of his pistol below Rankin's jaw. 'All of this was for the betterment of our country. Whether those cock suckers in Canberra believed me or not, I will be the one who was proven right.'

'They told you to retreat, didn't they?' Rankin said, sneering even as he felt the heat from the Hi-Power's muzzle under his chin.

The ground began to tremble around them, but Caitlin didn't seem to notice. He held his face close to Rankin, and he thought he could smell liquor on his breath.

'Oh *yeah*,' he said dramatically. 'But we just couldn't leave the wounded behind, could we now? His grin seemed to stretch further than what was natural. 'I was born here; I'll be fucked if I'd let these little slopes take over my hometown. I don't give a fuck how many die; they will not take my home.'

'You're fucked.' Rankin spat in his face. As he reached with one arm for his SLR, the trembling of the earth seemed to triple and finally, Caitlin noticed. Caitlin turned his head as the Huey began to shudder and Rankin lunged for his SLR. The captain felt Rankin move and pulled the trigger.

A bright light shot through Rankin's eyes and a pain seared up the side of his face, but he wasn't dead. He was far from it. He pushed Caitlin off of him and felt his hands clasp around the SLR. He gained his feet as his ear screamed in a bloody protest and he felt something run down the side of his face. The Huey had begun to shake violently and then suddenly Rankin saw it and he knew what had happened.

The third and final Chinese tank churned its way over the top of the grounded Titan. Rankin saw its frame buckle and twist as its rotors snapped. The whole thing was sucked under the enormous hull of the steel beast that was only mere feet away from him and Caitlin. Rankin turned to run as an enormous jet of flame spat out of its main barrel and engulfed Caitlin as he stood there and gaped.

If he could have heard anything, Rankin was sure that Caitlin would have screamed as he burned, but all he could hear was the high pitch that droned through his skull. All he could feel was the heat that radiated from the jet of flame and the wound to his face. The tank had stopped before Caitlin, as his burning body flailed about in front of it.

'Fuck you!' he roared over his shoulder as he retreated for the courtyard. His voice was high in his own head like he was under water. Rankin left Caitlin to die, like so many others that had fallen because of the captain's insane lust for glory.

He ran as fast as he could, and left it all behind. He left the dying, the wounded and maimed, he ran as fast he could to where the last line of Australian forces waited for him. So they could stand together at the end.

RANKIN

*'Do it in the name of heaven,
You can justify it, in the end.'*

The Original Caste – *One Tin Soldier* (1969)

Exhaustion. Every muscle in Rankin's body ached and groaned in protest as he ran. His stomach growled at its own dishevelled state while his heart held the rapid beat of 'The Black Dread's' fifty calibre. They had lost the gauntlet; they had lost at least half of their men. The Chinese losses seemed unfathomable, yet they kept coming. The new wave had chased him from the crumpled wreck of the Huey to the large white pillars of the courtyard, before they had finally let up and regrouped.

His boots hammered the pavers as he moved into the courtyard. He looked through the steel gates to his right and saw the path that led to the baron road to Melbourne and beyond. The courtyard was already littered with the corpses of the last of the Chinese vanguard. Those that had fought through the fires and the confusion of the street only to be gunned down on the white stone by the Australians that had given up their positions in the foxholes.

Rankin leapt over the small partition wall that bordered the grass and the pavers. He felt a cold shiver run up his spine as he saw the sights of every rifle left to Australians trained on him.

He didn't stop, nor did he call out as he moved up the steps, leaving the courtyard for the upper brick balcony of the office building.

As he reached the top of the stairs, he turned back and realised he stood in the same place that Caitlin had only hours before as he delivered his final speech.

'Caitlin's gone. Fucker went insane!' Rankin roared as he ducked behind cover. There was now a lull in the fighting: the calm before the storm.

Rankin looked at the faces of the platoon strength force that remained; none of them seemed to offer any expression of care or surprise for what he had just said. He looked from face to face: Men, boys, some old enough to be retired. Their expressions were solemn, their features hidden behind masks of dirt and grime. They didn't show the fear he had expected to see, only the determination to hold their line.

The last remaining tank grumbled and clanked in the distance; it drowned them in the dull tones of its diesel. The sound of it rolled around and around the brick walls, bounced and droned deep into their skulls. Rankin looked down the line and took in his surroundings. The Australians had managed to set up one M60 position high on the brick balcony, the office buildings to the right remained unoccupied and silent. Nothing moved, their sight was restricted beyond the pillars that bordered the most northern point of the unoccupied eastern coast of Australia. The wind swirled around them and stung their eyes with the silt that it carried. The smoke from the smouldering 'Titan' and, Rankin supposed Caitlin as well, burned their nostrils while the rolling cloud covered the Chinese advance.

Rankin was certain that the tank was stationary. The diesel rattled in the distance and barely moved above an idle. While the Australians heard voices from the black smoke that crept up on them.

They readied themselves, checked magazines and trained their sights on the smoke wall as it swallowed the pillars. Rankin thought he saw movement, to the right of the first pillar and swung his rifle to that position. He strained his ears and tried to concentrate over the drone. The soft sound of a boots sole on pavers, the sound of metal scrape against brick. He breathed in deep and held.

The smoke crept forward; it listed out and thinned as it moved further into the courtyard. Rankin saw a man standing bold as brass in the smoke. He didn't even attempt to hide behind cover. A shot rang out and every man in the courtyard jumped at its report in the deafening silence. The shot rolled off the brickwork and ripped back at the Australians with a more distant thud each time. The man in the smoke fell and the tension rose within their blood as they waited for a retaliation. Nothing came.

More sounds of movement echoed up to them. More shadows became visible as the smoke rolled through the steel gates to the left. Shapes of men, brazen against the smoke, shoulders and heads. As each figure became certain that it was indeed a man, they shot them. Shots ripped through the silence and drowned out the drone of the tank, if only for a short while before they subsided to non-existence.

Then the movement stopped as the smoke finally began to clear. They heard whispers as guttural exchanges only twenty feet in front of them and then the world seemed to explode in one single instant. Machine gun fire tore into the brick wall that stood proudly in front of the defenders. Rankin instinctually ducked his head as bullets raked the stone above his head. Rifle fire cracked down in front of them, sporadic yet timed shots as the Australians struggled to lift their heads against the suppressive fire.

Rankin tried to lift himself above the cover. He tried to get a sight picture long enough to take a shot, but no sooner had he started to raise himself had he become the focus of fire. He was the closest to the steps, the last on his line of the cover. The balcony he cowered on led beyond the stairs, covered once more by brick and led into the office building that sat to the right of the courtyard. He saw ramps lead down and knew that they would lead to the buildings to the right, and give them access to the Chinese flank.

He slid himself down, butted his shoulder against the bricks that protected him. His vision was mostly fine in his right eye, but the left side of his face was still raw with pain and he struggled to hold his left eye in focus. Rather than breach cover high, he leaned out low into the stairwell and kept the barrel of his SLR as far back as he could.

Chinese had already started to move into the buildings across the courtyard. Rankin swore. If they found their way up through the ramps there would be no way to defend against two fronts. He shot one man in the back as he climbed the steps to the office. Blood flew from his chest and ran from his mouth as he collapsed on the steps. Those that were behind him fell back to the courtyard and went to cover. Rankin pushed himself around further and saw the top of a soldier's helmet. He put a shot into it and it disappeared.

Other Australians achieved similar results; he heard the cracks of SLR's sporadic across the breadth of the brickwork, yet the M60 remained silent.

'We need that Sixty!' Rankin roared as he fired another round at a soldier who broke cover. The round smashed into the brickwork that he cowered behind and the soldier slunk back to safety before Rankin was able to get another shot.

'Too far out of cover and only one belt left. We need to save it for when we get a break,' one soldier barked at him; he raised his voice as he struggled to be heard over the hammering of the enemy machine gun fire.

'If we don't get a break, we'll be dead!' another piped up.

'Shut up!' Rankin roared while he fired a few more shots. 'We need men on this right flank, they're in the office.'

One Australian soldier had apparently stepped up to take command as Rankin heard the same barking voice rattle off names and sent them to the right flank, as per Rankin's suggestion. Men shuffled behind him as he continued to take pot shots. One round smashed into the brickwork just beyond his face and tore a section of mortar loose. Rankin swore again as he moved further back behind cover. He could now see further into the courtyard through the chunk that was torn out. Something touched him and he turned to see four soldiers crouched behind him as they checked their rifles.

One of them grimaced and said, 'Give us some cover as we move across.'

Rankin looked back at the chunk taken out of his wall and shook his head. 'You need more than just me, either that or you all rush at once and maybe two of you make it.'

The four soldiers looked at each other, and kept their heads low as the enemy machine gun continued to dismantle their cover.

Finally, the soldier who had first spoken racked the slide on his SLR. 'Two cover, two move. You two move beyond and cover the last.' They readied themselves.

Rankin rolled back into position, loaded a new mag into his SLR. He took a settling breath and moved his barrel out into the open.

This time he moved himself further out. He wanted to suppress the enemy machine gun position. Each inch he pushed himself out, the worse he felt. Finally, he saw the enemy machine gun. Positioned at the furthest most brick boundary wall three heads sat behind a smoking barrel of lead and fire. The gunner raked the gun back and forth over their lines as gunfire poured from its end.

'Cover!'

The SLR rapped against his shoulder as he fired over and over into their position. The two men who remained with him lifted themselves above their cover and fired into the Chinese below.

Again, and again, Rankin fired at the three soldiers. He hit one of them in the arm and saw him duck down. Shortly after, the machine gun fell silent as the other two ducked for cover.

Over the sound of the SLR's pounding he heard the hurried footsteps of the two soldiers as they bolted beyond the stairwell. Gunfire seemed to erupt from all directions, filled the lull left by the machine gun. More bricks broke to the front of him, and Rankin was forced to move back into safety.

He panted as he loaded another mag into his SLR. He looked over to the flank and saw two soldiers in wait, their sides pressed up against the full brick section. They made eye contact and nodded as Rankin racked his slide and shuffled out of cover again.

'Cover!'

Once more he hammered the machine gun position while the soldiers that had already made their safe pass leaned out and fired into the mass of Chinese in the courtyard. Rankin saw the gunner try and move up into a firing position, only to duck back down when his SLR started to break the wall he hid behind. He heard the pound of boots on concrete once more and continued to fire rapidly, he didn't care for his placements.

The SLR jammed.

'Fuck!' Rankin screamed as he moved himself back into cover. The soldiers whom he covered disappeared into the office buildings to his right. They had made it. He sighed a breath of relief as he cleared the jam in his rifle and slammed another round home in the chamber. He looked down the line of defenders. Men tried to move into firing positions, only to have the bricks above them smashed by the machine gun fire that returned with vengeance once his cover fire had relented. Holes had started to appear in their cover now, brick broken away by the hammering of the enemy fire. They weren't going to be able to hold the line for long.

'They're charging!' he heard a man scream. Those that could began to fire through the holes in their cover. Rankin saw four men charge up the stairs to his position. He whirled the SLR onto them and hammered the first man in the chest three times. The life went out of him as he ran and he collapsed on the stairwell, and partially blocked its access. The two men behind him tried to climb over, the one to the left started to spray automatic fire in Rankin's direction. Rankin shot wildly, panicked by how close they had made it to him.

He shot the one firing through the throat which, seemed to him pure luck more than anything, and he collapsed forward atop of the other. The remaining two turned to run and were shot down before they could make it back to their own cover.

The left stairwell was hit harder. The Chinese made it most of the way up the stairs before they were attacked by the Australian defenders. Automatic rifle fire ripped through the squad to Rankin's left and screams filled his ears. The Chinese stood tall, not worried about fire from their own guns, they fired down on the Australians who cowered for safety. Until finally the Chinese were cut down where they stood.

'Fuck this!' Rankin roared in desperation. 'We need to get the Sixty running!' He grabbed a soldier to his side and threw him down in the position he had covered. 'Switch out!' He roared to him as he began to move down the line.

He could see the M60, positioned up against the crumbling brick wall. He couldn't believe how much the wall had been reduced by. Men that had crouched behind it before the machine gun fire had started were forced to lie down for cover.

Rankin crawled along the broken brick, around men that were alive and fighting and over men who were dead. The whole time he kept his eyes on the sixty, which sat fixed by its mount positioned up on a portion of wall that remained intact for the most part.

He now knew, what they meant about the lack of cover. The wall had crumbled on either side of the mount's position, so that any man who stood behind the Sixty would be exposed at every angle.

Bullets ricocheted off stone and brick around him as he crawled, a man directly in front of him was shot through the forehead as he lifted his helmet to improve his vision on his sights. The sound of flesh and bone crack was horrid as his body jerked and he lay still.

'Charging again!' a man called, and through the broken cover Rankin saw Chinese charge the left stair well again. He raised his SLR and waited for them to crest the stairs. The SLR bucked as they crested and he managed to knock the first two flat, but more moved up behind them. At the risk of being overwhelmed he increased his rate of fire. The rounds he missed smashed into the brick by their heads and showered them with shrapnel and shards of clay.

Two more, then another three were felled, then his SLR clicked and it was empty. He reached for another magazine but he was out. More men charged up the stairs now while the machine gun fire ripped the building to pieces around them. He heard something scream, but it wasn't a man. He moved forward as the Chinese reached the stairs. The scream became louder and louder, as it rushed towards them.

Rankin got to his knees, exposing himself to the fire and leapt to the M60. He latched his hands onto the grip and the bricks that held the mount collapsed and fell backward onto him. Dust erupted from the bricks and mortar as it crumbled, while the scream turned into a powerful roar of exhaust and fuel.

Rankin lifted himself slightly and pushed the butt of the M60 into his shoulder. He trained the barrel on the left stair well when all hell broke loose in the courtyard, in a shower of shattered stone pillar, men and metal. While the unmistakable sound of a Chevrolet's V8 dominated the world around them.

CHRIS

'You can't say we never tried.'

The Rolling Stones – *Angie* (1975)

She felt powerful beneath him as he watched the charge of the men before him. She shuddered as if to tell him what she wanted him to do. He pressed his foot to the accelerator and her engine revved. The body twisted under her own power and her exhaust roared as the revs climbed, then fell and a backfire cracked through the air like a .303.

Pestilence was parked partway up the western side of the main road. The Chinese soldiers poured across the dirt paddock past a single dilapidated army truck. As if spectators, men sat on the motionless tank to watch the death of their own men. Screams echoed in the distance over the steady rapping of a machine gun. He was finally here.

A shudder overcame him as he took a breath. Everything hurt. He looked down at the wound in his guts and sighed. The blood had seeped through his clothes and had poured all over Pestilence's interior. The smell that came from him was enough to make him sick and his eyes felt so heavy. But when she powered up beneath him, it felt like he was living through her, like her power was more than enough to keep her and him alive.

His hand shook as he threw her into gear and she lurched forwards, eager for the kill.

'I'm coming, baby,' he said quietly as his vision reeled.

Then Pestilence roared and her back end came alive with power and churning rubber. She leapt forward like a beast that had finally been unchained. Her sound cut through him. He felt her, like she was just an extension of himself. The two speed Power glide whined as it shifted into high gear and the rubber spun hard as the 327 ripped power through the driveline.

She bellowed her crazed lust and grunt across the world before them and the earth gave way under her as she rocketed towards the mass of men. At first, they turned and just looked at them as the old Holden powered toward them. The soldiers seemed like they were in shock and did nothing to prevent what was coming, as the distance between them evaporated like cool water on a Darwin summer's day.

Chris's vision came clear as they rushed onward. He saw some of them turn and try to run. He saw others raise their rifles and fire. There was little glass left in her now and the bullets tore through the cabin, but she powered through it. Then finally, with a song of flesh and metal, they hit.

Her body seemed to float as she ploughed through the sea of men. The sound of her reinforced chassis as it ripped over the limbs while the railway iron broke them and forced them down under her was like heavy hale on a tin roof. The back end felt soggy as the front end was lifted upward over the soldiers, as they died either in front, underneath or behind, as they choked on her hot exhaust. Pestilence bellowed as the 327 fought against the added strain and still she pushed onwards, through the mass and over them.

The pillars stood like the gates of heaven before them as they ripped through. Chris was covered in the blood of the men that had been crushed on her bar. It was in his eyes, and he could taste it as it ran down his face. Still, she surged on and on.

The gunfire was the pitter patter of small feet underneath

the sound of her and she was the only thing that mattered now. Everything that had come to pass had led to her and this.

Her body bucked up hard and there was a crack as stone shattered as they burst through one of the pillars. She became airborne and Chris was showered with stone shards and pebbles as the archway crumbled and collapsed around them. Her motor spooled as the rear wheels spun freely in the air. He saw three men who were crouched behind a brick wall, a machine gun smoked wildly in their grasp. They turned and held their hands above their face as they screamed while Pestilence came down on them. Her engine coughed with the impact, then roared again as her nose bit in hard. Her bar work cut through the brick, the men and the stone pavers, and her back end came up.

He heard steel groan as she went over, end for end. Her driver's door opened and then disappeared. Her engine coughed, surged briefly and then stalled as the fuel was sucked from her carburettor. Chris held on for life, his fingers strained to hold onto her wheel.

He felt her die beneath him. She came down hard on her side and slid uncontrollably through the men and brickwork. An aluminium table was cut savagely from its mountings and thrown like it was nothing. Chris saw soldiers caught beneath it as it broke against them and the bricks that they hid behind.

She slid against the stone as she destroyed more brick and men that laid in her path. Then, with a groan of steel and the poor man that sat inside of her, she came to halt, and fell back on her wheels.

Gunfire filled the air around him and he fell out of her cabin. He tried to breathe as he dragged himself forward. Chinese soldiers raised themselves out of cover and turned their rifles onto him before they were cut down by a savage array. He heard a constant flow of machine gun fire rip through the world and his vision reeled. The sound became lesser and lesser as his vision came back. He felt cold and tired. He tried to breathe again but his chest felt so damned heavy. He looked before him and saw the gates, the ones he had dreamt about so many times. The ones that had always remained shut to him.

He dragged himself forward again. He felt as though he needed to breathe, but he still couldn't. A wave of dizziness rolled over him as he saw someone at the gate before him. The sound of gunfire seemed to dissipate, and the pain seemed to run from him.

Slender hands pulled the gate open and long golden hair flowed around her shoulders as she walked through. He tried to talk as she approached him. Her dress swept around her body as she knelt. A coughed racked him and the taste of blood filled his mouth again. She placed a finger on his lips and shushed him. Her touch washed all of it away. The coldness, the bad taste, the weariness.

She smiled as she helped him to his feet and he went to turn back to Pestilence. A soft hand touched his jaw and she directed his head back to the gate.

'It's okay, it's okay.' She soothed him, as she tried to direct him on. 'It's time to go through now, no one will stop you.'

'I tried…'

'Yes, I know.' Angie smiled, 'My brave, brave man. I know you've tried.' A tear trickled down her cheek as she kissed his hands. 'It's okay. Come now,' she said as she led him through the gate.

There was no smoke this time and he could see the road clearly before him. He could see the soldiers walking. Chinese and Australian, side by side. None of them fought, none of them even held weapons. Angie squeezed his hand as they walked the path. They joined the mass and departed together. Finally reunited as man and wife.

RANKIN

'The game of life is hard to play,
We're gonna lose it anyway'

Mike Altman – *Suicide is Painless* (1970)

Rankin felt that the world needed to stop for Pestilence as she ripped through the courtyard. The old Holden tore their lines to shreds before him in the instant that she broke through the pillar. He thought that after everything that they had all been through, the world at least owed her that much. Reality sunk in as the Chinese continued to move up the stairs. Rankin turned the M60 on them and fired. The machine gun ripped through them easily, brick, blood and bone tore around them as the sixties bolt hammered home.

The sound of grinding steel filled his ears as he moved up and Pestilence came to a halt before him. The other Australians rose from cover. Those that remained, beaten and broken, stood together as Rankin watched Chris fall from the Holden's cabin.

The Chinese were disorientated. They focused on Chris more than the soldiers above them. He saw the ground around his friend rip with the volley of automatic fire from the scared and broken attackers. He turned the M60 on them and rained hell down from above. They were so fixated on killing the man that had driven through their final assault that they didn't even drop down into cover as the Australians cut through them. They fell one by one, all of them with the hate in their eyes as it mixed with the desperation in their hearts.

Rankin eased off the trigger as Chris finally stopped moving. He had no time to move to his friend as he turned the M60 onto a mass of Chinese that moved for the office building. He tore through a large section, taking the legs of men out from under them as they scrambled to get to safety. Then he saw the doors of the building fly open and the four Australian soldiers that he had helped, broke out. They all fired into the Chinese. One of them threw a remaining Molotov at them and the steps erupted into a blaze of aviation fuelled fire. They burned as they screamed and the Australian's continued to fire into them, as desperate to lay them down as they had been to kill the Holden's driver.

Their hopeless defence and struggle against the Chinese had turned into a massacre. Chinese soldiers threw down their arms in hopes of surrender while Australians shot them where they knelt. Those that ran were cut down by SLRs while the others that continued to fight were killed.

Below the gun fire, the drone of the final tank's diesel had turned into a growl. The exhaust bored through their brains as the remaining Australians waylaid the enemy infantry. The M60 fell silent in his hands, and Rankin checked the belt. It had run dry, there was nothing left to run the pig, so he let it fall to the ground. Almost dazed, he walked back to his SLR and retrieved it, although he knew that it was empty. Beyond the broken pillars, a deep thud roared across the motor pool.

The entrance to the right flank caved in with a shower of dust and rubble. The Australians that had stood there were thrown forward from the steps and writhed on the ground in the middle of the courtyard. As if stunned that their victory was not assured, the Australians on the balcony stared blankly at their mates. As another wave of Chinese came through the smoke, they scrounged for cover.

Once more they cowered behind the last row of bricks that

remained to their cover while the barrel of the tank's main gun came through the smoke and the drone of diesel became overwhelming. Rankin watched as soldiers on either side tried to move into a position where they could fire and were in turn wounded or killed. An Australian man screamed as he held both hands to his stomach as blood poured through his fingers. Rankin moved to him and tried to keep every part of his body pressed to the ground. He felt brick and metal beneath him as it stabbed him and poked his ribs, but he didn't dare try to lift himself above.

Rankin moved over a dead soldier, pausing only to check for spare magazines; there were none. The tank had stopped in the middle of the courtyard, its coaxial machine gun rattled while the cupola opened. A man emerged from the top of the turret and the expression on his face filled Rankin with hate. Satisfaction is the only word could think of to explain that expression as the bastard looked up around at the carnage and what remained of the Australian defenders. He shouted down below him while he pointed in the Australian's direction. Rankin continued to move to the soldier that screamed as the hydraulic whine of the turret echoed around them.

He didn't hear the thud, like in Brisbane. He figured he was too close to hear anything. No sooner had he laid his hand on the collar of the screaming Australian solider, had the back wall of their balcony disintegrated. Rubble showered down on them while his ears rang. Bricks slammed into his face and his back while the gunfire from beneath them continued. He breathed in and took dust into his lungs but he didn't cough this time. He didn't have the energy.

He closed his fist around the collar of the screamer and pulled him close. Rankin brushed the dirt from his eyes while the Chinese tank shot a jet of flame across the far section of the balcony. The screamer was dead. Rankin didn't even have the energy to swear but dragged the body of the man in his hands over the top of him to try to protect himself from the coaxial fire. As he dragged him, he saw the butt of an SLR appear from under the rubble. He abandoned his idea and went for it.

The grip felt rotten in his hand and the butt was loose on the action. It didn't matter. He doubted there was going to be any ammunition in it or if there was, he wouldn't last long enough to fire it all. He threw the barrel down on the body of the screamer while bullets hit hard into the corpse. He trained the sights on the tank commander and with a final thought of only wanting to kill that man before he died, he pulled the trigger.

The SLR bucked in his hand and through the dust and gun smoke he saw the commander's head rock back. Blood flowed from his nose and his mouth as his arms flew up and his upper body hung back over the hatch. Rankin smiled as he lay there. He didn't bother to fire anymore; the fight had gone out of him. He felt bullets slam into the body that lay in front of him and he figured it wouldn't take long before one lucky bastard collected his head.

The gunfire continued, but the rain of bullets that fell around him ended. In his exhaustion he didn't understand at first. He pulled all of his strength into lifting his head above cover and he saw that the Chinese were firing through the gate to Rankin's left. Some men were atop of the tank and they tried to pull the officer out of the hatch while they screamed and pointed toward the gate. The hydraulics whined as the turret began to move and the barrel swung only inches away from Pestilence's rear end.

Rankin saw Chinese fall in the courtyard and his brow furrowed. He saw the men on the tank give up on their task and leap from the back of the iron beast as, in the distance once more he heard multiple deep thuds. Sparks flew as something heavy slammed into the tanks side armour. Metal screamed as the plating was torn to pieces and the tank shuddered. In the distance he heard more thuds, and this time the tank's turret was hit and it began to brew up. Sparks shot out from the gaping wounds in its armour and then deep black smoke begun to flood out of it.

The heavy steel gates that lay just before Pestilence's front end swung open, as Chinese soldiers stood up with their hands in the air. Soldiers walked through the gates, with rifles that Rankin remembered as M16's from his Vietnam days and the tell-tale U.S. Army uniforms. Then men with patches on their shirts, with flags that so closely resembled that of the Australian flag, came after them.

Those that ran before them were shot, but those that held their arms in air were taken prisoner. The newcomers were clean, they were fresh. They couldn't be anything but reinforcements.

Once more Rankin heard the drone of big heavy engines power from outside of the gate and then he heard the clatter of the tracks of the friendly tanks that had arrived. For once, they didn't strike fear deep inside of him. Hot tears blurred his vision, and he closed his eyes.

RANKIN

'And I can take or leave it, if I please.'

Mike Altman – *Suicide is Painless* (1970)

The American and New Zealand soldiers moved through the courtyard quickly. They moved beyond the motor pool and throughout the gauntlet. They chased down any Chinese that remained and immediately began to set up and take over Caitlin's base of operations.

Rankin climbed out of the rubble and couldn't believe his eyes when he saw more and more Australians beside him do the same thing. He sat there for some time with his hands on his knees as he looked at the filthy, broken men before him that had survived. He pulled the packet of cigarettes out from his pocket and looked at the state of them and threw them to the ground.

A group of Americans had begun to climb the stairs to his left. They walked on the bodies of the Chinese and smiled broadly up at them.

'Looks like we came just in the nick of time,' one of them said as he laughed and he looked down at Rankin's filthy face. 'You could have shaved for us though.'

'Mate, you give me a cigarette and I'll do more than shave for you,' Rankin replied as he clambered slowly to his feet.

The American laughed and pulled out an unopened packet and handed it to him, 'Keep the change,' he said and moved on.

Rankin lit a cigarette and sighed as he moved off the balcony. His eyes never left Pestilence the entire time. He smoked as he climbed down the stairs, the cigarette between his teeth as he walked amongst the bodies.

Chris Lowe lay dead only ten feet from the front of his battered old Holden. Rankin stood there and looked down on him for some time, studying each wound, and his friend's open grey eyes.

'I hope that you've found her, man,' he said softly. He sat and leaned his back against Pestilence's front end as he cried. His tears were for the loss of his friend but also, he was crying for everything. He had never shed a tear for Gary, Max, or Will and they had basically been brothers. The tears that poured down his face now could be for all of them.

He heard the shutter click of a camera, and he opened his eyes. A young man with glasses and a military uniform held a camera in his hands. He frowned down at Rankin and then moved on. Rankin sniffed as he watched the journalist move off to the destroyed Chinese tank and proceed to photograph it in sheer amazement. Rankin scowled as he watched.

'Captain Caitlin! Front and centre.' The voice cut through his thoughts and brought him back to the world around him. 'Captain Randal Caitlin, anyone seen him?'

Rankin turned his head and saw a pair of New Zealand MPs with furious expressions plastered across their faces. One of them locked eyes with Rankin and pointed toward him.

'You,' he grunted as the pair trudged over. 'Where is he?'

A soft smile spread over Rankin's face as he stood and brushed the tears from his cheek away. He never said a word to the MPs, he just jerked with his head in a 'follow me' gesture and headed out of the courtyard.

What struck him most of all in his journey out of the courtyard was the trail of carnage Pestilence had left. The stone pillar was shattered and spread out over the ground; bodies of Chinese soldiers lay twisted and broken along the road side; the machine gun crew were crushed between the frame of their gun and the undercarriage of the battered old Holden. Rankin looked from body to body as he led the New Zealanders.

Gunfire rippled off in the distant streets of Richmond. He wondered when this would ever end. Would each town in the series of run-down country miles just wait for their turn to be destroyed, then hope and pray for their turn to rebuild? The turn was here, he just hoped that it would turn hard enough and fast enough.

The MPs both lit a cigarette when Rankin stopped in front of the charred remains. Without a word, Rankin took one of the butts from the MP's hands and put it in his own mouth. Captain Caitlin's body had come to rest mere feet from where he had stood when the Tank had lit him up and instantly Rankin was taken back to the curling flames of the Napalm in Vietnam. One of the MPs squatted to his side and picked slowly at something on the corpse's chest. The flesh cracked like a well-cooked pork belly as the New Zealander pried a set of blackened dog tags from his chest.

'What happened to him?' he asked, a grimace across his face.

'The tank shot flames out of its main gun. It got a few more of us on the balcony too.'

'Shame,' the other MP muttered. 'Is it him?' He asked his partner, who had spat into his palm and rubbed at the metal stamping. The soldier who squatted next to the burned remains held the dog tag away from his face and squinted. Then a look came over his face and he nodded as he made eye contact with his partner.

'Shame fuckin' nothing.' Rankin spat. 'That pig should've hung.'

'It's a shame that he died,' the first MP said flatly. 'He's escaped the justice that waited for him, after all this.' The man waved his hand across the view in front of him and shook his head. 'After all this.'

Rankin left them at that. He had no need to stand there and bitch about the pig that had died. Nor did he have any interest in looking at his charred remains. The cigarette didn't seem to comfort him after the ghastly sight, and he let it fall from his hands. He walked through the courtyard and tried his best to hold his composure as he walked past the body of his friend. With a stiff jaw and a stern face, he walked out the gates and looked down the road to Melbourne. Army trucks, Centurions and men lined the road as far as he could see.

His apartment was only about fifteen miles from where he stood, but he thought about all the bad memories associated with it, and imagined what the milk that he had left in his fridge would smell like now.

'Melbourne,' he said to himself as he lit another cigarette. 'Sydney is a fucking shithole anyway.'

EPILOGUE

JACK

'Don't go 'round tonight
It's bound to take your life
There's a bad moon on the rise'

Creedence Clearwater Revival – *Bad Moon Rising* (1969)

It had taken longer than Jack had thought for the sounds of the gunfire and dying to fade behind him. He had stood in the shadows while men passed him on the streets. He watched from afar as he had continued south and south again, as columns of trucks and tanks had driven up the Northern Road.

Jack Baker had found a house that was far enough from any movement or noise that he felt safe enough to sleep. As exhausted as he was, mentally and physically, Jack was afraid to fall asleep. Weir had failed to cease his screams and he still swore to him at how much of a coward he was. Jack didn't care. If he had continued to fight in that mess, he either would have been killed or would have succumb to his anger and his rage, and would have lost control of himself all together.

'*The minute you rest, the second you close your eyes. I'll be there,*' Weir said to him.

With no idea of what to do, Jack sat around in the house for some time and even found blankets to wrap the Browning in. He didn't want anyone to see him with a rifle on his journey south. The last thing he needed was to be pulled back into the fighting.

He ate little, and less as the hours passed, finding only scraps of food that remained edible in the houses that he lingered in. Once more, his strength began to wane as he walked down the highway, with the Browning wrapped up in his hands. He didn't think about anything. He was too damned tired to bring it all back up again. Every time he thought about Michael, his family or Chinchilla, Weir wouldn't be far from the thought and he was the last thing Jack either wanted to listen to or think about.

In his exhaustion, reality became something else. His ears were full of a buzzing sound, like crickets in the heat of the night. His boots dragged along the blacktop as he shifted his heavy weight south and south again. He didn't even hear the bus pull up behind him, nor did he realise what was happening when the road began to illuminate in front of him.

'You okay there?' a voice sounded from behind him.

Jack stopped in his tracks and slowly turned around. His fist clenched around the Browning. He expected to see fear in the man's face, to see him cringe at the scars that lined him, to cower at his size. Yet the man who stood before him seemed concerned. He had a bald pate with a bushy white moustache. He was rounder than he was tall and he wore black suspenders over a white shirt. Even in this light, Jack could see the redness of his nose and his cheeks. He walked closer, with his hands out in a calming motion.

'It's okay, son. A lot of people have had a hard time lately. Come on, get on the bus.'

Jack swayed on his feet and blinked at him. He was spent. He took a short step and then another.

'Come and rest, take a load off. We'll get you somewhere safe,' the man said to him and took him by the arm as Jack walked alongside. 'We were surprised at how many civilians were still here. When they heard the invaders were on the retreat, they started coming out from everywhere.'

The bus was crowded with people. There were women and children, there were soldiers who had been wounded and were mostly patched up. A light flashed in his face and he blinked rapidly again. He turned and glared at a young man who wore glasses and held a camera in his hands. The anger flashed in Jack's stomach as he stared at him. He looked down and saw his military uniform.

'Sorry,' the young man muttered and looked down to his feet.

The suspension of the bus groaned as Jack walked sideways down the aisle. He needed to slouch so that he didn't hit his head as he walked. He made a beeline for the rear bench seat and glowered at the four men who occupied it. They all wore Australian Military uniforms, with bandages wrapped about various places of their bodies. The men exchanged glances and then changed seats.

Jack groaned, as did the bus when he lowered his weight onto the rear seat. He placed the Browning on the seat beside him and patted the blanket that wrapped it. Down at the front of the bus, the round, bald man sat back down behind the wheel and the doors closed with a hiss.

'Get some rest everyone, we will drive through the night,' he called back and the bus began to move.

Jack swayed as the suspension rocked over the road. He sighed and leaned his head back against the metal cabin. His eyes became heavy, yet he blinked against the sleep that had started to overcome him. He yawned loudly as he rubbed at his eyes.

'It's alright,' the soothing tones spread through his ears. *'I'll take care of us.'*

Jack blinked and tried to shake his head but he felt himself falling into slumber.

'It's alright,' The voice came again. *'No one will come between us again.'*

Jack wearily closed his eyes and soon after, he began to snore.

RANKIN

'When your rooster crows at the break of dawn,
Look out your window and I'll be gone.
You're the reason I'm traveling on.
But don't think twice, it's all right.'

Bob Dylan – *Don't Think Twice* (1963)

Darkness had come quicker than he had thought and he swore as he lit another cigarette. As he put his fingers to his mouth to pull the butt away, he tasted grease and old oil mixed with dirt and grime and shit. He spat and then took another drag. He leaned on the bar work of Pestilence and looked around the engine bay, in the little light that remained. If his friend had been anything in life, he figured it had to have been a mechanic. A builder's house was never finished and a mechanic's car was a fucking shit fight.

The bonnet groaned on its hinges as Rankin lowered it and let it clasp down on its latch. He sat down on the bonnet of the old Holden and finished his cigarette as he reflected as he looked over to the gate where Chris's body had once lain. What remained of Caitlin's camp was pretty much empty. The reinforcements had swept the captain's corpse away, had mobilised what was left of the forces, and had made their way through to Sydney proper.

Rankin, on the other hand, had remained. It hadn't taken him long to feel the unease of being around military men. It was surreal, how everything was fine until one just didn't want to fight anymore. As he packed the loose odds and ends that were scattered around when Pestilence had gone onto her side, he felt the gaze from the others fall upon him and he knew he would have to run. While the military cleaned up the bodies and burned them, he had taken Chris and laid him in the back of his Holden. He had covered him in an old tarpaulin and hidden him from view as best as he could and then, he had left his friend so that he could hide in the ruins of Richmond.

It was easier than he expected to slip away from the masses. The Yanks, Ram rooters and the Skips that remained were too busy picking up the pieces of the waste that had been left for them to worry about one man. He doubted they even noticed that he was gone. As far as he knew, they had no records of the men that had served, and he doubted they would stock take the men that they had massed to bury. However, the image of Caitlin's clipboard sprang forward in his mind and a seed of doubt was planted within his gut.

As he lay amongst the rubble of one of the houses, he thought about his decisions. He thought about the pistol that Caitlin had held to his head on more than one occasion. The war machine was something that was never satisfied, no matter the service an individual gave, it was like a boss that always wanted more for less.

It was on the floor of that house that Rankin swore to himself that he would never take up arms again in another man's war. He said this as he examined the jagged scar that ran up his arm, the remnants of a promise he had made to himself to never indulge in whiskey again. As the sun came down, and the last of the trucks left the motor pool, he laughed and mused that promises were only words. They didn't mean shit.

When the trucks had moved on, Rankin had emerged from the rubble which had concealed him and had carried Chris to a spot beyond the courtyard. The grass had remained green and lush, although only feet away the barrage of foot traffic and tank tracks had turned it to a muddy mess. He used a trenching tool that he had found in the mess and dug his friend a grave. He cried as he lowered Chris into it and placed his wallet with his faded photograph on his chest.

He covered him over and stood above his grave for some time and tried to think about words to say. But he had never been a wordsmith. Rankin smiled as he thought about their conversation about Chris' wife, when they had first met. Rankin had said he wasn't one for words and Chris, the want-to-be philosopher, had replied that painters and musicians were poor with words as well, that's why they either painted or wrote music. In the end, Rankin couldn't do anything but smoke as he looked down at his friend's covered grave. He figured that would be enough.

He sighed as he flicked the butt of his cigarette to the ground and he moved around the cabin of the Holden. The driver's door had come off and when Rankin had found it, the bolts had been torn out of the body. He didn't bother putting it back into place; he stowed the warped and battered door panel into the back of the utility. As he stood at the rear and looked at all the scars that the utility had suffered, he saw the place where the tailgate had once been. Metal was warped, creased and torn in the places where it had torn loose by the Wolf of Tamworth. Rankin frowned as he patted the back of the tray, it seemed that it wasn't just him that had a few more scars on his hide.

He sat in the cabin and looked about at the mess that remained. Blood had soaked the seats from the wound his friend had received that Rankin didn't notice. The fabric had almost turned black. He looked at the crack in the dashboard from where he had been thrown into it. He smiled and patted the dash above the cluster.

'I know I'm not him,' he said softly, feeling stupid. Then he didn't know what else to say. 'Fuck it, I'm not him. I don't need to talk to a car,' he grumbled as he turned the key.

With the first cycle of the key, the radio emitted a spray of static from its two speakers. The sound startled Rankin and his hand immediately went for the dial. Of all the times he had been in this car, he couldn't think of one time that he had heard the radio. His hand hovered over the volume dial for a second and then moved to the band width dial. The static squalled and cackled at him as he spun the wheel and then finally the tones of the Rolling Stones came through. No one could ever mistake the venerable voice of Jagger.

'Where will it lead us from here?'

Of all the songs, of all the times, it had to be that one. Rankin laughed as he turned the volume dial all the way and even though the speakers distorted the tunes and rattled in their frames, nothing had ever sounded so good to him. He smoked as he listened and at one point, he fumbled along with the words and then fell silent in his defeat.

'You can't say we never tried.'

As the song died out and an emptiness flooded his heart, Rankin dwelled on those final words. Over and over, they rolled around in his head, until he spat his cigarette out of the gaping door cavity as he reached once more for the ignition.

The starter motor clicked and nothing happened.

Rankin frowned and turned the key again. Click. He jiggled the key in the ignition as he turned it and the starter motor began to whir.

'Yes.' He hissed as he pressed his foot to the throttle.

The starter motor whirred, the engine coughed, spluttered shortly and then died.

'Come on, you old bitch.' He turned the key again.

The starter motor whirred, the engine coughed, and spluttered.

'You're not dead yet,' Rankin growled, as he pumped the throttle again, and the engine caught.

Pestilence roared into life and for the first time, Rankin knew exactly how Chris felt behind her. He blasted the throttle and her exhaust ran hot with gasses and unburned fuel. She echoed her power throughout the silent night. She made the earth tremble beneath her. She was everything, and more than what she was intended to be.

And now she was his.